TO...
TO...

BY
NANCY WARREN

AND

PLAY WITH ME
BY
LESLIE KELLY

MILLS & BOON

"I can't resist you."

"Oh, yes," Lexy whispered in a voice she barely recognized.

She felt the light stubble of his beard as he kissed his slow way up to her ear, then murmured, "You steal my breath away."

His clever thief's hands moved, tracing the front of her robe to the sash, which he untied, pulling the edges apart and revealing her in the deliciously lacy bra and panties.

The robe fell to the floor and it was his turn to make an incomprehensible sound, half sigh, half moan. "I want you."

Her body was on fire, she felt as much on display as the emeralds she wore and the experience was intoxicating. "I want you, too."

He touched her carefully, like a man who appreciates art and takes what he wants without asking permission. In the mirror she watched his hands tracing the shape of her breasts through the filmy cream colored lingerie. *Where was this leading?*

He was fully dressed standing behind her, dark and serious but for the gleaming eyes that showed how close to the edge of passion he was.

"This is a terrible idea," she said.

"I know." And then he turned her around and pulled her into his arms, kissing her so hard she felt the breath squeeze out of her.

TOO HOT
TO HANDLE

BY
NANCY WARREN

All the characters in this book have no existence outside the imagination of
the author, and have no relation whatsoever to anyone bearing the same name
or names. They are not even distantly inspired by any individual known or
unknown to the author, and all the incidents are pure invention.

First published in Great Britain 2011
Harlequin Mills & Boon Limited,
Eton House, 18-24 Paradise Road, Richmond, Surrey TW9 1SR

© Nancy Warren 2010

ISBN: 978 0 263 88055 7

14-0211

Harlequin Mills & Boon policy is to use papers that are natural, renewable
and recyclable products and made from wood grown in sustainable forests.
The logging and manufacturing processes conform to the legal environmental
regulations of the country of origin.

Printed and bound in Spain
by Litografia Rosés S.A., Barcelona

USA TODAY bestselling author **Nancy Warren** lives in the Pacific Northwest where her hobbies include walking her border collie in the rain and searching out unusual jewellery. She's the author of more than thirty novels and novellas and has won numerous awards. Visit her at www.nancywarren.net.

This is for my readers.
Thank you for your kind messages
and for reading the books I love to write.
With love, Nancy

Dear Reader,

What is it about a thief hero that we love so much? Is it that he will take what he wants without asking—and that just might be the heroine? Is it that he's a man who lives life on his own terms and makes his own rules? Of course, the thief hero is not some thug who hits little old ladies and steals their purses. No. Our kind of thief would risk his life to protect that little old lady and make sure she got her purse back. He's elegant, smooth, only takes things from not very nice people who can afford to lose the stuff. He's a pro. He's Cary Grant in *It Takes a Thief*, he's Robert Wagner in *To Catch a Thief*, he's Pierce Brosnan in *The Thomas Crown Affair*.

He is, in a word, dreamy. Tough, smart, a born rule-breaker, and yet the right woman can tame him. Mmmm. *Too Hot to Handle* is my first attempt at writing a thief hero. I've always wanted to and never had the story. Until now.

I hope you enjoy Lexy and Charlie as much as I did. As always, you can come visit me at www.nancy warren.net.

Happy reading,

Nancy Warren

1

LEXY DRAKE LOVED CONTRASTS. Delicate with bold, hot colors with cold, new mixed with old.

Hard rock music played as she peered through the binocular magnifier and looped a string of molten gold with infinite care around a ruby.

She loved every one of the creations that were slowly making her rich—this one a pair of wedding rings for a young couple who'd come to her with his grandmother's rings and a brooch that had been in her family so long no one knew its provenance.

Lexy would transform the old and forgotten into the new and now. It was the best kind of recycling, combining art, family history and love.

She worked alone, which was how she liked it. But never in silence. Her work might be delicate but her music provided much-needed contrast. Hard-driving rock and roll hammered the air around her. She'd have preferred to let the music reverberate off the walls, but since her tiny studio was tucked behind her SoHo store, she kept the volume low.

With the metal soft, she had a little time to bend it to

her will, but only a little. With a final twist, she had the look she wanted; a bold swirl of gold twining around a ruby.

A sudden prickling at the back of her neck told her she was no longer alone.

She turned sharply in time to surprise a man standing in the doorway. The way his gaze suddenly rose, she suspected she'd been shaking her booty in time to the music and her latest customer had stopped to watch her swaying hips.

He didn't look at all embarrassed to have been caught staring at her gyrations. If anything he appeared—interested—that would have to be the word.

"There's a salesclerk out front if you need help." It was rare for a customer to bumble back here to her private work space, but it happened.

"She's busy. So I followed the music."

"Oh." She picked up the remote and punched down the volume on her iPod. "I should hire more staff now we're getting so busy, but I haven't got around to it. Sorry."

"Don't be. It's fascinating to watch a master craftsman at work." He spoke in that perma-bored drawl with the crisp inflections she'd come to associate with the rich. She was pretty sure he'd been studying her ass—not her master craftsman hands—but he was a potential customer so she didn't call him on it.

Probably a lucrative customer, too. His handmade suit and shiny leather loafers screamed *Daddy owns a bank,* while his tie had one of those crests from a fancy Ivy League school. She could never keep them straight, wasn't interested enough to bother.

"I'm Charles Pendegraff III," he told her in that snooty tone, holding out his hand to shake hers.

"And I'm Alexandra Drake. Lexy." An imp inside her who would probably make sure she ended up broke, added, "The one and only."

His gaze sharpened on hers and she was struck by the gleam of powerful intelligence behind the laziness. The impression was gone in a second. He said, "I see you're working on a ring. I'm thinking of having one commissioned, myself. Do you mind if I take a look?"

"Sure." He had money to burn and she had self-defense skills that would flatten him in a New York minute if he tried anything. He strolled toward her and she figured he might be rich, but he wasn't idle. When he moved, his slacks molded around powerful thighs and as the blazer shifted she got the impression of a broad, muscular chest.

She loved contrasts and he seemed to have enough to be interesting. The lazy speaking voice was at odds with the sharp green eyes; the soft manicured hands didn't match the hard planes of his face.

And when he moved closer she felt the punch of his forceful sexuality.

Wowza.

"How did you hear about my studio?" she asked him. She nearly always started with a little market research and in this case a chance to distract her from the instant and powerful attraction she was experiencing.

"One of the fellows I play polo with, Jeremy Thurston, had you design an amulet for his mother. I bumped into her when she was wearing it at one of those tedious fundraisers. She was dull. The bracelet was stunning."

"Thanks." She remembered the piece, of course. She remembered them all.

"So, I'd heard of you, but I hadn't imagined you'd be

so young. And somehow one never imagines a jeweler as sexy, now why is that?"

"Oh, well…" She could not think of a thing to say. Lexy was rarely thrown off her stride, and getting hit on wasn't a completely foreign experience, so to be tongue-tied in front of this stranger was infuriating. But then she rarely felt the punch of attraction quite this strongly. And never from a guy with a number after his name.

No wonder she was speechless.

"Let me show you what I'm doing here," she said, deciding to ignore the sexy comment and reaching a hand toward the design she'd penned. "I'm combining elements—antique gold, a splash of platinum, those tiny rubies and the diamond solitaire, it's sort of my signature, you see—"

She stopped when he suddenly reached for her hand, taking it in his. "You've hurt yourself," he said, pointing to a red patch on her index finger.

"Oh, that's nothing, I burned myself on the soldering iron. I got careless."

She tried to pull away from the intimate warmth of her hand resting in his, but with a strength that surprised her, he prevented her. "Do you have a first-aid kit?"

"Yes, but I can't have cream or bandages on my fingers. I need them to do my work."

His gaze rose to meet hers and she thought he had the most amazing eyes she'd ever seen. "Then I'll use an old home remedy of my grandmother's." His words licked at her, soft, caressing. Intimate. "I'll kiss it better."

Her hand fluttered in his. She felt it, knew he must have felt the instinctive movement, too; she was completely annoyed by her reaction, but she didn't yank her hand away, either. She watched him raise her fingers slowly to his lips. Felt the lightest whisper of a kiss land on the sore spot and then he returned her hand to the worktable.

"I—um." She completely forgot what she was going to say.

He glanced through her magnifier at the ring. "This is exquisite."

"Thank you. What kind of a ring are you looking for, Mr. Pendegraff?"

"It's Charlie. And I need an engagement ring."

She blinked. "An engagement ring?"

"Yes." He raised his head and glanced at her. His green eyes were like cloudy emeralds, with too many occlusions to make them gemstone worthy, but it was the dark lines, the faults that made them so magnetic.

"You're getting married?"

"Yes."

She couldn't believe the balls of this man. He was kissing the fingers of the woman he wanted to design his wedding rings?

But then she reminded herself of one of her mother's favorite sayings. "The rich have different rules than the rest of us."

That was why she stayed away from them.

"Penelope and I are getting married in September. That's six months from now. Lots of time."

"I see." Ice coated her tone. "Well, if you'd like to come back out front, I'll show you what's in stock. All the designs are original, of course." Lexy was a certified gemologist and she'd apprenticed with a designer in London. When she'd returned to the States, she'd been unwilling to work in one of those design factories that turn out diamond solitaires and wedding bands by the thousand. So, she'd gone out on her own, building herself a perfect little studio in SoHo, a live/work loft that meant she and her livelihood were never far apart, and her commute was less than a minute.

One of the things she loved about New York was how quickly word spread when somebody found a new designer. She'd gone from complete obscurity, to a few select jewelers selling her unique creations, to becoming the go-to designer for wealthy trendsetters in less than two years.

She was so hot that men like Charles Pendegraff III came slumming in order to get his bride the trendiest engagement ring possible.

"Or, I could have something designed, just for me?"

"And for your fiancée. Yes."

As luck would have it, when she returned him to the storefront, her assistant, Amanda, was returning a ring tray to its display case. Her customer was walking out the door with one of their signature boxes made from recycled metal.

"Oh, good. Amanda's free now. Amanda? Would you help Mr. Pendegraff? He's looking for a ring. Goodbye, Mr. Pendegraff, and best of luck with the wedding."

"Bye, Lexy." He stuck out his hand and what could she do but return his clasp? Amusement lurked deep in his eyes as he gazed down at her. "I look forward to seeing you again."

She mumbled something inarticulate and retreated to her work space, shaking her head.

Poor Penelope.

CHARLIE STRODE AROUND a bundle of yellow garbage bags piled on the sidewalk, dodging tourists as he checked out the entire block around Alexandra Drake Designs.

As he took careful note of his Broome Street surroundings, snapping a few discreet photos, he pondered the nature of the woman he was about to steal from.

A woman of contrasts. Contrasts that intrigued him. When he'd first walked in, casually, a customer looking for some information, delighted to find the single sales-clerk busy, he'd followed the sound of some indie rock band into the workshop of Alexandra Drake. No more than an unlocked door separated the storefront from her work space. Was she really that trusting? Her back was to him and with the music pounding she couldn't have heard his approach.

Had he taken advantage of the perfect opportunity to check out her security system? Eyeball the safe sitting in the corner? He could have taken photos and she wouldn't have noticed.

No. He hadn't. He hadn't done any of the tasks a self-respecting thief would have accomplished in seconds.

His gaze had gone straight to the hips gyrating to the beat of the music, tightly clad in jeans, her legs not long, but shapely. She had small feet encased in boots. Above the swinging hips, her torso was still. She wore a navy tank top, not an ounce of extra flesh on her. Her bare arms revealed elegant swells of muscle. Her hair was black and wound into a big messy bun with what looked like chopsticks stuck through to hold it in place.

Her eyes were glued to a magnifier and he watched her hands. Those small, efficient hands. Using some kind of tool that looked like small pliers, she was twirling a strand of hot metal as though it were a piece of cooked spaghettini, draping it around a colored stone. He knew the moment she felt his presence. Those glorious hips slowed, her back stiffened.

Still, she finished the meticulous draping of the metal before setting the ring into a clamp. Then she raised her head and turned to him. Too fast for him to pretend he hadn't been watching her.

He couldn't have pretended anything, anyway. He was too stunned.

The woman was gorgeous. Cool gray eyes of a tilted almond shape that suggested there was Asian blood in her. Pale skin, full, sexy lips that begged to be painted red, but which she'd only touched with some kind of gloss.

He didn't have time for lust. He had a job to do.

And yet somehow he couldn't help himself. He'd come on to her. Enjoyed flustering her, finding an excuse to touch her.

And now, he was preparing to steal from her.

He had a bad feeling about this. A bad feeling that he was going to break every rule he lived by and get to know one of his marks. After the dust had settled, obviously, a few weeks from now when she'd have moved on and wouldn't think to connect a missing set of jewels with a visit from Charles Pendegraff.

He called himself every kind of fool as he made his preparations, but he knew he was going to be stupid.

As crazy as it was, he was going to see Lexy Drake again.

2

AT SIX, AMANDA PEEKED into Lexy's work space. "I've closed up. I'm heading out now."

Lexy glanced up and rubbed her tired eyes. "Good day?"

"Three engagement rings, a few pairs of earrings and about a hundred of those bracelets that were featured on *Party Girls of Manhattan.*"

Lexy laughed. It was amazing how slavish people could be when they saw their favorite star wearing something distinctive on a television show. She only had a small number of mass-produced designs, but since one of the women on the newest semireality show had discovered her work, her designs—especially the ones that appeared on the show—were snapped up.

"*Party Girls* will do for you what *Sex and the City* did for Manolo Blahnik," Amanda prophesied.

"Fine with me."

Her assistant glanced around the crowded space. "You planning to work all night?"

She rubbed the back of her neck. "No. A little longer. I want to finish this ring set, then I'll take a break."

"What did that woman and her daughter bring you, by the way? You seemed pretty excited. You know, that stylish woman with the perfect gray hair and her thin, pretty daughter."

"Mrs. Grayson and her daughter—" What was the daughter's name? She recalled the emeralds and diamonds with vivid clarity; she'd never seen such a perfect set, but recalling the details of the owners was always trickier. She closed her eyes for a second. "Judith, that was the daughter's name."

Lexy was becoming accustomed to the whims of rich people, and she was the first in line to recommend redesigning antique jewels into settings that would breathe new life into them, but as she'd opened the faded blue velvet box she'd had to suppress the urge to argue mother and daughter out of their idea to have this set broken down and reset.

The gems themselves were exquisite. Emeralds were funny things. The larger they came the more flawed they were likely to be. A few occlusions were expected but when she'd studied these gems through her loupe, she'd been astonished at the near perfection. And the color. Dark, clear green that she'd rarely seen outside a museum.

The setting was antique, no question. Like any personal ornamentation, jewelry went through fashions. But every age had its classics and this set was one of the most inherently beautiful she'd ever seen. Delicate strands of gold held the emeralds and diamonds in place but didn't compete, so the green fire flashed from the necklace. "These are exquisite. Are you sure you want to reset them?" she'd finally asked.

Mother and daughter exchanged a quick look. "Oh, yes," Mrs. Grayson had answered. "The set's a gift to

Judith, and she wants a more modern look. We both love your work. We're excited to see what you could do with these. You are such an artist and with these emeralds, I believe Judith will be breathtaking when she wears the jewels at the diabetes fundraiser next month." She smiled at her daughter. "I'd planned to give them to her when she got married, but now that she's twenty-five, and unmarried, I'm going ahead. Why wait? They've been in the family forever, and they really don't suit my coloring."

Lexy suspected what the older woman really intended was to display some of the family wealth around her daughter's throat in an unsubtle hint to potential suitors.

"You know, these emeralds are quite rare, and I suspect the pieces are hundreds of years old. You will compromise their value as antiques."

"Oh, they've been in the family forever. It's time they had a new look."

Lexy had accepted the commission, of course. It wasn't her business to talk clients out of her services and as lovely as the current set was, she knew she'd likely never have an opportunity to work with emeralds like this again.

Opening the safe, she withdrew the box and showed the emeralds to Amanda, who said, "Wow." They both studied the sparkle of diamond and deep, gorgeous green.

Amanda touched the edge of the swirled gold setting. "I've never seen emeralds that color. They're so rich-looking."

"I know. The color's spectacular. I think it's because they are so old. They must have come out of South

America centuries ago. Mayan stones are considered the purest and best."

"How much do you think they're worth?"

"Hard to say. But with the almost perfect diamonds and the unusual color and clarity of those emeralds, I'm guessing around a million."

"A million dollars?" Amanda squeaked.

"Yeah."

So Lexy had at least a million bucks worth of emeralds in her safe and a free hand to design settings that would help an unmarried twenty-five-year-old attract a rich man. Might be a little old-fashioned, not to mention Machiavellian, but this was also by far her largest commission ever.

"Don't tell anyone about this, okay?"

She knew she could trust Amanda. They'd worked together for about eighteen months. In her early twenties, Amanda Sanford was tall and thin, had slightly more than the fashionable number of tattoos and piercings and a penchant for painted leggings and army boots. She was also great with customers and seemed happy in her work.

Lately she'd been letting Amanda help her with some of the simpler settings. When she was swamped, it was amazing how useful an extra pair of hands could be. Amanda also possessed an artistic eye and Lexy often sought out her assistant's opinion when she was unsure.

AFTER AMANDA LEFT, Lexy finished the ruby wedding set. On a whim, she called her customer and let them know. As she'd half suspected the woman was so excited she wanted to come right over and pick up the rings.

So, her workday ended with a nice fat check, a happy and excited customer and one more peek at the emeralds.

Then, realizing she was starving, she opened the barely visible door that led upstairs to her living space. It wasn't nearly as fancy as the downstairs since she'd put every cent of her savings and a good chunk of the bank's into her business. Her tools, the display cases, lighting, decor, everything had to be consistent with her jewelry designs. Which turned out to mean expensive.

Which in turn dictated that upstairs she had little more than a bed, the most minimal kitchen and a couple of chairs and a table she'd found at Goodwill.

Pouring herself a glass of cool water, she noticed the familiar throbbing tingle of a burn on her hand. She regarded the spot, red and shiny, and recalled the guy who'd come in earlier, burdened by too much name and too little conscience. Charles Pendegraff III. Jeez.

He had a fiancée, and was going around staring at other women's butts and kissing their booboos all better. She shook her head. She gave that marriage a couple of years, tops.

So long as the happy couple lasted long enough to pay for her ring designs, she reminded herself, it was none of her business. For all she knew, Mr. Pendegraff III and Penelope had one of those open relationships where fidelity wasn't part of the contract.

She didn't understand that kind of relationship; she was firmly determined that if she ever decided to get married, she'd be the kind of woman who went after her husband with a shotgun if he ever strayed.

And, since her dad was a New York cop who worried about his single daughter, and had taught her all about self-defense and marksmanship, she could shoot the lying, no-good cheater right through the heart. Or any other part of his anatomy she felt like blasting holes in. Whoever married her better understand that.

Her mother, who was half Chinese and very traditional, would probably come back from the dead to help her bury the corpse.

The image of Charles Pendegraff rose up before her and she felt her trigger finger squeeze.

Odd that she should have such a strong reaction to a stranger, but she knew that the biggest part of her disgust was the undeniable attraction she'd felt to the man. But then she already knew her taste in men wasn't nearly as flawless as her taste in jewels.

As she finished her water the phone rang.

She checked the call display and picked up. "Carl. Hi."

"What's up, Sexy Lexy?"

"Just got home from work."

"All tired out from the long commute?" he teased. Carl Wiesenstein was one of her tight group of friends, all of them artists or craftspeople. He was a metalsmith who was making an amazingly good living considering that his specialty was house numbers and door knockers. "Come out and celebrate. I sold a five-thousand-dollar door chime today."

She laughed. "You've got to love New York."

"Oh, baby, I do. I'm getting the gang together tonight at Emo's. Nat and Bruce are coming, Ella if she can get a babysitter, a few others. You in?"

The thought of a night out with friends was tempting. She'd been working way too hard lately. But she knew she wouldn't go. Not tonight. "I'm so sorry. I've got to work."

"You work too much."

"I know." For a second she was tempted to tell him about the emeralds resting in her safe, but Carl wasn't known for discretion and all she needed was for him to be overheard while he was telling her friends about her big day—as she knew he would. Maybe when she got million-dollar pieces sitting in her safe every day she'd become blasé, but for tonight she was worried that some burglar might overhear Carl and it was dead easy to find her studio. Even though her safe was supposed to be uncrackable, she really didn't want it tested.

"I've got a rush commission. You know how it is."

Carl chuckled. "Not feeling sorry for you. You'll charge them through the nose to turn around a design fast."

"Gotta love New York," she said again. Frugality might be fashionable, but not to her clientele.

"If you decide to get a life, we'll see you at Emo's later."

"You got it."

She almost changed her mind when she opened her fridge and found nothing in there but half of an old pizza and a corked bottle of wine she didn't even remember opening.

She tossed both and called down to a Thai place for delivery, then she kicked back, cranked the music up, pulled out her sketchbook and started playing with ideas for the emerald and diamond set.

At midnight, she turned out the light, but Lexy couldn't sleep. A restlessness possessed her. She knew it was excitement. She loved her muse, she really did, but the damn woman was a workaholic slave driver. Ideas were chasing each other through Lexy's mind faster and more confusing than a stock car race.

After a couple of hours of tossing and turning, unable

to turn off her brain, she flipped on the light, looked at the sketch pad on the floor and knew that she needed to see those emeralds again. Her latest idea was bold, almost crazy, but she thought the gems were so unusually brilliant that they could dominate a bolder setting than the one they'd rested in for half a millennium.

THE ENTRANCE TO Alexandra Drake Designs was an eye-catching blue. Bight, shiny, as close to neon as paint can get, but the dramatic look suited her storefront and was oddly in keeping with the neighborhood, a place of avant garde shoe designers, exclusive little nooks selling nothing but handmade Italian bags, lingerie boutiques.

The woman was crazy not to have a decent security system, but then Charlie doubted she'd ever had to store anything as valuable as the emeralds that he assumed were currently residing in her safe.

It was almost too easy.

Broome Street was as quiet as it ever got. He could hear his soft footfalls on the pavement. In his black slacks, turtleneck and shoes he could pass for a man taking a walk after a night at the theater perhaps, or a meal at a good restaurant. The March night air was cool, crisp, and when the wind picked up, that man could as easily melt into the shadows of a doorway. And unlock the far-too-simple mechanism on the lock of Alexandra Drake Designs. This was the kind of lock he'd started his career with as a teenager. It took him less than a minute to take care of the main lock. The dead bolts took little more than a minute.

As the door of Alexandra Drake Designs opened and he slipped inside, he wished she at least had an electronic security system, something to give him a bit of excitement.

Charlie ought to be grateful he could be in and out in only a few minutes, with the Isabella Emeralds, but he had his pride. He might be a retired thief, but he was still the best. A little challenge would be good; otherwise a man could become complacent, lose his edge.

Silent and dark as a shadow he made his swift way past the dark shapes of her display cases to the back, to the door that separated the storefront from the small workshop. He was frankly insulted to find the door wasn't even locked. How was a thief to remain on top of his game when his marks were so damn sloppy?

He felt his way around her table, where he'd watched her work earlier, grinning at the memory of her body rocking out while her hands created magic. He'd been shocked at the punch of lust that damn near flattened him when she turned and he received the full impact of her eyes. Eyes that ought to be in a porcelain doll instead staring at him from that strong-looking body.

He'd be back.

He'd give the woman time to get through the shock of the break-in. A couple of weeks, then he'd casually stroll in here, with Penelope conveniently history. He planned to ask the jewelry lady out.

In silence, he knelt before the safe.

At least the safe put up a fight.

For the first time since he'd stood outside in the night contemplating the pathetic excuse for a lock, he felt his peculiar set of skills being called on.

The safe was an older, German model and he respected it. As safes went it was stubborn, thick walled, heavy, fireproof, blastproof, tamperproof.

But not Charlie proof.

They never were.

He flexed his fingers a few times to limber them, crouched, slipping into the zone, the blissed-out state that told him he was doing what he was born to do, and went to work.

ONE OF THE MANY ADVANTAGES of a live/work loft was that Lexy didn't have to commute very far to her job. She didn't even have to dress. Shoving on a pair of jeans and a sweatshirt, she pulled on a pair of purple and pink slipper socks and made her way downstairs.

Excitement was bubbling and she knew her imagination was working on overdrive keeping her from sleep. She'd learned to live with the quirk. Her creativity kept her designs fresh and edgy, sometimes surprising even herself. So she lost the odd night's sleep. She'd live.

She loved her studio at night. There was a hush that was almost palpable. Even though the traffic noise never ceased, and sirens pierced the night silence regularly, there were no customers, no movement, no commerce.

She could set herself to design knowing no one would bother her.

The door to her living space connected to the back room of the shop. As she neared the door she stopped, certain she'd heard something.

What?

A tiny scrape of sound, possibly nothing at all, but she couldn't shake the feeling that someone was behind that door.

Probably it was nothing. The creak of an old building, some animal she'd rather not think about nosing around in the alley, but not only had she been raised by a cop, she'd watched too many horror films to open any door behind which ominous sounds could be heard.

Instead she retraced her steps silently, grabbing the gun from her bureau drawer and taking her cell phone from its charger.

Deep breath, and down she went again. Silently.

At the door, she paused and listened. Was that a scrape? A click?

She eased open the door and flipped on the light.

And her eyes widened in surprise.

Charles Pendegraff III was standing nonchalantly in front of her safe. Her wide-open safe. The same one that was supposed to be unbreachable. And in his gloved hands, he was holding Mrs. Grayson's emeralds.

For a second neither of them spoke or moved. Then he motioned to the gun in her hand and said, "At least you have some idea of security. Is it loaded?"

Not that she'd ever surprised a burglar before, but she'd have expected a little more drama. Maybe false protestations of innocence or an attempt to run. At least you'd think the man would replace the emeralds in the safe, but he did none of those things. Simply leaned against the safe like it was an open refrigerator and he was in search of olives for his martini.

"Not only is it loaded, but I am an excellent shot. Put your hands up, Mr. Pendegraff. Or whatever your real name is."

"Oh, it's Pendegraff all right." His eyes crinkled with sudden humor. "And this is a very interesting situation."

"It's not interesting. It's disgusting. You're stealing from me."

"Not you, technically. Look, let me explain."

She raised the gun so it pointed at his heart. "Don't move another inch."

Somebody started banging loudly at the front door of the store.

The noise startled her. She'd never had so much action after hours before. "Open up, police," a harsh voice yelled.

Pendegraff glanced at the phone in her hand. "You called the cops? I wish you hadn't."

"I didn't. They must have followed you."

His lazy and most puzzling amusement vanished. "You didn't call them?"

"No."

"Then, sweetheart, those are not the cops."

"You're a pretty lousy thief, aren't you? Both I and the police nab you?"

She started for the door that separated her work space from the front of the store, keeping her gun trained on him. "Put the emeralds back in the safe and let's go talk to the cops."

"Think," he said softly. "If you didn't call them, how would they have tracked me? You don't have a security alarm I could have tripped." She could have sworn he sounded petulant. "No security cameras. And I've been in here ten minutes. If they'd followed me, they'd have been in long before now."

"Maybe—" A crash had her turning her head. The cops had broken down her front door without giving her a chance to open it? That was pretty aggressive.

One second, Pendegraff was leaning so lazily against the safe you'd have thought he was napping, and the next second he was behind her, one hand grabbing her hard against him, the other wresting the gun from her grip.

She was no weakling and she fought to keep control

of the weapon, jabbing him with her elbow, stamping on his foot, but her sweater socks were useless and her assailant was stronger than he looked.

Crashing sounds continued out front, she was sure she heard breaking glass, and then her own gun was jabbing her in the back. "Scream and I'll shoot. Let's get out of here."

3

HE HAULED HER OUT THE SAME door she'd come from and dragged her up the stairs to her apartment. "Fire escape. Where is it?"

"I'm not telling you." She was furious with both of them. With him for the whole escapade and with her for losing control of the situation. Not to mention her gun.

"Trust me, those guys downstairs are a lot meaner than I am. We really don't want to run into them."

She heard another crash. Pendegraff ran to her window and peered out.

She flipped open her cell, tried to call 9-1-1 but he grabbed it out of her hand before she could complete the call, tossing the phone onto her bed.

He yanked up the window sash. "Out," he said, pushing her through the window and onto the fire escape, dropping out beside her. "I swear to God if you make a sound or do anything I don't like, I'll shoot you. Now climb down."

"I'm wearing socks," she told him in a furious undertone as the crisscrossed wrought-iron bit into the soles of her feet.

"Good. It'll keep you quiet. Now move!"

He stayed right beside her as she stepped down, surprisingly as quiet in his shoes as she was in her slipper socks.

The fire escape was in good shape, but it was rickety and creaked as they made their way down. Still, no one came to investigate. *Thanks a lot, New York's Finest,* she thought bitterly.

They hit the pavement below and she felt a stone bite through her socks.

"Run," he ordered, grabbing her arm and breaking into a sprint, giving her no choice but to follow.

They ran, but cobblestone streets weren't designed for a woman in slippers. He didn't seem to care, hauling her along at a fast pace. She prided herself on being in pretty good shape, but she could barely keep up with his long-legged sprint. If his goal was to keep her too breathless to yell for help, he was doing an excellent job. She prayed she wouldn't step on broken glass or a nail or something.

"Hey," a man's voice yelled.

"Don't turn around," Pendegraff warned her. "Move."

They pounded down toward Canal Street and she saw a black limo glide toward them. She waved the vehicle down, almost sobbing in relief as it stopped.

Pendegraff didn't flinch, but with a quick glance over his shoulder, he dragged her toward the car, opening the back door and shoving her inside. The limo was sailing away before he'd closed the door. She heard the click of the locks sliding smoothly into place even as she grabbed for the door.

"Nice timing, Healey," Pendegraff said.

The limo took the corner at a sedate glide, and as it did so she watched through the tinted glass as a thickset guy in a cheap tweed jacket ran into view, gun in hand. When he saw the car, he slipped his gun under the flap of his jacket, then pounded past them.

"A getaway limo?" she panted. "Are you kidding me?"

She banged her head back against the leather headrest, frustration surging through her.

"It's very convenient. In New York a limo is barely noticeable and the tinted windows provide excellent privacy."

"Great. You stole the emeralds out of my safe, have your own getaway limo. And what are you planning to do with me?"

The gaze he sent her was speculative. He seemed relaxed and very cool sitting back in the black leather seat. "I haven't completely decided yet."

"Well, when you do, could you let me in on the secret?" She ought to be frightened, she knew that, but somehow she couldn't seem to work up any true fear.

"It's been a stressful night. Why don't you join me in a nightcap?" He reached for the bar built into the back, which was conveniently set up, right down to the fresh ice in the ice bucket. Swanky.

"I have a better idea. Why don't you drop me off at the next corner and I'll grab a cab home."

"Scotch all right?"

She rolled her gaze. "Fine."

"Rocks or straight up?" he asked in that lazy tone that was beginning to set her teeth on edge. As though they were at the yacht club for a social engagement.

"Rocks."

The ice tinkled into the crystal tumbler. "I promise I will let you go, unharmed, but I can't do it quite yet." He passed her a glass. Raised his own in a silent toast. "I promise, you can trust me."

She snorted. "You robbed me. I don't normally trust guys who break into my safe and confiscate my jewels. Call me a cynic."

She sipped her drink. She wasn't a big scotch drinker but he was right—it had been a crazy night and between the break-in, the police raid and the kidnapping, her nerves were a little jumpy. Naturally it was some ancient whiskey that had no doubt been lovingly distilled by kilted magicians a century or so earlier. The drink was smooth and rich.

He leaned back, and she thought that if she hadn't caught him red-handed, she'd never have believed the elegant man beside her was a thief. The knife pleats were still sharp in his black trousers, his Italian loafers showed not so much as a smudge of dirt despite racing through the streets of SoHo, his black turtleneck rose and fell with slow, even breath, as the man casually sipped his drink.

"Does Penelope know you're a thief?"

"Penelope?" His dark eyebrows rose. "I have no secrets from Penelope."

"Is she a thief, too?"

"She's more…" He seemed to consider his words carefully, and once again she caught the familiar amusement lurking in his eyes. "Support staff."

"You must be a pretty successful thief if you can afford limos and Italian loafers." She stumbled over the final word as a wave of fatigue washed over her. She was more tired than she'd realized.

"How about you?" he asked. "Do you have a significant other? Husband, boyfriend?"

"Worried someone will come looking for me?" she asked. At least she tried to ask the question. The words formed in her head but it felt as if there was a wad of cotton stopping them from making it to her mouth. Her head began to swim and in that moment she realized that there was more than scotch in her glass.

She jerked her head to face him. "You bastard."

He reached out slowly, oh, so slowly it seemed, his arm snaking like a Dali image, all long and loopy, to take the glass from her hand. "You'll be fine. I promise."

She struggled to keep her wits about her, jabbed the window control. If she could get some fresh air, maybe she could fight whatever he'd used to drug her. But even as she flailed for the button, she could feel herself slipping from consciousness.

LEXY WOKE WITH A SENSE of disorientation, as though she were on vacation and waking in a strange bed. But as her eyes opened slowly, the horror of what had happened to her came rushing back. She'd been in the back of a limo, she'd drunk scotch—not more than a few sips—and then she'd passed out.

Her mouth felt dry, her eyes were heavy and scratchy, and her head ached. She raised a hand to her face, rubbed her eyes. Then she looked around.

There was a little natural light coming in through a shuttered window. Enough to show her the ghostly outlines of a bedroom. She was in bed. Not her own. And she was alone.

She threw back the covers. Discovered she was in the same clothes she'd been wearing when she was

kidnapped. But someone had removed her slipper socks.
She pushed her bare feet to the floor and got up. Whoa.
A little wobbly. She waited for her legs to steady, then
padded to the shutters and opened them.

Gray light pushed sullenly into the room. As she
looked out, she saw snow and trees. Huge, dark green
trees and plenty of them.

Snow?

Something told her she wasn't in Manhattan anymore.
Her window was in an upper story of what looked like
an architecturally interesting house, which sat in a snow-
covered clearing in the middle of a forest. A single set of
tire tracks led to a parked 4x4. If there were neighboring
houses she didn't see them. All she saw were trees. Everywhere she looked, trees, a gray sky and it was eerily
quiet. It felt as though this place had been stuck in the
middle of nowhere. To a woman who'd spent most of
her life in Manhattan, all these trees and isolation were
a little freaky.

There was no sign of anyone around. She unlocked
the window and hauled up the sash, half surprised to
find it opened. But then what was she going to do?
Jump? At the very least a two-story fall would leave her
with broken bones. She stuck her head out the window,
filling her lungs with cool, moist air. The house was
gray cedar shingle, all sleek lines and modern angles.
A satellite dish perched incongruously from the roof.

A large bird swooped low over the trees and a chip-
munk chattered. Apart from pigeons and crows, she
wasn't really good at identifying birds, but she thought
this might be some kind of hawk. Some predator that
pounced on innocent animals, those that were smaller
and inoffensively going about their business. Rather

like she had before Charles Pendegraff III had pounced on her.

Lexy didn't like being a victim. And she most certainly didn't like that she'd been spirited to heaven knew where, with a thief who'd stolen property out of her safe. Not only did she have Mrs. Grayson's commission to design, but she had several other projects on the go. No time for a kidnapping.

When she crossed to the door she discovered it opened as easily as the window. She closed it softly and retreated back into her room. She needed to think before confronting her kidnapper.

She also needed to brush her teeth. This place seemed pretty ritzy. The furniture in her room was simple pine, but it had the high-end country look of simple furniture that cost a fortune. The bed was big and comfy; a couple of large armchairs flanked a fireplace and a partly open door led to an en suite.

The room reminded her of a luxury ski resort. Expensive, comfortable and in the middle of nowhere.

The bathroom thankfully possessed not only a toothbrush still in its wrapper but a basket of toiletries and a stack of fluffy white towels. The tap water tasted fresh and clean so she filled one of the two glasses she found on the granite vanity and filled it, drank the contents down in a couple of gulps and refilled the glass.

Sipping her second glass of water more slowly, she took stock of her reflection, which was a mess. Her hair was all over the place, her makeup had smudged and her clothes—which were pretty casual to begin with—looked as though she'd slept in them.

She brushed her teeth, then took a long, hot shower, washing away the last of her drug-induced grogginess.

A white bathrobe hung on the back of the

door—reminding her more and more of an upscale hotel—so she slipped it on and opened the drawers and cupboards in the bathroom hoping for a comb or brush.

She found both. Also hairstyling products and a limited supply of essential cosmetics still in their packaging. Her first instinct was to refuse to make herself pretty for a kidnapper, but she soon threw that idea aside. She had her own confidence to think of and it was amazing what a little lip gloss and some mascara could do.

Blow-drying her hair, putting on a little makeup, these small tasks steadied her and gave her some sense of normality.

When she returned to the bedroom and checked out the closet and drawers, she was only mildly surprised to find clean T-shirts, pajamas, track pants, a hoodie, outside jackets, rain boots and blessedly unopened packages of underwear and socks. He either had a lot of unexpected guests, or the kidnapping business had a high turnover.

She dressed swiftly—the only thing of her own she wore was her jeans—and then, pushing her shoulders back and her chin up, she left the bedroom in search of her captor.

Her feet were soundless on the thick carpet that covered the floors. The upscale mountain retreat look continued in the hallway. A muted palette of taupes and grays on the walls and woodwork highlighted several paintings and drawings that were so good she suspected they were originals. Hot ones, no doubt.

At the bottom of the stairs, she hit a slate entrance hall and landing. She listened, but heard no sound coming from anywhere. A flutter of panic in her chest as she wondered if she'd been abandoned here, but then she remembered the 4x4 out front.

She went searching. And discovered that Mr. Pendegraff had exquisite taste. Everything was of the finest from the leather furniture in the living room to the liquor in the cabinet.

She found the kitchen at last, and found Charles Pendegraff III sitting in a deep chair in a den area off the kitchen sipping coffee and watching a plasma TV. He glanced up when she entered the room and immediately flicked off the television.

He'd changed yet again, she noted warily. From rich fop to black-clad jewel thief, now he looked like an upscale mountain man. He wore jeans, a chambray shirt and hiking boots.

"Good morning. Would you like some coffee?"

"Is it drugged?"

His eyes clouded. "No. And I'm sorry about that, by the way. I couldn't think of another way to handle things."

There wasn't any point in him drugging her now, she was pretty certain. And she was a weak, weak woman unable to resist the scent coming from the sleek coffeemaker. "All right, then."

He rose, went behind the granite breakfast bar and poured a dark stream of coffee into a blue pottery mug that was much too ordinary and cheerful to be part of this house.

"Milk?"

"Yes."

He opened the door of a stainless steel fridge that she saw was fully stocked, withdrew a carton and placed it on the black granite countertop beside the coffee mug. "Sugar's in the pot there," he said.

She took her time preparing her coffee exactly the way she liked it. She was determined to stay calm. The coffee was delicious. Strong and rich and she felt the caffeine punching up her energy. Good.

"What would you like to go with your coffee?" he asked, as though he was her waiter. "I've got eggs, breakfast muffins, some—"

"I'd like some answers."

"I know. And you'll get them. Over breakfast."

"I'm not hungry."

"You will be. You like omelets?"

Frustration enveloped her, and forgetting her vow to remain calm, she marched up to him, right behind the granite breakfast bar and into his space. She stalked up until there were only a couple of inches between their bodies. She was so close she could smell him, hints of sandalwood from his shower gel or shampoo or something, the fresh laundered smell of his shirt, the smell of thieving hot man underneath it all.

His green eyes were wary and he'd missed a spot when he shaved. All that her mind processed while her anger boiled.

She slammed her coffee mug down on the counter. "I don't want eggs. I want answers. Yesterday you came into my life, into my store, into my work space." She began to list his crimes on her fingers, from mildest to most venal. "You lied to me, you broke in after dark and stole from me." Her third finger hurt when she hit it to emphasize the third item on her list. "You kidnapped me." Bang she hit her fourth finger. "And you drugged me. Now I have no idea who you are or where I am and I want to know." Her fingers curled into a fist. Even though she wanted to punch him as hard as she could, she wasn't foolish enough to do it. Instead she rapped her closed fist against the other open palm. Smack, smack.

"And I want to know, now."

For a second he simply stood, gazing down at her. She wished she were over six feet tall so she wouldn't have to look up to meet his eyes. It was infuriating being shorter and slighter than her foe.

It took her a second to realize that he was looking at her, not in a kidnapper to victim way, but in a man to woman way that made her blood stir. What was wrong with her?

How could her body respond to a criminal?

Needing an excuse to back away from this far-too-close contact, she picked up her mug of coffee. A tiny crack had formed in the bottom where she'd smacked the pottery on the granite. She only wished it was Pendegraff's head she'd cracked.

And she stepped back.

"Okay," he said. "You want to talk first, we'll talk."

"You'll talk," she reminded him.

THE DEEP, COMFY CHAIRS in the den made her want to curl her feet beneath her. Under different circumstances she thought she'd like this place. Wherever it was. There were no newspapers conveniently lying around, no phone book sitting by a phone that might give her hints to her current location.

She sat up straight, her feet on the floor.

He refilled his mug and took the other chair. Sipped, slowly, in a way that suggested he was stalling for time. Her foot began to tap against the floor.

"I actually am Charles Pendegraff," he began.

"The third?" Skepticism tinged her tone.

A brief grin lit his face. "Yes, though I only mention the number when I want to come off as a pompous ass."

"You're good at it," she said sweetly.

"As you've obviously gathered, I'm a thief." He paused, shaking his head. "*Was* a thief. I'm retired." He glanced at her and his gaze darkened. "And, until last night, I'd never been caught. I must be losing my edge."

"Caught by me and the cops."

"Lexy, those weren't cops."

"Oh, come on. Why would I believe you?"

He reached for the remote control. "You're not going to like this. I recorded a news broadcast from New York this morning."

He flicked on the screen and pushed a couple of buttons. A newscast she knew well, one she often watched as she was getting ready in the morning, told her it was going to be cooler in Manhattan today, then there was the usual banter between the show's host and the meteorologist. Then the news.

"I'm really not sure what the U.N. funding crisis has to do with—"

He held up a finger. "Wait."

And then there was news footage of a block of buildings she knew intimately. It was her street.

"A suspicious fire broke out last night at a well-known jewelry designer's SoHo premises, destroying the store and the living space above it."

"A fire?" she whispered.

The film that went with the voice-over showed her street, the blackened front of her store, the pretty blue paint all bubbled and black, all the windows smashed and uniformed firefighters spraying water into her apartment.

"Emergency crews responded at 4:11 a.m. when a neighbor saw flames coming from the building that houses Alexandra Drake Designs. Ms. Drake's residence was above the studio."

Like a horror movie, she watched as a man rushed to the store's entrance and had to be forcibly restrained by the police officers standing out front.

"Carl," she cried softly.

Next thing, her friend was being interviewed, clearly distraught.

"Lexy's a good friend. We asked her to come out with us tonight, but she said she had to stay in and work. I was walking home and saw the fire truck." He glanced around frantically. "I can't find her. Did she get out okay?"

The camera cut back to the on-the-scene reporter. "Police and fire crews aren't saying much at this point, only that they will be investigating the cause of the fire, which they are calling 'suspicious' and that robbery is suspected."

The pictures of the fire crews at work continued to play as the morning news anchor took up the story. "Investigators recovered the body of a woman from the scene. It will be several days before a positive identification can be made of the victim, but at this hour, Alexandra Drake is still unaccounted for."

Then there was video playing of her at a gala, taken a few months ago, wearing one of her own necklaces. A jeweled collar. Talking about her work.

The host continued: "Alexandra Drake was a fast-rising young jewelry designer in New York. Her work appears in the collections of movie stars, royalty around the globe, and has been featured in a handful of recent movies. Her specialty was wedding and commitment rings." Close-up of Lexy at the gala, speaking. "I believe every love story is unique, so shouldn't your wedding ring be as personal?" Back to the host. "Alexandra Drake was twenty-eight years old. And in the meat packing district today, a suspicious package in a garbage bag turned out to be—" Pendegraff flipped off the TV.

"*Was?* They said was." Her shock must have shown on her face; she couldn't have stopped it.

The man beside her nodded. Looking grim.

"They said there was a dead woman in my place. Why would there be a dead body in my apartment?"

"I don't know, Lexy. We'll figure this out."

She rose. Unable to sit still one more second. "Yesterday my life was so normal. Exciting even. And today, my business and home are destroyed, I have no idea where I am."

She glared at her companion. "Oh, yeah, and I'm dead."

4

"YOU'RE NOT DEAD."

She rubbed her eyes. "Right. Just kidnapped." Rage filled her and she welcomed the fiery anger; it was so much easier to deal with than the despair she felt tugging at the edges of her consciousness. Everything she'd worked for, her home, her business, gone. "This is all your fault."

"I know you aren't ready to believe this, but I saved your life."

It was the last straw. "You stole from me."

"Technically I was reclaiming stolen property. Look, you've had a shock. Let me cook you some breakfast and we'll talk this through."

She barely heard him. "I have to call my father. He'll have seen the news. He'll think I'm—" She couldn't finish the sentence. Since her mom had passed away five years earlier, her father had become increasingly protective of her, encouraging her to come home and live in the Queens home she'd grown up in. She knew part of his problem was simple loneliness and his years as a cop had put him in contact with too many horror stories.

She couldn't allow him to believe she'd become one of them. "Where's the phone?"

Pendegraff put a restraining hand on her shoulder as she began searching for a phone. "Until I figure out who is behind this, who set me up and burned down your place, the safest thing you can do is stay missing."

"But—"

"It's for your own safety, Lexy. Your father wouldn't want you to put yourself at risk, would he?"

"You don't understand. He's a cop. He lost my mother to cancer…I'm all he's got left. He'll go to my place, he'll think it was me in that fire and he'll drive himself crazy. I have to get hold of him."

He rubbed her shoulder briefly before letting her go. "Give me half an hour to explain. Then, if you still want to, you can call your father."

She glared at him, at the flawed emerald eyes, the expensive tough-guy face. How could she trust him? He wouldn't even give out her location.

"Where am I?"

"I value my privacy. You already know too much about me. I really don't want you being able to summon cops to my door."

She remained silent.

"You're in the mountains. Still in the States."

"Not good enough."

Maybe he understood how helpless she felt and how much she needed a little information to help her cope. "Colorado. It's fairly remote, but the closest town is Aspen."

"How did I get here?"

"Private plane."

"Stolen?"

A slight grin cracked the serious expression on his face. "No. I bought it."

"So you're a pretty rich thief."

"I do okay."

"Where's the pilot?"

"You're looking at him."

Somehow, she wasn't surprised. "This is like one of those nightmares where you want to wake up, and can't."

"I'm truly sorry about your home and business. This is not the kind of stuff I get involved in."

"Right. You're a gentleman thief, I bet. Somebody Cary Grant would play in an old movie."

He smiled briefly. "Sit down while I cook you breakfast."

She picked up her coffee and followed him as he strolled to the fancy-schmancy kitchen, pulling down a gleaming steel frying pan with all the confidence of a top chef. She watched as he opened the fridge and began efficiently removing butter, brown eggs, spinach, cheese and some kind of fresh herb she wasn't enough of a cook to identify. She topped up her coffee and perched on one of the sleek kitchen stools.

"He cooks, he breaks into supposedly unbreakable safes, he flies his own plane. What other talents are you hiding, Mr. Pendegraff?"

He turned from his task and the glance he sent her was so full of sexual heat she felt as if her skin would scorch. For a second she couldn't breathe. "One day, I'll show you," he promised softly.

Instead of returning the icy glare he deserved, she felt a response so strong it shamed her. Heat rushed through her, making her light-headed. Well, maybe he was the sexiest man who'd ever kidnapped her, but there was one thing she was certain of: it would be a cold day in hell before she'd be getting naked with this guy.

"You've got thirty minutes to explain what the hell is going on. Start talking."

It was amazing how he could crack eggs, chop herbs, grate cheese and still manage to calmly explain a story that grew increasingly complicated as she listened. Her headache was gone and if she still felt a little fuzzy, she had no trouble following the plot.

"I help people retrieve things," he explained. "Quietly, without a fuss."

"You steal."

"It's a gray area. I used to steal, no question about it, but after a while the thrill wears off. Besides, I figured I should quit while I was ahead. Never caught."

"I caught you."

A flicker of annoyance crossed his face. So, that bothered him, did it? Good.

"Had you at gunpoint, too."

"I was unbelievably careless last night." He flicked a glance at her...a quicker, softer version of the sexual scorcher he'd lobbed her way earlier. "On too many levels."

He chopped whatever the herb that was with a vengeance. "And so were you."

"Me?"

"What are you doing with no proper security? Candy-ass locks and no video surveillance? Anybody can get in."

She shrugged. His words echoed her father's uncomfortably. How many times had her dad nagged her about security? "I figured I could take care of things. I live on the premises." She glared at him. "And the safe is supposed to be unbreakable."

"No such thing. Not to a guy like me."

"So what was a guy like you doing there? Spinning me some tale about wanting a wedding ring, then robbing me."

The knife stilled. "Can we clear one thing up? I wasn't robbing you. Had no intention of doing so. The only thing I took was the emeralds."

She snorted. "Oh, is that all? Do you have any idea what they're worth? My insurance would never cover that amount. I'd be ruined."

He shook his head. "You can't put a price on that set. What story did the woman give you? The one who brought in the emeralds?"

"How do you know it was a woman?"

"Please. I'm a professional. I didn't pick your place to knock it over. I followed the gems to your studio."

She drank coffee, stalling for time. She didn't want to give out any information, but if he'd followed the woman to her place he must know something about her. "She said she wanted them reset, modernized to give them to her daughter to wear. I got the feeling she was hoping to attract a rich husband by hanging a fortune around that girl's neck."

He glanced at her sharply. "The older woman did the talking?"

"Yes."

"Who did she say she was?"

"Florence Grayson."

He laughed aloud. "Oh, you've got to give the woman credit. She's got some guts."

"Are you saying that woman isn't Florence Grayson?"

"Nope. Technically I suppose they stole the gems from Florence Grayson. The young one? Pretending to be the daughter? She's Edward Grayson's mistress. Or was. I'm guessing Edward gave her the heave-ho and Tiffany treated herself to a little goodbye gift. The Isabella Emeralds." He poured eggs into the pan and breakfast began to sizzle.

"Wait, I'm getting confused. The mother isn't the mother, the daughter's the mistress—and what are the Isabella Emeralds?"

"I've met Florence Grayson. That wasn't her. I've also met the mistress, Tiffany Starr if you can believe that's the name she picked for herself. And as for the Isabella Emeralds, they're part of a legend. Should really be in a museum."

Lexy had an affinity for jewels the way some people have for water, or music. They all but spoke to her. She recalled the sadness she'd felt at the idea of resetting stones that were so perfectly at home in the delicate antique setting. "I thought they were some of the nicest and best set gems I'd ever seen. That deep color was so unusual. I'd only ever seen it in jewels that came from Mayan mines in Columbia centuries ago. I actually suggested they might want to rethink the idea of having the set redesigned."

"Your instincts were right on."

Something was tickling her memory. She closed her eyes for a moment. And then it came to her. She'd actually read about the Isabella Emeralds back when she'd been studying antique gems. "I thought the Isabella Emeralds had been lost."

"Nope."

"Weren't they rumored to have gone down with the *Titanic* or something?"

"I suspect the owner set about the rumor. Rich collectors can do some pretty strange things. They've been in a private collection, which pretty much means the same thing as lost to the world. Grayson is so terrified of losing those emeralds that he never lets Florence wear them. I didn't know he even owned the set until I was called in to recover them."

"Then how did the mistress hear about them?"

He threw an amused glance over his shoulder. "I'm guessing Mr. G got a nice charge out of decking his mistress in his precious gems—and nothing else, for his private pleasure."

"Historical gems as sex toys? Oh, please."

He chuckled. "You asked. I was giving my opinion."

"Is that what you'd do if you had them?"

He folded the omelet expertly in two. "If I had the right model." Something about his tone reminded her that the Isabella Emeralds were currently in his possession.

As was she.

"If I remember correctly, the Isabella Emeralds were a gift to Queen Isabella of Spain from Christopher Columbus, right?"

He nodded. Cut the omelet in half and slid the pieces onto two thick blue ceramic plates. "As part of a thank-you gift for funding his trip to America."

"In 1492."

"Exactly. Not only are the gems themselves amazing quality—"

"I noticed that. The diamonds are flawless, and the emeralds as close to perfect as you can get in that size. The gems alone would be worth a fortune, but their provenance makes them—"

"Priceless."

He slid a plate to the counter in front of her, handed her a knife and fork and a blue linen napkin.

"Thanks."

He brought his own meal and sat beside her at the breakfast bar. It was undoubtedly cozy and she might have felt uncomfortable if she weren't obsessed with the notion that she'd very nearly unwittingly destroyed a piece of history. "How could that woman have been so stupid? By getting me to reset the gems she'd be decimating their value and annihilating a piece of history."

"They'd be a lot easier to sell, though. You can't exactly put the Isabella Emeralds on auction at Christie's or post them on eBay and not have somebody notice."

"Wow. So where do you come in?" She dug into the omelet, found it thick and fluffy and full of flavor, which didn't even surprise her. She was beginning to think that Charles Pendegraff did everything well.

"Edward Grayson hired me to retrieve the gems after he discovered they were missing. Oh, he doesn't know he hired me. My chauffeur fronts for me at all client meetings. I prefer to keep my identity to myself. I go along electronically."

"Sneaky."

"I prefer the term *discreet.* Anyhow, Grayson asked me to get the set back, with no publicity, no police, no embarrassment. In return I pocketed a nice fee. Everybody's happy."

"Except this one went sideways. Publicity, police and a very embarrassingly dead body. Somebody screwed up. Great omelet by the way."

"Thank you. Somebody was set up."

"But why? It makes no sense. And who is the dead woman in my studio?"

He frowned. "I don't know for certain, but I could hazard a guess."

5

THE EGGS SUDDENLY FELT like cement as she swallowed and made the obvious connection. "You think the dead woman is Tiffany Starr?" She had met the woman, talked to her even. She hadn't reached her thirtieth birthday, and now she was dead? It was foolish and vindictive to steal priceless jewelry from a former lover, but did she have to die for her crime?

"Who else could it be? You and I were there when the goons started to break in. There was no one else in the studio or your apartment."

She shook her head. "No."

"So they threw in an already dead woman, torched the place. Days will go by before anyone realizes it's not you in there."

"Why? If what you say is true, why didn't Grayson stick to the plan? He'd have got his emeralds back and no one would ever have known she took them."

"That, Lexy, is something I'm planning to figure out."

He was looking at her with an intensity she didn't like. As though there were more bad news on the way.

"What?"

"My guess is that Tiffany Starr wasn't the only one who was supposed to die last night."

An unpleasant queasiness rolled through her. "You mean…?"

"You'd seen and handled the gems and I'd been hired to retrieve them. As I said, no one has set eyes on them since the early part of this century. I pegged Grayson as one of those fanatics who want to keep all their toys to themselves."

"Like a spoiled kid?"

"A spoiled kid with his own private staff of thugs and killers."

She sank her head into her hands. "I should have listened to my mom. I should have gone into nursing. Or teaching. Something uncomplicated, with a pension."

"Somehow I can't see you in an ordinary profession."

She groaned. "I know. It's my curse."

"Finish your eggs. It's always been my belief that you can't commit a crime on an empty stomach, and I'm almost positive you can't solve one, either."

She toyed with an orange slice but in truth she'd lost her appetite. As she played his words back, she dropped the orange. "Wait a minute. You said your chauffeur went into the meeting with Grayson instead of you. They think he is you. He's the one who's going to get killed."

"Don't worry about Healey. He can take care of himself."

She didn't know why she should be concerned about a man who'd aided and abetted her kidnapping, but then she was the sort of person who bought non-kill rodent traps and had, on occasion, transported a very angry rat to a new home.

Amanda had been horrified and flat-out refused even to open the door so she and the rat could get outside. Her breath caught in her chest. "Oh, my God. Amanda. She saw the women. I even showed her the emeralds." She jumped to her feet, her heart hammering painfully. "I have to warn Amanda." She ran past Pendegraff, headed for the door of the house. If the Jeep was still sitting there, she could get to a town, somehow she'd find a way back to New York.

She was out of the front door. Good, the Jeep was still there. Keys inside would be nice, but if not she knew how to hot-wire a car. Her dad had taught her a lot of useful skills over the years.

The gravel bit into her socks and the sun blasted her eyeballs but she barely noticed. Amanda was her employee, a friend, her responsibility. She had to warn her.

The Jeep was parked, a gray shape against the snow. She sprinted blindly toward it, was almost there when a strong hand grabbed her arm, almost pulling it out of its socket.

"Ow. Let me go."

"Lexy. Stop."

She turned to him, and in turning found herself bashing hard abs, a chest that felt like granite, looking up into a face that was surprisingly understanding. "I have to go. You've got to let me. Amanda trusts me. She's my employee, my responsibility." She panted, trying to get the words out and pull away from his grip at the same time.

"I know. It's okay. Healey's watching things."

"Healey? The guy who helped you drug and kidnap

me? Pardon me if I don't feel superconfident in his abilities to guard my friend."

"Healey's the most capable person I know. It's why I hired him."

"Those men are killers. You said so yourself. Killer trumps thief. You know? Like Rock, Paper, Scissors? Killer would trump them all. Crush rock, shred paper, smash scissors. This isn't a game. You've got to let me get back."

"I can't, Lexy. It's too dangerous. I'm trying to protect you."

"Then you have to let me call my dad," she said as calmly as she could. "He deserves to know I'm alive, and he can make sure Amanda gets police protection."

The understanding expression in his eyes hardened to stubborn. "Not possible."

"This is not negotiable."

A glint of humor softened the hard planes of his face. "Are you in a position to negotiate?"

At that moment all she knew was she had to protect her friend and she'd do whatever she had to. "I think so. I will do everything I can to get out of here, and I'm a pretty resourceful woman. You'll either have to tie me and lock me up, keep me drugged 24/7 or give me one phone call."

"We're in the mountains. Miles from Aspen. You don't even know what direction it's in."

"Like I said, I'm resourceful. Do you really want to keep chasing me down?" She was gambling, she knew, but a man who didn't lock her door, and who made such good omelets didn't strike her as a guy who was going to be happy dressing her in duct tape the entire time she was here.

"You're a pain in the ass, you know that?"

"I didn't ask to be here."

He squinted up at the sky as though the answer might be written there. Finally he said, "And if I give you that one phone call you'll cooperate?"

"I want to get the people who tried to kill me as much as you do."

"Come on." He turned on his heel and headed back for the house. For a moment she hesitated. She could have the Jeep going in less than five minutes without keys, thirty seconds with, but she didn't know the area, the roads, she had nothing with her, not a cell phone, money, not even shoes.

Reluctantly she turned and followed Pendegraff. Seemed one phone call was her only option.

For now.

The phone was, predictably she supposed, a satellite phone, so the call would be untraceable.

Before he handed it to her, he said, "How easy would it be for an outsider to connect you with your dad?"

"Not easy." She hadn't thought until this second that her father could be in danger because of her and the missing emeralds. She'd never been more thankful they had different names. "My great-grandfather changed his Polish surname, Dabrowski to Drake. He figured it would be easier for the kids to fit in. My dad was a Drake and so was I, but when I was a kid he went through some kind of Polish identity crisis and wanted to go back to his roots." She found herself smiling, amazed she could. "We took one memorable family holiday back to the old country, saw the town where his people came from, looked up a couple of cousins who didn't speak any more English than we spoke Polish."

"How old were you?"

"Fifteen, I think. It was pretty cool and my mom

made him take us to Paris as well, so I had a great time. After we got home he decided to change his name back to Dabrowski. He wanted us all to be Dabrowskis but my mother refused. She said I already had a name, and I wasn't getting another one until I got married. So, my Dad's Dabrowski and I'm Drake."

"Even so, you'd better warn him to keep his guard up. I'm guessing Grayson will stop at nothing to get these jewels back. We have to be smarter than they are. Call your dad at the station. If he's not there, don't leave a message. Keep calling back until you get him."

"Okay."

She placed the call; for some reason her fingers weren't quite steady. What if she was wrong? What if somehow Grayson, or whoever was behind this, had made the connection between her and her father? Even as the phone was ringing she began to panic.

"Dabrowski," the familiar tone barked, sounding clipped and somehow toneless.

Relief washed over her and the familiar voice was so comforting to hear that she wanted to crawl into his lap and make all the ugly stuff disappear. "Oh, thank God. Dad, it's me."

For a second there was total silence.

"Dad? It's me, Lexy."

"Jesus, Mary and Joseph, you're alive."

"Yeah. I had to call when I saw the news. I knew you'd be worried sick."

"I gotta sit down." She heard fumbling and then he was back. "Where the hell are you? Your place burned, it's trashed, I thought you were dead." He sounded aggressive and angry, but also like he had a bad cold. She knew he was fighting back tears and her own eyes filled.

"I'm so sorry you were worried." She wrapped her hand tighter around the phone as though it were her father's hand. "It's a long story, and I don't have a lot of time, but I'm all right. I need you to do something for me."

"I'll come and get you is what I'll do. You seen what happened to your place?"

"Yes. I saw the news. Please just listen. I think I might be in danger."

"Then you get your ass back here so I can protect you."

"It's not that simple. Dad, if the people who burned down my place and killed that woman figure out you're my father, you could be in danger, too."

"What the hell is going on? Who's they? What are you involved in?"

"I honestly don't know, but it involves some jewelry I was working on."

Pendegraff was making wind-it-up motions with his hand. "I don't have much time, but it's really important you not go to the media or do anything that would make a connection between us. And watch your back, okay? You're all I've got."

"It's not my back I'm worried about. Honey, I need you to come home."

"I can't. Not until I figure out what's going on. Is there any ID yet on the body?"

"Too soon. Everybody still thinks it's you. Once they rule you out, then we start trying to figure out who the Jane Doe is."

"I might be able to help. There's a woman named Tiffany Starr...no idea what her real name is. We think it might be her."

"How do you know that?"

"I'm sorry, Dad, I've got to go. I'll call you again soon."

"Wait. Who's we? Who are you with?"

"I can't tell you that, but I promise I'm safe. I'll call again as soon as I can. Don't worry."

She hung up before he could get started on the worried rant she could feel building.

He was so concerned for her that she doubted he'd think for a second about his own safety, despite her warning.

And what was the point of her being stuck out here in the middle of Colorado when people she cared about were in danger? "I have to go back to New York," she said.

"Oh, I agree."

"You do?"

"Yes."

"Oh, thank God. When can we leave?"

"Thursday."

"Thursday? Why, do you have a dental appointment?"

He sent her one of his "James Bond superspy everything's a secret and women adore me anyway" looks that were really starting to piss her off. "A social engagement."

She opened her mouth to protest but he continued, "And you're coming with me."

"I thought you said—"

"What size do you wear?" He looked her up and down like he was Vera Wang's personal assistant. "Four?"

And he'd have made a good one. "I buy my own clothes."

"Fine. I'll make sure there are plenty of choices. Now,

if you'll excuse me, I've got work to do." He turned away and took a step.

"You're going to rob your own house?" she asked sweetly.

He turned back. "I'm a legitimate business person now. Mostly."

"Wait. You can't leave me here with nothing to do."

"I've got books, satellite TV, make yourself at home."

"To make myself feel at home, I'd have to torch the place," she snapped.

"I know this is hard for you, but I am trying to figure this thing out."

"By watching your stock portfolio and planning parties?"

"Oh, this is a very special party. A charity gala event in Manhattan. The Diamond Ball. You wouldn't want to miss it."

Something about his tone had her narrowing her eyes, amazed at how stupid she'd been. "Grayson's going to be there, isn't he?"

"You bet your sweet ass he'll be there. Since he and his wife are hosting the party, he can hardly avoid showing up."

"It's too bad I don't have any of my own jewelry with me. I could display my wares in front of New York's glamour crowd."

"Never mind. I've got a very nice set of emeralds you can borrow for the evening."

She swallowed. "You're serious, aren't you?"

"Absolutely. If Grayson's as obsessed with those jewels as I think he is, he'll go crazy when he sees them on you. And in public."

"Won't he try to get them back?"

"Oh, I hope so. But he can't do anything in the middle of a social gathering with hundreds of very well connected guests, now can he?"

"I don't know. The guy probably killed his ex-mistress, he tried to kill you and me, destroyed my home and business. I really don't think he'd stop at much."

"When are you going to start trusting me?"

"Oh, let's see. Probably when you stop holding me against my will."

He took a step closer. There was a glint in his eyes that made her want to take a step back, but naturally she held her ground. She had her pride. "From now on, I'll try not to do anything against your will."

There he went again, with his annoying sexual innuendos, which were so corny she should be rolling her eyes. Except that when he gazed at her in a certain way and his voice took on that deeper timbre, she responded in some deep and utterly female part of her that didn't care all that much about kidnapping or inappropriate behavior or sexual innuendo. That was the part of her that lit up like a rocket when he got close.

Heaven help her if he ever stopped teasing and actually made a physical move on her.

Of course, she'd drop him like a stone. Gun-wielding wasn't her only self-defense tool.

At least, she thought she'd drop him like a stone, but she hoped she wasn't going to be tested since she had a teensy feeling that the one doing the dropping might be her. Right onto her back.

He was looking at her mouth, the way a man looks at a woman's mouth when he's thinking about kissing her.

Her own lips started to tingle in anticipation as he drew closer, even as her brain was clamoring at her to stop acting like a fool. What, did she have Stockholm syndrome after one day of captivity that she should be thinking of locking lips with her kidnapper?

While she was trying to think of all the reasons why she shouldn't kiss the guy—and there were plenty—the decision was taken out of her hands. His mouth closed over hers. He kissed her slowly, thoroughly, then he raised his head, rested his hands on the wall above her head.

"I've been wanting to do that since the moment I saw you."

She was so surprised she could barely believe what had happened. The man stole everything, even kisses.

"What about Penelope?"

He was still staring at her lips so his voice was a little vague as he said, "Penelope?"

"Your fiancée?" She was pretty sure he'd made Penelope up, but she needed every defense she could muster against a man she found dangerously attractive.

"Oh. Right. Penelope." He traced her lower lip with his thumb. "We broke up."

He kissed her again.

He wasn't the only one having trouble focusing. She could barely form words. "When? When did you break up with Penelope your fiancée?"

"Right after I met you."

He was such a liar. He nibbled her lower lip. Good kisser, though.

"How did she take it?"

"Like a champ. You have the most kissable mouth I've ever seen."

"Thank you." He placed another series of kisses on her lips, then tilted her chin so he could kiss his way down her neck. She'd never noticed how sensitive her skin was there.

"Sounds like she was glad to get rid of you."

He nipped her lightly when he reached her shoulder. "She was brokenhearted, naturally, but she understood that I could never marry her if I was obsessed with kissing you."

"That would be awkward." She put her arms around his neck, looked up at him through her lashes. "So, do I look like her at all?"

"No. Totally different."

"She's tall?"

"A little taller than you. Not much."

"And she's blonde?"

"Redhead. And what they say about the temper is true, by the way." He came back for one more kiss on her mouth. "But to give Penelope credit, she never pulled a gun on me."

She didn't like remembering how easily he'd wrested that gun away from her. She was going to have to seriously get back in shape when she got home, and rev-up the self-defense lessons.

He straightened. "That was definitely worth waiting for. But, much as I'd like to stay here and make out all day, I've got to get to work. My office is back there if you need me," he said, gesturing to a hallway running to the rear of the house. "Try to stay out of trouble."

As she watched him walk away she thought he was too late.

She licked her lips slowly; seemed she was already in trouble. Deep trouble.

6

HEALEY'S ELBOW WAS JAMMED into a tree branch; he was pretty sure he'd ripped out the knee in his black trousers and something was crawling on the exposed skin of his leg. Something that felt like an ant.

He didn't care too much about any of that. Or the way his body was unnaturally folded into one of the ornamental trees that lined the block, the young leaves filling out the branches. What he cared about was feeling like a pervert. Looking through a window at a hot chick undressing would be great if the girl knew you were looking and wanted you there. But that wasn't the case.

He was doing a job because Pendegraff told him to and that was how he got paid. But when he'd crawled up here to check that Alexandra Drake's assistant, Amanda, was home, he hadn't imagined she'd be undressing.

Or that the tree would be so perfectly reflected in her dressing-table mirror. If he squinted, he could make out a darker shadow within the rustling leaves that was his own bulk. So long as he stayed still, she'd never clue in that he was here. But if he moved, she'd make him instantly.

So, acutely embarrassed, he stayed.

Amanda Sanford. That was her name. The assistant in Alexandra Drake's jewelry studio. A pretty small fish, but if Charlie was right, the same goons who'd torched the jewelry studio might well come after the only person who might know where Lexy was.

Of course, she didn't know her boss was alive, never mind where she was. Hopefully the two women would be reunited if he could keep Amanda alive and Charlie could do the same for Lexy.

Amanda was changing her clothes, which wasn't good news on a whole bunch of levels. First, it meant she was going out when he'd hoped she'd stay tucked in safe and tight. Second, she was taking her sweet time about the changing part and hadn't even bothered to pull the blind. Any fool with a pair of eyes could watch her.

A diamond stud glinted in her nose and when she turned the light caught the ring in her eyebrow.

A black shirt came off first. Her skin was tawny, and she had a long, lean torso. Her bra was one of those why-even-bother affairs that do more to show off than to hide the assets in question.

He dropped his gaze with determination. He couldn't shirk his duty, but he could for damn sure look away instead of staring at her like a Peeping Tom.

Resolutely he let his gaze slide, unable to help himself from noticing the tattoo of a sailboat on her left shoulder blade. He'd seen tatts on girls before, usually running to flowers or birds, or those tough-girl barbed-wire rings around the bicep, but he'd never seen a sailboat.

She put her hands to her waistband to undo her jeans

and he forced himself to look even farther down. Her feet were bare. The jeans bagged at the bottom as she pulled them off, then stepped out of them.

And he thought she had the prettiest ankles and calves he'd ever seen. Ankles? What the hell was the matter with him? He didn't have a thing for ankles. Never even noticed them before.

She turned, walked a few steps and he noticed another tatt. This one on her ankle. An anchor. Again, an odd choice for a woman and definitely at odds with the sailboat on her shoulder. From his peripheral vision, he could see her body moving, reaching into a closet but he kept his focus firmly on her feet and lower legs.

To his enormous relief he watched her step into a dress and pull it up over her hips. Giving her time to get the top part on, he waited a moment before raising his gaze. Her dress was short and floated around her. Feminine.

She opened a narrow drawer in the dresser and stared down into it for a long time. Then she drew out a necklace. She touched it as though it were an heirloom, running her finger along the edges of a chunky-looking design of gold and some other metals. In the mirror he watched her face crumple and tears started to fall. He wished he could reach out and wipe them away, tell her her friend and employer wasn't dead at all but alive and safe.

Naturally he couldn't, so he watched as she carefully fastened the necklace around her neck, then swiped her hands over her face. She walked out of sight, and returned a few minutes later, her face looking freshly washed. Her bangs clung damply to her forehead.

Without the heavy makeup she appeared much

younger and vulnerable. Her eyes were shadowed by lack of sleep and, he suspected, shock and grief.

She'd lost both her employer and her job in a pretty dramatic fashion when the studio burned to the ground and a woman's body had been found in the building.

He watched as she pulled herself together, touching the necklace from time to time as she lined her eyes with black pencil, smudged some other stuff in a complicated arrangement and then laid on the mascara brush. She left her face plain and merely added a swipe of glossy lip stuff.

He watched as she sat on her bed and yanked on black stockings with big diamond-shaped holes, and then stuck her feet into tough-guy black boots.

He kind of liked the mix of softly feminine with kick-ass toughness. Wondered if her personality reflected her clothing style and wished he had the luxury of finding out.

At last she grabbed a bag with a chain that she slung over her shoulder, and left. He looked carefully around before lowering himself from the tree but the side street was momentarily deserted. As he hit the ground, he noticed that it wasn't, in fact, deserted. An elderly woman walking a tiny dog jumped when he landed on the ground a few feet away. He hadn't seen her before because an arrangement of branches had hidden her. Damn. She was eyeing him as though she were about to whack him with her purse.

He smiled. Held out his ring of keys. "Found 'em. My wife threw them out the window during a fight." He shook his head, shrugged. "I love her, but the woman has quite a temper."

"Take her some flowers," the woman advised.

Her dog, meanwhile, peed on the tree he'd just vacated.

After walking down the street in the opposite direction of the old woman and her dog, he turned left, circling around in time to catch Amanda coming out of her building. She had a cell phone glued to her ear and as she talked, he noticed that she touched her necklace a few times.

She dropped down into the subway. He followed from a distance, keeping track of her whereabouts without getting too close and at the same time trying to figure out if anybody else was tailing her.

He didn't think so. But he wasn't taking any chances.

AFTER TOURING THE ENTIRE mountain retreat Lexy knew that there were four bedrooms, a nice workout room downstairs, a wine cellar and a media room, and that Pendegraff wore reading glasses when he worked and was vain enough to slip them off when she barged into his office to find him typing on a sleek laptop, ignoring a stunning view of the mountains behind him.

"I need boots," she informed him.

He blinked as though adjusting to looking at her after focusing on his computer screen. He then glanced down at her slipper-socked feet. "Why?"

"Because I need to get some air. I'm going stir-crazy." She'd been obsessively checking the news stations for any update on the fire and its aftermath. But, apart from feeling gratified to discover she'd rated a small mention on CNN, she didn't get much for her trouble but more depressing footage of her destroyed property. It was beyond strange to see her neighbors, a couple of fellow designers and even the star of the reality show, *Party Girls of Manhattan,* talking about how talented she was and how much they loved her and her jewelry.

"She was like her designs," a smarmy no-talent rival said into the camera. "One of a kind, and she'll never be replaced."

Lexy wanted to throw something. She stood up and shook her fist at the stupid TV. "I'm not dead," she yelled at the screen. That was when she knew she had to get some exercise.

Charlie seemed less than excited about the idea of her leaving the house but she'd had enough of being a victim. "I'm going out. There must be some kind of trail or something."

"I'll come with you," he said.

"No. I need to be alone. I don't want a jailor."

"But—"

She put her hands on her hips and glared. "Look, buster. You want me to trust you, which is a pretty tall order considering what you've put me through, how about you trust me. I said I'll come back, I will."

He nodded slowly. "What size are your feet?"

"Six."

"I've got some women's boots that are a seven. Best I can do. Wear an extra pair of socks."

"Ladies' shoes. Really. Can they be Penelope's?"

"My mother's."

She turned away. "Whatever."

"You'll find them in the mudroom closet."

As he'd promised, she did find a few pairs of shoes, hiking boots and snow boots. All sevens. The hiking boots fit okay when she tightened the laces. Pendegraff came into the mudroom as she was preparing to leave. He carried a white parka and a pair of ski gloves. He helped her into the coat, handed her the gloves, opened the door for her and stepped outside behind her.

This door opened to the back of the house, but the view was similar to that at the front. There was snow everywhere she looked, white and, except for some random animal tracks, untouched. And where the clearing ended, there were trees. Massive evergreens that marched toward the towering mountain peaks.

"You want some snowshoes."

"I do?" She was doubtful, never having been on a pair.

"Yeah. It's easy. Just walk normally. You'll get the hang of it."

He disappeared back into the mudroom and returned with snowshoes. Metal ovals that he strapped onto her boots for her.

"Thanks," she said reluctantly. She didn't want him to be thoughtful, any more than she wanted to be disturbed by his proximity, or find that his kiss was still imprinted on her mouth.

He extended his hand across the clearing to a gap in the trees. "That's the main trail. Stay on it and you'll be fine. Turn around when you get tired."

"Where does it go?"

He pointed to the summit of a mountain. "Take you a couple of days to get there, but on a sunny day, it's a great view."

She headed off without a backward glance, knowing he was watching her. Presumably to ensure she didn't sneak around to the front of the house and steal the 4x4.

Snowshoeing was a lot like normal walking, so long as she took her time. She practiced in the clearing until she had the hang of it and then attempted the trail. It was pretty rough with snow-covered rocks ready to trip the unwary. But the air was so clear and it smelled pure and heavenly when she filled her lungs. The trail headed upward meandering only slightly so she was soon puffing.

Oddly enough, as she got higher things started to fall into perspective. She wasn't dead; she was very much alive. And in the middle of an adventure the likes of which she'd never imagined.

She was also tough, resourceful and creative. Anybody who messed with her better be prepared for that.

A hawk circled in the sky, and a gray and white bird she didn't recognize landed on a tree and watched her, cocking its head as though wondering what on earth she was doing lumbering along on plastic and metal dishes.

By the time she'd stomped back into the mudroom a couple of hours had passed and she was starting to move beyond shock to "now what?"

"Hi, honey, I'm home," she yelled.

Pendegraff came out of his office. Took one look at her and grinned. If he was relieved she hadn't tried to steal the Jeep and take off, he was obviously trying to be cool. "You've got rosy cheeks."

"Had a great workout. Thanks."

He nodded. "Coffee's fresh. Help yourself." And he went back to his office.

She poured coffee and then checked the news stations again. Nothing new.

Went downstairs and made use of Pendegraff's very nice home gym, then showered and changed into a comfy pair of sweats and a T-shirt with a pink snow-flake embroidered on the front of it.

Not her usual look, but kidnappees, she reminded herself, can't be choosers.

7

AMANDA HOPPED ONTO a crowded subway car heading downtown and Healey squeezed himself in at the opposite end of the same car.

He was getting tired of following this restless woman around. She'd been to an avant garde art gallery for a couple of hours, gone shopping without buying anything, stopped for a coffee and stared sightlessly out the window. He wished she'd just go home and give them both a rest.

She got out near Third and Lexington. At first he thought she was going in to one of the Indian restaurants scenting the air and reminding him he hadn't eaten in a while. A black and white cat nestled in the doorway of a corner market regarded him with lazy interest.

They passed an Asian fusion place and then she joined a short lineup of people heading into a bar.

He studied the menu outside the Asian place feeling his hunger increase as he contemplated the possibilities.

She was in. He waited. When she emerged, he'd follow her home and make sure she got in safely. But what if Grayson's people somehow got her in the bar? He stared at the neon sign. Emo's. After an hour when she hadn't reappeared, he couldn't stop worrying about her. He entered the bar.

He was twenty-nine years old and walking into the bar made him feel ancient. The clientele was young and definitely tended to the alternative. In his jacket and dark pants he stuck out like a Wall Street banker at a folk festival.

Nothing he could do about it now, so he headed for the end of the long bar and checked the place out. It was pretty busy. Lots of Goth types, some college students, artsy folk. There were half-moon shaped booths along one wall and then mingling space, which was pretty crowded. Amanda sat at a booth with a group of friends. All had drinks in front of them but they didn't look like they were partying it up. He recognized the young guy who'd been on the TV looking for Lexy the night of the fire.

A couple of the women were wearing distinctive jewelry pieces, similar to that worn by Amanda. They kept touching their necklaces, or bracelets, or earrings as they talked, occasionally laughed. A digital camera appeared and was passed around, causing more laughter and a few tears. He had to believe this was a modern wake.

When it was Amanda's turn with the digital camera, he watched her expressions shift between fondness, amusement and grief. A grief so fresh it hurt him to look at her. Suddenly she passed the camera to the guy beside her, as though she couldn't bear to see the photos anymore. She looked up, his way, and before he could turn, their gazes connected.

Damn. He hadn't meant to make eye contact. Didn't

want connection between them. So he looked away, but not before recognizing the raw pain in those eyes and once more wishing he could ease it. Her eyes were blue. Bright, piercing blue under the tousle of short black hair. On a normal night, he'd go up to her. Say "hi." But this wasn't a social outing. It was work.

He turned away and took a pull of his beer.

A moment later he felt her beside him. As crowded as the bar was, and as full of women, he knew it was her without turning his head. Her presence was like a scent he couldn't ignore or get out of his mind.

"Hi," she said, her voice kind of rough, like a smoker's.

He turned to her. Saw that close-up her eyes were even prettier than he'd thought. Blue and dew-drenched, like flowers in the rain. "Hi." This was bad. So bad. He wasn't supposed to talk to her; he was supposed to be invisible. He absolutely wasn't to think about those contradictory tattoos, to wonder how that sailboat would taste under his tongue, to remember the lacy bra and the swells of flesh beneath it.

Nice going, Healey.

She leaned a slender arm on the bar and he realized she was a little the worse for wear. The diamond stud flashed. "I'm Amanda."

"Healey."

"I'm a little drunk."

"Sorry to hear that."

She giggled. "You shouldn't be. I'm so bad when I'm drunk."

He swallowed, hard. He could blow her off, should blow her off, but then she'd go hit on some other guy and that seemed an incredibly stupid and dangerous idea. She didn't know she could trust Healey, but he did.

"You seem kind of sad," he said.

"Buy me a drink and I'll tell you all my troubles."

Giving in to the inevitable, he motioned to the bartender. "Jaegar Bomb," she said. "We're sort of having a wake. You should have one, too."

He nodded and the bartender went to prepare the drinks.

"I can't sit there anymore. It's too depressing." She grabbed his upper arm, as though for balance. "Life is short, you know? I never realized how short it is. What's the point of dreaming about the future or worrying? You have to get out there and live it. Every day. Every minute. Every second." She laughed, a deep, sexy sound. "And definitely, every night."

The bombs came at that moment. She picked up the shot glass, popped it in the glass of Red Bull. And downed it. A drip of liquid ended up on her lower lip and he had to restrain himself from licking it off her.

She shook her head. "Wow." She laughed up at him. "Now, you."

He threw the drink back. The bitter and sweet mixing in his mouth. Which was pretty much how he felt about this woman coming on to him. He wanted her and knew this was the last thing he should be doing.

But then his usefulness as a tail was now completely blown, so he figured staying close to her was one way to protect her. And besides so far he'd seen no evidence that anyone was following her or watching her movements, except him.

"So, how come you're the only guy here in a suit?"

"Just got off work. Thought I'd come by and grab a quick beer and some food. What's good here?" He suspected that some food in her stomach would be a good plan.

"Nachos are pretty good. The burgers are okay."

He ordered nachos and a burger and she said, "So, what do you do where you have to wear a suit and work late?"

"I drive a limo. You?"

"I'm, ah, kind of unemployed right now." She didn't regale him with the dramatic tale of how her workplace had burned to the ground along with her employer, which he thought showed a lot of class.

"Taking some time?"

"Yeah. I'm not sure what I'll do next. I can't waste my time anymore, you know? Life's too short."

"So you said."

"Well, it is. There was a time, maybe last week, when I'd have noticed you, seen you checking me out and figured if you came to talk to me, great. If you didn't no biggie." She grabbed a nacho, piled it with sour cream and salsa, "Not anymore. What if you didn't come talk to me? I'd have missed an opportunity." She said the word *opportunity* very carefully. "I'm not doing that anymore. If I like the look of someone, I'm going to talk to them. Anything wrong with that?" She shoved the loaded chip in her mouth.

"Not a thing." But this oddly protective instinct he had about her kicked in. "You probably want to keep it in a public place until you're sure, though."

Her eyes lost their shadow of sadness as speculation took their place. "Are you telling me that you're dangerous, Healey?" Her voice took on a sultry edge. The filmy, floaty dress brushed his thigh as she moved closer. Her hand followed, rubbing up and down. "Is that why you want to keep this in a public place?"

Impossible not to feel aroused by her words and the blatant invitation of her hand on his thigh.

Her hand was moving, closing in on her target. He couldn't think what to do, so he grabbed her hand in his and said, "Let's get out of here."

He thought her friends would protest but they were deep in discussion and he doubted they'd even noticed. He led her out onto the street. It was dark, with pools of light spilling from the restaurant windows. The first shadowed patch they hit, she pushed herself against him, shoving him against a brick wall and pressing her body to his. She lifted her face, kissing him blindly.

He understood that she was seeking oblivion from her pain, even as he knew he should stop her. But the minute their mouths met, he was as lost as she.

He didn't have the excuse of alcohol or grief; all he had was this strange sense of connection, and lust as strong as anything he'd ever known.

Her hands grabbed his shoulders, ran down his back. Her body was lean and quick moving as she rubbed herself against him.

He pulled away. "Let's get you home, wildcat."

She giggled. "Thought you wanted to do it in public."

"Nope. What I want to do to you needs a lot of privacy."

"Yeah?" The word came out in a breathless rush. "What do you want to do to me?"

"I'll tell you on the subway. Come on." It occurred to him that she'd be a lot safer at his place than her own if anybody was looking for her.

As he kissed her, he smiled inwardly. Charlie had had to forcibly abduct Lexy to get her to go to his place. Amanda, on the other hand, was eager to get to Healey's place. Score one for him.

8

AMANDA WAS BURNING UP. There was something about this guy with his dreamy artist's eyes in the hard face that compelled her. Maybe because he was like one of Lexy's designs, all contrasts that went together in a delicious package, she couldn't resist him.

Impulsive, that was what she was being. And so what? She couldn't stand the heavy weight of grief anymore. She needed a couple of hours off. Maybe some hot sex with a stranger would kill the pain for a bit, since the drinks hadn't helped at all. In fact, if she let herself, she knew she'd become maudlin and start to cry. And the way she felt right now, she'd never be able to stop.

Lexy had been her friend as well as her boss. She'd started as a basic retail clerk but in the months they'd worked together she'd become a lot more. She ordered supplies, took care of the window displays and some-times—those very special times—Lexy let her help, asked her advice.

Amanda had been an art student when she'd applied for the job. It was originally a co-op placement, but she and Lexy had hit it off and the jewelry designer ended up hiring her. She'd been able to shuffle classes and work until she'd finished her program. Since then she hadn't done much in the way of art. She wasn't even sure what medium she preferred. She'd been happy working at the studio, helping Lexy with some of the simple tasks, hanging out with friends, being a young, carefree New Yorker.

Now she'd lost her job, her boss, her sense of the world as a normal place. She felt jumpy and vulnerable. If that awful, awful thing could happen to Lexy, anything was possible.

Maybe it was weird for Lexy's friends to go drinking the night after she'd died, but it was as if they had no rules or procedures to follow. None of them had ever been through anything so terrible. The bar provided the comfort of familiarity, they could share their stories, and maybe a few drinks would deaden the pain.

Hadn't worked, though. The drinks had only dulled the ache and left her with this burning need to do something wild. Sex was the most creative, life-affirming activity she knew. The second she saw Healey eyeing her, she knew she had to have him.

The subway had that eerie light that always seemed more bizarre at night. The people in their car—a couple of teenagers, tired people who looked like they worked shifts—were completely uninterested in the fact that she and Healey couldn't keep their hands off each other.

"My place?" she whispered against his lips.

"Mine." He kissed her, deep, until she felt weak with desire. "It's close."

She didn't care. She'd have done it right here if he'd asked her. "You said you'd tell me what you were going to do to me—you said you'd tell me on the subway ride."

"Did I?" He let his fingers toy with the hem of her dress, tracing the inside of her knee, finding the bump ridiculously exotic. "I'd rather show than tell. I think you have the sexiest knees I've ever felt," he informed her.

He traced a little higher, enjoying the landscape of bumpy stocking and satiny skin. The stockings looked like hell in his opinion, but they felt like sex.

They piled out of the subway, walked the few short blocks to his apartment, stopping frequently to push up against buildings in the dark and feel each other's bodies, tease each other.

He felt so good, surprisingly buff. His muscles were hard; work-out-three-times-a-day hard. The only other man she'd ever known like that had been a personal trainer she dated for a while. She loved the feel of his shoulders, his belly and chest when they rubbed against hers. The jutting evidence that he was into this as much as she was. But when she tried to slip her hands beneath his jacket, he stopped her, urging her on.

It felt as though they'd been teasing each other for hours; she was so hot she felt as if it must show.

Her dress brushing her thighs excited her, the size and solidity of the man beside her excited her, the scent of spring in the air aroused her and, most of all, the thrill of knowing she had no idea where they were going, where they'd make love, what his place would be like, what he would be like.

She was desperate enough that she didn't even care. He could lie on his back and think about the Knicks for all she cared. So long as he hung on to his impressive erection, she could do everything required to make sure they both had a good time. You could never tell with big, solid men.

He lived in a nondescript walk-up. No doorman. His apartment was on the second floor. She had a sense that the place would be full of workout equipment, a big-screen TV would dominate and his kitchen would be well-stocked with protein powder.

She couldn't have been more wrong.

He opened the door and flicked on a light, giving his place a visual sweep as though checking to make sure it was clean, which was what she'd have done. Except that this was the cleanest, neatest home she'd ever seen. Where was the junk? The dirty dishes? The clothes tossed in corners?

"I'll be right back," he said and disappeared through the doorway she assumed was the bedroom. She walked in. Usually she'd use these few moments to do some superficial snooping. What books were on his shelves? Did he have a collection of DVDs? Art on the walls? Trophies? Photos of old girlfriends?

But there wasn't much around that was snoop-worthy. One slim, sleek black bookcase held a few thrillers, some science books, a couple of volumes on natural healing. If he had family or old-girlfriend pictures they were hidden away somewhere.

She stepped into the kitchen, thinking maybe there'd at least be a few dirty dishes in the sink to make her feel more at home. Nothing. The sink was shiny.

"You want something to drink?" His voice startled her; she hadn't heard him return.

"Your sink is shiny." He must have a very good maid.

"I like to keep things neat." Finicky. Just great.

He came up behind her and wrapped his arms around her waist, running his lips up her nape so she shivered. "You want to stand here admiring my sink or get naked?"

Of course, maybe a man who shined his sink to perfection did everything to perfection. Maybe he wasn't finicky. But thorough. In the bedroom, she thought, thorough was very, very good. She sighed, leaned back into his warmth. "Get naked."

"I'm sure we'll get to the kitchen," he said, his voice low and sexy, "but for the first time, would you mind if we do it in the bedroom? I have this fantasy involving you and a mirror."

His voice was slow and heavy, like a drug in her ear, giving her a delicious shiver of excitement.

"You do?"

"Mmm-hmm. Come on," and he took her hand and led her into his bedroom. Predictably it was neater than a hotel room. The space was dominated by a low, European-looking bed with a simple gray comforter. Where a double closet had once been, he'd replaced it with a bank of drawers and one slim wardrobe cupboard. The mirror was a full-length one on the wall. She imagined him checking to see that all his buttons were done up correctly and that his socks were the regulation height as he dressed. A smallish flat-screen TV wall-mounted and a couple of Japanese block prints made up his art collection. Aside from the bed, the only furniture was a chair shaped like an *S*.

She considered going to check out the block prints since she liked art in all its forms, then he licked her shoulder and she decided she had plenty of time to check out his etchings. Later.

She turned, wrapped her arms around his neck and kissed him. Slow and deep. They'd been toying with each other now for what seemed like hours. She wanted the craziness to continue, to block out her pain, so she pushed her tongue boldly into his mouth, rubbed herself against him like a very passionate, sexually frustrated cat. "Why don't you tell me about this fantasy of yours?"

"You're standing in front of the mirror, undressing."

"Where are you?"

"I'm watching." He swallowed.

"From the bed? The chair?"

He shook his head. "I'm outside. I'm a stranger, watching you through the window."

"Peeping Tom. That's nice."

"You take your time undressing. You're kind of flirty about it."

"I'm doing a striptease for myself?"

Once again he shook his head. "You know I'm there, watching. You pretend you don't, but I can see the excitement in your eyes, the anticipation. I've been watching you, night after night, going crazy wanting you and you've been toying with me." His fingers tracked over her shoulder and his voice was so husky she felt as though the words were true. As though he'd been watching and wanting her for days. It was a good fantasy, one she could absolutely enjoy playing out, so she turned away, faced the mirror, wishing she was wearing more clothing.

She heard him settle into the chair—glad he wasn't going to go all method on her and climb out the window. She ignored him. Concentrating on her own reflection. Wow, she looked feverish. Her eyes overbright, her cheeks flushed, her breathing light and rapid. She felt a heat burning low in her belly and knew she wouldn't be able to drag this thing out very long.

For she knew that in teasing him she was tormenting herself and tonight of all nights she wanted release. Needed it with a fierce desperation.

She contemplated herself in the mirror; she had kind of a Twiggy-meets-Fight-Club look going on. No idea what she'd been thinking. Her hands went slowly to the neck of the dress. She thought her breasts were among her prettiest features so it only made sense to give him a hint of them and make him wait while she revealed the rest of herself to him.

This wasn't the first time she'd bedded a virtual stranger, but she'd quit one-night stands after college. She knew that it was grief making her act so foolishly but she was driven by forces she barely understood and certainly couldn't control.

There was a rush she'd all but forgotten in seducing a stranger, and with this game they were playing there was an extra level of sizzle in her blood.

Slowly she undid one of the buttons at her throat. A second button. The third revealed a hint of cleavage and the edge of a lacy black bra. The man behind her remained still but she felt his eyes on her reflection, was almost certain she heard a quiet "yes" as she began to reveal herself.

Taking her time about it, she lifted the hem of the dress and peeled it slowly over her head. She felt the burning intensity of his gaze as the fabric rose higher and higher until she'd pulled it over her head. He might be a neat freak but she wasn't. She tossed the dress into a corner, enjoying the way the crumpled dress stuck out in the neat room like graffiti on a white wall.

Boots next, she decided, bending slowly to untie them, giving him a good view of her rear and of her breasts straining against the lace of her cups. One by one she removed her boots, sending them sailing across the room with twin thunks.

The stockings were next. With infinite patience she peeled them down her legs, feeling his impatience burn in a way that only ignited her own and yet perversely made her slow her movements, torturing them both.

She straightened again and regarded herself in the mirror, knowing he was watching the same refection. Did he like what he was seeing? Her breasts weren't showgirl size, but they were shapely and held their own. Her hips were narrow, her legs long and lean. Not exactly a centerfold, but she liked her body, enjoyed sharing it.

She put her hands to her back to unsnap her bra and as she did so she glanced behind her. She was only checking to make sure he was paying attention, but as she looked at him their gazes connected and she felt as though lightning had struck. Heat, fire, sizzle, shock, she couldn't look away. Neither, it seemed, could he. So, while her body was displayed for him in the mirror, he gazed into her eyes. The snap gave, she eased the fabric away, and still he stared into her eyes. It probably wasn't the most intimate act of her life, but it sure felt like it.

The game ended.

He rose from the chair, fully dressed while she wore only a black lace thong.

He pulled her to him wordlessly, crushing her lips with his mouth, his hands going everywhere at once. She dragged at his shirt, his belt, bumped into his hands trying to perform the same tasks. If her striptease had been a thing of slow seduction, his was one of clumsy haste.

She almost growled in frustration as she fumbled at his belt until he pushed her hands away and did the job himself, though not all that suavely. He jammed his slacks down his legs, kicking them off in a way she knew had to be totally out of character. His briefs followed; his shirt was over his head and sailing into the corner to join her discarded clothing.

Pushing back the coverlet on the bed, he tripped her back so she fell into the soft, cool sheets. He followed, his body so hot against hers. His hands were everywhere, molding her, learning her. She felt soft and pliable compared to his boot-camp-tough body. And yet his mouth was so soft, tender almost as it traced her collarbone, her breasts. He licked the underside and she felt like screaming. The sensations were racing too fast for her to keep up. He reached down, slipping his hand into her panties, reaching for her center where she knew she was already slick with desire.

Suddenly he flipped her so she was on her tummy. His tongue traced the outlines of her tattoo. "Why a sailboat?" he asked in that gruff, deep voice that resonated with banked passion.

"To remind me I'm always free to sail away."

He continued rubbing her hot spot even as his mouth toyed with the tattoo and his lips traced the bones and ridges of her back.

He paused to remove her panties, sliding them slowly down her legs.

Then he was back, teasing her once more. "And the anchor?"

What anchor? She could barely think clearly with his hand moving in rhythmic circles. "Anchor?"

"The tattoo on your ankle," he said as though realizing she couldn't think straight.

"To keep me grounded," she panted.

He reached over and she heard a drawer open, then the familiar rustle and tear of a condom wrapper.

Heat rushed through her. Soon he'd be inside her, and she didn't think she could wait another second.

Sure enough she felt him nudge between her thighs, heavy and warm, finding the hot, open place. He entered her slowly, stretching and reaching, up, up to that magic spot. When he hit it she groaned.

He kept up the motion of his fingers working her clit and began to drive into her.

Wild, crazy sounds spilled out of her mouth, nonsense words and cries, as she bucked against him, driving them both to the edge of madness.

He took her up and over the edge and then as her cries subsided, he grabbed her hips and pumped, long, deep strokes that drove her up again until they both fell off the edge of the world. She sailed, and the weight of his body kept her grounded.

9

Lexy's stomach reminded her that it was dinnertime. Pendegraff's stomach must be on the same schedule for he'd emerged into the kitchen and was peering into the well-stocked fridge.

"Does someone shop for you or did you carry me unconscious into the grocer's to get all these supplies?"

He turned, and she noticed he'd showered also. And changed into a dark blue cashmere sweater and black pants. She thought that dark green would have looked better with his eyes, and wondered if he didn't wear dark green for that very reason. "Much as I like the mental image, I've got a housekeeper who cleans the place and shops when I let her know I'm coming."

"Handy."

"Grilled chicken okay? Or there's tofu. I wasn't sure what you eat."

"Chicken's fine." She washed her hands. "What can I do?"

"Salad?"

"Sure."

From the fridge he drew out a bottle of white wine

and, without asking her, opened it and poured two glasses.

"I feel like we should have a toast," she said. "I mean, this is probably the strangest situation I've ever been in."

He held his glass aloft. "Here's to the pleasure of meeting you. I only wish I had you here alone under different circumstances."

Their gazes connected along with their glasses. She didn't say what she was thinking, which was that she wished she had her own wardrobe with her if she was going to be alone with him. The pink snowflake put her at a disadvantage.

While he prepared the chicken, she dug through cupboards and found one of those gourmet packages of fancy rice and seasonings and put that on to cook. Then she put together a salad.

It was oddly homey making dinner with an attractive man. And completely strange at the same time. She thought he felt it, too, for they ended up having typical first-date conversation. Books they liked, movies they'd seen, music, sports, even New York politics.

When the dinner was almost ready, he said, "Okay with you if we eat in the den?"

"Yes, sure."

He had little fold-out tables, kind of like the TV trays her folks used to use only way fancier. Brought the food out and he flipped the switch to bring the gas fire to light. Normally she'd have been disappointed not to have a real wood fire, but right now she thought gas flames that could be controlled with a switch were just fine.

She'd wondered if they'd end up watching TV with their dinner but the screen stayed blank. Instead he turned his chair so he was facing her. "I've got the makings of a plan to catch Grayson," he said.

"That's very good news."

"I'm glad you think so, because the plan involves you." He glanced over at her. "How quickly could you make a piece of jewelry?"

"Depends what it is."

"Let's say I wanted you to copy the Isabella Emeralds."

She shook her head immediately. "Can't be done. There's no way I could source emeralds of that quality and color. You wouldn't have to be a jeweler to spot the fake. Grayson, or anyone who knew the piece, would see that the color was off. And while I can re-create the setting, getting the gold to exactly the right patina would take a lot of trial and error."

He nodded. Ate a bite of chicken. He'd put some kind of a rub on it and grilled it to perfection, naturally. "What if you wore the original to the gala? And the copy only had to fool somebody who believed they were getting the original? And only for a little while?"

"Bait and switch?"

"Exactly. In fact, this might work out better. Maybe we leave a trail of bread crumbs, make it easy for Grayson to get the necklace back, but we want Grayson to know he's ended up with a fake."

She blew out a breath. "If I had all my tools and an operating workshop, and all the supplies, and Amanda to help me, I guess I could have it done in time for the gala." Mentally she went through the steps and the time each would take, but of course in her imagination, she was working in her own space. "But I don't have my tools, or my studio and Amanda thinks I'm dead."

"None of those are insurmountable obstacles," he said in a voice of reason that made her want to hit him.

"Well, I could come back from the dead pretty easily, I've got friends who would lend me their studios and tools, but what I don't seem to have is the raw materials or the substantial wad of cash I'd need to buy them."

He turned to her and grinned. "See, I told you it was easy. You solved all the problems but one. And I can buy the raw materials." There was a light shining in his eyes that she thought was excitement. It was like he couldn't wait to waltz into Grayson's gala escorting her and a million-dollar heirloom he'd stolen. "We're a great team."

Instead of answering, she rolled her eyes.

"But I really don't want you back in New York yet. Somebody could spot you, or one of your friends could accidentally let slip that you were alive and well and working on a secret commission."

She opened her mouth to tell him that her friends were completely loyal. Then she closed it again. They were loyal, every one of them, but did she really want to burden them with her presence? Especially if someone was out to kill her?

"So you don't want me to copy the necklace."

"I do. I've got a…connection with a jeweler here, in Colorado. We've done some work together in the past."

She didn't want to speculate aloud on what relationship a thief and a jeweler might have that was mutually beneficial, since she was pretty sure he wouldn't tell her anyway. In truth, she didn't want to know. Having watched footage of her burned and ruined business over and over again, and hearing people talk about her as though she were dead, had given her a burning desire to bring Grayson to justice. If she had to work with people who operated in a murkier area, legally, than she, she guessed she was going to get on with it.

"I see. And does this jeweler have a full workshop?"

"Yes."

She considered the feat he'd proposed to her. Copying someone else's masterpiece felt like forgery to her. Like trying to rip off the Mona Lisa. The emerald and diamond set had been created by a master of the day. But there was also something exciting about trying to re-create the artistry, using her own methods. No one who knew the original intimately would be fooled for long, but could she copy the original well enough to fool the casual eye?

"I wonder if we'd be better with synthetic emeralds," she found herself saying aloud.

"Lexy, if it's the money—"

"No. It's the color. Synthetic emeralds are often darker. Obviously a jeweler would know right away that the stones were man-made, but if we're going for visual illusion, then I might be able to pull it off." Her mind was spinning over possibilities. "I'll need real diamonds, though."

"Absolutely."

She glanced at him curiously. "Will you get them back?" Was it worth it to him to invest a fortune on getting revenge?

"I hope so. But it's not the most important issue." He seemed to hear her unspoken question. "I do not like being cheated, and I sure as hell don't like having people trying to kill me. Grayson pissed me off. If it costs some money to bring the guy down, so be it."

"Pretty high moral ground for somebody who made

their money from stealing things that didn't belong to them."

He rose, went to the fridge for the wine bottle and topped their glasses. "Oh, come on. You think Wall Street's not full of crooks? Name a profession that's never been touched by scandal. Law? Medicine? The clergy? At least I was an honest crook. I only stole from people who could afford to lose things."

"Did you need the money?"

He returned the bottle to the fridge and sat back down before answering.

"What kind of question is that?"

"A direct one. Sounds to me like you already come from a wealthy family, probably have a fat trust fund. I'm just asking whether you needed to steal to support yourself."

"Not technically." He picked up the pepper grinder and cranked it, adding spice to chicken that was already perfectly spiced.

"Okay, I'm curious. Why did you go into the larceny business?"

He seemed to realize there was nowhere he could go to get away from this conversation and that she wasn't going to give up. He shot her an irritated glance. "I didn't want to go into law, politics, finance or any of the other professions that were considered suitable." He shrugged and gave a wry grin. "It's the sad plight of the poor little rich boy. He can never be better than his father or whatever ancient relative amassed the fortune in the first place. I didn't want to follow...I wanted to set my own path."

"Really."

"I probably would have bummed around for a while and ended up toeing the line eventually, but luckily, when I was alone in the house one weekend, a guy broke in and tried to steal mother's jewels." He grinned in memory. "He was good, too. He'd have got away clean if I hadn't come home late and on my way up to bed heard something. Not even much of a noise, just one of those sounds that don't belong, you know? So you stop and take notice."

It was exactly like when she'd heard Charlie cracking her safe. The sounds hadn't been loud, simply out of the ordinary. She nodded.

"Anyhow, I snuck into my parents' room and he had the safe open and my mother's jewelry laid out on the bed, all nice and neat, like he was shopping. Naturally, being nineteen and thinking I was one tough dude, I tackled him."

He laughed. "The guy was pretty surprised. But he didn't seem like my idea of a thief. He was intelligent, well-spoken. If you'd passed him in the street you'd have pegged him for a university prof or a scientist or something, never a thief. Well, long story short, I agreed not to call the cops if he'd teach me everything he knew. We were partners for four years before he retired. Then I worked alone for a few years and now I mostly steal things back for people. Ironic, isn't it?"

"Oh, it's ironic all right. Especially as I'm the one who ended up homeless and dead."

"Well, bringing you back to life in the middle of the Diamond Ball, and wearing the necklace that supposedly got you killed, should go a long way to making up for that. As for the studio, I'm sorry it happened. Truly sorry. Did you have insurance?"

"Yes, but that's not the point. Of course I can rebuild, but it's going to take time and will really mess with my schedule."

"Right."

She rubbed her forehead with her hand. "But there's no point whining is there? Okay, I'll make a list of what I'll need. Maybe Amanda can contact my suppliers and get the gems."

"No. My jeweler can source what he doesn't have in stock."

She snorted. "Please yourself. But I guarantee you'll pay too much."

"Understood."

"How soon can you get Amanda here?"

"Tomorrow. I'll get Healey to put her on a commercial flight to Aspen."

He walked over and put a hand on her shoulder. "We'll get them, Lexy. I promise. We'll get them."

She nodded, looking up. His face was serious and yet she felt the excitement in him. He could tell her all the stories he wanted about being a rebellious teen, and maybe part of that was the truth, but the real reason he'd become a thief, and still continued to operate in the shadows, was that he was hooked on the thrill.

She caught a hint of his excitement and felt her fingertips tingle. She was going to forge a masterpiece starting tomorrow. She found she could hardly wait to get started.

Their gazes locked and she felt her breath hitch. She'd been absurdly drawn to this man from the first moment she saw him, knew he felt it, too, but she wasn't thinking clearly enough right now to be embarking on an affair.

Then his hand turned, rubbing her shoulder, moving slowly upward to cup her cheek. Abruptly he dropped the hand. "I'd better get back to work. Watch whatever you want on TV. Or there's some movies and stuff. I'll see you in the morning."

She watched him go, a slightly smug smile pulling at her mouth. She knew why he'd bolted. He wanted her, and he knew he couldn't have her.

Damn straight, he couldn't. Not yet, anyway.

Of course, she suddenly had all this sexual energy coursing through her body. She supposed she might as well make use of it and get to work herself figuring out how she was going to replicate the Isabella Emeralds.

"Hey," she called him back. "I'm going to work tonight, too. I'll need to study that necklace."

"I'll bring it to you."

"And I'll need that jewelry studio to myself. I don't want interference."

"You're not much of a team player, are you?"

"No. I work alone. It's how I like things."

"I also work alone. I guess the next few days, trying to work together and trust each other, should be interesting."

"Honey, you and I are never going to be a team."

He chuckled. "That sounded very much like a challenge. I have a weakness for challenges." He turned and went to get her the emeralds. Maybe he thought he was out of hearing range, but she heard him mutter, "And gorgeous smart-mouthed jewelers."

10

"YOU PICK UP STRANGE MEN in bars very often?" Healey asked Amanda over breakfast the next day, a bowl of healthy grains—far more than she could eat, with fresh bananas and frozen blueberries sprinkled on top and a healthy dollop of white stuff that she doubted very much was whipped cream. If she had to eat yogurt she liked it flavored with a lot of fruit. Somehow she thought Healey would disapprove. And she'd better not even mention that she was more a bagel and cream cheese and a quick coffee kind of gal.

She really didn't feel like getting a critique on her lifestyle so early in the morning, but his tone didn't sound judgmental, more genuinely curious. She pushed away the cereal and picked up her coffee. At least he had coffee. For a horrible moment she'd feared green tea.

"No. Not really. I was kind of crazy last night, you know? I really, really needed to get my mind off my problems and find an outlet."

A rare grin lit his face. "I'll be your outlet anytime."

He reached past her and pulled a bottle of disgusting

green stuff from the fridge that he said was full of spirulina. Which she was pretty certain was a kind of moss.

He drank right out of the bottle. "You want some?" he asked after he'd taken a few gulps.

She shuddered. "No, thanks." His refrigerator featured things like tofu and wheat grass. Organic fruits and vegetables, free-range eggs. No junk food.

"What happened to the guy who ordered a hamburger in the bar?" she asked in frustration.

He kissed her shoulder, leaving a green spirulina smudge. "I order the odd hamburger to impress girls like you. Plus, I crave them once in a while."

"We are total opposites. I crave healthy food once in a while. But mostly I live on the tasty stuff."

At least he had coffee. Free-trade organic blah, blah, blah that needed to be ground in small quantities and put into a French press, but the result was almost worth the effort, she thought, when she got up to make another pot.

"Want some coffee?"

"You drink too much caffeine. It's why you're so jittery," he commented.

"I'm not jittery. I'm in junk food withdrawal."

She dug a spoonful of yogurt and berries from the bowl and ate it, trying not to screw up her face at the sour burst of yogurt. She put down the spoon.

"Someone close to me died. Well, we were all close to her, those people I was with last night? It was sort of a wake. We were all immersed in grief and sharing our stories and pictures and suddenly I couldn't stand it anymore. I didn't want sympathy, I didn't want friends. I wanted sweaty sex with a stranger."

He was looking at her almost as though he understood.

"I wanted to disappear for a while. Have you ever wanted to be invisible?"

He chuckled, like he was having a private joke. "Frequently."

They chatted for a while until she'd made a respectable dent in her breakfast and finished her coffee.

"Well," she said, "I guess I should be going." She never knew how to exit gracefully from a one-nighter. Did she leave her number? Ask for his? Play it cool and say nothing? How did anybody have a night of intimacy and passion of the kind they'd shared and not want to see each other again?

He looked at her almost as though he was wondering the same thing. "What are you up to today?"

She shrugged. "I should probably start looking for a job."

"Or you could hang around for a couple of days."

"Don't you have to work?"

"I've got a pretty flexible schedule." He rubbed a hand along her shoulder, above the sailboat. "I'd like to spend some time with you."

And like that, her burden lifted a little. After Lexy's death she'd felt so unbelievably alone. Now, even for a short time, she had somebody who cared what she did all day. Who wanted her.

"Okay. Yeah. Sure."

It was only for sex, but right now? Sex was about all she had to give.

"So, what do you want to do today?"

She was hovering between responses. Did she most want to go shopping for junk food? Because if she was staying here she couldn't survive on nuts and berries, or did she want to take him to see some art that would blow his mind—or did she just want to drag him back to bed? She hadn't remotely made up her mind when his phone rang.

He checked the display and excused himself to the bedroom to take the call.

Her stomach did a weird dippy thing. Secret calls could only mean other women in his life. Not that she, a one-night hookup, was in any position to complain, but she'd felt like he maybe wanted to start something with her. Who'd said anything about it being exclusive?

She heard him arguing. And then he came out, holding the phone.

"Look," she said, "if my being here is messing anything up for you...I can leave."

He shook his head. "It's not that." He sank down heavily on the chair beside hers and took her hand. He looked so serious he was starting to freak her out. "I want you to know that last night was...amazing. And I wouldn't have changed a thing. You need to believe that."

"Okay." What the hell was he getting at? It was over? He had a girlfriend? Sure, she got it. Why not show her the door and be done with it? This hand-holding thing was a little strange.

And he still had his phone open.

"I'm a big girl, Healey."

"Okay. I know. There's someone on the phone who wants to talk to you."

He said into the phone, "Put her on."

She threw her hands in the air and backed away. "Oh, no. I'm not talking to her. You got woman trouble, you deal with it on your own. Don't get me involved." She looked around for her purse. "It was a hookup. We had fun. I'm out of here."

"Amanda, it's not what you think."

"Sure, okay, whatever." Where were her shoes?

"Amanda, stop. It's Alexandra Drake on the phone."

The air went out of her lungs and she felt the room sway. "What?"

"Lexy. It's Lexy on the phone. She wants to talk to you."

"Lexy's dead," she replied. And how the hell did he know about Lexy? She was sure she'd never mentioned the woman's name.

"No. She's not."

"I don't know what's going on, but I've got to get out of here. This is too weird."

He grabbed her arm, not hard, but firmly enough to get her attention. "Please, just take the phone."

He held it up but she shook her head. "Amanda?" The voice came faint and familiar. "Amanda?"

She grabbed the phone and plastered it to her ear. "Lexy? Oh, my God, is it really you? You're alive?"

"Yes. Alive and unhurt. I'm so sorry I couldn't call before. I'm fine."

"But…" She put her other hand to her head and collapsed on the couch before she fainted. "I don't even know what to ask first. I… We had a wake."

"You had a wake? For me?"

"Yeah." She laughed shakily. "Me and Carl and well, you know, the usual bunch. We met at Emo's and had a wake for you. Last night." She wiped her cheek, not realizing she was crying until the back of her hand came away wet. "And I thought about you and how I should have stayed that night and helped you. I... What happened?"

"It's kind of a long story. And I'm going to tell you everything, but I can't tell you on the phone. Look, I really need your help. I'm in Colorado. I need—"

"Colorado?"

"I know it sounds crazy. But I need you to come here and help me with a project."

"In Colorado?"

"Yes. Today. Healey, the guy with the phone, he'll get you a ticket. You've met Healey, right?"

"Oh, yes. We've met."

"Good, so—"

"Wait a minute. Why didn't you call me on my cell?"

"It's not secure. Amanda, criminals burned down my place and I'm pretty sure they murdered a woman. We need to stay safe. Healey's there to protect you."

"Huh, is that what he was doing?" She glared at Healey, who was standing across the room, watching her.

"I know this is a shock."

"How do I even know you're really Lexy?" she snapped.

"Don't you recognize my voice?"

"Not enough. Tell me something about me that no one knows."

"You've got a sailboat tattooed on your back."

She thought of Healey tracing the pattern with his tongue. Yeah, that was a real secret. "Something else."

"Um, your middle name is Jocelyn and you never tell anyone that. Ah, you're allergic to pistachios, when your mom threatened to throw you out of the house if you got your nose pierced, you got your nose pierced.

Oh, and you got the ring in your eyebrow when a drummer called Stephan broke up with you and went back to Frankfurt."

"Amsterdam." But that was exactly the kind of mistake a friend would make.

"Really? I thought it was Frankfurt. Okay, I remember his band was called Bionic Piss."

Amanda snorted with laughter. "What was I thinking?"

A familiar giggle echoed back. "I have no idea. So, did I pass the test?"

She glanced at Healey. Right now she trusted nothing that he was involved with. "Not so fast. I have some questions for you. What's your father's name?"

"Jed Dabrowski."

"Name the last commission you refused."

"Easy. Two weeks ago. The skull and crossbones wedding rings. So banal."

"What's your favorite sexual position?"

"Amanda, I'm not alone."

"You put me through hell, Lexy." The pain was still there. Weird. She wanted to believe Lexy was okay but on some level couldn't. "Besides, anybody could find out all that other stuff. This is more personal."

"I am never going drinking with you again."

Amanda was feeling better and better. She still remembered the night she and Lexy had gone for a drink after a late night at work. Somebody had left behind a sex manual and the two of them had looked through it and discussed favorite positions. Laughed at some of the names. "Quit stalling."

"Could you leave the room for a second?" she heard Lexy ask someone. "Hell, no," was the amused male reply.

A long suffering sigh whistled in her ear. "This is the last question I'm answering. The Lyons Stagecoach."

But she wasn't done punishing Lexy yet. The woman should have called her much sooner. "Man on top or woman on top?"

"It's a woman-on-top position," Lexy said, sounding as though she was speaking through gritted teeth.

Even though she'd pretty much accepted that the woman on the phone was Alexandra Drake it was still a huge relief to have the confirmation. "'Kay. I guess you really are Lexy."

"So, will you come to Colorado?"

"Sure." She gave Healey the evil eye. "It's not like I have anything better to do."

She gave the phone back to Healey, who spoke briefly to God knew who and then clicked off.

He came to her and tried to take her hand. She shook him off. "Don't even bother," she warned him.

"But you have to let me explain. I should never have slept with you."

She snorted. "That's my line."

"Amanda, please, let me explain."

"Fool me once, shame on you. Fool me twice, shame on me. You won't make a fool of me again. Clear?"

Reluctantly he nodded. "I never meant to hurt you."

She forced herself to sound casual. "Hey, you got me through a rough night. Gave me a few orgasms. I needed the release. You did your job, kept an eye on me. Now you need to get me to Colorado."

11

ASPEN CHARMED LEXY the moment she saw it. The town was quaint, European feeling, but you couldn't forget this was a ski destination. A glance up showed the wide, white ski runs like open hands, white fingers pointing to the collection of ski lodges, shops and restaurants in the village.

The drive to town from Charlie's house took fifteen minutes. Once the Jeep had powered over the unpaved private road, they hit a well-marked, well-trafficked area. Had she hot-wired the Jeep she'd have made it to civilization in minutes. "You lied to me," she said, incensed as the town came into view.

"No, I didn't. I told you the closest town was Aspen."

"You didn't say it was on your doorstep."

"You assumed you were in the middle of nowhere. I let you believe it. That's all."

Incredibly soon he was parking on a snow-covered road. A line of brick-faced buildings that looked like old warehouses contained a string of stores. Pottery, clothes, ski equipment and, surprise, surprise. Three jewelry stores. He took her into one of them where a young woman in jeans and a sweater asked if she could help them.

"Marcus is expecting me," Charlie said.

She nodded. Pressed a button under the counter. "You can go on back."

He led her through a back door and up a flight of stairs.

He knocked on the locked steel door at the top of the stairs and after a minute, during which Lexy felt herself to be under scrutiny, the door opened. "Charles, my friend," an older man with a beard and tiny round glasses said, shaking his hand.

"Good to see you, Marcus. This is the woman I was telling you about."

Marcus shook her hand. Not asking her name or seeming perturbed that Charlie hadn't introduced her. "Come in. I think I've got everything you requested."

He led them to a jeweler's workbench and handed her a loupe. From a locked drawer he withdrew several black cloth bags and a velvet-lined tray. He shook out diamonds from one, true emeralds from a second and synthetic emeralds from a third.

"Excellent," she said, as the raw materials she'd need tumbled out and caught the light. He'd followed her instructions exactly. She began to study the diamonds and found them of reasonable quality and the cut was right. It was the emeralds, however, which dominated the set and she was excited at the assortment she could choose from.

She glanced around a well-equipped workshop. "Ah, you've got the Black Max, excellent." The chemical, when applied with steel wool, would give the new gold an ancient patina. It wouldn't fool a professional, but she reminded herself, it wouldn't have to.

Marcus removed a heavy wool coat from a tree stand and eased himself into it. "I'm taking a couple of days off. Please make yourself at home. Charles knows how to contact me if you need anything."

Charlie leaned down to speak quietly into her ear. "Have you got everything?"

"Yes. I'll be fine."

"Okay. Don't let anybody in until I return." He gestured to the security camera in the corner that showed the stairs and landing. "I'll be back with Amanda in a couple of hours."

"Good. Excellent."

She barely waited for the door to close behind Marcus and Charlie before drawing out the Isabella Emeralds from her bag.

She opened the case and carefully took the necklace out and placed it on a velvet tray. She'd studied it at length the night before, making extensive notes and she thought she had a pretty good idea of how to duplicate the piece.

She pulled a second item out of her bag, the iPod she'd borrowed from Charlie. His playlist wasn't entirely to her taste, but by skipping the classical, the podcasts and anything remotely resembling folk, she had pretty good background sound.

She rubbed her hands together, stretched and flexed her fingers as though getting ready to play a piano concerto, and then she got to work.

Two hours later, Amanda arrived.

They screamed like young girls, hugged and rocked and laughed. "I am so glad to see you," she exclaimed.

"Not as glad as I am to see you!"

"Wow," Amanda said, looking at the work in progress. "I've never seen you copy anything before."

"No. It's not exactly my style. But I think I've figured out how to copy the necklace."

"Cool. Oh, Charlie said to tell you he's getting sandwiches. I told him you like ham and cheese and egg salad and you hate mustard."

"You are an assistant in a million."

Five minutes later, Charlie showed up with a paper sack containing sandwiches, coffee and a couple of bottles of water. Then he left and they munched sandwiches and drank coffee while Lexy filled Amanda in on everything that had happened.

Her eyes fairly bugged out when she heard the story. "I can't believe it. Were you scared?"

"Yeah. I was at first, but mostly I was angry, you know? And for some reason Charlie never really frightened me." She shrugged.

"It's 'cause he's so good-looking," Amanda said around a bite of egg salad. "In the movies they always cast good-looking actors as the heroes and ugly ones as the bad guys. But I don't think real life works that way. A guy can be totally hot and still be evil." She chomped into her sandwich as though biting someone's head off.

"Are we still talking about Charlie?"

Amanda shook her head. "Healey," she mumbled, her mouth full.

"What did Healey do?"

The young woman scowled. "Had sex with me."

"Oh, my God, Amanda, he didn't..."

She waved a hand and shook her head. "No. Picked him up at Emo's. But he was only there because he followed me. He was doing his job. He shouldn't have let me pick him up." She looked angry, but Lexy also saw the hurt in her eyes.

"Bastard."

"Yeah."

"Is he here?"

"No. He stayed behind in New York. Charlie had stuff for him to do, but I swear, Lexy, I love you like a sister but I would not have gotten on a plane with that man."

"Don't blame you. Did he have any explanation for why he let you, ah, pick him up?"

"Oh, the usual. It's not what you think, I have feelings for you, give me another chance, the usual bullshit." She waved her hand as though swatting a mosquito.

"I can't—"

"Forget about it. How 'bout you? You and Charlie tried out the Lyons Stagecoach yet?"

"No. And I will never forgive you for making me tell Charlie my favorite sexual position."

She got an unrepentant grin in return. "Has he teased you about it?"

"No. He never said a word."

"Huh. Maybe he doesn't know what it is."

Lexy licked butter from her thumb. "Charlie looks like a guy who knows every move in the Kama Sutra. And a few more."

"Yeah. I think so, too. He hasn't mentioned the Lyons Stagecoach, he hasn't teased you about knowing your favorite sex position." She shook her head. "That's not good."

"Why? What do you think it means?"

"Wild guess? He's planning to ride in your stagecoach." She stood up and moved her body provocatively until they were both snorting with laughter.

"Come on," Lexy said at last. "We've got work to do."

Some time later Amanda said, "So, are you going to let him?"

Lexy raised her gaze from the magnifier. "Ride my coach? I haven't decided yet."

"At least he didn't lie to you."

"No. He only kidnapped me. His excuse is he did it to save my life."

"Men. They always have some story."

"Yeah. Pass me that hammer."

12

"YOU SURE YOU KNOW HOW to fly this thing?" Lexy asked as the twin-engine Cessna chugged its way up into the sky. Maybe if they were in Kansas wheeling over flat fields of corn she wouldn't have her heart backing up into her throat, but in Colorado? The little plane had to fight its way up over the Rockies. Charlie seemed pretty calm, which she guessed was a good thing, except he always seemed calm.

"Enjoy the view," he said.

Which didn't exactly answer her question. She turned and rolled her eyes at Amanda, buckled into one of the backseats and seeming a lot more at home in the small plane than she felt.

"So, what's the plan when we get back to New York?"

"A simple one. We're doing some shopping. We've got a little prep work to do before the gala. And then we're going to hide out where no one will find us."

"Mexico?"

He glanced at her, looking very piloty with his headset. "The Plaza."

"You're insane."

"Probably."

He didn't seem nearly as bothered by her accusation as she was, but then he had all the power in this relationship.

For now.

She was nothing if not a fighter and so long as they seemed to be on the same side, she was content—well, resigned—to the idea of him in her life. Temporarily.

She didn't want to distract the man while he was flying a plane, so she took his advice and stared out the window. The plane hit a patch of turbulence and bounced up and down a couple of times. It had been doing that for most of the trip and she had to force herself not to squawk.

The peaks were snowcapped and jagged, gorgeous in the sunshine as they flew east toward New York.

What Pendegraff had planned seemed bold to the point of insanity, but she had to admit the idea of walking into the lion's den and out again wearing the very jewels Grayson coveted was exciting.

Besides, she had a score to settle with Mr. Grayson.

She raised her voice to be heard above the noise of the engine and the wind rattling at the windows. The idea of waltzing into the Plaza and going to a fancy charity gala all while she was presumed dead seemed absurd and oddly satisfying. "I hope Grayson has a heart attack when he sees us."

"But not fatal. I want him in jail."

She smiled. Maybe they could work together after all.

They landed without incident; in fact Lexy had a reluctant admiration for how easily he brought the small plane down into the private airfield.

After filling out some paperwork in the office they walked out the other side.

Lexy's step hitched when she recognized the limo waiting for them. "Last time I rode in that thing it didn't end so well."

Amanda also stalled when she caught sight of the driver. "Oh, no."

Pendegraff put a hand on each lower back and urged the women on. "Don't be too hard on Healey. He kept a good eye on Amanda. And he's making sure we have some people we can trust on security tomorrow."

The driver moved to the rear door as they approached and opened it, very properly. She slid inside the familiar interior.

She heard him say, "Amanda? Why don't you ride up front, with me?"

"In your dreams." And Amanda got into the back.

Charlie slid in beside Lexy. "Everything all set?" he asked.

"Yes," the man in front said and slid him a hotel key folder.

The March day was gray and overcast, already depressing, and the thought of everyone here at home thinking she was dead didn't do a thing to make her feel better. There was something about returning to New York that made her current dilemma more real to her than it had appeared when she'd seen the news reports. Here she was. She could ask the driver to take her home, but she had no home. All her stuff, from her clothes to her tools to her tax returns. Gone.

She supposed she was in shock of some sort because she felt numb. Everything was gone and she didn't seem able to grasp what that meant for the immediate future.

She leaned forward. "Could we drive past my studio?"

Healey glanced instinctively at Charlie, who shot her a concerned glance. "You know you can't stop or go inside."

"I know. I need to see the place, to make it real. I feel like the fire was something that happened in a TV show, that it's fiction, not that my home and business are really gone."

"Okay." He spoke to Healey. "Don't even slow. Cruise by and—" to her "—don't even think about putting down a window. We're only doing this because no one will see you through the tinted glass."

"Okay." He didn't have to do this, so she managed a small smile. "Thanks."

The limo cruised through the insanity of midtown traffic. After the utter peace of the mountains, the honking and sirens and noise of millions of people living their lives seemed loud and jarring, even in the relative quiet of the limo.

As they got closer to SoHo, her spine began to tingle. It was a stress reaction she'd had since she was a teenager. Her stomach felt strange, too, as though she were coming down with something.

The streets grew familiar, her neighborhood was upon them busy with shoppers and tourists and the residents of the area. Her neighbors and customers.

She all but pressed her face to the glass of the window, straining for the first glimpse of her place. Maybe they'd played some kind of cruel joke on her, maybe her studio was standing, its bright blue door as inviting as ever. Her store full of customers buying her ready-to-wear collection and ordering custom pieces.

Then she saw it.

She didn't realize she'd made a sound until she heard a cry of distress bounce through the air.

A warm hand took hers in a hard grasp and she held on tight to Charlie.

Amanda didn't say a word. In fact, she didn't even turn her head, as though she couldn't bear to look.

Traffic crawled so Lexy had plenty of time to take in the bubbled, blackened paint, the broken windows, the dirty trickles where the fire hoses had done their work. Charred beams were visible, her pretty window display a sooty mess.

Crime scene tape stretched across the doorway and yellow wooden barriers kept the pedestrians streaming around the building—she supposed there was some danger that something could fall on them from above. But her home and business were like an infected patient no one would go near.

From nowhere, tears blurred her vision and clogged her throat. That was her life, her business, her future. Black, burned, over.

There were commissions, of course. Clients and customers who had hired her to do a job. Her spine straightened against the leather upholstery as hot, cleansing anger roared through her, sweeping away her feelings of loss and self-pity.

She would do her job. She'd finish those commissions, just as soon as she and Pendegraff nailed whoever was responsible for this senseless destruction.

"You okay?" he said softly beside her.

She shook her head. Not ready yet for anyone to see her face. "But I'm angry. And getting angrier by the minute. I want whoever did this nailed. And I'll do whatever it takes to make sure that happens."

"That's the spirit."

He squeezed her hand and let go and she missed the warmth, the sense that he might be a thief and a kidnapper and a thousand other things she wouldn't approve of, but for some reason, she trusted him.

"Let's get to the hotel and get planning."

"Can I go home?" Amanda asked. "I need to check my messages and water my plants."

Charlie asked Healey, "Can she?"

The man in the front nodded. "Nobody's shown any interest. She should be fine. I'll keep an eye on her."

Amanda narrowed her gaze. "You stay away from me or I'll call the cops."

Suddenly the limo jerked sideways, pulled over to a curb and Healey turned around. Lexy had never seen him show expression before, so his anger was impressive. "Charlie, how long have I been working for you?"

"About five years."

"And in those five years have I ever had sex with one of our clients, or anybody remotely connected to our business?"

"No."

Amanda made a rude noise. "And I would believe that why?"

"Because it's true," Charlie said. "Amanda, I'm as pissed off with Healey as you are. What he did was dangerous, unprofessional and completely out of character for him. I can only assume that he's lost his mind or he has feelings for you." He turned to the driver. "Which is it, Healey?"

The man glared at all three of them in the back. "There's nothing wrong with my mind," he informed them with dignity. Then faced forward and pulled the limo back out into traffic.

13

THE PLAZA WAS LIKE Central Park, or the MoMA, or Saks, part of the fabric of her life, but not a place where Lexy spent a lot of time. She'd had brunch or drinks at the Plaza a few times, but she'd never even seen one of the guest rooms, so even with the sick feeling in the pit of her stomach since she'd seen the fire damage, she still managed a jolt of anticipation as they entered the landmark hotel.

Charlie didn't check in. It seemed Healey had done so on his behalf. He didn't even explain the room arrangements to her, but he wasn't a man who wasted a lot of words. She supposed she'd soon find out what was going on.

The elevator made its expensively quiet ascent to the eighteenth floor. Charlie strode to the door of their room as though he was a regular visitor. Maybe he was.

When he opened the door he stepped aside for her to enter first. She thought those kind of manners were so inbred he didn't even think about his actions.

It was nice.

She entered and her jaw dropped. "Are you kidding me? This is a suite."

"Yes."

She stepped in and glanced around. "I feel like I'm in Versailles."

The old-world charm of the room was distinctly European in flavor. No simple bedroom this; it was a full two-bedroom suite including butler's pantry, and two sumptuous bathrooms, so any idea she'd had that Pendegraff had more than business in mind could be put away for now.

They stood there for a moment. She'd unpack, but she didn't have any luggage.

"What do we do now?" she asked.

"We shop."

"That sounds great since I have no clothes whatsoever and certainly Cinderella has nothing to wear to the ball tomorrow night, but I thought you wanted me to stay hidden?"

"I do. The shopping is coming to us."

"Rich people really do have different rules of life."

He put the black briefcase he was carrying on the table and carried a black leather bag into one of the bedrooms. "You seem pretty hung up about rich people. We're not all that different, you know."

"Putting aside our different views on morality, you fly your own plane, you book a suite at the Plaza on a whim, you don't go shopping, you bring people to you, I'd say we have nothing in common." She sighed, flopping back into the luxury that was the couch. "My mom and dad always worked hard. They took pride in that, and so do I. I guess I don't have a lot of respect for people who lounge around all day living on trust funds." She flicked him a glance. "Not to be rude."

"Of course not."

There was a discreet knock on the door. He glanced at his watch. "Right on schedule."

When he opened the door and a stylish middle-aged woman sailed in with two assistants, a rolling wardrobe rack, boxes and several wardrobe bags, Lexy felt a spurt of annoyance. Where did he get off snapping his fingers and getting all this special treatment? Money, that's how, and not honestly earned money, either.

The woman had a slight French accent and introduced herself as Francine. Her helpers she ignored. She didn't seem to need any introduction to Charlie and was so uninterested in any details about Lexy that she almost choked not being able to tell the woman who she was and why she was here. She had no choice but to let these people think she was another Pendegraff possession, a mistress to be decorated and dressed according to his lordship's whims.

Her temper simmered while Francine fawned all over Charlie, who seemed accustomed to the attention and not at all bothered by it. She motioned one of the helpers to the closet and after some zipping sounds and a few soft directions, she returned with her assistant holding two dresses, one in each hand.

"Black or color?" Both dresses were beautiful. She suspected Charlie had insisted on a simple gown with a low neck to showcase the emeralds. From the fact that Francine was willing to run all over town with a selection of dresses for a private showing, Lexy had to assume they were devastatingly expensive.

Charlie considered them both, then turned his gaze to her. She ought to be amused, but the way he sized her up as though he'd seen her naked a hundred times and owned her body incensed her.

"Black, I think," he said.

"I prefer color," she snapped. She was determined to have some say in choosing her own dress.

His slightly amused expression told her he'd read her mind. "Try them all on," he instructed.

She stomped into the bedroom that didn't contain his bag, only hanging on to the shreds of her temper in the knowledge that she needed to be dressed properly for the gala in order to catch Grayson tomorrow.

One of the assistants followed her in and opened a display case full of lingerie.

Lexy's annoyance melted like ice cream on a hot sidewalk. "Oh, my," she said, leaning forward to touch the exquisite filmy things in the case.

"Monsieur said you were thirty-four B but I brought a few sizes."

"Monsieur was right," and the fact that he'd checked her out so thoroughly was mildly unnerving.

The helper's name was Marie-Anne and she became Lexy's new *bff* as they matched lingerie with the first dress, a long black evening gown paired with black high heels.

The moment she was in the first of the dresses, she knew the style was wrong. It was a one-shoulder arrangement that drew attention to the sweep of fabric from shoulder to hip. Jewelry would be overkill in this dress. She was about to shake her head and step out of it when she thought, what the heck? Mr. Pendegraff wanted to sit around and look at dresses? She'd oblige. She'd never known a man who hadn't grown bored in five minutes of shopping with a woman. Let's see how Charlie liked a parade of dresses, spaced out as he waited for her to change. And she didn't plan to hurry.

She walked slowly out into the main room.

Francine immediately launched into an effusive gush of praise about how beautiful it was, what a magnificent figure mademoiselle had, but she ignored the woman and concentrated on Charlie's reaction.

Lexy was female and vain enough to be gratified at the way his eyes grew intent as they looked at her, at the drape of fabric that accentuated her curves, but his verdict was the same as hers.

"I've got a fine necklace I want you to wear, darling. You definitely need something with a lower neckline."

"All right, sweetheart," she murmured in the way she imagined a well-pampered mistress might. Not that she had any experience in the matter, or desire to find out.

She found the perfect dress on the third try. The gown could have been designed for her, so lovingly did it hug her curves, accentuating her small breasts, and leaving her shoulders bare. It was an antique-gold color, which would highlight the necklace to perfection. She looked delicate and slightly mysterious. She'd never worn a prettier dress. Or, she suspected, a more expensive one.

"It's perfect," Marie-Anne whispered. "Like it was made for you."

"I know." And she slipped the dress off.

"You're not going to show monsieur?"

"Yes, I'm going to show monsieur. But we should save the best for last, don't you think?"

The Frenchwoman shrugged in a "who can understand Americans" kind of way, and pulled out the next dress.

"I always think it's good to keep a man waiting, don't you?"

A very Gallic shrug of the shoulders. "Some men,

yes. But this one? I would not care to cross him, mademoiselle."

"How funny. I'm absolutely looking forward to it."

14

HOW COULD WOMEN STAND shopping? Charles wondered as he tried his hardest not to look bored and to continue to speak politely to Francine. He had a strong suspicion that Lexy was dragging this thing out as long as she could to make him suffer. And it was working.

After the fifth dress he was ready to cry truce. Enough already. She looked fabulous in all of them, as she must know, but still she insisted that this one wasn't quite perfect. The hem was too frilly, the fabric not what she had in mind, the neckline too high, too low, too wide, too wavy, frumpy, décolletage and he'd lost track of what else was wrong. He felt like yelling to her that all the dress had to do was show off the emeralds, she was meant to be a frame, that was all. But she already knew that, which was why he was pretty sure she was yanking his chain.

He guessed he deserved retribution. He'd kidnapped her, as she kept on reminding him, which seemed to trump the fact that he'd also saved her life.

Women.

"I think this is the last one," Francine said in her smooth way as though she could read his boredom.

"Good."

The door opened behind him. He turned his head.

And felt his eyes bug out. Totally cartoon style. Wowza.

He'd imagined he'd seen everything a dress could do to that sweet little body, but he had been wrong.

The dress didn't just fit her, it caressed her when she moved, making a man want to put his hands in all the places the fabric was allowed to linger and he wasn't.

Off the shoulder, low-cut, her bosom was a white expanse waiting for the perfect jewelry.

Once you got past the small, shapely breasts, the dress showed him a trim waist without an ounce of fat, and curvy hips. He wanted to say something but he felt as if his tongue was welded to the roof of his mouth.

Even Francine's gushing actually sounded genuine this time. She oohed, and ahhed and ooh-la-la-d and still he stared, dumbfounded.

Being in such close quarters with a beautiful woman and not being allowed to touch her had been an effort from the moment he saw her, but now that he'd seen her in this dress, he didn't think he'd be able to stop himself wanting her. Who was he kidding, anyway? Since he'd been fool enough to kiss her, he couldn't get the feel of her body out of his mind, the taste of her, the way her lips fit against his.

Lexy ignored the fussing Frenchwoman and concentrated on him. Finally, when he still hadn't spoken, she said, "You like?"

He nodded. Enthusiastically.

Her amusement deepened. "You speechless?"

He nodded again.

"Good," she said, her lips smiling in a mysterious fashion that hid her thoughts. "I like that in my dates."

She nodded brusquely and he was reminded that she was a very competent businesswoman. "We'll take this one. Including the shoes and lingerie I'm wearing."

"An excellent choice, mademoiselle."

"I'm also going to need two pairs of jeans, some shirts and some everyday underwear. Marie-Anne knows me pretty well by now. She can pick them out for me. Could you have them delivered today?"

"With pleasure, mademoiselle."

When the women had all but bowed themselves out, Lexy said, "I could get used to being a kept woman." She contemplated her new shoes. Then struck a sultry pose in front of the long mirror. The vision made him instantly, humiliatingly hard.

"I've never been a mistress before."

"Not to burst your bubble, but there's more to being a mistress than shopping." He eyed her hungrily. "There are certain…services you're expected to provide."

Her gaze rose and connected with his and passion flared as it did pretty much every time they were close.

"Catch me a killer and we'll see what we can do about that."

"That's a pretty tall order."

"Oh, believe me, I'm worth it."

He had no trouble believing it.

LEXY WENT BACK TO HER bedroom and slipped off the most gorgeous dress she'd ever worn. Not that she didn't have a certain style all her own, but she tended to vintage pieces and young designers she knew who were just starting out. She'd even been known to barter jewels for frocks. But this? This dress was in a whole other league. Charlie's league.

She shook her head, hanging it carefully in the closet and pulling her jeans and one of the shirts from Colorado back on.

She swept back into the living room to find Charlie immersed in his computer.

He glanced up when she entered the room and politely stopped what he was doing.

"Maybe you could Google the guest list. I'll need a rundown of all the inbred, pampered socialites I'll be rubbing shoulders with. Bare shoulders, too. I hope my plebian roots don't freak them out."

"You know what your problem is? You're a snob."

She drew in her breath so fast she almost choked on it. "I am not. I'm working class and proud of it."

"Exactly. That's what I meant. You look down your nose at me because I have a certain background and possessions without knowing anything about who I truly am."

"That is blatantly untrue. I know you're a thief."

He crossed his arms over his chest and sat back. "What else do you know about me?"

"Aside from the fact that you're arrogant, pushy and annoying, what more do I need to know?"

"Right back at you, sweetheart."

She went to the kitchen to make tea. After a minute, she said, "I'm nervous. It makes me bitchy. Sorry."

She didn't realize he'd moved until she heard him behind her say, "Don't be nervous. It's going to be fine."

"I'm going to walk under Edward Grayson's nose wearing the necklace his mistress stole from him, the one he murdered her for stealing."

"Allegedly."

"Well, I am allegedly nervous."

"You don't have to do it."

"I said I'm nervous, not that I'm a quitter. Of course we're doing it. I like the audacity of the plan."

He gripped her shoulders. "That's the spirit. Look, I need to go out for a few hours. Will you be okay?"

"Why? Where are you going?"

"Some business to attend to."

"Aren't you afraid I'll run away?"

He turned to her, his eyebrows lifting in surprise. "Are you planning to run away?"

"Probably not." He didn't point out the obvious. That she didn't have a lot of places to go.

"But I'm going to call my father."

He nodded. "Great idea. Tell him to come by. I'd like to meet him."

"You would?"

"Sure."

"But he's a cop."

"So you said."

"And you're a thief." She made an up-and-down motion with her two hands. "Cop, thief, I'm seeing a conflict of interest here."

"Oh, we're on the same side on some things."

"Such as catching Grayson?"

The look he sent her was inscrutable. "Among other things." He came forward and kissed her swiftly. "Use the peephole before you open the door."

After he left, she was restless. Keyed up. Her spine continued to tingle. What happened over the next twenty-four hours would be critical. And she had to trust a man who was a thief and a kidnapper. Not exactly a résumé that filled her with confidence. And yet, oddly, she'd come to trust this man.

Half an hour later, her clothes arrived. If it wasn't the full Julia Roberts wardrobe from *Pretty Woman,* the clothing she'd asked for was a lot more practical. She wasn't planning to attend any polo matches or fancy dinners while she was here, only the one gala, then she'd have to go back to rebuilding her business. And her life.

Marie-Anne brought her the jeans she'd asked for, a couple of shirts, sweaters, a tweed car coat, walking shoes and a pair of boots. There was even a funky scarf to wear with the coat. "This is great, thanks."

"You're welcome." The woman hesitated. "I know you said your luggage went missing."

"Yeah. Stupid airline. Still haven't found it."

"I was wondering if you also need some makeup."

She slapped a hand over her mouth. "Yes. I totally forgot."

A quick smile. "We sell these kits at the store. It's not everything you need, but it's a start."

"Thank you so much." She gave the woman an impulsive hug.

The next visitor was her father, who enveloped her in a crushing hug the second the door shut behind him. She knew he was emotional from the way he squeezed her so tight she thought her ribs would snap.

"Don't ever put me through anything like that again," he warned.

"No. It was awful."

He set her away from him and glanced around. He wasn't a tall man but he was solid and she could feel his temper simmering. "Where is he? Where's the guy who put my baby in danger?"

He stalked around the suite long enough to figure out that there were two bedrooms and her things were in one while Charlie's were in the other. It helped cool his temper a degree or two.

"He had to go out for a while but he said he's looking forward to meeting you."

Her dad grunted, never a good sign. "I got a few things I want to say to him."

"Do you want some tea or coffee or something?"

He shook his head.

She sat beside him on the couch. "Tell me everything you've found out."

"You were right. That name you gave me? Tiffany Starr? How'd you know she was the dead girl?"

"It's a complicated story."

"I got all afternoon."

So she told him how the woman and her supposed mother had come into her studio, the story they'd given her and she told him about the emeralds.

"Seems to me there's some details you're leaving out."

"The rest of the story is Charlie's. He'll have to tell you himself. He should be back any minute."

Her father looked very grim. She hadn't seen him like this since her mom died. She put a hand on his arm. "What is it, Dad?"

"That girl was murdered."

Even though she'd suspected this news, it was like a blow to the gut. "Oh, no." She swallowed, had to know. "How?"

"She was shot."

"Oh, poor woman."

"It gets worse."

"Worse? What could be worse than being murdered and then burned?"

"She was killed with your gun."

15

LEXY'S HORRIFIED GAZE flew to her father's. "What?"

He had his cop face on, but she knew him so well. He was angry, frustrated, confused. And a little bit helpless, which he would hate more than anything.

"She was killed with my gun? That means, oh, God, that means she was still alive when they brought her to my place. They killed her there." Then the implications of the murder weapon struck her. "Dad, am I a suspect?"

"Of course you're not a suspect," he barked at her.

She licked her lips, thinking back to that terrible night. "But I had my gun out that night. There'd be fresh prints." She remembered threatening Charlie with the gun, the pounding and breaking glass in her front studio that had distracted her long enough for him to overpower her and grab the weapon. But Charlie, consummate thief that he was, had been wearing gloves. And she'd be willing to bet that whoever else had handled her gun, whoever had killed Tiffany Starr, had also worn gloves.

She felt like she was twelve again and in trouble. Only this time she knew her trouble was serious. She found herself pleading her innocence. "I'd never met the woman until that day. She came in and gave me a false name. She wanted an expensive necklace reset. A necklace she stole. But why would they use my gun?"

"You got any idea who might have killed her?"

They were interrupted by the door opening. Charlie came in, took one look at her face and strode to her side. "What is it?" He held out his hands and without even thinking, she put hers into them. His clasp felt warm and reassuring.

"They used my gun to kill that poor woman."

"Bastards."

"You mind telling me who you are and what you know about all this?" her father commanded.

"Oh, Dad, I'm sorry," she said before Charlie could speak. She released his hands. "Charles Pendegraff, meet my father, Jed Dabrowski."

Charlie extended a hand. "Pleased to meet you, sir."

Ignoring the hand, her father stood and glared at Charlie. "If anything happens to my Lexy while she's with you, I'll shoot you dead."

"Dad—"

Letting his hand drop back to his side, Charlie pulled himself up to his full height. "If anything happens to Lexy while she's with me, I'll load the gun myself."

The two men stared at each other, both tense and wary, and then to her amazement her father nodded, once, like he'd made up his mind about something. His prizefighter stance relaxed. "Good. We understand each other."

He sat down on the luxurious couch and motioned them to do the same. "Now, suppose you tell me what the hell is going on?"

And, to her amazement, Charlie did. He explained that he'd been hired to retrieve the stones, and pretty much gave a full description of everything he knew and everything that had happened up to and including the moment she caught him stealing the necklace.

At this point, she took over the story before Charlie did anything stupid like incriminate himself. "Charlie saved my life, Dad. He got me out of there and convinced me to get right out of New York with him." She didn't tell her father that he'd "convinced" her using unorthodox methods.

"Damn it, Lex, you shoulda come to me," her father said.

"I'm sorry, Dad. I wasn't thinking straight." Ha, and wasn't that the truth. At the time, she hadn't been thinking at all. She'd been drugged into unconsciousness.

"It would have been a good thing if you had. Well, you're not a suspect, but they'd sure like you to come down to the station and give a statement."

"And I will. But not until after the gala. They wrecked my place and now it turns out they killed that woman in my home. Using my gun. I am so bringing that Grayson down."

"I'll help you," Charlie said.

There was a tense pause. She looked at her father with appeal in her eyes.

"And so will I," her father echoed.

And suddenly they were a team.

Another knock sounded on the door. She stiffened.

"That'll be Healey," Charlie said.

He rose and opened the door to Healey, who came in and swept a swift glance around the room, as though checking for weapons, before entering. Amanda came

in behind him. She held herself stiffly away from him.
Wow, Lexy thought, *she really doesn't like this guy.*

"Healey, this is Jed Dabrowski, Lexy's father.
Jed, Healey's my associate. And I assume you know
Amanda?"

The two men shook hands, sizing each other up as
they did so. The suite seemed to be pulsing with testos-
terone all of a sudden.

Thank heaven for Amanda, Lexy thought as her father said, "Hi, sweetheart," and enveloped her in one of
his bear hugs.

They sat around the ornate living area sharing information, and throwing out ideas.

"I want my daughter protected," her dad said.

"Absolutely." Charlie turned to Healey. "How many
security guards do they usually hire for the Diamond
Ball?"

"They call in twenty men from a private security firm.
Six outside making sure nobody gets in who shouldn't
be there and that the guests get inside the mansion with
all their jewels intact and back to their limos. Another
six patrol the grounds and eight men work the interior.
In addition, Grayson has a few permanent employees
who wander around."

"Okay. Could be better, could be worse. But I think
we can make it work."

He glanced at Jed. "I'm guessing, based on the
bling at these events, that the NYPD has some kind of
presence?"

"Sure. But I don't get involved in that kinda crap."

"This year, I think you should. See if you can get
assigned to the detail. Lexy and I will both feel better
if you're on the premises."

"Consider it done. Anybody who doesn't already owe me a favor, soon will."

"Excellent."

Jed Dabrowski was looking at Charlie through narrowed eyes. "You've got something in mind?"

"Yeah. How 'bout I bring in some pizzas and we'll go over the plan?"

So they sat over pizza and sodas making plans, contingency plans, thinking of everything that could go wrong and how to prevent disaster.

Hearing Charlie explain the details to someone new, she realized how simple his plan was. So simple she almost laughed. Except that nothing about murder and arson was funny.

After everyone left, there was a moment of awkwardness. She didn't know what to do. It was nine-thirty, too early to go to bed, too strange to sit out here chatting with Charlie.

He seemed equally restless. He picked up a sports magazine, put it down.

Finally she said, "I apologize for my father. He's very old school. You hurt his daughter and there'll be hell to pay."

"I respect his position. He seems like a good man."

Her lips relaxed into a smile. "He is a good man. But tact was never his strong suit."

"He's worried about you."

"I know."

"Damn it, he's right. Lexy, you don't have to do this. I was crazy to suggest it. I'll find another way."

"Hey, I'm in this, too. Grayson burned down my house and business, remember?"

"Grayson's a dangerous man."

"So it seems. But he'll be in a public venue with no

idea that I'll show up with his necklace on. What can he possibly do to us?"

"I don't know, but I don't want anything to happen to you."

"Hey, you're not getting sentimental on me, are you?"

"No. Don't want your father using me for target practice."

He came closer, looked as though he were going to reach for her and then suddenly turned away. "Think I'll get an early night. Busy day tomorrow."

And he was gone.

16

SHE WAS KEYED UP, excited, nervous and—if she was honest with herself—a little nauseated.

She was like a little kid, getting ready hours too early for a birthday party. Charlie was mysteriously gone again and so she'd indulged in a bubble bath, shaved and plucked and polished herself. The manicurist, hairdresser and makeup artist had already been and she'd slipped on the lacy black underwear. All she was waiting for was the time to crawl along so she could slip into her dress.

Her freshly manicured fingers drummed against the upholstery. She tried to read the paper, but she couldn't concentrate. She flipped on the television, flicked a few channels and then punched the off button.

She considered having a drink to calm her nerves, but decided she'd better keep a clear head for tonight.

She opened the closet and considered the dress hanging there. It wasn't simply a dress. It was a net to catch a killer. The Isabella Emeralds the bait.

And they planned to snag a very sharp-toothed shark tonight.

She put a hand to her stomach. Phew. Pressed her lips together and the unfamiliar thickness of lipstick on her mouth reminded her of the unfamiliar amount of cosmetics she was wearing. The makeup felt oddly protective like a mask.

The shoes were in their box sitting on the bottom of the closet. She eased the box open, slipped the shoes on. Maybe if she walked around the suite in the unfamiliar gold heels it would ensure she was smoother tonight. At least the activity would give her something useful to do while she waited for time to pass, for Charlie to return, for the big night to begin.

She walked around the suite once, twice, until it felt more like pacing than walking.

Then she heard the key in the door.

Thank goodness.

It opened and Charlie walked in. He caught sight of her and it seemed as though he stopped, going completely still. He glanced at her hair, her face and all the way down to her new shoes. "I see the salon people have been," he said at last in that lazy drawl.

The air between them felt suddenly electric and she'd never been more conscious that she was wearing nothing but a hotel robe and, under it, the skimpiest lingerie imported from France and a pair of gold heels.

"I always get ready early. It's a curse. Then I have nothing to do with myself."

"You look beautiful," he said. It didn't sound entirely like a compliment, more like an inconvenience.

"Thanks."

He went to the hotel safe, punched in the code and popped the door. Out came the jewelry case that had started this nightmare. He opened the case and brought it to her.

The Isabella Emeralds.

"The jewels will look spectacular against your skin," he said, like a connoisseur considering a painting for his house.

"I usually wear my own creations when I go out socially. It's good advertising."

He smiled briefly, stepping closer to her. "Next time I take you out, I promise you can wear your own merchandise. For tonight, you'll have to settle for the emeralds."

Even though she'd seen them, studied them, copied them, she was still awestruck by the brilliance and clarity of the gems. By the setting that was so perfect. The intricate setting that was both ornate and delicate had been designed and executed by a master craftsman. She'd handled a few pieces that might compare in value but never anything that also had historical importance, or that she would actually wear.

"Do you know the legend?" he said as he carefully lifted the glittering mass from its case.

She'd read everything she could find on the set and was fairly certain she knew the legend to which he was referring, but she chose to say, "Which legend?"

Charlie moved behind her, nudged her until she could see herself in the ornate mirror. Her hair was styled in a simple knot to keep it out of the way. She wanted nothing to distract the eye from the necklace.

As he moved behind her she felt his presence, felt the heat coming off his body, his breath stirring the skin at her nape. She felt the coolness of the stones and metal as they rested against her upper chest, under the white hotel robe.

"There's a story that Isabella wanted so badly to finance Columbus's voyage to the new world that she pawned her jewelry to raise the cash."

He fingered the gems at her throat. "Among the other bounty he brought her, this gift was a nice repayment for her pawned stones."

They both watched the green wink in the mirror. "I've rarely seen such a deep green but it's characteristic of emeralds originating from the ancient Muzo mines of Colombia."

The thought that Christopher Columbus had handled these gems, that Queen Isabella of Spain had worn them around her own neck, sent a thrill through Lexy.

"It's also rumored that the stones inflamed the royal lust, giving her back the pleasure of youth."

As he spoke, his fingers traced her collarbone, softly caressed the skin of her shoulders and neck in a gesture that felt both intimate and arousing.

"You made that up," she said, her voice not much more than a whisper.

"Want me to cite my sources?"

She felt her breath hitch. He was so close. His fingers were smooth and sure as they fastened the complicated clasp.

"Magnificent," he said, his words stirring her hair. Their gazes connected in the mirror and it was as though an electric storm passed through her.

She felt transfixed, mute, could neither turn around nor throw out some flip remark. Instead she remained rooted to the spot, feeling her breath grow shallow. With every breath she felt the weight of the gems, could see the flash of light, the deep green and hot white diamond spark in the reflection. She needed the extra makeup, she realized, to match the drama of the jewels, and the sophisticated side twist of hair was perfect.

In slow motion she watched as Charlie eased the fluffy white robe to the side, revealing the jewels in their full glory. He didn't remove his hands, so she felt the heat of his fingers burn into her flesh.

He bent closer, his eyes growing heavy with an emotion she recognized as desire because it so neatly mirrored her own. In slow motion she saw his lips come nearer, felt his breath on her shoulder and then the soft, warm press of his lips. "I've tried to stay away from you, but I don't think I can do it any longer."

A tiny tremulous sigh escaped her lips and she felt his curve slightly as he pressed his mouth to the pulse beating at her throat.

"You arouse me, bewitch me, make me crazy with wanting you."

"Oh, yes," she whispered in a voice she barely recognized. Must be all the stress, she thought dimly, causing both of them to act so crazy. She felt the light stubble of his beard as he kissed his slow way up to her ear, then whispered, "You are so beautiful. I want you."

His clever thief's hands then moved, tracing the front of her robe to the sash, which he slowly untied, pulling the edges apart and revealing her in the deliciously lacy bra and panties.

The robe fell to the floor and it was his turn to make an incomprehensible sound, half sigh, half moan.

Her body was on fire; she felt as much on display as the gems and the experience was intoxicating. "I want you, too."

He touched her slowly, carefully, like a man who appreciates art and takes what he wants without asking permission. She saw herself being touched, watched his hands tracing the shape of her breasts through the filmy lingerie. His fingers looked dark against her pale skin.

He was fully dressed standing behind her, dark and serious but for the gleaming eyes that showed how close to the edge of passion he was.

"This is a terrible idea," she said.

"I know." And then he turned her around and pulled her into his arms, kissing her so hard she felt the breath squeeze out of her. His arms held her tight, hands running up and down her back as though he couldn't get enough of her.

Her passion flared brighter than the flash of the gems as she ground herself against him, panting against his mouth, opening to him, offering generously and taking greedily at the same time.

She wanted everything, all of him, and she needed it now. His erection was strong and hard as she reached between them for his belt buckle.

He toed off his shoes, she tugged at his shirt. A jagged scar on his shoulder caught her attention as she pulled the shirt off him; she pressed her lips to the spot, tasting heat and salt on his skin.

He dragged his boxers off, and then he was naked and magnificent before her.

He sucked her through the lacy bra, making her moan as her tingling nipples sprang to life. He peeled the lacy thong down her legs, then rose slowly, kissing whatever part of her was in reach of his mouth, her knee, her upper thigh, her belly, her breasts and finally her mouth, kissing her deeply while he reached between them and began to play in her curls, finding her slick and hot. When he rubbed her clit she found herself thrusting forward into his hand; when he pushed a finger inside her she cried out.

In her lust-fogged brain she managed to pant, "condom," and he sped to the bathroom, returning with a package, which he ripped open as he ran back. In seconds he was sheathed and then his hot length was pressing against her, her arms wrapped around his neck. He scooped her up, and she opened for him, wrapping her legs around his waist. He backed her up to the wall, and with his eyes open on hers, thrust up and inside her body.

Oh, he felt so good, so absolutely right as he pushed deeply inside her, giving her a moment to adjust before moving, driving her up, up, until she was wild for release, her hips riding against him, her breasts pressed hard against his chest, the necklace pressing against their hearts.

Their mouths were fused, their bodies locked together and as they moved with a kind of frantic desperation she felt the delicious ache begin to spread, build, until she shattered against him, crying out into his mouth, feeling her body busting with light.

He muttered nonsense words against her mouth and then she felt him stiffen and cry out as he climaxed deep inside her.

She felt boneless as she slid down the wall and back to her feet, though she still needed to hold on to him as she was afraid she'd collapse to the floor if she didn't.

He didn't let her go. He was breathing heavily, his heart thumping hard against hers. She stroked his back, waited for both of them to come back down to earth.

She tilted her head back, eyed him through half-closed eyes. "Maybe I believe in that legend after all," she said.

17

AMANDA'S CELL PHONE RANG. Healey again. She was about to turn the thing off and then decided to answer it. Maybe if she told him once and for all to leave her alone, he would.

"What do you want?" she snapped.

"What was I supposed to do?" he snapped right back. "You came onto me, remember? Sure, I could have blown you off, and then you know what you would have done?"

"Gone home. Alone." She squeezed her eyes shut, knowing it was a lie.

"Bullshit. You'd have found some other willing stud. And you know what? I couldn't stand the thought. I'd been watching you, okay? Not because I'm a pervert but because it was my job. You were lost and grieving and messed up."

She opened her mouth to blast him. But he was right. So right. "I know," she said softly.

"And I was seriously attracted to you."

"You were?"

"Yeah." A pause. "Still am."

"Oh. Are you still my bodyguard?"

"No, ma'am. I'm off the case."

"Well, thanks for, you know, keeping me safe."

"You're welcome. Now it's just you and me. No job getting in the way. I want to see you again. Start over."

She stifled a smile. "When?"

"How about now? I'm outside your door."

She ran to the peephole. And there he was. Standing outside her door. She figured she had two choices. She could trust him. Or not.

He was so different than anyone she'd ever been with. More serious, way cleaner living, and he really seemed to care about her. Which was probably good.

Also, she hadn't been able to stop thinking about him.

So, she flung open the door and before either of them could speak, they were in each other's arms.

He kicked the door shut behind him. "I missed you," he said into her mouth.

"Me, too." She dragged at his shirt, he stripped off her hoodie, her T-shirt.

Their jeans ended in a single mass on the floor and then they were naked on her unmade bed. Light streamed in the window onto their naked bodies.

She wanted him so badly she literally ached. But he seemed to have other ideas.

He was stroking her in slow, delicious ways, keeping her in the zone but not letting her climax. She groaned, partly from pleasure, partly from sexual frustration and partly from annoyance.

"Are you punishing me?"

He laughed softly. "No. Can't you simply trust me?"

"I have trust issues," she admitted. "From a long string of bad decisions in the guy department."

"How about giving trust another try?"

She hooked a leg over his hip, angled her hips so she could add her own friction. "Will you let me come if I do?"

He grinned down at her. "Maybe."

Her lips curved in response. "I won't make it easy." And then she took over, torturing him until sweat was beading his forehead and he was breathing like a man in pain.

"You gonna let me come?" he finally asked when she'd brought him to the edge and backed off one too many times.

"Maybe."

She put her hand back on him and suddenly found herself flying through the air, hitting the mattress with her back. She squeaked with shock, and found her legs being pushed apart. She gazed up at him, torn between need and satisfaction that she'd won this round. "You in a hurry or something?"

"Yeah." And then he plunged into her. He managed to hold on to his control long enough for her to catch up and she could see the effort it was costing him. He stroked her with his body, stoked her excitement with his own until they hit one of those magic moments where they shattered simultaneously. Usually she closed her eyes at the fateful moment, but she hadn't known how close to climax she was and so was swept away, her gaze locked with his. She felt as if she was looking into the deepest part of him, where all his secrets, his memories and his essence lived.

His eyes went dark, seemed to focus on whatever he

saw inside her open eyes, which she suspected was her secrets, her memories and her essence.

As her orgasm swamped her, she felt a connection so powerful with this man who was a virtual stranger that a mist of tears clouded her vision.

He didn't say anything for a moment, simply held that intimate gaze and then, bending slowly, kissed her. She tasted the salt of his sweat, the softness of his lips and then they were holding each other tight. As though they'd never let go.

When they'd come back to earth, he said, "I'd love to stay and make love to you for days, but I've got to get ready for the gala tonight."

"I know."

"I'm going to go shower." She watched him walk naked to the bathroom, feeling lust stir once more. She was seriously turning into a nymphomaniac.

He paused in the doorway of the bathroom. Didn't turn around. "You staring at my butt?"

Damn, he was good. She could lie, but then he might start wearing clothes around the place. Trust, she reminded herself. Maybe she could trust him with the truth. "Yeah. I am. It's one of your best features."

He chuckled. "Maybe I should turn around and you might want to revise your opinion."

"Egotist. Go shower."

"Come with me."

"Okay."

They made love in the shower, wet and slow. And as they were drying off in her too-small bathroom, bumping into each other, he said, "When this is over, how would you like to go sailing?"

"In March? It would be freezing."

"Not in the Caribbean. I figure both our bosses owe us some time off."

She fought the excitement that roared through her like a flash flood. "You barely know me."

His hand traveled down her spine, tracking the bumps as he went. That hand was warm and sure. "I know the sounds you make when you climax." He dropped a kiss on her damp shoulder.

"I know that when I lick the back of your knees you giggle, and when I touch your sailboat tattoo with my tongue you get goose bumps."

"Do not."

He licked at the tattoo on her back. "Do, too. I know that you're a good person who eats way too much crap and that it makes me happy to wake up with you."

She turned to stare at him. "I've gone out with guys for months, years, who never made a speech half that romantic."

"Bet they were thinking it."

She snorted. "Ah, no."

He kissed her lips softly. "Then they didn't deserve your time. You deserve romance."

"I don't need—" He cut her off with his mouth.

"I know you don't need it, or me, or anyone. You're tough. I get it. So, you don't need romance. I still say you deserve it."

He kissed her one more time and she was embarrassed at the way her hand clung to his shoulder when he pulled away.

He dressed swiftly and she knew that he was going to make sure Charlie and Lexy got in and got away from the gala safely. She wanted to ride along, but she knew it would only look suspicious. She understood she had

to stay out of the way even as it killed her to sit home
and worry. About all of them.

"I have to go," he said.

"Be careful. And come back tonight."

He kissed her hard. "I'll see you later."

18

LEXY HAD BEEN TO THE ODD charity gala, of course. Impossible to live in Manhattan and work in the fashion world without ending up at one glitzy benefit or another. But she'd never seen anything like the Diamond Ball hosted by the Graysons. The ball had been going for half a century, but Florence Grayson took over the chairmanship in the late eighties and had held it ever since.

The Diamond Ball raised an enormous sum for charity, but it was also a chance for the rich and connected to polish up the best of their gems and adorn themselves with all the sparkle they owned.

Traditionally they wore diamonds.

She'd wanted to get in these doors for years so she could showcase her own designs to the wealthy, fashionable and fabulous. However, the price tag put the party way beyond her reach. The price of a single ticket was the equivalent of a small car, and a table cost as much as a house in most parts of the country.

If she wasn't slightly apprehensive about being in the company of a possible killer and wearing jewels that were controversial to say the least, she'd have been wildly excited to be here.

Charlie walked at her side, the perfect escort in a Dior tux. They chatted idly as they entered the magnificent ballroom of the Grayson mansion.

"I've always wanted to come to this event," she admitted, trying to ignore the tingle in her spine, "but I've never been able to afford it. I can never pay you back for the cost of my ticket."

He smiled. "Relax. We're both here as guests. We're part of a table."

"A table? I thought those were reserved by big companies and superrich families."

He put a hand to her lower back and urged her forward. "We're here as guests of my mother."

She stopped as though she'd run face-first into a plate-glass window. Smuck.

"What did you just say?"

He seemed amused at her obvious horror. "My mother gets a table every year. She was delighted that I actually accepted her invitation for once. Even more so that I'm bringing a guest."

"I can't meet your mother." Panic was beating at her breast much worse than when she'd thought all she had to deal with was a possible killer. "She'll know what we were doing before we came here tonight. Mothers always know." She put a hand to her hair. "I'm mussed. I'm definitely mussed."

He took her hand in his and lightly kissed it. "You look absolutely perfect," he said, studying her carefully. "I like your hair slightly mussed, and your heavy eyes and swollen lips, you look like you've spent the afternoon being pleasured in my bed, which is exactly how I want you to look. Like a well-pampered mistress."

"Listen, Pendegraff, I don't do mistress. We are equal partners in this thing. And I didn't spend all afternoon in your bed. It was up against the wall." She paused, reliving the afternoon in all its glory. "And on the living-room sofa." She touched her thumb to the corner of his mouth. "And we ended up in my bed. Not yours."

Beneath her thumb his lips quirked. "It was a hell of an afternoon."

"You certainly don't need my mussed hair to broadcast your sexual exploits. That smug expression on your face should do the job just fine."

She made to walk past him but he stopped her, holding on to her elbow. "I'll be as equal as you want me to be, but for tonight we're playing parts. You're the hot, slutty mistress and I'm the rich playboy so smitten with you that I've hung a fortune in jewels around your neck. Think you can handle that?"

"I can handle anything. You worry about yourself."

He chuckled softly and they continued on their way, mingling with gorgeously gowned women sparkling with diamonds. Suddenly he leaned forward and whispered in her ear. "When we get home tonight, you'll be in my bed. That's a promise."

Based on what could happen between now and then? She seriously hoped he was right.

"I was hoping to make some business contacts among these people. It is demeaning to masquerade as your hot, skanky mistress and it won't do my credibility as a businesswoman any good."

"Look at it this way. You're also being resurrected from the dead. That's got to be a reasonable trade-off."

"You are such a smart-ass. I don't know why I put up with you."

"I've been wondering the same myself for years." An older woman's rather amused voice said from behind Lexy. The voice was rich sounding, a little slow and lazy. It almost reminded her of— No. Please let the woman behind her not be—

"Lexy, darling. I'd like you to meet my mother."

Pulling every bit of backbone she could access, she turned to face Charlie's mother.

The woman gazing at her with an amusement that was eerily familiar and was astonishingly chic. She was probably in her early sixties and wore her naturally white hair in a stylish bob. Her gown was peacock-blue and brought out the blue color in her eyes and emphasized a clear complexion that she'd allowed to age naturally. Her diamond set, earrings, necklace, brooch and bracelets, was almost stunning in its brilliance.

"Mrs. Pendegraff, it's wonderful to meet you. And thank you for inviting me to this party. I've always wanted to attend."

"It's my pleasure, dear. And you must call me Sarah."

Charlie's mother extended her hand and she shook it, feeling the woman's scrutiny of her and immediately being certain she could tell what she and her son had been doing all afternoon, which naturally made her blush and feel guilty.

"May I say that in a room full of amazing jewels, your set really stands out? Those emeralds are spectacular."

"Thank you. I know I'm supposed to wear pure diamonds, but Charlie gave me this necklace so I wanted to wear it." She blushed even deeper. This was the lie they'd decided on and didn't it just figure that the first person she'd have to tell it to would be the man's mother?

Of course, if he'd told her his mother was going to be here, she'd never have agreed to the preposterous story in the first place.

"Really?" Sarah Pendegraff shot a piercing look at her son. "How long have you two been going out together?" And the subtext was so clear she might as well have shouted it out. *And why haven't I met this girl or heard a word about her when you know her well enough to hang a fortune in jewels around her neck?*

She decided to let Charlie answer that one. This was his mother, after all.

He took her hand in his. "Be nice, Mother. You know I only introduce women to you when I'm serious. Lexy is serious."

Her hand jumped in his. He must have felt it for he squeezed her fingers reassuringly. Of course it was a lie, but for a moment her heart had done a strange bump-bump thing. Which was crazy. She didn't want to be important to Charles Pendegraff III any more than she wanted him to matter to her.

Sarah glanced searchingly between the two of them. Then smiled. "Well, I'd better get to know Lexy then, hadn't I?" She gestured to a small group standing and chatting, all of whom were fiercely elegant. Lexy knew that in the stolen jewels and a dress she couldn't possibly afford she'd fit right in, but she'd never felt more of a fraud. "Come and meet the rest of the table."

"Where's Charles II?" she asked Charlie in an undertone as they trailed his mother.

"The major British royals don't usually come unless they're in town, but we've probably got some minor royalty around."

"I meant your father."

"Ah. He passed away a few years ago."

"Oh. I'm sorry." There wasn't time for more, but she realized how very little she knew of this man who'd been inside her body. He was full of contradictions. A thief who moonlighted working for law enforcement and insurance agencies, a man who stole for a living and yet belonged to a family wealthy enough to buy a table at the Diamond Ball, a man who could be ruthless when he chose, as in when he'd grabbed and kidnapped her, who could also be a gentle and romantic lover.

Unfortunately she was a woman who loved contrasts.

She had a feeling it was safer in her jewelry designs, however, than in her choice of men.

Not that she'd chosen, really; she and Charlie had been thrown together by circumstances that were more than strange. But now that they'd been intimate, she didn't think she was going to be able to go back to her old life exactly as it was.

"My dear," Sarah Pendegraff said, drawing her forward. "I'd like you to meet some of my friends."

The friends turned out to be people she'd mostly heard of. They were either quoted in the *New York Times* business pages, or they were featured in the society pages, which she tried to keep up with for business reasons. There was so much bling in the group flashing and twinkling that she wished for sunglasses.

She shook hands all around and soon discovered she wasn't the only one who kept up with what was going on around town. "What did you say your name was?" one of the gray-haired captains of industry asked her.

"Alexandra Drake. Lexy."

His yachting-tanned forehead crinkled. "You're not the jewelry designer from SoHo, are you?"

She smiled. Resisted glancing at Charlie. Showtime, it seemed, had arrived. "Yes. That's me."

"But you're alive."

"Very much so. I was out of town when the fire broke out in my studio. I didn't hear about it until I returned."

"I believe there was a fatality involved," the man said, with a delicacy that barely masked his curiosity.

"Yes. The police are still trying to identify the woman. I don't know who she was."

"Stanley loves current events," Stanley's wife interrupted smoothly. "He'll talk your ear off if you let him. May I just say that is a stunning necklace you have there."

"Thank you." She reached for Charlie's hand in a coquettish gesture. "Charlie bought it for me."

He took her hand. Gave it a squeeze.

"My goodness." The woman who had obviously been attempting to steer the conversation into smoother channels seemed to lose her bearings. "Stanley's never given me anything half so precious." She glanced at her husband accusingly. "And they aren't even married yet."

"Do you mind if we mingle for a few minutes, Mother? I'd like to introduce Lexy to a few people."

"Of course not, dear." She glanced over his shoulder, and stopped him with a hand on his shoulder. "Oh, but before you go, you should say hello to our hosts."

Lexy's hand twitched in Charlie's as a jolt of nerves zapped her. He squeezed reassuringly, but she could feel the current of energy coming from him.

"Sarah, darling," a cultured female voice crooned. Lexy watched a woman with shoulder-length ash-blond hair and a face that belonged to a forty-year-old approach. She suspected that face would always look forty.

Apart from a waterfall of diamonds hanging from her neck, she wore a diamond tiara. Victorian era, judging by the style.

"Florence." The women air-kissed and then a man kissed Sarah's cheek in his turn. "Edward, how good it is to see you."

Edward Grayson was a dapper man of about seventy, with silver hair and red cheeks. His eyes were blue and protruded slightly behind horn-rimmed glasses.

"A lovely party, as always," Sarah continued. "I think the floral arrangements are spectacular this year."

Florence beamed. "I found this darling florist. He's from Prague, if you can imagine. He said to me, in his delightful Czech accent, 'I don't do floral arrangements, madam, I create fantasies.'"

While the women talked, Mr. Grayson smiled and nodded at the group. He got to Lexy and his smile grew rigid, his eyes bugged out and his already rosy cheeks grew scarlet. He didn't say a word, simply stood stock-still, staring at her chest. She pretended not to notice, but she felt herself beginning to blush.

"Well, it's certainly a gorgeous fantasy. Doing all the flowers in white was inspired. And the glitter on the feathers is—"

"Diamonds. They are all diamonds. Tiny industrial diamonds, he insisted on it. He had seamstresses working night and—" At this point Florence Grayson's gaze wandered and, as her husband's had, landed on Lexy's chest and stuck there.

The woman made a horrible sound in the back of her throat, like an asthmatic cat with a hair ball.

Maybe the Botox prevented her from any facial expression, but her eyes were feverish as she stared.

"Florence, are you all right?"

"Yes," the woman gasped. "Fine. The air's very dry in here." She sucked back her drink with an unsteady hand. Then tried to pull herself together.

"And how is everyone? I know you all of course, no introductions necessary, except I don't believe I've met you?" she said in a questioning tone to Lexy.

Sarah, hostess born and bred that she was, immediately introduced them. "Alexandra Drake. Charlie's friend."

"Please, call me Lexy," she said, extending her hand. She knew one thing: this woman was definitely not the same person who had come into her shop and introduced herself as Florence Grayson.

"It's lovely to meet you."

Lexy had watched carefully and while Florence Grayson hadn't reacted to hearing her name, her husband had gone rigid and, if it was possible, even redder in the face.

"Lexy Drake?" the man sputtered. "You're Lexy Drake."

"I am."

"But you're dead."

Mrs. Stanley laughed, a slick society laugh, the kind of laugh that could smooth over any awkward situation. It was getting a workout tonight. "We've already been through that, Edward. Fortunately Lexy was out of town when that awful fire happened."

"Out of town? Where?"

Charlie cleared his throat delicately. "She was with me. In a quiet, secluded not-to-be-revealed location."

"That's a lovely necklace, Lexy," Florence Grayson said, her hand reaching forward as though she were going to touch the gems, or perhaps attempt to rip them from her neck, and then drawing back.

"Isn't it gorgeous?" Mrs. Stanley gushed. "We've all been admiring it. Charlie bought it for her."

"Charlie bought it?" Mr. Grayson spoke again, his face still as red, his eyes still as buggy, as when he'd first caught sight of the necklace.

"That's right," Charlie said.

"Fine-looking piece. Where did you get it?"

"Private sale. Friend-of-a-friend sort of thing. Frankly I got it at a fire-sale price."

She had no idea how he could be so cool. All she had to do was stand here and show off the goods, but Charlie had to play a part. Cool, calculated. Giving Grayson enough information to freak him out, not enough to really tell him anything. Except for the two crucial pieces of information he was now absorbing.

Charlie had the Isabella Emeralds.

And Lexy was alive.

Grayson's gaze jerked up to Charlie's and she didn't like the expression in those protuberant blue eyes.

She had no idea what would have happened next, but luckily—or had Charlie's mother made a graceful motion?—a society photographer appeared in front of them. "May I?" He motioned with his big-lensed camera and they all dutifully arranged themselves. Charlie made sure to position Lexy at the front of the grouping so her necklace would be photographed, no doubt as yet another part of his obscure plan.

The photographer took their names and checked spellings for the photo cutline, and when he got to Lexy, paused, stared up at her and then said, "Are you the same Lexy Drake who had a fire?"

"Yes."

"That sucks. I got sent out to take the pictures. Nasty."

She nodded, feeling queasy just remembering the gutted black hole that had once been her home and business.

"Wait just a second. Didn't you die in that fire?"

"No."

He thought that over. "So, you're alive."

"As you see."

"Cool. Wait right here. There's a reporter wandering around. This could be, like, a scoop." And he tucked his notebook into his back pocket and sped off.

"Let's hope he takes good pictures," Charlie said in her ear.

"I guess it was inevitable, but I really feel strange having all this media fuss."

"Has to be done."

"I suppose. At least Amanda knows, and my dad, so they won't find out from the paper tomorrow."

Charlie turned to his mother and her friends. "If you'll all excuse us, I was about to introduce Lexy to a few people I'd like her to meet."

"Yes, of course," Grayson said, pulling himself together with an effort and finally raising his gaze from her chest. "We'll catch up with you again later."

Charlie and Lexy made their slow way through the crowd. He knew a lot of people. They hadn't gone far when a redheaded woman about Lexy's own age wearing a green strapless dress appeared, the photographer at her elbow.

"Lexy Drake?" she said. "Is it really you?"

"I'd show you my ID but I think it all melted in the fire."

"Oh, wow. This is amazing that you're alive. I was really upset when I heard the news. I've bought earrings from you before and always dreamed of being able to afford one of your custom pieces. Now I guess I can still dream."

Lexy smiled at her. She liked the woman immediately. She had freckles and a wide, innocent smile, that no doubt made people tell her all their secrets. Very handy in a journalist.

"You showing up at a charity gala very much alive is going to be news. Do you mind if I ask you a few questions?"

"No. I suppose not."

"Fantastic. First I guess I have to ask where you were and how come you didn't call anyone to say you were alive."

They'd rehearsed this story but it still felt a little awkward. Lexy didn't make a habit of distorting the truth, at least not until she got mixed up with Charlie. They'd come up with a story that was essentially true, though not entirely.

"Charlie and I were away together and—well, we didn't see or hear the news. We only returned today and I found out…"

"So you were on vacation?"

"More like a dirty weekend," Charlie put in helpfully.

Lexy glared at him. She really didn't need that being printed in the newspaper.

"This must be a huge shock for you. How did it feel when you got back to find out your studio was gone?"

"It's like a part of me died," she said, recalling the sick feeling she'd experienced when she drove by.

"I hate to ask you this, but it's my job. Do you know there was a body found in the rubble?"

"I heard that, yes."

"Any idea who it could be?"

"No. The police are investigating and of course I'll help in any way I can."

"It's strange to see you in public and not wearing one of your own designs, but I have to say this is a truly stunning piece."

"Thank you. Charlie gave it to me. It's especially precious to me now that I have no jewelry of my own to wear. Though, of course, I'll get back to work as soon as I can find a new space. And, if it's possible, could you please print that I will honor all of my orders and commissions. I'll put something on my Web site so customers can get hold of me."

"Of course. So how does it feel to discover everyone thought you were dead?"

Lexy thought about it for a moment. Her mind darting to the activities of the afternoon. "I'd have to say, I've never felt more alive."

"I'm really happy you are." She turned to the photographer. "Can you get a picture of Lexy and her boyfriend?"

"Sure, yeah."

"Do a great job. I think we're looking at our front page," the woman said with all the satisfaction of a society reporter who just stumbled on a front-page news headline.

He snapped off a few photographs of Charlie and Lexy standing together.

After the photo session, Charlie whisked her away and toward the opposite side of the room. "How are you doing?" he asked in a low voice, a caressing smile on his face presumably to convince anyone watching that they were exchanging sweet nothings.

She pasted a matching smile on her own lips. "I'm

sweating in places I didn't know I had sweat glands," she said.

"You're doing great," he said, leaning forward and giving her a little kiss. Which definitely helped steady her.

"Security guards closing in," she whispered against his lips. "Three o'clock."

He smiled, as though he were quite happy about this turn of events. She supposed they'd provoked Grayson hoping for some reaction, but right now she really wished she were curled in bed in her pajamas with a good book.

"Let's dance," he said, not bothering to look over his shoulder and confirm what she'd seen.

The game of cat-and-mouse had begun.

The gala was packed. Due to the high net worth of everybody here, except her, the age range was predictably on the upper end, but there were some younger celebrities, up-and-coming hotshot business types and trophy wives and dates to balance things out.

When they got to the dance floor, the live orchestra was playing a waltz, which she probably hadn't danced since the last time she attended a wedding. But she loved dancing, and when Charlie pulled her into his arms, she had no trouble following his moves.

As their bodies touched and brushed she found her mind filling with images of their sex games earlier and in spite of the nervous tension she was experiencing, or maybe because of it, her senses seemed heightened. She felt the brush of his wool jacket against her bare arms, the heat of his body where they touched, the subtle movements of his hips and legs, his arms guiding her as they swooped in circles around the dance floor. She didn't need to keep him informed of the location of the two goons dressed as security guards, since he could see them for himself.

She tried not to stare, but it was impossible not to stay aware of them as they watched from the edges of the dance floor, waiting.

When the second security guard turned and stared directly at her, she stumbled slightly.

In that second she was back at the night her place was broken into and later torched. She remembered clearly staring out of the limo window and seeing the guy running, a gun held in his hand.

"You all right?" Charlie asked, smoothly guiding her back into the dance.

All right? She'd never been less all right. Her heart was hammering and she felt her breath hitch. "The second security guard? I recognize him."

"Shh. I know."

"You saw him, too? It's the one from that night. The one who ran out after us the night my place was torched."

He winced as she accidentally stepped on his toe but she barely noticed.

"The guys who were pretending to be cops. You were right. They were hired by Grayson. But imagine the nerve, having them here tonight."

"Remember, they have no idea that you saw them. And they couldn't connect me with any of this until tonight."

"We should call my dad right now. He can arrest that guy."

"On what charge?" The song ended and they clapped politely along with the other dancers. A few left the floor, more joined them.

"How about murder? Arson? Impersonating an officer?"

"Did you actually see him do any of those things?"

She opened her mouth. Closed it again. Damn. A few reruns of *Law & Order* would tell her she had no case. Never mind years of living in the same house as a cop. Her excitement fizzled. "Nope. All I saw him do was run down a street with a gun in his hand."

"It's not enough. The only thing we have going for us is that they have no idea how much we know. Let's keep it that way for a while."

"I wish they'd stop staring at us. It's creeping me out."

"Relax. They won't do anything here—not with my mother, your father and half the power players in the city watching."

She knew he was right, theoretically, but she couldn't rid her mind of the image of that brutish guy with the short neck running along her street with a gun. What if he'd caught up with them?

She remembered the news report about the body in her apartment and she knew the answer.

They left the dance floor and he scooped them two champagne flutes from a passing tray and handed her one. She needed the false courage, so she sipped the dry, bubbly wine on the theory that it was hard to take anything too seriously when champagne was involved.

Charlie introduced her to a few more people he knew, as though this were a normal social event. Then it was time for dinner.

No doubt the most fabulous, delicious dinner ever created. It might as well have been boxed mac and cheese for all she could taste.

She couldn't stop noticing that she was always

watched. She worked out that there were four of them, paired off so that one team would keep her and Charlie in their sights and then they'd trade off. As though she might not notice the surveillance if it was always a different thick-necked type in a bad suit eyeing her.

There were speeches, of course, more dancing, more mingling. Charlie seemed the epitome of relaxed charm. He laughed, he joked, he ate with the apparent relish of a man who could actually taste his food. She wanted to hit him.

Once the speeches were over and people had begun to circulate, the event she'd been dreading occurred. Mr. Grayson approached, without his wife.

He was all smiles as he patted Charlie on the back all hail fellow well met. She could almost feel his eyeballs longing to stray to her neckline, but he controlled himself with an effort.

"Charles, I've got something to discuss that I think you might find interesting."

"Really?" Charlie managed to combine surprise with flattery in his tone to a degree that would have impressed Stanislavski.

"If you can spare me a few minutes in my study, there's something I'd like to show you."

"Of course." He turned to Lexy with a smile and the ghost of a wink. "All right if I leave you for a few minutes, darling?"

Before she could reply, Grayson said, "Come along with us, Ms. Drake. I'd value your expertise."

"All right."

He led them to a private elevator in a corner and they rode it up two floors. She knew he couldn't do anything violent to them, not during the gala and certainly not with Charlie's mother downstairs, but still she felt her anxiety ratchet up a notch. She had to restrain her fingers from floating to her necklace and toying with it nervously. She gripped her clutch bag instead, squeezing and releasing the poor thing as though it were a stress ball.

The elevator opened on the quiet hush of a well-insulated home. No noise from the party penetrated. She hadn't realized how noisy it was downstairs until she felt the heavy quality of the silence.

"I keep my offices up here. I do most of my work from home, these days. Much less exhausting."

The hallway was lushly carpeted so her heels were soundless. He punched a code on a heavy door, which opened on a luxurious office, like something out of a men's club. Deep maroon leather club chairs, a desk big enough for a king to run a country from.

A second desk held several top-of-the-line computers, but the desk Grayson eased himself behind was bare of clutter, either technological or paper based. Somehow she found the gleaming bare surface kind of creepy.

In a gesture so clichéd she could barely believe he did it, he went to a cabinet and pulled out a humidor. Offered it to Charlie. "Cigar?"

Charlie chose a Cuban.

Grayson chose one for himself and soon the two men were puffing, adding a fog of sweet-scented smoke to her already addled brain.

Grayson didn't waste any time in getting to the point.

"I couldn't help but admire your necklace, my dear."

Now, at last, she allowed her fingers to touch the sparkling confection at her chest. "Isn't it something? Charlie bought it for me."

"Which brings us to the point of this little chat," the man said smoothly, his gaze still locked on the emeralds and diamonds. "Of course, discretion is assured, but I must tell you that I recently was burgled and a necklace identical to that one went missing."

Charlie raised his eyebrows. She felt equally surprised. She hadn't imagined the man would honestly tell them the jewels belonged to him. "Really? That's quite a coincidence."

A small smile that looked somehow dangerous appeared on the aging cherub's face. "I don't believe in coincidence. In my experience there's usually a logical explanation."

And she knew exactly what the explanation was. She couldn't believe he could act so cool.

Charlie didn't speak, merely puffed his cigar, leaning back in his chair as though he had nothing to do and all evening to do it in.

Grayson said, "Who sold you the piece?"

"Sorry. It was a private sale. As I said, an old friend needed some quick cash and I liked the look of the piece."

"You've got a good eye. What did you pay for it?"

A low chuckle was his answer. "It was a gift for Lexy. I don't want her knowing how much I paid."

The smile was growing thinner by the moment. "Ms. Drake, you're a jeweler. What's your estimate of the value of the piece you're wearing?"

She paused, as though she'd never considered anything so vulgar as value. She glanced down at the sparkling stones winking up at her.

"I'd estimate that a collection of emeralds and diamonds of this size and quality would run close to a million dollars."

"That's a pretty good guess, my dear. To me, of course, there's the added sentimental value. That necklace holds fond memories."

"Forgive me," said Charlie, "but I don't ever recall seeing it before. Surely if your wife had worn it I'd have noticed. I've a good memory for jewelry. That's one of the reasons I bought this piece. It was unique."

"You're right. As I said, it's got sentimental value and also I've kept it very private."

"Well, I guess there's more than one of them around after all. I assure you, the person who sold this to me is no thief."

Grayson's fingers tapped his immaculate desk surface sounding like machine-gun fire.

"I'm sure your insurers will be able to compensate you for the loss if the police don't have any luck locating your property." Charlie blew a few smoke rings.

"Well, that's the problem right there. I never insured the piece. As you've noted, my wife never wore it, and I thought I had it safe. Somehow, it was discovered and stolen."

"Odd that your wife's truly stunning collection of diamonds that she's wearing this evening weren't also taken."

"Yes. That was a lucky thing." Grayson opened a desk drawer and drew out a bank ledger. Old-fashioned and somehow commanding. "Let me get right to the point. I'd like to buy the necklace from you. Never mind what you paid. If we take Lexy's rough evaluation and add, let's say another half a million for your time and trouble, shall we say a million and a half?"

"You want to buy my necklace?" Lexy said, doing her best to appear astonished and hurt. "But I couldn't part with it. It was Charlie's first real gift to me."

"With a million and a half, I'm sure *Charlie* could buy you something more useful. An apartment perhaps. I believe you are currently homeless, Ms. Drake."

An apartment was not the most tactful item to bring up since he must know that she'd been burned out of her last home thanks to him. A shiver ran over her skin as she thought how truly deadly this old choir boy was.

Charlie looked perfectly unconcerned. "Up to you, babe. The necklace is yours." Like the most useless playboy bazillionaire, as though a million here or there didn't really bother him so long as it didn't make him late for his polo match.

"I'm sorry, Mr. Grayson. I've had so many compliments on my necklace tonight I'd hate to part with it. Besides, I'm not the kind of girl who sells presents somebody bought her." She shot Charlie a particularly intimate smile. "Particularly not somebody really special."

Grayson hadn't become a bazillionaire himself by wasting his time. It was obvious she wasn't going to change her mind, so he put the ledger carefully back in his drawer. She had a moment when she wondered whether he'd pull out a gun next and force her to give up the goods but as Charlie had predicted, he couldn't do that, not with the party going on downstairs. Not when half the people there had complimented Lexy on her fine necklace.

"Well, my dear, if you ever change your mind and decide to sell, do let me know. It's astonishingly like the one I lost."

"I will. And I hope you find yours." What she really meant was, *I hope you get yours.*

"Let's go back and join the party, shall we?"

The men put out their cigars and the three of them

retraced their quiet steps, whooshed down in the elevator and rejoined the gala.

"And the curtain closes on Act One," Charlie said softly.

19

THE LINE OF LIMOS stretched as the guests made their way home at the end of the evening. Lexy caught her father, one of the cops on the detail, and he looked visibly relieved when he saw her and Charlie get into their limo, driven, of course, by Healey.

"They following?" Charlie asked as they pulled away and headed toward the hotel.

"Yep."

"You know what to do."

"Sure do." Healey shot a glance at the pair of them. "Be careful."

The limo dropped them at the hotel and after the doorman helped Lexy out, followed by Charlie, it pulled away.

They walked into the hotel lobby. Charlie checked for messages. There were none.

They rode the elevator up to their floor. Entered their suite. Charlie flipped on lights. Came up behind her.

He kissed the back of her neck, making her shiver. "I'd love to peel you out of these clothes and make love to you right now, but honey, we've got to move."

She nodded. They'd rehearsed this part already.

He unfastened the necklace, placed it carefully in a plain black jewelry case. Then he opened the original Isabella Emeralds box where an identical necklace lay. The one Lexy and Amanda had sweated over. "You did an amazing job."

"Let's hope I didn't waste my time and your money."

He put the box into the in-room safe, locking it carefully. Then he and Lexy stripped out of their clothes and slipped into their waiting jeans and sweaters. She was thankful for her new boots and the coat. She wrapped the scarf around her throat. Gloves would have been nice but she didn't have any. It couldn't be helped.

She took their discarded evening clothes and scattered them in a seductive trail toward one of the bedrooms while he took pillows and made two vaguely human-size sausages in the middle of the bed.

Within ten minutes they'd turned out the lights and exited the suite. He was carrying a black leather bag. She didn't even ask. Moving swiftly to the stairs, they ran lightly down, and down, and down.

She was out of breath by the time they'd scooted out a back door and headed to where a slick, powerful-looking black motorcycle waited.

He unzipped the black bag and pulled out a helmet. "You ever ridden on one of these?"

She grinned at him. "All around Europe. The summer of my Italian boyfriend."

He tossed her the helmet. Also black. "You're experienced, then."

"Oh, yeah." She put the helmet on, tucking her hair underneath. Charlie put his own helmet on and then climbed onto the bike. She swung a leg over and snugged up behind him on the pillion, settling into a posture she remembered well.

They roared off into the night. Even though she had her arms wrapped around Charlie's waist, her hands still quickly chilled against the cool night air. It was three in the morning and New York was still busy with cabs, emergency vehicles and garbage trucks.

She had no idea where they were going and it was typical of this bizarre adventure that she hadn't bothered to ask. She knew Charlie had a plan, had thrown him her trust as easily as he'd thrown her the bike helmet. Maybe it was crazy, but ever since he'd entered her studio mere days ago, her life had been nothing but insane.

If the adventure ended well, and she really, really hoped it did, there'd be no reason for them to stay together. She wasn't the kind of woman men showered with million-dollar necklaces. She never aspired to wear the big-ticket bling; she'd always appreciated individual design rather than the number of karats something represented. Style over dollar value.

She didn't belong in Charlie's world any more than she belonged at that fancy gala tonight. Still, it had been fun playing Cinderella at the ball. Now, her dress had turned into jeans, her limo into a motorbike and her fancy necklace into evidence to catch a murderer.

That was the plan, anyway. But plans, as she knew well, didn't always go, well, according to plan.

The motorcycle dipped as he took turns fast and she stayed with him, leaning into his body, letting the bike do its thing. She didn't fight the movement, so the three of them—bike, Charlie and her—moved as one.

The adrenaline was still pumping through her system and somehow a ride through the night was perfect.

He slowed, pulled out a pass and brought it to a

sensor; then a gate opened and they sped through into a garage. He parked and they dismounted.

"Where are we?" she asked.

"My place." He kissed her swiftly. "I promised you I was going to make love to you in my bed."

He walked to an elevator. He needed to punch in a code to use it, she noted. Pretty good security in this building. The elevator took them straight to the top floor and then opened into a small foyer with only one door.

Another code, and a finger scan, and then the door opened.

"Cool," she said and walked inside.

And her mouth fell open. It was like walking into an interior designer's vision of what Lexy had always secretly dreamed of. The apartment was huge, with high ceilings, open beams, a circular staircase to a second level.

The walls were decorated with bold, original art. She walked straight to the window and looked out on the river.

"This is amazing."

"Thanks."

"You took me to a hotel when you have this?" She waved her arm around the apartment.

"Didn't know you well enough."

"Now you do?"

He walked toward her, put a hand to the back of her head, pulled her forward for a kiss. "Now, I do."

His cell phone rang. He answered, "Yeah, Healey." Checked his watch and nodded. "Right on time. No. Let Jed know, make sure you follow them."

"Yeah. I will."

He ended the call. Turned to her. "Dumbass One and Dumbass Two just entered the hotel."

She let out a breath she hadn't realized she was holding. "Grayson took the bait."

"Yep. Now let's hope those boys can manage to break in to the safe and steal the emeralds." He sighed and rubbed the back of his neck. "Maybe we made it too difficult for them putting the jewels in the safe. I should have left them out on the bureau."

"We talked about this," she reminded him. "If we made it too easy he might sense a trap. I'm sure they'll figure out a way to get into that safe."

"And lead us straight to Papa."

Charlie withdrew a flat box from inside his leather coat. Opened it carefully.

"How'd they survive the trip?" She peeked over his shoulder. The Isabella Emeralds winked at her.

"I guess they've survived shipwrecks, airline travel and who knows what else in five centuries. A motorcycle ride wasn't going to bother them."

She touched a deep green emerald with her fingertip. "I wonder how long it will take him to spot the fake."

"Initially he'll see what he wants to see. His necklace. We have the element of surprise on our side, plus his own greed and mania working against him. A man who would be willing to kill three people to keep those gems all to himself couldn't be too sane."

"No. Which only makes him more dangerous."

"I agree. So we play it safe. Your part in this little drama is over."

She wasn't going to argue with the man at this time of the morning, but she really didn't think her part was over. Not yet.

"I know that necklace wasn't the real Isabella one,

but even so, you put out a lot of money buying real stones."

He shrugged. "The man tried to kill me and you. I have a vested interest in taking him down."

"I just hope the tracking device is hidden well enough. If I'd had more time, I'd have done a better job."

"Honey, you are way too much of a perfectionist. I swear when I first looked at them side by side, I couldn't tell the difference. Besides, we don't want him believing he's got the real gems or we'll never get him. He's got to figure out we conned him."

"That's twice now he's tried to get the necklace back and failed. He seems like the kind of guy who's going to be very unhappy when he figures that out."

"And I hope I'm around to see it." He took her arm in his. "Let's go track our package."

She ought to be dead tired, but she still felt wired, so she followed him to his office on the upper level. She wasn't really surprised to see another set of security measures before the heavy door opened and she entered a large office with enough equipment to run NATO.

"Have a seat," he said, pulling out a high-tech office chair and pulling it next to a similar chair that sat in front of a large-screen monitor. He fired up the computer, typed in a few commands and chuckled. "There it is. On the move."

It was amazingly cool to watch the blip that was the GPS tracking device making its way through a computerized street map. As they'd hoped, it was headed toward the Grayson mansion.

"I guess they figured out how to break in to the safe after all."

"Guess so."

"You sound awfully pleased with yourself."

"I am." He gripped her thigh in a warm clasp. "We did it. He swallowed the bait."

They watched until the blip stopped moving. "Do you suppose it's in his safe?"

"Or under his pillow. I doubt he's going to put it around his next mistress's neck."

She shuddered. "When do you think he'll figure out it's not the original?"

"If he's the fanatical collector I think he is, he's going to have an expert verify that it's unharmed. That's when he'll figure it out. If we're lucky, that will be tomorrow."

"What if he doesn't call anyone in?"

"Then we call the cops. Tell them about the break-in and about the lucky security measures we took to protect the necklace. They'll track the stolen goods to Grayson."

They watched the stationary blip for a few more minutes. "Well, looks like the action's over for tonight." He glanced at her. "Ready for bed?"

She nodded.

"Tired?" The skin around his eyes crinkled and just the tips of his lips tilted up. It was one of the sexiest things she'd ever seen.

Slowly she shook her head.

He spun her chair so they were facing each other. "So, you want to go to bed, but you're not tired?"

"That's right."

He leaned over, cupping her face with his palm, reaching around to the back of her head and unfastening her hair so it tumbled, glossy and dark, bouncing around her shoulders. "I do like your hair," he said, sifting the strands through his fingers.

"Thanks."

"Know what else I like?"

She shook her head.

"A little something called the Lyons Stagecoach."

She clapped her hands over her eyes. "A gentleman would never bring that up."

He was laughing as he pulled her hands away and kissed her fingers. "A gentleman always tries to give a lady what she wants."

Half embarrassed, half turned on, she followed him as he led her to his big, gorgeous bed. He undressed her slowly, as though her jeans and sweater were a fancy evening gown, then he stripped off his own clothes.

She was so hot for him she couldn't believe they'd had sex most of the afternoon.

He pushed her back onto the bed and they rolled and played, naked and silly. The relief that everything was going according to plan was enormous. He kissed her, touched her everywhere, then sitting in the middle of the bed, he pulled her onto his lap, her knees on either side of his hips. While they kissed, he reached down and began to play with her, getting her hot and juicy. She climbed onto him, easing him into her body, then leaned back on her hands; he leaned back on his and they started to rock the stagecoach.

"Why do you like it so much?" he asked, half panting.

"I like the slide, the way you hit my G-spot, the amount of control I have."

"I like the view," he said, grinning.

Excitement was building, building, she could hear them both panting, and then her head fell back, her hair cascaded down her back and she came in a great swamp of feeling. Seconds later she heard his cry of release.

She leaned forward, slumped on top of him, knocking him onto his back, falling with him.

"Is it really your favorite?" he asked when they could speak again.

She kissed his chest. "It's right up there." But then so was everything else they'd done. "I'm glad you knew," she murmured drowsily.

He kissed her hair. "Me, too."

20

"GOOD MORNING."

Charlie turned from contemplation of the morning paper to see Lexy wrapped in his robe. Her hair was a glorious mess, mostly because he'd had his hands in it so often in the night, and then she'd done some mussing of her own, he recalled, thrashing her head back and forth on the pillow.

"Good morning."

Her skin looked extra pale against the navy silk of the robe, and its size made her appear particularly dainty. Her bare feet were long and he loved the dark purple color on her toenails.

"Want some breakfast?"

She stifled a yawn with the back of her hand. "Coffee?"

"Fresh pot."

"Heaven." But she didn't head straight for the kitchen; she came toward him and gave him a quick kiss. "Did we get any sleep last night?"

He grinned. "Not much."

Stifling her own smile and another yawn, she headed for the kitchen. "Time is it?"

"After eleven."

He'd thought about waking her earlier, but she'd been sleeping like a woman who needed the sleep. He folded the paper, watched her sip coffee the way a vampire might suck blood, greedily, as though her very life depended on it.

"I need to run back to the hotel and discover the break-in. You want to come or hang out here?"

She looked startled. "You'd trust me here alone? What if I pushed the wrong button in mission control up there and started a war?"

"Of course I trust you. I'll even tell you the good places to snoop."

She snorted. "Please. You're not that interesting. Anyhow, I want to come with you. We'll discover the break-in together."

He pushed the now-closed paper toward her. "You're front-page news."

"Oh, right. I forgot."

She wandered over and looked down at the photo. "'Missing Jeweler Turns Up Alive At Diamond Ball.' Not the most imaginative headline." She tilted her head. "Good picture, though. And that necklace really photographs well. No need to describe the missing piece of jewelry. We can simply point to today's paper." She glanced up at him admiringly. "Nice."

"Grayson is going to have a cow."

"That thought makes me very happy. Let me grab a shower and dress. I'll be ready in twenty."

"Want some toast or something?"

She was already sprinting up the stairs. "Sure. Anything."

He had to give her credit. She was one of the few women he could think of who could actually shower and dress in twenty minutes. Impressive. One more attribute in a growing list of things he adored about this woman. Not the least was the way she gave her body with absolute joy and abandon.

"What's that weird smile about?" she asked as she came down the last couple of stairs eighteen minutes after she'd gone up them.

"I was thinking about last night. You are very flexible."

She grinned at him. "Yoga. And pole dancing."

He offered her the whole-grain toast and peanut butter he'd made her. "Pole dancing?"

"Okay. Mostly yoga. But I did take pole dancing once. It's harder than it looks. Takes a lot of arm strength."

"You never stop surprising me."

They were still teasing each other when they arrived back at the hotel. Since they knew the jewels were gone he couldn't think of any reason for Grayson's thugs to be waiting in their room, but still he called Healey to meet them and made Lexy wait while he and Healey entered the room first.

A five-second run-through told them there was no one in the suite but them, so he motioned Lexy inside.

"Oh, my God. Why would they make such a mess?" she asked, surveying the damage.

"Could be to make it look like a real robbery," Healey suggested. "They had to trash your stuff looking for money and stuff. Then hit the safe."

The door of the safe swung wide, the empty gray metal box bereft of its contents.

"Wow. I hardly had anything, just a few new things,

now it's all ruined. Again." She sounded upset. He and Healey exchanged a glance.

"Don't touch anything."

"I won't."

She walked toward one bedroom, obviously forcing herself not to pick up the belongings that were scattered on the floor. The sexy trail of last night's clothes mixed with tossed cushions and broken cosmetics. She entered the bedroom and made a strange, choking sound.

"Lexy?" She didn't answer. Her back was stiff and she seemed rooted to a spot just inside the doorway.

"Lex? You okay?"

"I think…" she began in a strange, high-pitched tone not at all like herself. "I think…"

He didn't wait for more. He sprinted to her side. "Babe, what is it?"

She pointed a trembling finger to the bed. "I think those are bullet holes."

"Holy shit." The quick sausagelike mounds he'd made in the bed to fool any intruders into thinking they were asleep now sported charred holes. He put an arm around Lexy and pulled her to his side. "Healey, you'd better see this."

Healey joined them. He stepped closer to the bed. "From the size of those holes, looks like a .38, maybe a 9 mm. Must have used a silencer." He regarded them with hard eyes. "Grayson sure wants you two dead."

"I'm starting to feel the same way about him."

He pulled Lexy gently from the room. Her face was pale and she was trembling lightly. Shock. She'd been amazing, shouldering the strain of the past few days, but this was one bad experience too many. He sat her down on a chair. Got to his knees before her and rubbed her hands. "It's okay. It's going to be okay. I won't let anyone hurt you. I promise." Over his shoulder he said to Healey, "Make the calls."

"Sorry." She blinked a few times as though clearing her eyes of a gruesome sight. "I'm not going to fall apart, I promise. That just... What if we'd..."

"Shh. We didn't. He won't get another chance."

She nodded.

The police and hotel security arrived about the same time. And for the next half hour they went through their story. Ballistics experts were brought in, a photographer, fingerprint guys, a pair of detectives. Which impressed Charlie until he realized the bullet holes upped a theft charge to attempted murder.

His mind flipped to what could have happened and a cold, ruthless anger began to surge inside him.

Lexy's dad was through the door in seconds, out of breath and red in the face. He took one look at his daughter's pale expression and jogged to her side. "What happened here?"

He didn't coddle her, Charlie noticed. Probably never had, but his concern was evident in every cell of his belligerent body.

"The break-in went exactly as we hoped. With one added detail." He didn't like looking up at Jed Dabrowski when he had this kind of news to deliver, so he gave Lexy's fingers a quick squeeze and rose. "They shot up the bedding we'd rolled up to make it look like we were sleeping."

It hadn't occurred to him until the words were out that he was admitting to a very irate father who happened to carry a gun for a living that he was sleeping with his only daughter. Also, putting her life in danger. From Jed's expression, he'd just made himself number one on the shit list.

"Show me."

He led him into the room, crawling with photographers and the fingerprint experts while a security guy from the hotel stood there seeming not to know what to do.

"Detective," Jed said, nodding to a man in plainclothes about his own age who was studying the bed.

"Sergeant."

"So, what do you think?"

It seemed like they knew each other, probably respected each other's abilities because the detective said, "Six shots fired, probably from the doorway."

"Somebody wanted those two real dead. Obviously the perp thought these two were sleeping."

"Or did they? Maybe they knew they were shooting into pillows." The detective sighed, walking out of the room and motioning Jed and Charlie to follow. Removed his latex gloves when he got to the outer room. "Problem is, even if we find the guys who did the shooting all they have to say is that they knew there was nobody in the bed. It was a warning. Target practice. They can say anything they want. If they claim they knew there was nobody in that bed, we can't get them on attempted murder."

Jed stalked back over to his daughter. She was looking better now, Charlie was glad to see. Her color was back and she seemed steadier. He was pretty sure her dad was going to try to bully her into going home to his place. He was about to go on over there and explain why that was a terrible idea. His place was as close to impregnable as he could make it.

She needed to stay with him. He looked across at her, her dainty features, the long dark hair he loved to push his hands through, the lithe body that made magic with his. He needed to protect her.

As though she sensed his scrutiny, she glanced up at him and smiled. And that was when it hit him.

He was in love with her.

Perfect. In the middle of a crisis, when their lives were in danger and a madman was after them, now he had to fall in love?

Well, he'd never made things easy on himself. Why would he start now?

He took a step toward Lexy and her dad, feeling suddenly awkward with this new knowledge. Felt good, though. Right.

His phone rang. His mother.

"Hi, Mom."

"Hello, sweetheart. How are you?"

Well, if he couldn't tell his mom, who could he tell? "I'm in love."

She laughed softly. "I know that, dear. I saw you look at her last night." She sighed. "It's how your father used to look at me."

"I remember." He did, too. They fought, his mom and dad, they weren't the bloodless "everything's fine" types that so many of his friends' parents were. His were passionate people. Not demonstrative in public, but sometimes he'd catch his dad planting a good one on his mom, or she'd pat his dad's butt in passing. Stupid little things, but they'd always made him feel good as a kid. "I wish Dad was around. I wouldn't mind his advice."

"I know." She cleared her throat. "I was actually calling to speak with Lexy. Is she there?"

"What do you want to talk to Lexy for?" He was standing in front of her now, and she raised her eyebrows at his words. He mouthed, "My mother." At the words, his brand-new love looked startled and mildly panicked.

"Never you mind. If she had a phone I'd have called her directly. Put her on, please."

It was a tone he'd never yet been able to argue against. He was a grown man but he doubted he ever would be able to hold out against that particular tone of command.

With a shrug, he handed his phone over.

Lexy ran her tongue over her lips and took a quick breath before saying, "Hello?"

She listened for a moment.

"Oh, lunch. Today. Well, that's very nice of you, but—"

"Of course. Yes, a late lunch is fine. Two o'clock." She sent an S.O.S. with her eyes. "Yes, that's perfect."

She flipped the phone shut. Turned a stunned face to his. "How does she do that? I was going to say no, and then she said, 'I'd really love it if you could make it today,' and suddenly I'm saying yes.'"

"I know. It's the tone. My mother could rule the world. It's very scary."

"But why does she want to have lunch with me?"

"Probably to tell you how much she wants grand-children."

"Sounds like a sensible woman," Jed chimed in. "Lunch with a nice woman would do you good." He turned to Charlie. "How's the security at your mother's?"

"Adequate. But don't worry. I'll be there."

Lexy handed him back his phone. "Um, you're not invited."

"I know. I'll keep an eye on the house. Until this thing is over, I'm not letting you out of my sight."

She looked as though she were going to argue, but her father nodded in approval. "If she won't come home with me, I guess you're the next best choice."

He nodded. "Jed, can I talk to you privately for a second?"

Lexy bristled at that. "What? What could you possibly want to talk to my father about that I couldn't hear?"

"I'm going to ask his permission to marry you."

"Oh, very funny. Ha-ha. Okay, don't tell me. Have your little guy talk and I'll sit here and look pretty. If anyone needs a sandwich or a foot rub or something, just let me know."

The two men stepped outside into the hallway.

"Well?" Jed asked. "Something you need to tell me?"

Now that the moment had arrived Charlie felt stupidly nervous. He'd imagined this moment would come someday, that he and the father of his intended would enjoy a brandy and a cigar in comfort while he laid out his plans for the future and formally asked to marry the man's daughter. Sure, it was old-fashioned, but it was what his father would have expected of him.

But there was no brandy to sip in a bid to steady his nerves, no cigar to puff and avoid speaking for a second or two. It was him, a guy who had every reason to hate his guts since he'd endangered his only daughter, and a security guard down by the elevator looking at them curiously.

"Look, I know my timing pretty much sucks, but I want something out in the open."

Jed crossed his arms over his ample belly. "You're sleeping with my daughter. I got eyes. I figured it out.

You should know I'm not some modern-type father. You hurt her and I kill you. Simple as that."

"I love her, Jed."

"Words are cheap. I'm not impressed."

He blew out a breath. "You're not going to be one of those easygoing fathers-in-law, are you?"

For the first time the pugnacious expression disappeared from Jed's face. "Father-in-law? Did you say father-in-law?"

"That's right. I'm bungling this badly, I know, but I really did want to ask your permission to marry your daughter."

A deep chuckle resonated from the man standing in front of him. "She doesn't know anything about this, does she?"

"No. I know it's all moving pretty fast, but I'm thirty-four years old. I've never been in love before, never wanted to marry anyone before. Now, I can't imagine my life without Lexy. I want to live with her and love her and have children with her. And I'd like your permission before I ask her."

Jed rocked back on his heels, every inch the cop. "Well, this is an interesting situation." He chuckled. "Gotta tell you, not one I ever thought I'd find myself in. Lexy, she's not the kind of girl who believes in stuff like this. She's modern. But not me. I think you did fine." He scratched at the back of his head. "So, before I give my permission, I guess there's some things I should ask you. Let's see. I know she's a successful business gal, but she's taken quite a hit recently. You gonna be able to provide for her?"

"Yes. Money's really not a problem. I've got a very high net worth."

"Look, Charlie, no offense, but I got no time for

hedge funds and collections of old brandy and fancy cars. I'm a simple man. You got money in the bank? A house? Real assets?"

"I own quite a bit of property. All mortgage free. And I can have my accountant go over my other assets. Trust me, Lexy will only work because she wants to."

"Okay. Are you a gambler? A drinking man?"

"Only moderately."

"Ever been in trouble with the law?"

Damn it. He supposed he'd always known it would come out. But he'd hoped there'd be a better time. "Not exactly. But I should tell you something you won't like." Of all the men he could be having this conversation with, a cop wouldn't be his first choice. "I've never exactly had trouble with the law, but I have to tell you the truth. I used to be a thief."

"Come again?"

"I was a thief. A pretty good one, too. Never caught."

He shrugged. "I guess I was bored. Didn't want to go into my father's law firm, and I figured the financial industry was full of crooks. I decided it was more honest to be an actual crook than one who wears a suit to the office every day."

"That's a puny justification for breaking the law."

"I know. If it's any consolation, I only stole from people who could afford to lose things. Now I've turned my talents to an honest business. I work to get stolen goods back. Kind of a nice switch."

A noncommittal grunt was his only reply.

They stood there in the hallway for an uncomfortable minute. He supposed he'd imagined the asking-for-permission thing would be a quick run-through for form's sake. It had never honestly occurred to him that Jed Dabrowski might turn him down.

Then he'd be stuck in a nice dilemma. He wasn't going to give up Lexy, not because her father said so. As it was he had no idea if his feelings were returned. Did she love him?

They'd known each other such a short time. Intense, but short. Obviously they had incendiary passion between them, and they seemed to get on well together, which had to be a miracle considering the stress load they'd been under since the beginning. For him, the pressure cooker of tension and passion had turned to love. For Lexy? He had no idea. Maybe she'd walk away from him the second Grayson was in police custody and this adventure was over. Which would be soon.

The thought of that happening was too painful to contemplate. If she didn't love him now, he could wait. He'd give her time, let her rebuild, be the supportive boyfriend. Friend even if that was all she'd give him. But he wouldn't give up.

Finally his hopefully future father-in-law spoke. "I spent my whole career enforcing the law. I'm not happy about what you've told me. But you were man enough to come clean, and I appreciate that. I'm not saying yes, I approve of you marrying my daughter, and I'm not saying no. I think we all need to slow down a little. Ask me again in a month."

Okay, so it wasn't the pat on the back and fatherly approval he'd hoped for. It wasn't cuffs and getting shoved in the back of the paddy wagon, either. All in all, he figured Jed had handled the news pretty well. "Thank you, sir." He stuck out his hand and this time Lexy's dad shook it.

The door to the suite opened and Lexy swept out. "What are you two doing out here?"

"Man talk, young lady. None of your business."

"You and your man talk." She grabbed Charlie's arm. "I need to go shopping again. I can't wear jeans to your mother's for lunch."

She could and his mother wouldn't care, but he understood there were deep-seated female rituals he knew nothing about, just as Lexy would no doubt never comprehend why he'd felt compelled to ask her father for her hand in marriage.

Or that he respected the cop more for bluntly telling him he needed to prove himself worthy than he'd have felt if the man had been all smiles and "welcome to the family."

They said their goodbyes and then he and Lexy headed out of the hotel.

"If I ever get a day when people aren't trying to kill me, I really need to get to my bank and get new cards and checks and things. It's so weird not even having a debit card so I can use the ATM."

"I know. I feel terrible about all the trouble I've cost you." He put an arm around her. "So, get your revenge. Go ahead and max out my platinum card."

She sent him a taunting look. "Don't tempt me. We're on Fifth Avenue and I have very good taste."

He took that moment to kiss her, finding her lips soft and full. He felt them curve beneath his as his arms came around her and a little kiss turned into something much more.

"Yep," he said, pulling away, "Definitely good taste."

21

WHEN THEY DREW UP at the gates of Charlie's mother's mansion she realized that Charlie's family was even richer than she'd realized. The place was one of those huge old mansions built in the boom times of lumber magnates, railway barons and oil tycoons.

He drove her about two hundred miles up a tree-lined driveway to the mansion. "Don't worry," he said, when she hesitated to get out of the car. "You'll be fine."

She drew in a breath. Nodded. Put her hand on the door handle.

As she was getting out of the car, he said, "By the way, I love you."

She stuck her head back in and stared at him. "What did you say?"

His eyes laughed up at her, but she saw the earnestness behind them. "I said, I love you."

"And you tell me now?"

"I figure it will take your mind off being scared of my mother."

Her hand went to her heart. She searched his face for a "gotcha" sign, but there wasn't one. If anything he appeared uncertain for the first time since she'd met him.

"You're serious," she whispered.

"Yeah."

"But—"

"No buts. My ego can't take them right now. We'll talk later. I just wanted you to know. Have a great lunch."

In a daze she shut the car door and heard him pull away. She tottered to the door and knocked on the shiny lion's-head knocker. This was the kind of door that could afford one of Carl's knockers, she realized.

The door was opened promptly by a uniformed maid. "Good afternoon, miss."

"Good afternoon. I'm Alexandra Drake."

"Come in, please. Mrs. Pendegraff is expecting you." The woman had a Polish accent. From a working-class half-Polish family herself, she suspected she'd have a lot more in common with this woman than with the WASP down the hall.

The maid led Lexy past exquisite paintings and antiques and into a salon where Sarah Pendegraff awaited her.

"Lexy dear, how nice of you to come on such short notice," Sarah Pendegraff said, rising gracefully from a pretty little writing desk where she'd been penning a note. It was a vision out of an era gone by.

She gave Lexy a quick hug scented with Joy, and led the way to a pair of floral chintz sofas. Her dress was also a soft floral print and there were bowls of roses throughout the room.

After pouring out two sherries into tiny crystal glasses, she said, "I'm so glad you could come today. Normally I wouldn't have lunch at this hour, but after being out until all hours I thought a late meal would be more appropriate."

"Yes. Thank you again for last night. It was a wonderful evening."

"Mmm. I was just writing a thank-you note to Florence Grayson. The trouble is finding something fresh to say about an event one attends every year. The flowers, I suppose, they were certainly different."

"Yes." Should she have sent a thank-you note to Charlie's mother? What with thefts and attempted murders she really hadn't had a moment to keep up her social correspondence.

"I, um, this is a lovely home," she managed.

"Thank you. I've always liked it. Of course, it's getting too big for me now, but I plan to live here and keep it up until Charlie settles down. Then I'll move into an apartment I own on 83rd."

She smiled. "Well, you're obviously important to Charlie and that makes you important to me. I thought we should get to know each other."

His words echoed freshly in her head. *I love you.* Not exactly words she'd imagined she'd hear from him, and definitely not after they'd known each other only a few days. If he'd intended to rock her world, he'd definitely done it.

"May I ask you a somewhat personal question?" Lexy asked.

"Of course you can. Ask me anything."

"Am I like Charlie's other girlfriends?"

"Hmm. That's not a terribly easy question to answer. You're very beautiful, of course, which I must say all his women have been. You're also hardworking and ambitious, which probably about half of his women have been."

It sounded like a cast of thousands had come before her. As though his mother read her thoughts she said, "But I'll tell you one way in which you're different. He's never been in love with any of them."

"He told you he's in love with me?" She almost croaked the words.

"Yes. But he didn't have to. I could see it when he looked at you last night."

Sarah sipped her sherry. "And pardon me if this is too personal, but I saw it when you looked at him, too."

"Oh, but, I'm…I mean. You did?"

"Maybe it was a mother's fond hope, but yes, I did."

"I, this is all so… We haven't known each other very long."

"I'm not sure you need to. Love isn't something you can plan or schedule. It doesn't happen when it's convenient or you're the right age, or your partner has the correct pedigree. Love happens in entirely inappropriate and glorious ways." She laughed. "Not that I have a great deal of personal experience, of course. The only man I ever loved was my husband. Charlie's father. Charlie's a lot like him."

"I doubt it."

"Why? Because he's a thief?"

Her eyes bugged open and she almost dropped her sherry glass down her brand-new Gucci wrap dress. She'd even run into one of the boutiques that carried some of her costume jewelry so she could wear one of her own pieces to give her confidence. Dropping her drink down her front wouldn't do much to keep up the image, but she was so shocked she could barely hang on to the thing. "You know about that?"

"Of course. We don't have a huge number of secrets

from each other, Charlie and I. Perhaps it's because he's an only child, but we've always been close." She sighed. "Of course, it's never a mother's dream, but honestly, dear, I think larceny is in the blood."

"In the blood?" This conversation was taking the most extraordinary turn.

"Yes. We can trace our family back quite far. On my side, we were pirates," she said with relish.

"Pirates? Like Johnny Depp pirates?"

"A little more bloodthirsty than that, I believe. My many times great-grandmother was a well-born young lady expected to make a great marriage. When returning from her convent school to her parents' home in France, the ship she was on was attacked by pirates. Her kidnapper was the son of a deposed duke, there were so many in those days, who'd been stripped of everything. So, the son turned to piracy and did quite well for himself, if you disregard the price on his head and the fact that he couldn't turn up in decent society without immediately being taken out and hanged."

"My goodness."

"Well, my many times great-grandmother, whose name was Veronique, by the way, and the pirate fell in love. It's an extraordinary story because he actually escorted her to her home, in spite of the price on his head. She was completely unharmed and quite determined to marry him. When they got to her home, he formally asked for her hand in marriage. Of course, her family was so relieved to have her returned to them that they almost agreed on the spot. But he was a pirate and a rascal and she was their only daughter so they said that if he could reestablish his reputation, he could have her."

"Lunch is served, Mrs. Pendegraff."

"Ah, thank you, Sophia."

The women moved into the dining room, which had been laid for two.

"I thought something simple. It's just salads and quiche. Is that all right?"

"Oh, it's perfect."

When they were seated, Lexy said, "So, what happened to your many times great-grandmother and the pirate?"

"It's like a fairy tale, really. He had so much money that he could afford to buy a pardon from the Pope and then he bought himself a nice estate in France and renewed his addresses. Veronique had, by this time, made it clear that she wasn't interested in any other man, so they were allowed to marry. It was a very successful marriage, by all accounts, and they had twelve children."

"Twelve children?"

"Veronique wrote about her adventures in a diary, which was passed down through the family. That's how I know so much about her. Anyway, on my side at least, there's historical evidence of thievery. So, when Charlie went into the business, I had to wonder if it was hereditary." She passed a bread basket to Lexy. "Of course, all that's behind him now."

"Are you sure?"

"As much as I can be. I think he was bored more than anything. His father was a truly wonderful man and a brilliant lawyer. I think Charlie felt that he couldn't compete and, as boys are wont to do, decided to do whatever was the opposite of what his father wanted for him."

"He couldn't have become a used car dealer or a stockbroker or something?"

The older woman smiled. "Charlie tends to go all out when he puts his mind to something."

"So I've noticed."

Lunch was surprisingly pleasant after that. There was something about a woman admitting her family tree contained thieves and pirates that encouraged intimacy. They discussed jewelry, food and fashion. They were enjoying coffee when Sophia entered the room.

"Excuse me for interrupting, but Florence Grayson is on the phone. She says it is urgent."

"Florence Grayson? Good heavens. Whatever can she want? Do you mind if I take it, Lexy?"

"No. Of course not." But internal alarms were going off. Why was Florence Grayson phoning Charlie's mother? And where was the murderous Mr. G.?

The phone conversation made its meandering way through the evening before, compliments were exchanged, while Lexy wished Charlie were here. How could she tell his mother that one of her oldest friends was married to a psychopath?

She tried not to eavesdrop, but it was impossible not to when she heard her own name. "Lexy?" Sarah Pendegraff's voice trailed upward in surprise.

Lexy waved her hands, "No," but Charlie's mother was busy fixing one of the blooms in the rose bowl in the middle of the table and didn't see her. "As a matter of fact she's here now. We were enjoying a late lunch."

Only then did she glance up at Lexy and must have read horror in her face. "But unfortunately she's about to leave. Yes, of course, I'll tell her. All right. Thank you again for a lovely party last night. Goodbye."

She hung up and turned to Lexy. "Florence Grayson would like you to call her at your earliest convenience."

"Did she say why?"

"No. Florence sounded odd. She seemed very anxious to talk to you. In fact, now I think about it, she was rather strange last night when she first met you. I—" She slapped a perfectly manicured hand over her mouth. "Whatever is wrong with me? Forgive me, dear. I feel I've been horribly gauche. Never mind. I've put her off, now. Told her you're about to leave."

But Lexy was still puzzling over the woman's odd comments. "Gauche? Why would you think you were being gauche? Mrs. Grayson did act strangely when she met me, but—" Then the obvious conclusion came to her. If Charlie knew about Grayson's mistress, she supposed a woman as plugged into the social network as his mother obviously was would be bound to know that the man had a wandering eye.

"Oh." Lexy felt herself becoming flustered. She had Charlie telling her he was in love with her, his mother thinking she'd had an affair with Grayson, the man's wife wanting to talk to her. This really was the craziest day. "If you're thinking that Mr. Grayson and I...um, knew each other, well, no. I never met him before last night."

She fidgeted in her chair. Glanced at the French ormolu clock atop the marble mantel. Where was Charlie? "I'm hoping when your son gets here he can explain everything."

She didn't like the feeling of vulnerability that possessed her. Here she was in a house she didn't know with an older woman who seemed more adept at flower arranging than self-defense and the wife of a murderous criminal knew where she was. If Florence happened to mention to her husband that Lexy was here, what was to stop the man from sending his thugs to try to get at her?

Charlie said he'd arranged security, but she still felt a little nervous. A scratching sound at the window had her jumping out of her seat and assuming a defensive posture. She wasn't going down without a fight.

"Lexy. What's wrong? It's only Buttons, my cat."

Before her bemused gaze, a sleek Siamese slinked its way from the window into the room. "You're not allergic, are you?"

"No." She took a slow, deliberate breath and sat back down feeling incredibly foolish. "I'm a little jumpy, that's all."

Charlie's mother regarded her steadily. "Perhaps you'd better tell me what's going on?"

"You won't like it."

Sarah smiled slowly. "Then we'd better take coffee back in the sitting room."

They'd barely got their coffees when Sophia's voice was heard in the hall, coming toward them, a man answered her and Lexy wilted with relief. Charlie was here. Somehow he made her feel that everything would be all right. On her own, she felt overwhelmed by all that was going on, but with the two of them working as a team, she felt like they could do anything.

The door opened. "Mr. Grayson, ma'am."

22

"OH, NO," Lexy said, and without conscious thought, rose and went to stand by Charlie's mother's side determined to protect the woman to the best of her ability.

Grayson entered and if his reddened cheeks and frantic eyes gave away his agitation, she could see that he was trying to hold on to his facade of composure. "I'm so sorry to trouble you, Sarah, but Florence left word that she was on her way here and I must speak to her about something important."

"You two can't afford cell phones?" Lexy snapped.

He blinked at her, then made a helpless gesture with hands that shook slightly. "I know it's silly, but neither of us can bear them. At a time like this, it would be useful, though. It's really very important that I find her." He glanced around the room as though his wife might be hiding behind a piece of furniture. "You're sure you haven't seen her?"

"No," Sarah said. "She telephoned earlier, but obviously, it's not convenient for me to have a visitor. I'm having lunch with Alexandra."

"Yes. Of course. I'm so sorry to bother you." He

scratched at his face and she could see the bulge of a hive. "If she shows up, will you let me know?"

"Yes. Certainly."

As he turned, the door behind him was thrust open and Charlie appeared. "Oh, thank God," Lexy murmured, feeling somehow that everything would be all right now Charlie was here. His gaze took in the scene at a glance and settled on hers. The smile in his eyes was relieved, intimate.

"What are you doing here?" he demanded of Grayson, maneuvering his body so that he was between the man and the two women.

"Not that it's any of your business, but I am looking for my wife."

The man looked as though he wanted to say more, but ended up turning slowly toward the door. Which opened again before he reached it.

Mrs. Grayson flew in the room. Her eyes were wild, her hair askew.

"Florence, thank heaven."

"Don't you Florence me." The woman opened her purse, one of those with designer logos printed all over it that Lexy always found tacky. She pulled out a mass of gold and green and just as Lexy realized it was the necklace, she squeezed her fist around the gems and threw the jewelry at Lexy.

Transfixed, they all watched the flash of diamond, emerald and the duller shine of gold as the necklace sailed through the air. Reflexively Lexy grabbed it before it could fall to the floor.

"You bitch!" the woman screamed. "You've ruined everything."

"Florence, dear, please," her husband said in a soothing tone. More hives had broken out on his face in bright red raised patches.

"Don't you talk to me, you sniveling fool. It's not the right necklace. She switched it." And the woman broke down into tears.

Edward Grayson patted his sobbing wife awkwardly on the shoulder but she shook him off.

"My wife's very upset. You see, she believes you've got her necklace. It's very important to her. Sentimental value and all that."

Charlie and Lexy exchanged another glance.

Charlie moved closer to Edward. "You must be pretty surprised to see Lexy and me alive."

"Of course I'm not. I saw you last night. You both appeared perfectly healthy."

"Yeah. That was before your thugs came in and stole the necklace and tried to kill us. If you're here to finish the job, you're wasting your time."

"I don't believe it's stealing to retrieve your own property. If there's a thief in this room, Pendegraff, it's you."

"Retired thief," Charlie corrected him.

Mrs. Grayson was sobbing quietly into her hands. "The necklace was mine. Why did he take it?"

Sarah moved to her old friend. "Can I get you something, Florence? Coffee? A glass of water perhaps?"

The distraught woman nodded and allowed herself to be led to the sofa and gently seated. Charlie's mother poured water from a pitcher on a side table. Lexy imagined the Polish servant keeping the water refreshed all day so it was always fresh. Like the rose bowls.

Sarah pressed the glass into Florence Grayson's hand.

"Thank you," the woman whispered and sipped her drink.

"I didn't take your necklace, Mrs. Grayson. I was hired to steal it back. Your husband hired me. But he also hired thugs to kill me, kill Lexy and take the necklace back by force. Why would you do that, Grayson? Why?"

"I don't know what you're talking about. Why would I want to kill you? I wanted the gems back quietly."

"And you wanted a certain young woman who stole them disposed of quietly, didn't you?"

Grayson was scratching at his face again. He jerked his chin at his wife and then shook his head violently. "Don't know what you're talking about."

"Lexy crafted the second necklace. It was enough to fool your henchmen, wasn't it? When they broke into our suite and stole it. But they tried to finish their handiwork, didn't they? Shot up the bed where they thought we were sleeping?"

"What?" his mother gasped, putting a hand to her heart.

"No." Grayson jerked the word out. "All I want is my property back. That was the original necklace she was wearing last night. Where is it?" He shot a glance at his distraught wife. "It belongs to me. I want it back."

"That necklace is your ticket to jail."

"Do not pass Go. Do not collect two hundred," Lexy added.

"Putting your mistress's body in Lexy's place wasn't too smart. The cops will connect the dots easily."

"Stop. Please. Ladies present."

"Oh, come on, Grayson. Drop the act. You let your girlfriend try on the famous Isabella Emeralds and she took a liking to them, didn't she? Maybe you got tired of her so she decided to give herself a little goodbye present…is that what happened?"

"No." The man was frantic, gesturing to his wife again and again. "This is nonsense. I don't have a mistress."

Lexy took up the interrogation. If they could get Grayson to admit what he'd done in front of witnesses, they had him. "Everybody in town knows about your infidelities. I'm sure your wife's always known. Wives always do." She sent Charlie a steely-eyed look. "Which is why I don't recommend the practice. If you're interested."

His implacable expression softened. "Noted. And not planning on it."

Maybe this was a strange time for her to realize she was as much in love with Charlie as he could possibly be with her but the truth hit her with a solid punch. "Good." Something zapped between them, a spooky unspoken communication that no greeting card could ever duplicate. If she had to put it into words it would be something like, "I love you. Back at you. We're in this together. We're going to make it."

But of course no words were spoken, the entire exchange took place in a millisecond and then Charlie turned his attention back to Grayson. "The body found in Lexy's studio, the female body burned beyond recognition? It's already been ID'd by the cops. It's Tiffany Starr."

Grayson made a strange gurgling sound in the back of his throat, like he'd choked on his own spit.

"Stop it," Florence suddenly screamed. "Don't mention that horrible name to me."

She jerked to her feet and to Lexy's horror, she saw that from her handbag, the woman had taken out a gun. And she was pointing it right at Lexy.

"Florence, sweetheart, what are you doing?"

"You're so stupid you never did figure it out, did you? You're all stupid." Her eyes were wet and haggard but also gleaming with madness. "Did you really think I didn't know? I found your pictures of your little girlfriend wearing my necklace. My necklace! She was naked. It was the most disgusting thing I'd ever seen. I couldn't let her live after that."

"You killed Tiffany?"

"Sure. And I hired my own people to make sure I got the necklace back and that nobody who handled it would live to talk about it."

"But—"

"Quiet. Now, Edward, you and Charlie are going to get the real necklace. If I get it back, then you're free to go. If I don't get it back in one hour, Lexy dies." She glanced at Charlie's mother. "Sorry, Sarah, but I'll have to kill you, too. Nothing personal."

Charlie was rigid. Ever since the gun had appeared she'd felt his coiled tension, his readiness to spring. All he needed was an opening. But Mrs. Grayson wasn't giving him one. And Lexy was cursing herself all over the place for being so focused on the husband she hadn't noticed the wife pulling a gun until it was too late.

"You don't want to do this, Florence," Charlie's mother said in the soothing voice she'd probably use on a toddler having a tantrum. "You'll never be able to host another of your lovely Diamond Balls if you kill my son and Alexandra Drake. Why don't we put the weapon down. I'll get Sophia to make us a pot of tea and we'll discuss this sensibly. I'm sure, if the necklace is yours, that Charlie will get it for you, won't you, Charlie?"

"Yes, Mother," he said.

"I don't want tea, I want my necklace. And if I don't

get it in one hour, Charlie, I will shoot Alexandra and
then your mother! Do I make myself clear?"

"Florence, please," her husband begged.

The gun made a definitive and deadly sound as she
released the safety. "Fifty-nine minutes. And with my
low blood sugar I'll start to shake. You really don't want
my trigger finger getting shaky."

"No, dear. Of course not."

"You try anything, anything at all, and Lexy dies.
I've killed before. I'll do it again."

Once more Lexy and Charlie shared a glance. He
was telling her to stay calm and not try anything to
overpower her captor. She was telling him to be careful.
Oh, yeah, and that she loved him.

"I'll be back," he said aloud. "Don't worry."

She nodded.

"I'm sorry, Mom," he said, turning to Sarah.

"We'll be fine," she assured him.

Grayson and Charlie turned to the door and Lexy
realized that Grayson didn't have a gun or any kind of
weapon. Florence must believe that her threat to kill
Lexy and Charlie's mother was all the incentive he
needed.

And maybe it was, but Lexy had finally found the
person who was responsible for destroying her business,
her home and who had used her gun to commit a murder.
She didn't intend to stand by and let Charlie walk back
into the gun sights of a madwoman.

Not if she could help it.

Grayson opened the door and held it for Charlie, as
though they were two old friends lunching at their club.
The gesture was so automatic, and so absolutely foreign
to what was going on in this bright, rose-scented room
that she could barely take it in.

As the door opened, a large bulk in a flak jacket bar-reled in, a series of dark shadowed figures behind him, all holding semiautomatic weapons.

"Hold your fire," Charlie shouted frantically, turning and diving to protect Lexy.

After the first second of startled realization that the security guys had followed the tracking device in the necklace, she threw herself to the floor, grabbing Florence Grayson's feet—encased in Chanel pumps—and yanking them out from under her in a move she'd learned years ago from her father.

The woman screamed with rage. She felt her try to focus her aim, but in a blur, a floral-print angel of vengeance grabbed her gun arm and shoved it upward, so the shot that rang out hit the crystal chandelier.

A sparkling glitter, like a cache of enormous diamonds, rained down onto Edward Grayson before he could jump out of the way.

As Florence Grayson fell back onto the sofa, trying to tug the gun away from his mother, Charlie got hold of her wrist and wrested the firearm from her clawlike grasp.

"My necklace," she panted. "I want my necklace," she shouted as a burly guy shoved her arms into handcuffs.

"You okay, Mom?" Charlie asked.

"Yes. Fine."

He then tumbled to the floor. Cradled Lexy in his arms. "Hey, how you doing?"

"It's been quite a day."

He kissed her and she clung to him, feeling the emotion pulse between them. She kissed him back, hungry, urgent, knowing how close they'd come to disaster, possibly even death, and celebrating the fact that they were still so vitally alive.

"It's not every day I tell a woman I love her," he said against her lips.

She smoothed back his hair, looked up into his eyes.

"It's not every day I tell a man I love him back."

"Really?"

"Hell, yeah."

Epilogue

THANKS TO THE ISABELLA EMERALDS, the Manhattan auction house was packed.

After Florence and Edward Grayson's arrests, it had been determined that, while he had originally hired Charlie to steal the necklace back, it was Florence who had killed Tiffany Starr. Florence had hired the thugs who'd tried to kill them, who'd burned down Lexy's studio and who'd broken into their hotel suite and stolen the copy of the Isabella Emeralds and once more tried to kill Charlie and Lexy.

Now, Edward was raising the money for his wife's defense. In a nice twist of justice, Edward Grayson was auctioning the Isabella Emeralds to pay her team of top-notch lawyers. Ironically the burst of publicity as the story hit the media only upped the estimated value of the ancient jewels.

Grayson was going to need all the money he could raise, too, since it turned out that Tiffany's accomplice, the older woman who'd masqueraded as Florence Grayson, had been hiding in Tiffany's apartment when Florence came by for a visit. The woman's testimony that her young friend had been kidnapped by a gun-wielding

Florence Grayson would go a long way to putting the murderous Mrs. behind bars for a long time.

Lexy and Charlie didn't buy the necklace, but they were present at the auction where it was sold. After spirited bidding among collectors from London, Frankfurt, Kuwait and New York, the winner was a museum in Spain.

"Very appropriate," Charlie said, as he and Lexy walked home arm in arm. "Now everyone can enjoy the Isabella Emeralds."

"And I guess they are home where they belong."

"It's finally over."

They hadn't talked about the future and she felt silly bringing it up. So far they were happy; she'd been spending her days in her new studio and her nights at Charlie's place.

Amanda was back as her assistant and, if anything, seemed to be more focused. She was certainly happier than Lexy had ever seen her. She and Healey were an odd couple, but so far their relationship was working. After spending two weeks in the Caribbean, they'd returned tanned and happy. Amanda had removed the ring from her eyebrow, and sported a tiny new tatt: a tiny bird flying above the sailboat, which seemed to have some kind of personal significance since twice she'd caught Healey placing his lips there when he thought no one was looking.

Lexy liked Amanda's way with customers, her artistic eye and was already thinking of promoting her to assistant designer and hiring someone else to take over the retail part of the operation.

Amazingly her business had never been better. She supposed that since her fame had increased due to the

Isabella Emeralds and the murder trial, she shouldn't be surprised that her business was booming.

Charlie halted her, turned her to face him and kissed her. He did that a lot. As though he couldn't wait until they were back at his place and had privacy.

She put a hand to his cheek. How she loved this tough, tender man.

"Now I've got my new studio up and running, I should really think about getting my own apartment."

"You could do that."

Her heart fell a little. It wasn't that she didn't know she couldn't stay with him forever, but it would be nice to have him argue with her.

"Or you could marry me."

Her jaw dropped. "What?"

He pulled out a jewelry box. "I know this is kind of strange, since you probably figured you'd design our rings. But this is a family ring. Jeez, I'm totally blowing this already." He took a breath and she realized he was nervous.

"Lexy, will you marry me?"

He opened the box and she saw an exquisite diamond solitaire, an art deco design that she fell in love with on sight. "Oh, Charlie. Are you sure?"

"Are you kidding me? Ever since I kidnapped you, I've known I was never going to let you go."

"That pirate blood really does run through your veins, doesn't it?"

"I promise that you are the last thing I'm stealing. From now on, I'm an honest businessman. So, will you?"

"I don't know. My dad's a cop. He might freak out that I'm marrying a thief. Even if you are a reformed thief."

Charlie wrinkled his face, like he was in pain. "I have to tell you something and you probably won't like it."

"What?"

"I already asked your father for permission to marry you."

She jerked her head up and stared at him in growing wrath. "You did what?"

"I asked your father for your hand in marriage. A month ago. I told him I used to be a thief. He took the news pretty well, but he made me wait a month and then ask him again. So, I did. Yesterday, when the two of us went for a beer, I asked for his permission to marry you. And he said yes."

"You're just doing this for hot sex, aren't you?"

"What are you talking about?"

"I know you. You're getting me mad so then we can have hot makeup sex."

Charlie threw back his head and laughed. "Yep, that's exactly what I'm doing. And after the hot makeup sex, what do you say to trying out 'will you marry me?' sex."

A sudden lump of emotion clogged her throat but she managed a cocky grin. "I've never tried that. I bet it's hot."

"Especially if you say yes."

He nibbled her lower lip while she ran her hands up and down his back. Sometimes, she realized, you just knew. In the same spooky way she could look at gemstones and know instantly what their setting should be, so could she realize at this moment that she and Charlie were meant to be together forever.

"Yes, Charles Pendegraff III, I will marry you."

He pushed the ring on her finger and she wasn't a

bit surprised to find it was a perfect fit. "I love you, Lexy."

"I love you, too." They continued on, hand in hand, the diamond sparkling on her ring finger. "So, if I'm going to marry you, I guess I should know what your favorite sexual position is."

He grinned. "Let's get home and I'll show you."

* * * * *

PLAY WITH ME

BY

LESLIE KELLY

All the characters in this book have no existence outside the imagination of the author, and have no relation whatsoever to anyone bearing the same name or names. They are not even distantly inspired by any individual known or unknown to the author, and all the incidents are pure invention.

First published in Great Britain 2011
Harlequin Mills & Boon Limited,
Eton House, 18-24 Paradise Road, Richmond, Surrey TW9 1SR

© Leslie A. Kelly 2010

ISBN: 978 0 263 88055 7

14-0211

Harlequin Mills & Boon policy is to use papers that are natural, renewable and recyclable products and made from wood grown in sustainable forests. The logging and manufacturing processes conform to the legal environmental regulations of the country of origin.

Printed and bound in Spain
by Litografia Rosés S.A., Barcelona

Leslie Kelly has written more than two dozen books and novellas for Blaze® and Temptation. Known for her sparkling dialogue, fun characters and depth of emotion, her books have been honoured with numerous awards, including a National Readers' Choice Award, and three nominations for the RWA RITA® Award.

Leslie resides in Maryland with her own romantic hero, Bruce, and their three daughters. Visit her online at www.lesliekelly.com.

To loyal romance readers everywhere.

In this economy, I know it's got to be really tough to indulge your reading habits. I sincerely appreciate each and every one of you who keeps buying books so that I can keep writing them.

Thank you so much.

Dear Reader,

After my title *One Wild Wedding Night* was released in 2008, I heard from a lot of readers. Most of them especially enjoyed Tony and Gloria's story—the last one in the collection—about a married couple trying to recapture the sizzle by playing a little game of strangers-in-a-bar.

The idea of playing sexy games is definitely an exciting one. Years ago, I was one of those readers who snapped up *101 Nights of Grrreat Sex*, the book where you tore open an envelope that suggested an entire sensual scenario for you and your partner (the things we do for research). And the concept of keeping things fresh by enacting role-playing fantasies never left my mind.

So when I got the chance to contribute to the popular Forbidden Fantasies series in the Blaze imprint, I wanted to do the theme justice. Having a secret affair and indulging in lots of sexy, role-playing games sounded both forbidden…and extremely sexy. Blazingly so, in fact.

I love hearing from readers. If you would like to let me know what you think of *Play with Me,* please drop me a line through my Web site, www.lesliekelly.com, or visit me on my blog, www.plotmonkeys.com.

Thanks and happy reading!

Leslie Kelly

Prologue

Columbus Day

"Do you know what your problem is?"

Reese Campbell didn't even look up as the door to his office burst open and the familiar voice of his extremely nosy, bossy great-aunt intruded on what had been a relatively quiet October morning. Because that was one hell of a loaded question.

Hmm. Problem? What problem? Did he have a *problem?*

Being thrust into a job he hadn't been ready for, hadn't planned on, hadn't even wanted? That was kind of a problem.

Being thrust into that job because his father had died unexpectedly, at the age of fifty-five? Aside from being an utter tragedy, that was absolutely a problem.

Battling competitors who'd figured him to be a pushover when he'd stepped in to run a large brewery while only in his mid-twenties? Problem.

Dealing with longtime employees who didn't like the changes he was implementing in the family business? Problem.

Ending a relationship because the woman didn't appreciate that he—a good-time guy—now had so many responsibilities? Problem.

Walking a tightrope with family members who went from begging him to keep everything the way it was, to resenting his every effort to fill his father's shoes? Big effing problem.

"Did you hear me?"

He finally gave his full attention to his great-aunt Jean, who had never seen a closed door she hadn't wanted to fling wide open. He had to smile as he beheld her red hat and flashy sequined jacket. Going into old age gracefully had never entered his aunt's mind. Keeping her opinions to herself hadn't, either.

"I heard," he replied.

"Well, do you know?"

What he didn't know was why she was asking. Because she didn't *want* an answer. Rhetorical questions like that one were always the opening volley in the elderly woman's none-of-your-damn-business assaults on everyone else's private life.

He leaned back in his chair. "Whatever it is, I am quite sure you're about to tell me."

"Cheeky," she said, closing the door. "You're bored."

No kidding.

"You're twenty-nine years old and you're suffocating. For two years, you haven't drawn one free, unencumbered breath."

He remained still, silent. Wary. Because so far, his eccentric, opinionated great-aunt was absolutely, one hundred percent correct.

Suffocating. That was a good word to describe his life these days. An appropriate adjective for the frequent sensation that an unbearable weight had landed on his chest and was holding him in place, unable to move.

As Aunt Jean said, his breath had been stolen, his momentum stopped. All forward thought frozen in place, glued to that moment in time when a slick road and a blind curve had changed everything he and his family had known about their former lives.

"You need some excitement. An adventure. How long has it been since you've had sex?"

Reese coughed into his fist, the mouthful of air he'd just inhaled having lodged in his throat. "Aunt Jean…"

She grunted. "Oh, please, spare me. You need to get laid."

"Jeez, can't you bake or knit or something like a normal great-aunt?"

She ignored him. "Have you gotten any since that stupid Tate girl tried to get you to choose her over your family?" Not waiting for an answer, she continued. "You've got to do something more than deal with your sad mother, your squabbling sisters and your juvenile-delinquent brother."

He stiffened, the reaction a reflexive one.

"Oh, don't get indignant, you know it's true," she said. "I love them as much as you do, we're family. But even apples from the same tree sometimes harbor an occasional worm."

The woman did love her metaphors.

"So here's what you do."

"I knew you would get around to telling me eventually."

She ignored him. "You simply must have an adventure."

"Okay, got it. One adventure, coming right up," he said with a deliberate eye roll. "Should I call 1-800-Wild Times or just go to letsgetcrazy.com?"

"You're not so old I can't box your ears."

A grin tugged at his mouth. "The one time you boxed my ears as a kid, I put frogs in your punch bowl right before a party."

An amused gleam lit her eyes. "So do it again."

Reese's brow furrowed. "Excuse me?"

"Be wild. Do something fun. Chuck this cautious-businessman gig and be the bad-ass rebel you once were."

Bad-ass rebel? Him? The guy most recently voted Young Businessman of the Year? "Yeah, right."

He didn't know which sounded more strange—him being that person, or his elderly great-aunt using the term bad-ass rebel. Then again, she *had* just asked him when he'd last gotten laid—a question he didn't even want to contemplate in his own mind.

She fixed a pointed stare at his face. "Don't think I've forgotten who I had to bail out of jail one spring break. Which young fellow it was who ended up taking two girls to the prom. Or who hired a stripper to show up at the principal's house."

Oh. That bad-ass rebel. Reese had forgotten all about him.

"The world was your playground once. Go play in it again."

Play? Be unencumbered, free from responsibilities?

Reese looked at the files on his desk. There was a mountain of order forms, requisitions, payroll checks, ad copy, legal paperwork—all needing his attention. His signature. His time.

Then there was his personal calendar, filled with family obligations, fixing his sister's car, talking to his brother's coach…doing father stuff that he hadn't envisioned undertaking for another decade at least.

All his responsibility. Not in a decade. Now.

It wasn't the life he'd envisioned for himself. But it *was* the life he had. And there wasn't a thing he could do about it.

"I've forgotten how," he muttered.

She didn't say anything for a long moment, then the elderly woman, whose energy level so belied her years, laughed softly. There was a note in that laugh, both secretive and sneaky.

"Whatever it is you're thinking about doing, forget it."

She feigned a look of hurt. "Me? What could I possibly do?"

He knew better than to be fooled by the nice-old-lady routine. She'd been playing that card for as long as he could remember and it had been the downfall of many a more gullible family member. "I'm going to leave a note that if I am kidnapped by a troupe of circus clowns, the police should talk to you."

She tsked. "Oh, my boy, circus clowns? Is that the best you can come up with? I'm wounded—you've underestimated me."

"Aunt Jean…"

Ignoring him, she turned toward the door. Before she exited, however, she glanced back. "I have the utmost confidence in you, dear. I have no doubt that when the right moment presents itself, you will rise to the occasion."

With a quickly blown kiss and a jangle of expensive

bracelets decorating her skinny arm, she slipped out. Reese was free to get back to work. But instead, he spent a few minutes thinking about what Great-Aunt Jean had said.

He didn't doubt she was right about the fact that he was bored. Stifled. Suffocating. But her solution—to go a little crazy—wasn't the answer. Not for the life he was living now. Not when so many people counted on him. His family. His employees. His late father.

Besides, it didn't matter. No opportunity to play, as she put it, had come his way for a long time. Not in more than two years. The word wasn't even in his vocabulary anymore.

And frankly, Reese didn't see that changing anytime soon.

1

Halloween

IT SHOULD HAVE BEEN a routine flight.

Pittsburgh to Chicago was about as simple an itinerary as Clear-Blue Airlines ever flew. In the LearJet 60, travel time would be under an hour. The weather was perfect, the sky like something out of a kid's Crayola artwork display. Blue as a robin's egg, with a few puffy white clouds to set the scene and not a drop of moisture in the air. Crisp, not cold, it was about the most beautiful autumn day they'd had this year.

The guys in the tower were cheerful, the Lear impeccably maintained and a joy to handle. Amanda Bauer's mood was good, especially since it was one of her favorite holidays. Halloween.

She should have known something was going to screw it up.

"What do you mean Mrs. Rush canceled?" she asked, frowning as she held the cell phone tightly to her ear. Standing in the shadow of the jet on the tarmac, she edged in beside the fold-down steps. She covered her other ear with her hand to drown out the noises of nearby aircraft. "Are you sure? She's been talking about this trip for ages."

"Sorry, kiddo, you're going to have to do without your senior sisters meeting this month," said Ginny Tate, the backbone of Clear-Blue. The middle-aged woman did everything from scheduling appointments, to book-keeping, to ordering parts, to maintaining the company Web site. Ginny was just as good at arguing with airport honchos who wanted to obsess over every flight plan as she was at making sure Uncle Frank, who had founded the airline, took his cholesterol medication every day.

In short, Ginny was the one who kept the business running so all Amanda and Uncle Frank—now 60-40 partners in the airline—had to do was fly.

Which was just fine with them.

"Mrs. Rush said one of her friends has the flu and she doesn't want to go away in case she comes down with it, too."

"Oh, that bites," Amanda muttered, really regretting the news. Because she had been looking forward to see-ing the group of zany older women again. Mrs. Rush, an elderly widow and heir to a steel fortune, was one of her regular clients.

The wealthy woman and her "gal pals," who ranged in age from fifty to eighty, took girls-weekend trips every couple of months. They always requested Amanda as their pilot, having almost adopted her into the group. She'd flown them to Vegas for some gambling. To Reno for some gambling. To the Caribbean for some gambling. With a few spa destinations thrown in between.

Amanda had no idea what the group had planned for Halloween in Chicago, but she was sure it would have been entertaining.

"She asked me to tell you she's sorry, and says if she has to, she'll invent a trip in a few weeks so you two can catch up."

"You do realize she's not kidding."

"I know," said Ginny. "Money doesn't stand a chance in her wallet, does it? The hundred-dollar bills have springs attached—she puts them in and they start trying to bounce right out."

Pretty accurate. Since losing her husband, the woman had made it her mission to go through as much of his fortune as possible. Mr. Rush hadn't lived long enough to enjoy the full fruits of his labors, so in his memory, his widow was going to pluck every plum and wring every bit of juice she could out of the rest of her life. No regrets, that was her M.O.

Mrs. Rush was about as different from the people Amanda had grown up with as a person could be. Her own family back in Stubing, Ohio, epitomized the small-town, hard-work, wholesome, nose-to-the-grindstone-'til-the-day-you-die mentality.

They had never quite known what to make of *her*.

Amanda had started rebelling by first grade, when she'd led a student revolt against lima beans in school lunches. Things had only gone downhill from there. By the time she hit seventh grade, her parents were looking into boarding schools…which they couldn't possibly afford. And when she graduated high school with a disciplinary record matched only by a guy who'd ended up in prison, they'd pretty much given up on her for good.

She couldn't say why she'd gone out of her way to find trouble. Maybe it was because *trouble* was such a bad word in her house. The forbidden path was always so much more exciting than the straight-and-narrow one.

There was only one member of the Bauer clan who was at all like her: Uncle Frank. His motto was *Live 'til your fuel tank is in the red and then keep on going. You can rest during your long dirt nap when you finally slide off the runway of life.*

Live to the extreme, take chances, go places, don't wait for anything you want, go out and find it or make it happen. And never let anyone tie you down.

These were all lessons Amanda had taken to heart when growing up, hearing tales of her wild uncle Frank, her father's brother, of whom everyone else in the family had so disapproved. They especially disliked that he seemed to have his own personal parking space in front of the nearest wedding chapel. He'd walked down the aisle four times.

Unfortunately, he'd also walked down the aisle of a divorce courtroom just as often.

He might not be lucky in love, but he was as loyal an uncle as had ever been born. Amanda had shown up on his Chicago doorstep three days after her high school graduation and never looked back. Nor had her parents ever hinted they wanted her to.

He'd welcomed her, adjusted his playboy lifestyle for her—though he needn't have. Her father might hate his brother's wild ways, but Amanda didn't give a damn who he slept with.

From day one, he had assumed a somewhat-parental role and harassed her into going to college. He'd made sure she went home for obligatory visits to see the folks. But he'd also shown her the world. Opened her eyes so wide, she hadn't wanted to close them even to sleep in those early days.

He'd given her the sky…and he'd given her wings to

explore it by teaching her to fly. Eventually, he'd taken her in as a partner in his small regional charter airline and together they'd tripled its size and quadrupled its revenues.

Their success had come at a cost, of course. Neither of them had much of a social life. Even ladies' man Uncle Frank had been pretty much all-work-and-no-play since they'd expanded their territory up and down the east coast two years ago.

As for Amanda, aside from having a vivid fantasy life, when she wasn't in flight, she was as boring as a single twenty-nine-year-old could be. Evidence of that was her disappointment at not getting to spend a day with a group of old ladies who bitched about everything from their lazy kids to the hair growing out of their husbands' ears. Well, except Mrs. Rush, who sharply reminded her friends to be thankful for their husbands' ear hair while they still had husbandly ear hair to be thankful for.

"Well, so much for a fun Halloween," she said with a sigh.

"Honey, if sitting in a plane listening to a bunch of rich old ladies kvetch about their latest collagen injections is the only thing you've got to look forward to…"

"I know, I know." It did sound pathetic. And one of these days, she really needed to do something about that. Get working on a real social life again, rather than throwing herself into her job fourteen hours a day, and spending the other ten thinking about all the things she would do if she had the time.

Picturing those things, even.

She closed her eyes, willing that thought away. Her

fantasy life might be a rich and vivid one. But it was definitely not suitable for work hours.

Problem was, ever since she'd realized just how dangerous she was to men's hearts, she really hadn't felt like going after their bodies.

Her last relationship had ended badly. Very badly. And she still hadn't quite gotten over the regret of it.

"What a shame. Mrs. Rush would have loved your costume."

"Oh, God, don't remind me," Amanda said with a groan.

It was for the benefit of the ladies that she'd worn it. Mrs. Rush had ordered her to let loose on this one holiday trip.

Gulping, Amanda glanced around, hoping nobody was close enough to see her getup. She needed to dart up into the plane and change because while the old-fashioned outfit would have made her passengers cackle with glee, she didn't particularly want to be seen by any of the workers or baggage handlers on the tarmac. Not to mention the fact that, even though the weather was great, it *was* October and she was freezing her butt off.

The Clear-Blue uniform she usually wore was tailored and businesslike, no-nonsense. Navy blue pants, crisp white blouse, meant to inspire confidence and get the customer to forget their pilot was only in her late twenties. Most customers liked that. However, the older women in the senior-gal group always harassed Amanda about her fashion sense. They insisted she would be one hot tamale if she'd lose the man-clothes and get girly.

She glanced down at herself again and had to smile. You couldn't get much more girly than this ancient stewardess costume, complete with white patent-leather go-go boots and hot pants that clung to her butt and skimmed the tops of her thighs.

She looked like she'd stepped out of a 1972 commercial for Southwest Airlines.

As costumes went, it wasn't bad, if she did say so herself. Shopping for vintage clothes on e-bay, she'd truly lucked out. The psychedelic blouse was a bit tight, even though she wasn't especially blessed in the boob department, and she couldn't button the polyester vest that went over it. But the satiny short-shorts fit perfectly, and the boots were so kick-ass she knew she would have to wear them again without the costume.

"Now, before you go worrying that your day is a total wash," Ginny said, sounding businesslike again, "I wanted to let you know that the trip was not in vain. I've got you a paying passenger back to Chicago who'll make it worth your while."

"Seriously? A sudden passenger from Pittsburgh, on a Saturday?" she asked. This wasn't exactly a hotbed destination like Orlando or Hartsfield International. Mrs. Rush was the only customer they picked up regularly in this part of Pennsylvania and most business types didn't charter flights on weekends.

"Yes. When Mrs. Rush called to cancel, she told me a local businessman needed a last-minute ride to Chicago. She put him in touch with us, hoping you could help him. I told him you were there and would have no problem bringing him back with you."

Perfect. A paying gig, and she could make it home in time to attend her best friend Jazz's annual Halloween party.

Then she reconsidered. Honestly, it was far more likely she would end up staying home, devouring a bag of Dots and Tootsie Rolls while watching old horror films on AMC. Because Jazz—Jocelyn Wilkes, their lead mechanic at Clear-Blue and the closest friend Amanda had ever had—was a wild one whose parties always got crashed and sometimes got raided. Amanda just wasn't in the mood for a big, wild house party with a ton of strangers.

Being honest, she'd much prefer a small, wild bedroom one—with only two guests. It was just too bad for her that, lately, the only guest in her bedroom had come with batteries and a scarily illustrated instruction manual written in Korean.

"Manda? Everything okay?"

"Absolutely," she said, shaking the crazy thoughts out of her head. "Glad I get to earn my keep today."

Ginny laughed softly into the phone. "You earn your keep every day, kiddo. I don't know what Frank would do without you."

"The feeling is most definitely mutual."

She meant that. Amanda hated to even think of what her life might be like if she hadn't escaped the small, closed-in, claustrophobic world she'd lived in with the family who had so disapproved of her and tried so hard to change her.

She had about as much in common with her cold, repressed parents and her completely subservient sister as she did with...well, with the swinging 1970s flower-power stewardess who'd probably once worn this uniform. When she'd stood in line to get doused in the gene pool, she'd gotten far more of her uncle Frank's reckless, free-wheeling, never-can-stand-to-be-tied-down genes than her parents' staid, conservative ones.

She had several exes who would testify to that. One

still drunk-dialed her occasionally just to remind her she'd broken his heart. *Yeah. Thanks. Good to know.*

Even that, though, was better than thinking about the last guy she'd gotten involved with. He'd fallen in love. She'd fallen in "this is better than sleeping alone." Upon figuring that out, he'd tried to *make* her feel something more by staging a bogus overdose. She'd been terrified, stricken with guilt—and then, when he'd admitted what he'd done and *why,* absolutely furious rather than sympathetic.

Making things worse, he'd had the nerve to paint her as the bad guy. Her ears still rang with his accusations about just what a cold, heartless bitch she was.

Better cold and heartless than a lying, manipulative psycho. But it was also better to stay alone than to risk getting tangled up with another one.

So her Korean vibrator it was.

Some people were meant for commitment, family, all that stuff. Some, like her uncle Frank, weren't. Amanda was just like him; everybody said so. Including Uncle Frank.

"You'd better go. Your passenger should be there soon."

"Yeah. I definitely need to change my clothes before some groovy, foxy guy asks me if I want to go get high and make love not war at the peace rally," Amanda replied.

"Please don't on my account."

That hadn't come from Ginny.

Amanda froze, the phone against her face. It took a second to process, but her brain finally caught up with her ears and she realized she had indeed heard a strange voice.

It had been male. Deep, husky. And close.

"I gotta go," she muttered into the phone, sliding it closed before Ginny could respond.

Then she shifted her eyes, spying a pair of men's shoes not two feet from where she stood in the shadow of the Lear. Inside those shoes was a man wearing dark gray pants. Wearing them nicely, she had to acknowledge when she lifted her gaze and saw the long legs, the lean hips, the flat stomach.

Damn, he was well-made. Her throat tightened, her mouth going dry. She forced herself to swallow and kept on looking.

White dress shirt, unbuttoned at the strong throat. Thick arms flexing against the fabric that confined them. Broad shoulders, one of which was draped with a slung-over suit jacket that hung loosely from his masculine fingers.

Then the face. Oh, what a face. Square-jawed, hollow-cheeked. His brow was high, his golden-brown hair blown back by the light autumn breeze tunneling beneath the plane. And he had an unbelievably great mouth curved into a smile. A wide one that hinted at unspilled laughter lurking behind those sensual lips. She suspected that behind his dark sunglasses, his eyes were laughing, too.

Laughing at *her*.

Wonderful. One of the most handsome men she had ever seen in her entire life had just heard her muttering about groovy dudes and free love. All while she looked like Marcia Brady before a big cheerleading tryout.

"Guess I should have worn my bell-bottoms and tie-dyed, peace-sign shirt," he said.

She feigned a disapproving frown. "Your hair's much

too short, and not nearly stringy enough." Tsking, she added, "And no mustache?"

The sexy smile was companion to a sexy laugh. Double trouble, either way you sliced it. "I hate to admit it, but I'm not a Bob Dylan fan, either. I guess I really can't turn on, tune in and drop out."

"What a drag! If you say you can't play 'Blowin' in the Wind' on the guitar, I'm afraid I'm going to have to shove you into the engines of that 747 over there."

He held both hands up, palms out. "Peace! I really do dig the threads, sister," he said. "They're pretty groovalicious."

"Ooh, how very Austin Powers of you."

Wincing as if she'd hit him, he muttered, "Do chicks really go for dudes with bear pelts on their chests?"

"Not this one," she admitted with a laugh, liking this stranger already, despite her initial embarrassment. "Obviously, if you own a calendar, you know today's Halloween."

"Yeah, I heard that somewhere. That could explain why I passed a group of Hannah Montanas and Sponge-Bobs walking down the street on my way here."

"I don't know whether to be more sad that kids have to trick-or-treat in the daytime, or that you know who Hannah Montana and SpongeBob are."

"Nieces and nephews," he explained.

The affectionate way he said the words made her suspect he liked kids, which usually indicated a good nature. One point for the hot guy.

Correction, one *more* point for the hot guy. He'd already scored about a million for being so damned hot.

She also noted that he'd said nieces and nephews... not kids of his own. *Single?*

He glanced around at the other small planes nearby, and the few airport employees scurrying around doing the luggage-shuffle waltz. "So, nobody else got the invite to the costume party?"

Just her. Wasn't she the lucky one? "I was supposed to be picking up a regular passenger and she made me promise to dress up. This is definitely not my usual workplace attire."

"Rats. Here I was thinking I'd suddenly been let in the super-secret club. The *true* reason charter flights are so popular. You're saying it really *is* just to miss the long lines at security, and have some travel flexibility? It's not the hot pants and go-go boots?"

She shook her head. "'Fraid not. But don't forget, you also get to drink more than a half-cup of warm Coke and eat more than four pretzels."

"Well, okay then, we're on."

Amanda suddenly sighed, acknowledging what she'd managed to overlook. For just a minute or two, she had been able to convince herself that some sexy, passing stranger had noticed her and come over.

Passing by on a private, secured tarmac? Don't think so.

He wasn't some random passerby, she just knew it.

"Oh, hell. You're my passenger."

"If you're headed for Chicago, I think I am." He stuck out his hand. "Reese Campbell."

Cursing Mrs. Rush and Halloween and that stupid vintage clothing store on eBay, she put her hand in his. "Amanda Bauer."

Their first touch brought a flush of warmth, a flash of pleasure that was unexpected and a little surprising. The handshake lasted a second too long, was perhaps a hint more than a casual greeting among strangers. And while the exchange was entirely appropriate, she suddenly found herself thinking of all the touches she hadn't had for so long, all the *in*appropriate ways that strong, masculine hand could slide over her body.

Instant lust. It was real. Who knew?

She stared at him, trying to see the eyes behind the sunglasses, wondering if they had darkened with immediate interest the way hers probably had. Wondering what she might do about it if he returned that interest.

Get a grip.

Amanda regretfully tugged her hand away, pushing it down to her side and sliding it over her satin-covered hip. Her fingertips quivered as they brushed against the bare skin of her upper thigh and she suspected her palms were damp.

Forcing herself to take a deep, calming breath, she managed a smile. "Well, thanks for choosing Clear-Blue Air. We…"

"Love to fly, and it shows?"

It took her a second, then she placed the old Delta slogan. Her smile faded. The guy was way too hot to also be quick-witted and flirtatious. She could handle one at a time—it just became a little more distracting when they were all wrapped up in one extremely sexy package.

You can handle him. No sweat. Just stay professional.

Professional. While she was dressed for a love-in with the local beatnik crowd and this guy was both gorgeous and freaking adorable. *Right.*

"It'll be a quick trip," she said, gesturing toward the

steps and moving back so he could ascend them ahead of her.

No way was she going in first, not with the length of the damn hot pants. Her cheeks were pretty well covered as long as she remained still. If she walked up the steps with him behind her, however, all bets would be off. He'd get an eyeful, and it wouldn't be of London, *or* France. Because the stupid shorts were too form-fitting to wear even the most skimpy of underpants, unless they were ass-flossers, which she didn't even own.

"Wait," he said, pausing on the bottom step. "Aren't you going to say 'Fly me' or at least 'Welcome aboard'?"

She didn't. The softly muttered word that came out of her mouth was a lot less welcoming. And had fewer letters—four to be precise.

He shook his head and tsked. "Not exactly the friendly skies. Haven't caught the spirit yet this morning?"

"Make one more airline slogan crack and you'll be walking to Chicago," she said.

He nodded once, then pushed his sunglasses up onto the top of his tousled hair. The move revealed blue eyes that matched the sky above. And yeah. They were twinkling. Damn it.

"Understood. Just, uh, promise me you'll say 'Coffee, tea, or me' at least once, okay? Please?"

Amanda tried to glare, but that twinkle sucked the annoyance right out of her. Something irrepressible deep inside made her smirk and order, "Stop flirting. Start traveling."

He immediately got the vague Southwest Airlines reference. "Gotcha." With a grin, he added, "I'm starting to suspect I'm going to experience something pretty special in the air."

She groaned. "You do realize you're a total nerd for knowing all these old slogans."

The insult bounced right off him. "Nerd, huh?" Then he threw his head back and laughed. Innate good humor flowed off this sexy man who, though dressed like a businessman, wasn't like anyone she'd ever shuttled before. "Something tells me this is going to be a trip I won't soon forget," he said, something warm and knowing appearing in those deep blue eyes.

She could only draw in a slow breath as he climbed into the plane, thinking about that laughter and that twinkle, wondering why both of them made her insides all soft. As she watched her passenger disappear into the small jet, she also had to wonder about the trip she was about to take.

Coffee and tea they had, and he was welcome to them. But her? Well, she'd never even considered making a move on a customer before. Talk about unprofessional. Even the original hound dog himself Uncle Frank would kill her. He swore he never mixed business with pleasure.

And yet, how often was it that she actually met someone new, someone sexy and funny and entertaining? Considering her moratorium on anything that resembled dating, maybe a one-night stand with somebody from out of town, somebody she would never see again, was the perfect way to go.

Something inside her suddenly wanted to take a chance, to be a little outrageous. Maybe it was the playful, dangerous holiday—she'd always loved Halloween. It could have been the fortuitous change in passengers from wild old ladies to supremely sexy young man. Maybe it was the costume. The damned hot pants were hugging her open-and-alert-and-ready-for-business sex, the seam doing indecent things to her suddenly throbbing girl bits.

How long since she had done indecent things—or decent ones, for that matter—with a sexy man? Not since before they'd thrown all their energies into expanding Clear-Blue Air, at least. She hadn't had time for a lunch date, much less anything like the lust-fests she'd enjoyed in her younger years. The kind that lasted for entire weekends and involved not leaving a bed except to grab some sort of sensuous food that could be smeared onto—and eaten off of—someone else's hot, naked, sweat-tinged body.

She closed her eyes, her hand clenching tight on the railing. Her heart fluttered in her chest and she tried to make herself move. But she couldn't—not climbing up, but not backing away, either. Not physically, and not in her head.

Was she really considering this? God, she hadn't even looked at Reese Campbell's left hand to make sure he was available. She had no idea if he was actually attracted to her or just an irrepressible flirt. Yet something inside was telling her to take a shot with this complete stranger.

It was crazy, something she'd never considered. Yet right now, at this moment, she was definitely considering it. If he was available…could she do it? Seduce a stranger? Have an anonymous fling with a random man, like something out of a blue movie on late-night cable?

She didn't know, but it sounded good. Given the

current craziness of her life—her work schedule, travel, commitment to her uncle and his company, plus her aversion to anything that even resembled "settling down" as she'd always known it, this whole fling idea sounded *damn* good.

The trip to Chicago was a short one, so she had to decide quickly. Really, though, she suspected the decision was already made. And as she put her foot on the bottom step and began to climb up, Amanda suddenly had the feeling she was about to embark on the ride of her life.

2

Pittsburgh to Chicago was a short, easy trip even on a bad day. Fortunately, aside from the fact that he was taking his first flight in a vehicle that didn't look much bigger than his SUV, today was shaping up to be a very good one. And he wasn't just thinking about the weather, which was cool, crisp and clear.

As they took off, Reese went over the situation again in his mind. One hour in the air—that was good. For a mere sixty minutes, he could trick his brain into believing he wasn't *really* sitting inside an oversize tin can, hurtling across a couple of states.

After that, he faced a short taxi ride to the newest location of a brew-pub chain owned by a wealthy Chicago family, the Braddocks. They had recently agreed to offer Campbell's Lager as a house beer in a couple of their bars. It was a foot in the door, and Reese hoped to grow the account and get them to expand their order to include every one of their establishments. So he couldn't refuse when he got a call from old Mr. Braddock himself this morning, asking him to come to put in an appearance at tonight's opening.

He wouldn't have to stay long—just had to shake a

few hands and say a few thank-yous. He should be in and out in under an hour.

And after that...what?

He had intended to hop a commercial flight back to Pittsburgh tonight. The trip had been too impromptu to fly that way this afternoon, but there was one regional jet leaving at 10:00 p.m. that he could undoubtedly find a seat on. If he wanted to.

But ever since he had walked across the tarmac toward the small private plane and seen the woman standing at the base of the steps, he hadn't wanted to. Because one look at her and he'd been interested. One word and he'd been intrigued. And one brief conversation and he'd been utterly hooked.

It wasn't just that she was beautiful. He knew better than to think beauty was ever more than a surface pleasantry. Besides, he was no chauvinist. He had four sisters, three of them unmarried and living at home, the fourth a divorced single mom. Since his brother was only in his early teens, Reese bore the full brunt of female judgment against his sex. The only other adult male in close proximity was Ralph, his black lab, who had lost his claim to maleness at the hands of a ruthless vet when he was just six months old. A female vet.

So, yeah, Reese knew better than to ever judge a woman solely on appearance.

Amanda Bauer's amazing body, her thick reddish-brown hair that hung past her shoulders and her damn-near-perfect face might have stilled his heart for a moment or two. But her smile, her husky voice, the shininess of her green eyes and the snappy humor had brought about the full stop.

So what are you going to do about it?

He needed to decide. And he now had only about forty-five minutes in which to do it.

In any other situation—if they'd met at a business meeting or a local bar—he might not have considered it. He'd been living in a fishbowl for the past two years, with his every move analyzed and dissected by his family. Bringing a woman into the picture was just inviting the kind of microscopic commentary he did not want.

But this was totally different. His pilot was someone he'd never seen before and, after today, probably would never see again. The thought made him suddenly wonder about the ways in which they could spend that day.

Fortunately, thinking about all those things had distracted him from the whole terrifying takeoff business. They'd chatted while she'd prepared for flight, but since the minute the tires had started rolling down the runway, Reese's throat had been too tight to push any words out.

He forced himself to swallow. "So, a full-time pilot, huh?" he asked, knowing the question was an inane one. But it was better than the silence that had fallen between them while she'd been occupied getting them up into the air.

It also beat looking out the window at either the ground, which was getting farther away by the minute, or the wing of the plane, which looked far too small to be the only thing keeping him from a twenty-thousand-foot crash back to mother earth.

He looked away.

"Yep."

"Must be pretty interesting."

"It beats being a kindergarten teacher, which was what my folks wanted me to do."

He barked a laugh. Her. A kindergarten teacher. Right. In his mental list of other careers this woman could have, being a sedate, demure teacher wasn't even in the top gajillion.

Actress. Seductive spy. Rock star. Designer. Sex goddess. Yeah, those he could see. But definitely not teacher.

She glanced back, one brow up, though her tiny smile told him she wasn't truly offended. Reese sat in the first passenger seat on the opposite side of the cabin and their stares locked for just a moment before she faced forward again. "What? You think I couldn't be a teacher?"

"Uh-uh." He quickly held up a defensive hand. "Not that I don't think you're smart enough. You just don't seem the type who'd like working with children."

She did, however, seem the type to be fabulous at the physical act that led to children. Not that he was going to say that to a woman he'd known for less than an hour.

That'd take two, minimum.

"I'm good with kids, I'll have you know," she insisted. "My friends' and cousins' kids love me."

He didn't doubt it. "Because you bring them cool stuff from your travels and you fly an airplane?"

She shrugged, not denying it. Nor did she turn around, keeping her eyes on the sky ahead of her. Which was good. He much preferred his pilot to be on the lookout for any random high-flying helicopters or low-flying space shuttles.

"I'm not knocking it," he said. "I'm the king of doling out loud toys to my sister's kids. I know the gifts will drive her crazy long after I'm gone."

She laughed, low and long, as if reminiscing at some personal memory. Amanda Bauer's warm chuckle seemed to ride across the air inside the cabin and brush against him like a soft breeze on a summer day. He could almost feel it.

Reese shifted in his seat, trying to keep focused on small talk and chitchat. Not on how much he wanted to feel her laughter against his lips so he could inhale the very air she breathed.

"Believe it or not, I think I'd have been a hell of a good teacher."

"Uh-huh. I can hear five-year-old Brittany coming home to tell Mommy she had a hell of a good time learning her ABCs that day."

She still didn't turn around. She didn't have to. Her reaction was made plain by the casual lift of her right hand and the quick flash of her middle finger.

"Hey, both hands on the steering wheel, lady," he said, his shoulders shaking in amusement. His sexy, private pilot had just flipped him off. Damn, he liked this woman. He took no offense. In fact, he was more grateful than anything else that she had already grown so comfortable with him.

It was strange, since they'd just met, but he felt the same way. Oh, not with the fact that he was in a tiny plane far above the ground…but with her. Like he could say just about anything and it would roll off her back. She had such an easygoing way about her. It went well with the adventurous spirit that put her in the cockpit of a plane wearing go-go boots and booty shorts.

Personally, he had the feeling they were going to get along tremendously. He felt more relaxed with her than he had with anyone—including just himself—in months.

Except for the whole being-in-a-small-plane thing. Which he was trying to forget.

"Okay, I apologize," he said. "I'm sure you would have been great. But I think any mother with a brain cell in her head would insist her kid be moved out of your class before the father attended his first parent-teacher conference."

She didn't respond. But the middle finger didn't come up, either.

"Now, back to the subject. Your job. I guess you like to fly, huh?"

Before she could answer, the plane rose suddenly, then dropped hard, though not far, just like a kite being lifted and gently tossed by an unexpected gust. "Jesus…"

"Don't worry, it was just an air pocket. It's completely normal. In a jet this size, we just feel the turbulence a bit more than you're used to."

Why one little pocket of air was any different than the rest of the big, vast atmosphere, he had no idea. He just knew he didn't like it. "Okay, uh, stay away from those pockets, would you please?"

"Sure," she said with a snort and, though he couldn't see it, probably an eye roll. "I'll just watch for the yellow hazard signs and steer around them."

"Your empathy would have been a real help in a job teaching young children."

Instead of being insulted, she snickered, a cute, self-deprecating sound. "Sorry." Then, though she didn't turn completely around, her eyes shifted slightly. Enough to catch a glimpse at his probably tense face. "I like flying better than you, I take it?"

"It's not my favorite thing to do."

"And I bet it's even worse when you're not tucked

inside the belly of a huge 747, trying not to catch the mood of all the other nervous flyers who are envisioning the worst?"

"Exactly."

She nodded once, then offered, "Doesn't it help to think something smaller would be easier to keep aloft than some big, monstrous commercial airliner? Just like a feather on the breeze?"

"No," he admitted. "Actually, all I keep thinking about is the whole man/wings thing."

"Relax. I haven't crashed in, oh, a good month at least."

Not appreciating the joke, he stared, his eyes narrowed. "My luck, I get the comedian in hot pants for the pilot."

"Sorry. Just figured if you laugh a little, you might relax."

"Say something that's actually funny and I might." Though, he doubted it. A tranquilizer or a shot of gin might help him calm down. Or this woman's hands. Then again, if this woman's hands ever did land on him, *calm* almost certainly would not describe his mood.

"Why don't you try closing your eyes and just pretending you're somewhere else?"

"Pretend?"

"You know. Fantasize." Her voice melodic, as if she were a hypnotist, she provided a fantasy. "You're in a safe, solid car driving up a mountain pass toward a beautiful old hotel."

"Okay, this isn't helping. I'm thinking Jack Nicholson heading toward that hotel in *The Shining*."

She huffed out a breath. "It's an exclusive ski lodge,

glamorous, not haunted. Around you is nothing but pristine, white snow, blue sky, clear air."

"Guys with axes…"

"Don't make me come back there!"

"Okay, okay," he said with a grimace.

Reese closed his eyes and tried to see it. He really did. But he could conjure up no mountain pass. No car. No ski lodge.

A curvy snow-bunny wearing a fluffy hat, skimpy shorts and skis…that was about as close as he could get.

He sighed. Not necessarily because it was a bad thing, but because the vision was so damn hot, it had him a little dizzy.

"Don't use your imagination much, I guess. I should have known."

His eyes flew open. "I have an imagination."

"Uh-huh. Let me guess, most of the time what you imagine is getting through the next sales meeting or closing some big business deal."

Reese shifted a little, not answering. Up until he'd walked up to her on the tarmac, that had been pretty accurate. Since then, though, he'd been imagining a few other things. But to tell her she was wrong meant to spill those thoughts, which he wasn't about to do—again, at least not after a one-hour acquaintance.

Though, two was looking better all the time.

The plane bounced again, quickly, up and down. Reese's stomach bounced with it—at least, on the way up. It didn't go all the way down and settle back into place.

He felt the blood drain from his cheeks. "I think we just ran over a moose. Or a lost skier."

"There's a small fridge between the seats. You look like you could use a drink." She chuckled. "Or a Valium."

"Wow. That is first-class service."

"Kidding."

"Yeah. I figured that," he said, ignoring the offer. He didn't need a drink. He just needed a distraction.

Fortunately, one of the sexiest ones he had ever seen was sitting just a few feet away. As long as he didn't humiliate himself by losing his lunch on the floor of her pristine jet, he fully intended to enjoy spending this flight in her company.

And maybe more than that.

After all, why shouldn't he? He already liked her sense of humor, the competent way she handled the controls, the low laughter. There was a lot to like about this woman beyond her killer legs. Not to mention the rest of the physical package. She was quick and witty, sharp, smart. Lots to like. Lots to want.

And he could like her, want her…maybe even have her, without any of the complications that would arise if he were within fifty miles of home. There, he never felt free to do something for no other reason than the fact that he wanted to. The idea of heaving aside all that responsibility for a little while, of grabbing on to a good thing and enjoying the hell out of it just because he *could,* was incredibly appealing.

"Is this your first time chartering?" she asked.

The plane jiggled the tiniest bit and he instinctively clutched the armrests. "That obvious, huh?"

"You have that first-timers glow."

Huh. Did vampires glow? Because he figured his face was probably as white as one.

"Must be a pretty important trip."

He shook his head. "You'd think so, right? But I'm actually headed to a Halloween party."

She glanced over her shoulder in surprise. Reese waved toward the front, "Keep your eyes on the road, please."

"Don't worry. I'm not about to drive into the back of a slow-moving semi doing fifty during rush hour."

He'd just be happy if she didn't drive into the back of a slow-flying goose. A big Canadian one.

Oh, God, one of those had brought down a huge airliner, hadn't it?

Stop thinking about it.

Right. He had much better things to think about. The way his family business was booming under his management, even in this bad economy. The success of their first nationwide marketing campaign. The house he'd just finished remodeling and considered his private fortress in the middle of his crazy world. The sexy pilot in hot pants whom he now kept picturing on skis, and whose downhill slopes he would very much like to explore. Much better things.

"So, Halloween party, huh?" she said. "If this is you dressing up, what do you regularly look like? I mean, in your real life, are you a biker-dude who usually wears black leather and chains? Only for the occasion, you're dressing up as a boring businessman?"

Reese leaned forward, dropping his elbows onto his knees, and stared at the back of her silky-haired head. "Ahem. Boring?"

"It was a joke. I was just trying to distract you."

Maybe. Or maybe she really did think he looked boring.

He should have felt a little insulted. Reese had been fending off most of the single women in his small home-town since his high school days. *Most* of them. He defi-nitely hadn't fended off all, at least not before two years ago when his life had gotten so out of whack. And he had enjoyed his share of discreet flings through the years. Could've had enough to qualify as a half-dozen guys' shares if he'd felt like it. His sisters were forever cackling over some of the ways in which the hungry local females tried to get his attention.

True, the females in question were no longer the twentysomething party girls who'd gone through his revolving bedroom door a few years ago. They were now career women who saw the steady businessman with a nice income and a reputation as being a great guy who stepped up for his family. But there were still quite a few of them and they definitely wouldn't say no if he *ever* started asking again.

He wasn't the hottest dude in the known universe, and he suspected the money that flowed from his family's successful brewery was partially responsible for the at-tention. But nobody had ever called him boring before, that was for sure.

Damn, that was harsh.

And damn, she was right. To hell with all the mental pumping about how great business was, and how many women had made plays for him. His personal life was *exactly* what this beautiful woman imagined it to be.

Boring.

Boiled in mediocrity and steeped in sameness, he'd allowed himself to disappear into a daily life that wasn't ever what he'd imagined for himself. Ennui had grabbed him by the lapels of his stuffy suit and forced him to remain in his small box of family, business, responsibility. He hadn't even tried to step outside that box in a long time.

Maybe it was time. Maybe he should heed his great-aunt Jean's advice: live, go a little wild, have an adventure.

It had sounded crazy, impossible a few weeks ago when she'd burst into his office. Now? Not so much. Especially because he'd suddenly found someone he wanted to go a little wild with.

There was, of course, one obstacle.

"Are you single?" he asked, direct and to the point.

Her shoulders stiffened the tiniest bit and she hesitated. Then, with a small, shaky exhalation he could hear from back here—as if she'd made some decision—she nodded once.

"Yes. Completely unattached. You?"

"The same."

He didn't give it any more thought. She might have thrown the word *boring* at him, but he had seen the look of interest in her eyes before they'd gotten aboard the plane. The tiny hitch in her breath just now, and the sudden tension that had her curvy body sitting so stiffly in her seat told him her thoughts had gone in the same direction as his.

Have an adventure.

Sounded like a good idea to him.

"So how do you like Halloween parties?"

AMANDA HAD TO ADMIT IT…Reese Campbell made one hot-as-blazes 1970s-era airline pilot. Eyeing him from the other side of the backseat of the taxicab, she wondered what strange whim of fortune had sent such a sexy, charming, single man across her path right when she needed one most.

And she definitely needed one. It had been a long time since she'd felt so sure of herself as a woman, so in tune to the sensations coursing through her body. All the late-night blue movies that had played in her mind lately, replacing any semblance of a real love life, had been mere placeholders, no substitute for the great sex she wasn't having.

Those mental movies were going to have a new leading man in them after tonight. Because she had the feeling that before the night was over, she was going to be saying, "Welcome aboard," and "Fly me," and meaning *exactly* what those old ad execs had wanted passengers to think the sexy stewardesses meant.

She wanted Reese. He wanted her. It was a wild, reckless Halloween night and they were both single and interested.

So why not?

Okay, so she'd never done the one-night-stand-with-an-utter-stranger thing. But her best friend, Jazz, had. She hadn't ended up with a scarlet *A* branded on her chest or any nasty diseases, nor had she needed therapy to get rid of some nonexistent guilt.

Considering she sometimes thought Jazz was the only woman her age in the world who was the least bit like her, or who completely understood her, she didn't figure the example was a bad one to follow.

Besides, Amanda had indulged in short-term affairs before. In fact, considering how badly her last few relationships had ended, a one-night stand sounded just about perfect.

She liked sex. She liked it a lot. This time, she'd just

be having it without the two requisite dates—drinks, then dinner—first. Or the worrying about a phone call the next day. Reese would go back to his life in Pittsburgh, she'd stay here, and they'd both smile whenever they thought of the night they'd gotten a little down-and-dirty with a stranger in Chicago.

Best of all…there'd be no crazy fake suicide attempts. No drunk-dialing complaints that she was a feckless bitch who enjoyed breaking guys' hearts. And Reese wouldn't become the newest member of the Facebook group "Dumped by Amanda Bauer," which had actually been set up by a guy she'd dated during her junior year of college.

God, men could be such fricking babies.

Back to the subject: one-night stand.

Okay. Sounded good. She just had to feel her way around to make sure Reese was on board with it. Judging by the way he'd been devouring her with his eyes since the minute they'd met, she had a feeling that was a big, fat yeah.

"How in God's name did they breathe in these things?" he muttered as he tugged at the too-tight collar of his shirt. "I can't believe there weren't crashes due to lack of oxygen in the pilots' brains."

"It's only a suit, for heaven's sake," she said, rolling her eyes at the typical male grumbling. "It just happens to be too small for you."

They'd found the antique uniform Reese was using as a costume at the airport after landing in Chicago. It hadn't been difficult. Lots of the companies at O'Hare had been around for decades, and Amanda had friends at just about all of them. A few inquiries had put her in the office of a guy who'd worked as a baggage handler since the days when there'd been a Pan in front of American. He'd known where lots of interesting old stuff was kept and had put an only-slightly-musty uniform, complete with jaunty pilot's cap, in her hands within an hour of landing.

It was too tight across Reese Campbell's broad shoulders, but loose around the lean hips and tight buns. Whoever Captain Reliable from the 1970s had been, he definitely hadn't had Reese's mouthwatering build.

"You're going to rip it," she said as he continued to tug. "The thing is flimsy enough."

Brushing his hands away, Amanda reached up to his strong throat, her fingers brushing against the warm, supple skin. A low, deep breath eased in through her nearly closed lips and she suddenly felt a little lightheaded. There was such unexpected strength in him, tone and musculature more suited to an athlete than to the boring businessman she'd accused him of being.

Not that she'd meant it. Not at all. The clothes he'd been wearing might have been conservative, but the look in those eyes, the sexy twist to his lips, the suggestive tone of his conversation…none of those things had indicated anything but exciting, intriguing male.

A thin sheen of sweat moistened the throat where the shirt had cut into the cords of muscle. She had to suck her bottom lip into her mouth just to make sure she didn't do something crazy like lean closer and taste that moisture, sample that skin. She ignored the sudden mental command to just *do* it, focusing instead on unfastening the top button and loosening his tie.

Reese said nothing, just stared at her, his expression hard to read in the low lighting of the cab.

When she was finished, she dropped her hands to her

lap, twisting her fingers together on top of her long winter coat. It didn't quite match the costume, but despite the mild autumn they'd been having, it had become freaking cold out when the sun went down. She honestly didn't know how the hippest 1970s chicks had stood it.

"So, this client of yours, he's not going to mind you showing up with a…" She considered her words, decided against saying *date* and concluded, "…guest?"

"It's a pub," Reese replied, his sensual lips curving up a little at the corners. "I think they can handle one extra."

"That's some job you've got, *having* to go to pubs for Halloween parties," she said, trying to think about something other than his mouth. How much she wanted that mouth. And *where* she wanted that mouth.

"I don't think it quite stacks up to yours—having to jet off to the Caribbean to ferry the rich around to their sinfully expensive vacations."

"I usually ferry obnoxious, spoiled executives to their sinfully expensive corporate retreats."

He tsked. "I'm sure they consider it bailout money well spent." He hesitated for a split second, then added, "So I guess I should be glad you called me boring rather than obnoxious and spoiled?"

"Not obnoxious," she immediately replied.

A brow went up. "Spoiled?"

Amanda tapped her fingertip on her chin, pretending to think about it. She didn't suspect this man was spoiled in the way some of her clients were. He didn't come off as rich, used to everyone bowing down before him at the first request. And he definitely wasn't the kind of guy who expected a woman to spread her legs at the first mention of something sparkly.

Yeah, she'd met a bunch of those guys. Amanda had always been left wondering what kind of woman would trade a night beneath a sweating, out-of-shape, pasty old man for a pair of diamond earrings.

Reese wasn't like those men, not physically, not mentally. She had the feeling he was successful but he was not financially spoiled.

Spoiled in other ways? Maybe. Something about his self-confidence, his half smile when he'd asked if she was single, told her he was used to getting what he wanted when it came to women. The way he sat just a few inches away—casual and comfortable when she, herself, was tingling with excitement at his nearness—said he was sure of what he wanted to happen and his ability to make it happen.

Sexually confident, yeah. *But spoiled?* No. The guy who'd looked like he was going to lose his lunch during the flight had been adorably sexy and vulnerable. Not one creepy, jerky, I'm-good-and-I-know-it thing about him.

"Not spoiled," she admitted.

"I should hope not. As the oldest of six kids, I learned at a very young age not to count on anything I owned remaining unbroken, unborrowed or unlost."

"Six kids!" The very idea horrified her. One sibling— one perfect, good, just-like-their-parents sibling who did exactly what was expected of her and never stepped off the approved path—was quite enough for Amanda, thank you very much.

"My God. Six. I can't even imagine it," she muttered.

"Oh yeah." A small chuckle emerged from his mouth as he added, "It was never *boring*."

Amanda nibbled her bottom lip before replying, a bit sheepishly, "Sorry I said that earlier. I was just trying to get you to relax."

Reese might dress the part of executive, but no man with those looks, that mouth and that gleam of interest in his eyes could possibly be called boring.

"So how's that strategy work for you?"

Confused, she asked, "What strategy?"

"Throwing insults at guys to relax them. Working out okay?"

Hearing the laughter in his tone—knowing he was laughing at himself, too—she had to admit, she liked Reese Campbell.

Wanted him. Liked him. Two points checked off her mental I'm-no-slut-and-don't-have-one-night-stands list.

Tonight was looking better by the minute.

"It worked on me, by the way." He leaned back farther in the seat, turning a little to stare at her. The dim reflections from streetlights they passed striped his handsome features in light and shadow. His breaths created tiny vapors in the chilly air that couldn't be banished by the car's weakly blowing heater. His voice was low, thick as he promised, "Because I'm looking forward to proving you wrong, Amanda."

Her heart skipped a beat. Just one. Something about the way her name rode softly, smoothly, on his exhalation, thrilled her. But she managed to keep her own breaths even. "Oh?"

He nodded. "There's nothing boring about what's going to happen between us."

A shiver of excitement coursed through her. It started with her lips, which quivered and parted, then moved down her entire body, which suddenly felt so much more…alert, somehow. The cold was more biting, the coat scratchy against her bare thighs. Her breasts tingled under the slick, polyester fabric of her blouse, the sensation sensual against her tight nipples.

Excitement had awakened every inch of her. It had been there, sparking right beneath the surface, for hours, since she'd first spied him on that tarmac back in Pittsburgh. Now the spark had caught and spread into a wildfire of interest and arousal, even though he hadn't touched her.

He knew. He had to know. The very air seemed thick with her sudden certainty of just how much she wanted the man. That certainty must have communicated itself to him with her shallow, audible breaths, the almost imperceptible way she leaned closer to him, irresistibly drawn to his heat. His size. His scent.

The big, strong hand sliding into her hair and cupping her head came as no surprise. She smiled in anticipation as he turned her face, tilted her chin up, then bent toward her. Their breaths mingled in the cold evening air and an almost tangible sizzle of excitement preceded the initial meeting of their lips.

A heartbeat later, the cold air disappeared. Nothing separated them at all.

Their first kiss was no tentative brush of lip on lip, nor was there any hesitation, or even a gasp at the thrill of it. It was instead strong and wet. Sensuous. Confident and hungry, Reese parted his lips and slid his tongue against hers, tasting deeply, thoroughly, with enjoyment but not desperation.

Enjoyment could easily lead to desperation, she had no doubt. But despite the fact that they were in the backseat of a random cab, and had a one-man audience, courtesy of the rearview mirror, Amanda didn't care.

She wanted this. Craved it. So she didn't resist or even hesitate. Instead, she reacted with pure instinct, wrapping her arms around his neck. Tilting her head to the side, she silently invited him deeper. She moaned at the delights provided by his soft tongue, tasting him and exploring the inside of his mouth.

He was warm and solid, the spicy, masculine smell of him filling her head even as his heat against her body chased away any last remnants of chill.

Finally, he ended the kiss, slowly pulling away far enough to stare down into her eyes. She saw want there. And something else—excitement. Pleasure.

His lips quirked. And she saw even more: self-confidence. He confirmed it with a broad, satisfied smile.

"This is going to be so much fun."

"The party?"

He shook his head. "You and me."

3

ALMOST FROM THE MOMENT they'd met, Reese had known he was heading in one direction: toward Amanda Bauer's bed.

They were going to have sex. Soon.

Reese knew it. Amanda knew it. The two of them were savoring that knowledge, building the anticipation as the evening wore on.

He'd done his bit for the business. Then, when old Mr. Braddock and his family had left for the night, he'd taken off his official Campbell's Lager title and gone back to being Reese, the man who'd picked up his sexy personal pilot.

Every look asked and answered the same question. Every smile was a seduction, each casual word a hidden code and every brief brush of hand on hand had become the most sensual foreplay. The way they intentionally tried *not* to touch more intimately increased the incredible tension, each non-caress promised unimaginable pleasure when they finally did come together.

Reese couldn't remember a time in his life when he'd been more excited by a woman. He just knew, as he stared at her across the crowded bar, that he'd never desired one more.

They hadn't kissed again since that brief encounter in the cab. They hadn't needed to. The want they were both feeling had been building by the minute.

When they'd danced, and his hand cupped her hip, or her thigh slid against his, the anticipation of how this night was going to end had nearly sent him out of his mind.

It had also sent him in search of something to try to calm down his body's heated reactions.

"So, are you supposed to be, like, the president or something?"

Reese didn't bother glancing over at the vapid little redhead dressed as a sex kitten—one of at least a dozen in the packed-to-bursting bar. She'd been trying to engage him in conversation for a full minute, but he was busy focusing on the dance floor. And frowning.

Because there, in the middle of a writhing crowd full of zombies and witches, mad scientists and vampy angels, was his sexy stewardess…dancing with another guy. He'd made his move when Reese had gone in search of a cold shower, but had had to make do with a cold glass of water.

"Or, like, a James Bond spy?"

Right. 'Cause James Bond always wore stupid navy blue uniforms and captain's wings on his lapel.

"You're way too hot to be an accountant or something."

"Pilot," he mumbled, barely paying attention. All his attention was focused on Amanda.

She looked better than any woman in the place as she shook her stuff with a man Reese recognized as one of

Braddock's low-level employees. Steve something or other.

Reese had never had a problem with him—at least not until he'd realized Steve was seriously moving in on his date.

Steve hadn't been able to keep his covetous eyes off Amanda since the minute they'd arrived. Reese had figured the hands-off-she's-here-with-someone-else code would prevent the other man from actually doing anything about it. But when Steve's hand accidentally brushed Amanda's luscious ass for a second time, Reese realized he was either too drunk, or too hot for her, to even remember the code.

He tensed, ready to stride out there and do something that could cost his company a major customer, depending on how much Mr. Braddock liked Steve, even as he wondered what this crazy, unfamiliar jealousy was all about. But before he could do anything, the redheaded feline jiggled around in front of him, purring, "Dance with me?"

She didn't wait for an answer, just grabbed his arm and tugged him forward. He wasn't the first man she'd been gyrating up against tonight. An hour ago, she'd been wrapped around some guy dressed as a caveman, complete with fur loincloth. Captain Caveman was now groping a woman in a Little Red Riding Hood costume cut so low it barely covered her nipples.

Was there a law somewhere that said Halloween costumes for twenty-something-year-old women had to be slutty? God, he hated parties like this. How could he possibly have forgotten?

The only good thing about tonight's was the moment he and Amanda had hit the dance floor themselves. After he'd officially gone "off duty" they'd had a couple of drinks. Drifting into the crowd, they'd danced not to the loud music, but to the intimate, primal beat that had been thrumming between them for hours.

He should never have left her alone. He should have just lived with the hard-on, trusting that the crowd on the dance floor would ensure nobody else knew he was dying to rip his date's hot pants off and screw her into incoherence.

"C'mon, it's a party, in case ya haven't noticed!"

The redhead was the one who wasn't too observant. She obviously didn't notice that every ounce of his attention was focused on another woman. Or else she just didn't care. He figured that was it because she had dragged him to within a few feet of Amanda and Steve, then proceeded to pole dance against his thigh, rubbing so hard he could feel the heat of her crotch through both sets of their clothes.

Nasty.

Grabbing her shoulders to push her off, he grimaced when she reached up and clasped onto his hand. Holding tight, she then turned her head and tried to suck his thumb into her mouth.

Repeat: You hate Halloween parties. And he was so far over the bar scene, he honestly couldn't remember why he'd once enjoyed it.

Before he could disentangle himself, he glanced over and met Amanda's stare. Her eyes narrowed and hardened. Her pretty lips compressed as she saw the strange young woman practically riding him, the pouty suction-cup mouth trying to simulate a sex act on his thumb.

He knew how it must look—as if he was pulling the bimbo closer rather than pushing her away. Amanda

obviously saw it that way, because she rolled her eyes
and grimaced, her jaw rock-hard and her slim form
straight and tense. Considering she had been fending
off the groping hands of one of Reese's customers, she
had every right to be angry as hell.

Reese was on the verge of just sacrificing his thumb
to death-by-the-jaws-of-drunk-ho and pushing over to
Amanda's side. He needed to explain, and to get her the
hell out of there. But she suddenly changed the game.
With a look that verged between anger and challenge,
she wrapped her arms around Steve's neck. She slid
closer to him, swaying slowly to the pounding music
that had everyone else gyrating and bouncing. Steve all
but stumbled as her beautiful mouth came close to his
neck. Over the other man's shoulder, her stare sought out
Reese's and she lifted one brow in a deliberate taunt.

Damn. She was tormenting him. His sexy pilot had
claws much sharper than this intoxicated little cat who
was still trying to use his thigh as a scratching post and,
now, his neck as a lump of catnip.

He should have been annoyed—he'd never liked
women who played games. But somehow, as his heart
started thudding hard against his rib cage and all his
blood again rushed to his cock, he realized he was incredibly excited by Amanda Bauer instead.

Their stares locked, intense and hot. She licked her
lips, and Steve tugged her closer, as if he'd almost felt
that sweet, wet tongue. But her attention wasn't on Steve,
it was entirely on Reese. Her eyes sparkled, as if she
knew he was torn between wanting to laugh at her for
trying to make him jealous or pick her up, throw her over
his shoulder and out-caveman the guy in the loincloth.

Reese lifted a questioning brow, silently asking her

how far she was going to take this. In response, she leaned toward Steve's ear and whispered something. The other man froze, dropping his arms and watching as Amanda turned away from him. She eased through the crowd, winding a path across the dance floor, heading toward a back hallway that led to the restrooms. A number of men turned to watch her go, and she earned more than a few glares from their dates. Just before she slipped down the short hallway, she cast one more glance over her shoulder. Her half smile taunted Reese, daring him to follow.

Reese spun the horny little cat around and pushed her toward the still-frozen Steve, who appeared almost shell-shocked. When he met Reese's eyes, he flushed, then mumbled, "Sorry, man."

Whatever Amanda had said, it had worked. He should have known she needed no help in taking care of herself. Still, he couldn't help smiling tightly and saying, "I think my date and I will be leaving now. Before you do something that requires me to break your jaw."

Not waiting for a reply, Reese moved in the same direction Amanda had gone. Easier said than done, as the dance floor swelled when the deejay put on a campy version of the "Monster Mash." He couldn't find an inch of clear space and had to push his way through couple after couple.

Finally, though, he reached the short hallway. A woman had just disappeared into the ladies' room, and a guy in a toga passed him as he left the men's. Stepping into a corner to wait, he started when he felt a hand on his shoulder.

"I knew you'd follow me," a throaty voice whispered.

Amanda.

She'd appeared from the shadows of a storage room, ignoring the Private: Employees Only sign. Standing in the doorway, she watched him with heat in her green eyes and a pant of audible hunger flowing across her moist lips.

"I knew you wanted me to."

He didn't resist when she tugged him inside the small room, dark, damp, smelling of yeasty beer and booze.

"Your girlfriend isn't going to come after us, is she?" Amanda whispered as she pushed the door shut behind him, trapping them inside.

He made sure everyone else was kept out by twisting the lock on the knob. "My girlfriend?"

She reached up and ran the tip of one index finger over his bottom lip, hissing lightly when he nipped at it. "Uh-huh. She looks very *catty*." Leaning up on tiptoe, she pressed her wet lips to his throat, swiping her small tongue against the hollow. "I don't usually go after other girls' guys but the way you've been looking at me all night has me feeling a little reckless."

He got into the spirit of her game. "She's not the one I want." Reese stared down at her, able to see her beautiful face more clearly as his eyes adjusted to the glimmer of moonlight spilling in from a small window. He leaned into her, knowing by her groan that she felt his raging erection pressing into the juncture of her thighs. "She's not the one who's had me hard and desperate for the past six hours." Being honest now, he added, "You're a stranger and yet I'm dying for you."

She lifted one slim leg, tilting toward him so his cock nested against the warm seam of her silky hot pants. He swallowed hard, desperately wanting to yank down his zipper, tear her shorts off and thrust into her hard, fast and deep. But a bigger part of him wanted it slow and hot, erotic as hell, with every sensation building upon the last, until the tension of anticipation had them both ready to explode.

"Sex with a stranger is a very enticing fantasy, isn't it?" she asked. "How lucky that we saw each other across the bar and both knew exactly what we had to have."

Wicked. Erotic. So damned sexy.

"Aren't you afraid your boyfriend is going to come looking for you?" He was half-curious about what she'd said to the other man before abandoning him. But not curious enough to ask, or do anything that might distract them from what was happening right here, right now.

"I don't care," she mumbled, her fingers tugging at his tie, slipping the top button of his shirt open. "He can't satisfy me."

Her fingertips brushed his bare chest and he hissed at the sensation of skin on skin. "No. He can't. But believe me, I'm going to."

Hearing the sexy confidence in Reese Campbell's voice, Amanda melted a little. Okay, a lot. Coming from another guy—like the drunk ass she'd just ditched on the dance floor—the pronouncement might have come off as arrogant. But to her ears, Reese's certainty about the pleasure he intended to give her was utterly intoxicating. There was no conceit in it; he simply knew, as she did, that their chemistry was enough to take them both to places neither of them had ever gone before.

"One thing we have to make clear up front," she said, staring up at him, dropping the game for a moment.

"Yes?"

"This is just a one-night stand."

Instead of taking offense, he laughed softly. "Why don't you wait until after you've actually tasted something off the menu before deciding whether or not you want dessert?"

"I suspect you're going to fill me up very nicely the first time," she said, trying to sound seductive but knowing that had come out almost prim.

His continued laughter confirmed it.

She nibbled her bottom lip, her heart beating in excitement at all the ways she wanted to taste him. But the demands of her job, her travel, her commitment to the company and her allergy to anything resembling a relationship made her persist.

"I'm not looking for anything serious or long-term. No entanglements."

Sounding almost relieved, he replied, "Then we're on the same page. My life is so full of people right now, the Health Department is gonna cite me for overcrowding."

She hammered the point home. "So we're clear. One night, then it's done. We'll just enjoy ourselves because it's a holiday and we're both unattached and we want each other. We play all night and then walk away in the morning?"

"Sure," he said with a half grin that promised he didn't really mean it. But she had the feeling it was as close to a promise as he intended to give her.

"Okay. Good…perfect."

He stared at her in the darkness, running the tip of his index finger across her cheek. "Yeah. Perfect. That's exactly the word I'd use."

For her? For them? For this moment and this night

and this wonderful, unexpected interlude? All of the above?

Who gave a damn?

"I want you, stranger," she said, feeling bold, crazy, wild with need and want. "I want you *now*."

He groaned, sinking his hands into her hair, tugging her face to his to capture her mouth in a deep, hard kiss. Without breaking away, he maneuvered her around so her back was to the door, and he crowded her there. Every inch of her body was enveloped by his, every curve, angle and point, and she whimpered and writhed at the feeling of being so utterly in his control.

She wasn't used to the sensations, had never been so enslaved by a person, a feeling, a need. She felt powerless, immobilized, able only to enjoy what he was doing to her, give herself over completely to his every sensual whim.

Somehow, she just didn't care. Maybe because she had gone for so long without any kind of physical connection. Or because it was Halloween and she was dressed in a crazy costume. Or that she had never played sexy, sultry games like they were engaging in tonight and had suddenly discovered she liked them. Or simply that she found Reese more attractive and exciting than any man she had ever met. It didn't matter.

This mattered. Just this.

"Please," she whispered, not even sure what she was asking for.

Moving his mouth to her jaw, he pressed hot kisses to her even hotter skin. He tasted her neck, before traveling on to her pulse point and licking lightly. "Have I told you that I really like your costume?"

That mouth moved lower, down to her nape, and he

scraped his teeth across her collarbone, ever so lightly. She shivered. Ever so lightly.

"I do, too," she admitted, meaning it. Arching against him, she groaned at the feel of her own silky blouse against her hard, sensitive nipples. The hot pants had never felt so tight, and the seam did wonderfully wicked things to her highly sensitized clit.

"I think I'll like it even more when it's on the floor." His strong hands moved down, brushing her shoulders, sliding the length of her arms. His fingertips brushed hers in a caress so light and delicate she shivered with the need for more.

He cupped her hips, holding her in place. Pressed against him, she almost cried with the need to see, feel, taste and be filled by the massive erection pressed into her groin.

"Don't you think we should hurry before somebody comes looking for us?" she asked, helpless and desperate for him to go faster. Harder. Now.

"Nobody's going to come looking for us."

She wasn't giving up. "Not even your girlfriend?"

He smiled a little, his white teeth gleaming in the low lighting. "Oh, we have a very open relationship. She told me to come back here and have a fabulous time with you, then tell her all about it."

God, he was so sexy, tempting her with all that was forbidden and hot. He was still playing, but changing the rules of the game to suit his whim. He made it more taboo, more erotic.

"So does that mean you like handling two women at the same time?" she asked, intentionally trying to inflame him. She wanted him to go faster, give her more, *immediately*.

She should have known better. Reese merely continued to kiss her mouth, her jaw, her earlobe. "I'd like to have two yous."

"Why don't you have one me first before deciding whether you want a double portion?"

Though he chuckled, Reese continued to take his time, dragging this out. He was going to torture her with a slow, seductive ignition rather than just making her explode in a hot, sexual inferno the way she wanted him to.

"You evil man," she muttered.

Reese moved his mouth back to her throat, kissing his way down, licking, nibbling. Amanda could only wriggle and moan as sensations washed over her. When his rough cheek brushed the upper curve of one breast, she instinctively arched toward him, wanting a much more intimate connection.

Reese complied, rubbing his cheek against the silky blouse as he moved his mouth to her nipple. He breathed over it, hot and anticipatory, then covered the taut peak and sucked her through the material.

"You wonderful man," she groaned.

Her legs going weak, she sagged against him. His body in front of her and the door at her back seemed to be the only things holding her up.

As much as she wanted him to, he didn't pull her blouse open and suckle her bare breast, seeming content to torment her through her clothes.

"Reese, touch me, please," she whispered.

He *was* touching her, gripping her hips, his fingertips digging lightly into her bottom. But she wanted so much more.

Reese's strong hands traveled up her sides in a slow,

deliberate slide. The palms nestled in the indentation of her waist, cupped tenderly, then rose to her midriff, right beside her breasts.

"Beautiful," he murmured as he tightened his hands, plumping her breasts up so the top curves almost spilled free of the blouse. Then the ancient top button gave way, popping open. He took immediate advantage, lowering his face and nuzzling against her, even as he worked the next button free, and the one below that.

When the silky blouse fell off her shoulders, Reese stepped back so he could look down at her, his appreciative stare turning into one of pure, raging hunger. This time, she didn't have to ask him to touch her, taste her. Instead, he immediately bent down, covering a nipple with his mouth and sucking hard.

She tangled her hands in his hair, holding him there, feeling every deep pull right down to the quivering spot of sensation between her thighs. Tweaking her other breast with his hand, he rolled the tip between his fingertips. A firm pluck brought a shaky cry to her lips. Reese moved his mouth over to kiss and suck away any twinge of pain, though he knew—he had to know—that what she felt was utter pleasure.

Desperate for skin-on-skin contact, she yanked at his shirt, pulling it apart, not giving a damn that a few buttons went flying. He didn't seem to care, either. He simply shrugged out of it, continuing the lovely, erotic attention to her breasts.

Then, once he, too, was bare from the waist up, he moved back to her mouth and kissed her deeply. Their tongues tangled and played as their bare chests sizzled against one another. She didn't know that she'd ever felt anything as delicious as the crisp hairs on his chest scraping across her moist nipples.

Except, perhaps, for his mouth. And his hands. And, she suspected, just about anything else he chose to press against her in the next fifteen minutes.

They didn't end the kiss, not even when they each reached for the other's waistbands. His deft fingers easily unfastened her hot pants, and his costume was so loose on him, she only had to unbutton, not unzip, before she was able to push the trousers down over his lean hips.

He'd had something on under his clothes—boxer briefs that strained to contain an erection that literally made her suck in a shocked, delighted breath.

All that hugeness. All hers. At least for tonight.

Before he let the pants fall away, he reached into the pocket. "I hope you don't think I was taking you for granted, but I bought this from a machine in the men's room."

She saw him tug the condom from his pocket and grinned. "My purse is over there. And if you look inside, you'll see that I stopped at the airport gift shop and bought an entire box. So I think I'm the one who could be accused of taking you for granted."

"Anytime, anywhere, beautiful."

She liked the way he called her that, liked the way he silently repeated it with his eyes as he stared at her. His gaze was covetous as he stepped back enough to look down at her middle, her hips, the juncture of her thighs.

That look was so hungry, she should have been warned about what he was going to do. But she wasn't. It took her completely by surprise when he dropped to his knees on the bare cement floor and pressed his mouth to the hollow just below her pelvic bone. Then his soft, seeking tongue was dipping low, licking the moisture off her damp curls.

Oral sex was, to quote the song, one of her favorite things. But she had never gotten it quite so quickly from a man. Or quite so....

"Oh, God," she groaned when he moved lower, sliding that warm, sweet tongue between the lips of her sex and swirling it around her throbbing clit. "That's fantastic."

She sagged against the door, helpless to do anything else under the onslaught of such intense pleasure. And she didn't make a sound of protest when he encircled one of her bare limbs with a big, strong hand. Without a word, he guided it over his shoulder, tilting her sex even closer to his hungry mouth.

"Reese, you don't have to..."

"Yeah, actually I do," he mumbled, continuing what he was doing.

She looked down at him, seeing her own booted foot resting against his back. Only now it looked incredibly hot and sexy, the ultimate do-me boots from the original era of free love.

She suddenly felt like the girl she'd been portraying. Like she was some sexy stewardess having a crazy closet interlude with a pilot, just because she *wanted* to. No explanations, no questions, no regrets. Live in the moment and love the one you're with.

Sounded pretty damn fine to her.

"Stop thinking. Let go," he ordered, not looking up.

Amanda did what he asked, giving up any effort to pretend she didn't want him to finish what he'd started.

Finish it he did. Within moments, she felt the sparking, zinging waves of heated delight that had been focusing tightly in on her clit turn around and explode outward. They rocketed through her entire body, wave upon wave, delighting her to the tips of each strand of hair.

Amanda cried out, rocking her hips. He stayed with her, continuing to taste her as she rode the orgasm out, milking it and squeezing her muscles tight to wring out every last bit of sensation. And only after it was over did he slide out from under her leg and ease his way up her naked body.

She was panting and nearly desperate by the time his face was level with hers. His eyes gleaming, he licked at his moist lips and whispered, "Definitely want to keep ordering off this menu."

Dying for him now, needing to be filled, she grabbed two handfuls of his hair and pulled his face to hers for a deep, drugging kiss. This time, she was the one who lifted her leg. Wrapping it around his thighs, she tilted her groin against that thick erection still covered by his briefs.

"Off," she ordered, mumbling the command against his mouth.

He moved a few inches away, far enough to strip out of the last of his clothes. Far enough for Amanda to look down and take measure of the delightful present that was headed her way.

Whoa. As she'd suspected, Reese's "present" was far greater than any she'd ever seen before. She nearly panted with the need to have all that male heat slamming into her, filling the hollow core that had practically grown dusty with disuse.

"Damn. I wasn't exaggerating," she whispered.

He didn't even glance up, tearing the condom open with his teeth and rolling it onto his cock as he mumbled, "Hmm?"

"I told that jerk on the dance floor that if he thought he could measure up to you, he obviously needed to get a new ruler because his had to be broken."

He barked a laugh, but that immediately faded when he moved between her thighs. Amanda lifted her leg again, opening for him, arching toward the massive tip and rubbing her body's natural juices over it.

He put a hand on the door behind her head, palm flat, his strong arm just above her shoulders. She turned her head for a moment, wanting to taste his wrist, feel his blood pounding in his veins. She did so, licking the sweat off him, feeling the strength of his pulse against her tongue. His excitement merely fueled her own as she looked back up into his face, losing herself in those blue eyes.

Their stare never broke as he eased into her. He moved slowly, with utter restraint. Amanda's mouth fell open with a tiny gasp at the feel of him as he went deeper, inch by inch. He was solid and thick, stretching her, making a place for himself within her body.

A temporary one, she knew that. But she also knew it was one she would never *ever* forget. This was the one-night lover every woman fantasized about at least once in her life. And for tonight, he was hers.

"Perfect," he said, echoing his earlier claim.

This time, she knew what he was talking about. Knew as he slid home, burying himself to the hilt inside her, that he meant their connection was perfect. Being joined with him felt about as wonderful as anything on this earth possibly could.

"You okay?"

She nodded, unable to speak. Sensations battered her, his smell, the heat of his skin against hers, his warm breaths against her cheek. She even felt his heartbeat, realizing at once that its rhythm was perfectly matched to her own, as if they shared one single organ.

"Perfect," she finally agreed.

As if he'd been waiting for her, to make sure she was really okay with his incredibly deep possession, Reese finally began to move. He dropped his hands to her hips, holding her still as he slowly withdrew, then slid into her again, making her feel so damn good she let out a tiny sob.

The next thrust was a little harder. The one after that harder still. Each wrung a louder groan from her throat.

"More," she ordered, digging her hands into his broad shoulders, still stunned by the strength of the body he'd hidden beneath that conservative suit.

"You got it."

He lifted her, his hands holding her bottom, controlling every thrust, every move, every sensation. Wrapping her legs around his hips, Amanda kissed his cheeks, stroked his hair and held on while he brought her to another intense orgasm.

It rocked her, hard. She threw her head back and cried out, banging into the door but not really caring. Nor did she care when Reese seemed to lose whatever remnants of control had been restraining him. As if her cries of pleasure had stripped away his every thought, he drove into her mindlessly, until finally, with a cry that was twice the volume of her own, he climaxed, too.

He held her there for a long time, still inside her, his breath sounding ragged and his heart pounding crazily against hers. Finally, though, he let her down to stand on her own two shaky legs.

He didn't let her loose entirely, keeping his arms draped around her shoulders. Finally, after a few minutes during which her pulse dropped back from the red zone to orange, he lifted a hand to her face and cupped her chin.

"Amanda?"

"Yeah?"

"Where do you live?"

"I have an apartment not too far from here."

He nodded, then disentangled himself from her with one last, regretful caress. "Let's get dressed. Or, get as dressed as we can given the missing buttons." He stared at her intently, as if he were looking for some clue to her mood. "If you really meant it, if we've only got one night…"

Her heart skipped a beat. She knew what he was asking. Did she *really* want to stick to that original condition?

Oh, God, was she tempted to tell him to forget what she'd said. Having had him once, it seemed almost inconceivable that she wouldn't have him again after tonight.

But a small voice inside her head—the one that kept reminding her of just how badly every one of her previous affairs had ended—wouldn't let her do it. So she said nothing.

He nodded once, then pressed a hard kiss on her lips.

"Got it." He handed her her clothes and began pulling on his, as well. "Let's hurry up, then. If we've only got this one night, I want to spend as much of it as I possibly can in your bed…making love to you."

Her hand shook a little. Because with those words, those sexy, tender words, a sneaking suspicion crossed her mind.

One night was not going to be enough.

$$4$$

Veterans Day

From: mandainflight@hotmail.com
To: Rcampbell@campbelllagers.com
Sent: Tuesday, Nov 10, 2009
Subject: One more time?
Reese—
Another holiday...whaddya say? Want to meet me for a Veterans Day game of captured enemy soldier vs. ruthless interrogator?
Manda

From: Rcampbell@campbelllagers.com
To: mandainflight@hotmail.com
Sent: Tuesday, Nov 10, 2009
Subject: One more time?
Affirmative. Where. When.
R.
PS: Tell me I get to be the ruthless interrogator.

BEING INTERROGATED had never been so much fun.

Lying in bed in the Cleveland hotel room, Reese

watched as the sexiest woman he knew emerged from the bathroom. She was wrapped in a white towel, her skin slick and reddened from the steamy hot shower she'd just taken. It was probably also that way because he'd been touching her, tasting her, adoring her all afternoon. And though he'd already spent almost as many waking hours today inside her body as he had out of it, he already wanted her again.

He still couldn't quite believe this had even happened. Not the sex—God, yes, that was bound to happen whenever the two of them were in a room with a flat surface. But them being together again at *all*.

He'd tried calling Amanda a couple of times after they'd said their goodbyes in Chicago the morning after Halloween. She hadn't responded. Nor had she returned his e-mails.

Finally, he'd had to accept the fact that she'd meant it—one night only. He'd have to live for the rest of his life with the knowledge that the most desirable woman he'd ever met, and the best sex he'd ever had, were both in his past.

He'd tried to get his mind back into his real life. So much needed his attention: the business, the family, his own house. Responsibilities seemed to weigh heavier on his back every time he answered the phone or opened his front door.

Then, out of the blue, this morning, her message.

He hadn't hesitated. Inventing an out-of-town meeting, he'd thrown a few things in a bag, dropped his dog off at a buddy's and headed to Cleveland. He'd needed no further details than the name of the hotel and the time she'd be there.

There was nothing that could have prevented him

from making the trip. Absolutely nothing that would have stopped him from accepting her invitation to sin.

And oh, sin they had.

"You know, I might have been lying about where the top-secret orders were hidden. They might not really be inside Jimi Hendrix's guitar at the Rock and Roll Hall of Fame. Maybe you should torture me again to get the truth out of me," he offered.

Reaching for her purse, Amanda grabbed a hairbrush from within it, and turned to face the mirror. She caught his eye in the reflection as she began to brush the wet strands. "Sorry. Not buying it. I don't think anybody could have held out against that last round of—" she licked her lips "—questioning."

God. He began to harden again, just at the thought of it. That last round of *questioning* had been unforgettable.

Well, to be honest, the whole afternoon had been unforgettable.

She'd been playing her role from the minute he'd walked through the door of the hotel room. He was her prisoner and he had to do what she said. He'd gone along, liking the wildness in her. She was aggressive, demanding. So damned sexy.

Amanda had insisted that he strip. Threatening to punish him if he didn't cooperate, she had then instructed him to sit in a chair right beside the head of the bed.

Half curious, more than half turned-on, he'd agreed to her terms. He wanted to see how far she would go, just what she had in mind. So he'd given his word he would not rise from that chair, no matter what she said or did.

He'd been certain he could do it. Absolutely positive.

He'd told himself he wouldn't get up, not even if the room caught fire.

Then it did. Or, at least, she'd made it *feel* that way, filling the place with so much intense heat he'd thought his skin was going to peel off his bones.

It took every bit of his strength to remain still, just an observer. Because with pure wickedness in her eyes, Amanda had slowly slid out of her clothes and gotten comfortable on the bed, directly in front of him. There she'd proceeded to thoroughly pleasure herself.

Seeing her hands move over that amazing body, being an observer, unable to participate, had been *exactly* the torture she'd anticipated. He'd begun to sweat, to pant, to strain and to clench his fists in a quest for control.

Not content to just run her hand across her bare breast or delicately stroke her long fingertips over her gleaming slit, she'd actually pulled out a vibrating sex toy. He'd had to sit there, silent, nearly dying, while she'd used it to bring herself to orgasm three times.

Then, still ordering him to stay still and leave everything in her control, she'd climbed on top of him and slid down onto his shaft, taking him deep inside her body, controlling their every move, every thrust, every stroke. At one point she'd even turned around to ride him like a cowgirl, all while smiling at his reflection in the same damn mirror she was using now.

He was pretty sure he'd come at least a gallon when she finally did let him go over the edge with her. And that had been only the beginning.

"You're incredible."

"Must be Stockholm Syndrome," she quipped. "You're infatuated with your captor, right?"

"Uh-huh." *Infatuated*. Good word. Maybe even on the verge of obsessed.

"Don't worry, it'll pass."

He very much doubted it. "I don't think so."

Her smile faded a little at his intense tone, and her eyes shifted as she busied herself finishing her hair. He suddenly wondered if he'd touched a nerve.

"You might say you like all of me, but I bet there are certain parts you like better than others." She pursed those lips, reminding him of everything else they'd done so far today. Amanda's second round of torment had involved her luscious mouth.

He had loved giving her oral sex their first time. But Reese had never even contemplated how mind-blowing it would be when she wrapped her lips around his cock. Again and again, she'd brought him to the very edge, taking him as close to orgasm as she could get him, then backing off, cooling things down.

He'd held out as long as he could, liking this reckless, wild side of her. Not to mention loving the feel of her lips and tongue sucking him into oblivion. Finally, though, it had gone too far and he knew he couldn't wait much longer. So he'd played his role in the game, giving her the "information" she had been asking for.

But instead of ending it, pulling him down on top of her so he could finish things in the sweet channel between her legs, she'd ended the game with her mouth. She hadn't even given him the chance to do the polite guy thing—or the standard porn movie one—and pull out before reaching the end of the countdown.

Wild. Erotic. Intense.

She was his every fantasy. And about as far from his real life as a woman could possibly be.

He forcibly pushed that thought away. Because, though they'd done almost no talking so far today, he didn't imagine Amanda's feelings about what they were doing—and what they were going to do in the future—had changed. A one-night stand had evolved into a holiday affair. He just didn't know how far out on the calendar she'd want to go. She might be his Thanksgiving feast or his ultimate Christmas present. If fate was kind, perhaps she'd be the one coloring his Easter eggs.

Or they might have tonight and nothing else. Ever.

Not knowing drove him crazy, in both a good way and a bad one. The possibility that this might be all made him desperate to have and take and possess her as much as he could.

It's not all. It can't be all.

"I'm hungry," she said.

Thrusting away his thoughts of tomorrow, he knew he had to focus on tonight. He rolled over to sit up on the edge of the bed. One thing was sure—he needed to eat in order to have the strength to spend the rest of the night the way he wanted. "Me, too. Please tell me I've been cooperative enough to get more than bread and water."

"How's cold gruel sound?"

"Uh-uh. I need protein. Let me take you out to dinner."

Her mouth fell open, but quickly snapped closed again. After a hesitation, she murmured, "I don't know…"

"I've got to keep up my strength. How else can I hope to resist you?"

Her head turned a little and she averted her gaze. "Resist me? That's what you call resisting?"

"Come on, cut me a break. It's kinda hard to say no to a woman when she has your cock in her mouth."

Amazing. They'd done the most intense things to one another, but he'd swear a slight flush rose in her face at his words. And she still wouldn't look at him.

Embarrassment? That seemed crazy, given all they'd shared. Besides, her unease hadn't started with his crass comment, but when he'd suggested that they go out to eat. Or maybe a few minutes before that when he'd admitted to being infatuated with her.

"Let's stay in. We can order room service," she insisted.

She'd play sex games with him all afternoon, but didn't want to go on anything resembling a date?

Interesting.

Reese stood and walked up behind her, dropping his hands to her hips and pressing a kiss on her nape. "Room service for breakfast," he whispered. "Tonight, though, let's get out of here for a little while."

She still looked uncertain. As if, now that the game was over, now that they were played-out and talking about something as simple as food, she didn't know what to say, how to act.

Or who to be.

"We both know that's not what this is about…"

"Look, I'm not proposing, okay?" he said, forcing a noncommittal laugh. "It's dinner. Eating together, not any kind of a declaration. Sharing a meal doesn't elevate this to anything more than the two-night stand you've decided we can have."

Her eyes flared in surprise, as if she hadn't guessed how easy she was to read.

Reese shrugged. "I'm not stupid, okay? I know what

you want, and what you don't. I accepted that when I showed up here today."

She still hesitated.

"No pressure, no hidden meanings, just food," he said, coaxing her as carefully as he would a wild bird with a piece of bread. "You can choose where we go. As long as it's someplace that serves red meat, I'll take it."

She nibbled her bottom lip, than finally said, "Do you consider pepperoni red meat? Because I could really go for some pizza."

He almost breathed a sigh of relief. Both that she'd said yes, and that she wasn't a woman who liked to nibble on a few carrots and pieces of lettuce and call it a meal.

"Perfect."

She managed a weak smile. "You say that a lot."

"You *are* that a lot."

He met her stare in the mirror. Amanda didn't exactly pull away at the gentle push into more personal, intimate territory that fell out of the boundaries of their sexy games. But the muscles beneath the silky skin tensed ever so slightly. Enough to warn him to back off.

He did. "Give me ten minutes to grab a shower."

Gently letting her go, he walked toward the bathroom, figuring she needed a chance to pull herself back together. Hell, so did he. Because in the past few minutes, it had hit him—hard—that despite being more intimate with the woman than he'd ever been with anyone in his life, he didn't know much about her.

Sure, he knew he liked her. Knew she had a great sense of humor, was smart and hardworking. Knew that right before she came, she emitted this adorable little high-pitched sound from the back of her throat.

Beyond that—not so much. He'd been to her place, in an old downtown Chicago highrise, but even seeing where she lived hadn't offered many answers about her personal life. She had no pets, no plants, no pictures, nothing that personalized her apartment at all. Entering it, he'd immediately known it was just a place for her to eat, sleep and chill—not really what anyone would call a home.

So maybe this time-out for dinner, with no play-acting, no innuendo…no sex…would be a good thing. Maybe it was time to take a step back, drop the pretense and actually get to know the real people playing the games.

She might not like it, she might not want it. But Reese did. Because he had the feeling the woman behind the wild seductress was someone he really wanted to get to know better.

AS THEY WALKED INTO a nearby Italian restaurant recommended by the hotel's maitre d', Amanda found herself starting to sweat. And not just because Mr. Hot-ness was walking so closely behind her, his hand resting possessively on the small of her back.

This was too much like a date. Way too much like a date. And while she liked Reese Campbell a lot, dating him hadn't been part of the deal. Dating made this too real, when all she'd set out for from the beginning was a fantasy. A one-night stand that had somehow segued into two.

And only two. This was it, tonight *had* to be the end of it. Her life was just too complicated, and Reese was too incredible a guy for her to get any more involved with. He was too stable, too solid, too nice.

She…wasn't. Amanda wasn't dating material. She was sex material, oh, yes, she was good for flings and wild affairs, even if she'd had no time for any in recent months.

But dating? Romance? Relationships?

Uh-uh. She was the bitch who broke hearts. The one who panicked and took off whenever anybody got a little too serious or tried to tie her down in one place, instead of letting her live her life in flight, as she'd done for the past ten years.

This isn't a date. Just food so we can build up more energy to have lots more anonymous, no-strings sex.

"Would you relax?" Reese murmured as they followed the hostess, a fiftyish brunette in a full-skirted dress who'd yelled something in Italian as they passed by the swinging door to the kitchen. "It's just pizza, for God's sake."

Amanda drew in a long, shaky breath, trying to force the stiffness from her spine. Although, that was hard to do when his fingers were branding her.

"Is this all right?" the older woman asked as she reached a small, intimate table set for two.

"Just fine," Reese murmured.

Thank heaven he didn't say *perfect*. That word coming off his lips just had too many associations. Sometimes it made her incredibly horny, sometimes nervous as hell.

With its red-checked tablecloth, and an old Chianti bottle plugged with a candle and dripping wax, their table looked like the one where Lady and the Tramp had shared a romantic plate of spaghetti. All they needed was a pair of Italian singers with an accordion and a violin to serenade them.

God, this was *so* a date.

She almost bolted. If he hadn't already pulled out her chair and gently pushed her down into it, she probably would have done so.

It wouldn't have been the first time. One guy she'd been involved with had, despite all her warnings, told her he was in love with her. And she'd run to the airport, hopped on a flight to Paris and stayed away for two weeks.

No wonder he still drunk-dialed her.

But maybe this time could be different. Because he's different.

Reese was so different. So fun and sexy and playful. Daring and imaginative. He made her feel unlike any other man had before.

She sighed heavily, forcing those thoughts away. The way he made her feel couldn't possibly be a good thing. Not when it left her so confused, off-balance, unsure. Completely un-Amanda-like.

"Thank you," Reese said as he took the seat opposite her and smiled up at the hostess. Despite being at least twenty years his senior, she preened a little, as would any woman under the attention of a man as handsome as her companion.

Companion. Not date.

"So are you locals?" the woman asked.

Reese shook his head. "Just visiting."

"Excellent! Contrary to what you might think, Cleveland is a wonderful vacation spot. Very romantic," the woman said with a wag of her eyebrows. "Lots for a young couple in love to do."

Amanda opened her mouth to respond, lies and denials bubbling to her lips. They were just playing here...

just two wildly compatible people playing naughty games. Nothing more to it.

But before any could emerge, Reese reached for her hand and clasped it in his on top of the table. Their hostess nodded approvingly, then turned away to greet some newcomers standing in the entranceway.

"You were going to make up some outrageous story, weren't you?" he asked, casually releasing her hand, lifting a napkin and draping it over his lap.

"How do you know?"

"Are you denying it?"

"Of course not. Just wondering how you know."

"Oh, believe me, I'm starting to understand how your mind works. Romance, love…those words aren't in your vocabulary, right?"

She nodded once. "Right."

The hostess had left a basket of bread sticks on their table, and Amanda took one, nibbling lightly on the end, not elaborating even though she knew he probably expected her to. That kind of talk was for dates. This was just a…nutrition break.

"So what kind of story were you going to tell?" He sounded genuinely curious.

"I don't know." Thinking about it, she tapped her finger on her chin. "You're a witness against the mob in protective custody and I'm your bodyguard?"

"You're obviously not a very good bodyguard if you go around blabbing about me being a witness."

"I didn't say I was a good one. Maybe I'm a too-stupid-to-live one, like in one of those really bad movies."

"Hmm, possible." He looked around the restaurant, at the tables full of people who all looked much like their very-ethnic hostess, Rosalita. "But that might not be such a good idea in this place. I think half the diners in here are one generation out of Sicily. You might get me whacked."

"Got any better ideas?"

"Playboy bunny and mogul?"

"Keep dreaming." Giving him an impish look, she added, "Besides, I don't think you'd look very good in bunny ears."

He laughed out loud. Before he could reply, though, a busboy came over and filled two glasses of water, leaving them beside their untouched menus. A not-uncomfortable silence fell once the bored-looking teen had walked away.

Finally, Reese broke that silence. "So, why don't we just go with a pilot from Chicago hooking up with a businessman from Pittsburgh?"

She snorted, forcing herself to remain casual when her first reaction to the idea of just being who they really were more resembled panic. "Boring."

"You keep using that word…I do not think it means what you think it means."

Delighted that he'd quoted one of her favorite movies, *The Princess Bride,* complete with Spanish accent, she said, "Well done."

"Wow, we have something in common? A movie we've both seen?"

She gestured toward the table and the candle. "If we had the same taste in movies, you'd know just how ter-rified I am that some Italian dude is going to come up and start singing 'Bella Notte.'"

"At least tell me I'd get to be the Tramp in that one."

Something about his put-upon tone, plus the fact that

he knew exactly what she was talking about, made her relax and offer him her first genuine smile since they'd arrived. "I'm a pain in the ass, I know. I doubt you'd understand."

"I might. Why don't you try me?"

She thought about it. But how could she? How, exactly, did you go about telling your lover—*no, not lover, sex partner*—that you had a reputation as a bitch, that men faked suicide attempts because you couldn't love them, that you'd rather just not be bothered with the whole romance thing anymore? It wasn't exactly ladylike to admit you didn't want a guy who'd bring you chocolate and flowers and had long ago realized you were much more the fuck-buddy than the girlfriend type.

She couldn't say those things. And suddenly, she didn't want to. Not to him.

Why the very thought of it bothered her so much, though, she honestly didn't know.

When she didn't respond, he finally prompted, "Sometimes it's just easier to pretend than to be who you really are?"

"Yeah, something like that."

He shook his head ever so slightly, either disapproval or disappointment visible in the tightness of his mouth.

"Hey, you agreed to the terms."

"I agreed to a one-night stand." His eyes sparkled as he added, "You *changed* those terms with your e-mail."

He had a point.

"So maybe it's time to renegotiate."

Wary, she asked, "How so?"

"Maybe we should agree to at least one open, honest conversation, without any, uh, embellishments."

Figuring great sex would make him forget that idea, she licked her lips. "I don't see why you're complaining. I thought you were pretty happy about how things turned out this afternoon."

"As I recall, so were you. At least three times."

She licked the tip of her bread stick. "Mmm…six."

Reese crossed his arms over his chest and leaned back in his chair, eyeing her steadily. "I'm not counting the ones I wasn't involved in."

"Oh, honey, you were most definitely involved."

A brow arched over one blue eye. "Oh?"

"Mmm-hmm. And you've *been* involved every other time I've played with that little toy in the past two weeks."

He dropped his crossed arms onto the table, leaning over it, closer to her. Close enough that she saw the way his pulse pounded in his throat. "Is that so?"

"Yes."

He reached for his water, bringing the slick glass to his mouth. As he sipped, the muscles in his neck flexed. And when he lowered the glass, his lips were moist, parted. "Did that happen often?"

"Probably more than it had in the past year."

A masculine expression of self-satisfaction appeared on his incredibly handsome face. "You thought about…"

"Everything," she purred. "I thought about it a lot."

"Ditto."

She swallowed, immediately knowing what he was admitting. "I don't suppose you had any toys to play with?"

"'Fraid not. Had to go the old-fashioned route."

Squirming a little in her chair as she thought of him needing to gain some relief because he'd been thinking about her, she echoed his question. "Did that happen often?"

He lowered his eyes, gazing at her throat and the soft swell of cleavage rising above her V-necked sweater. "What do you think?"

Realizing she'd bit off a little more than she could chew, and that images of Reese pumping that long, thick shaft into his own tight fist were going to intrude on the rest of her meal, she cleared her throat and bit hard on the bread stick.

Reese didn't let it go, however, going right back to where he'd been headed before that detour into Lustville. "So what happened, your little toy was no longer enough so you decided to break your own rules and come back to order something else off the menu?"

She opened her mouth to answer, but before she could, a chirpy voice intruded. "Something else? Wait, has somebody already taken your order? Gosh darn it, I told her I was coming right over!"

Amanda bit her lip in amusement at the realization that a young waitress, whose name tag said Brittani, had overheard part of their conversation. Of course, she'd obviously misinterpreted it. Thank God.

The girl was probably only about seventeen, and she looked extremely annoyed that someone else had been poaching on her table. She apparently feared losing her tip. Considering they'd been left sitting here unattended for a good ten minutes, she was apparently the optimistic type.

"It's okay," Reese said, "we were talking about something else."

Amanda couldn't resist being a little mischievous. "Oh, yes. Definitely something else. Just reminiscing about something we ordered off a menu in Milan last week."

The girl's jaw opened far enough to display the chewing gum resting on her tongue. "You been to Australia? For real? Did you see any koala bears?"

Amanda managed to hide either a laugh or a sigh at Brittani's less-than-impressive geography skills.

"No koalas," Reese interjected smoothly. "Just a few dingoes. Now, if you don't mind, I think we're ready to order."

They did so, asking for the pepperoni pizza she'd been craving since they'd first talked about food back in the hotel room. Their perky waitress, whose mood had picked up once she realized nobody was horning in on her table, nodded and sauntered away, not even asking if they wanted anything other than ice water to drink.

The ice water that was just about gone.

When they were alone again, Reese said, "To be sure I've got it, let's clarify. Honest conversation is just as forbidden on your planet as actual dinner dates, right?"

Damn, the guy was tenacious. "Depends on the conversation."

"Can we talk about sports?"

She wrinkled her nose.

"Movies?"

"Sure. Though I haven't seen a new one in a theater in at least two years."

He shrugged. "Me, either. Moving on. Politics?"

"Only if you're a right-down-the-middle moderate like me."

"Progress. We have one thing in common."

Grinning impishly, she said, "I think we have more than one."

"Touché."

She lifted her glass and drained the last few drops of water from it, then sucked a small piece of ice into her mouth. "I think there's another thing we can safely agree on. Brittani's tip is getting smaller by the minute."

"I think we can also agree that world geography should be a required course in high schools."

She snickered, liking his deadpan sense of humor. Liking so much about him. Too much.

Maybe...

No. She wasn't going to go there, not even in her own head. She wasn't going to evaluate the possibility that this thing between them might be about anything more than having fun and incredible sex.

She'd take fun and incredible sex over angsty emotional dramas and minefields of feelings any day.

Despite her best efforts, for a few minutes Amanda let herself actually converse with the man. Nothing too heavy, definitely no sharing of past relationships or deepest fears. He got her to admit she'd once had a mad crush on every member of the Backstreet Boys, and he'd come clean about his secret desire to be a drummer for a rock band, even though he'd never held a drumstick.

"Backstreet Boys never had a drummer," she pointed out.

"Too bad. To think we could have started all this fun fifteen years ago."

"Fifteen years ago, we would both have been seriously underage."

"But think of all the interesting things we could have learned together."

Frankly, she was learning lots of interesting things from the man, right here and now. At fourteen, still the rebel trying to survive in good-girl wonderland, she didn't think her heart could have taken meeting someone who excited her like Reese Campbell.

Well, her heart probably could have. Her parents, however, would have lost their minds.

Their light chatting seemed to satisfy Reese, at least for now, and he didn't try to steer her toward any more personal subjects. That was fortunate. Amanda honestly didn't know if she'd have been able to explain her aversion to such things. Not without giving him all the information he was looking for in the process. Her past heartbreaks, her rigid upbringing, her bad reputation for being a little too footloose and coldhearted…all explained who she was today. But none were topics she particularly cared to talk about. Teenage fantasy was about as intimate as she wanted to get.

"Okay, here you go. Enjoy!"

Brittani had returned with their pizza right on time—before Reese could slip through any conversational back doors she might have inadvertently left open. She was so anxious that it remain that way, she grabbed a slice and bit into it right away.

Bad move.

"Ow!" she snapped when the gooey cheese burned the roof of her mouth.

Reese immediately scooped a piece of ice out of his own water glass and lifted it toward her. Dropping the pizza, Amanda gratefully parted her lips, sucking the cube he offered into her mouth. Her tongue swiped across his fingertips as she did so, and suddenly the pain wasn't so bad. Seeing the way his eyes flared at the brush of her tongue against his skin, she had to acknowledge it wasn't so bad at all.

"Watch it. Don't want any injuries that could cut short our two-night stand," he teased. Then, looking at his own pizza, he added, "I think I'll wait a while for this to cool off. I have definite plans for my mouth tonight."

She quivered in her seat at the very thought of it. Because oh, the man did know how to use his mouth. And there were such wonderful things he could do with it that did not involve the conversation she suspected he would want to get back to as soon as they finished eating.

She thought about it. Stick around here and deal with lots more talking? Or just seduce the man back to their hotel room?

No-freaking-brainer.

"Reese?" she said, speaking carefully, the ice now just a small sliver on her tongue.

"Yeah?"

"Can we please take this to go?"

He stared at her, as if gauging the request, and her motivation for making it. She didn't have to feign her interest in getting back to where they'd been a couple of hours ago: in a hotel room bed. But she did have to hide the fact that her motivation was at least partly to get out of having to talk anymore.

Something that looked like understanding crossed his face, though she would swear she saw a hint of frustration there, too. "You're sure?"

"I think you need to kiss this better," she said, pushing him just a little more. She swiped her tongue across her lips to punctuate the point.

He shook his head, smiling ruefully. "I guess I should be thankful just to have found out you're a political moderate who doesn't go to the movies. That's more than I knew two hours ago."

"And don't forget—not a sports fan."

"We're really getting somewhere."

"Now let's get somewhere else," she insisted, leaning across the table. This back-and-forth conversation was reminding her of how much she liked his quick wit, his easygoing personality. Physically, she'd been attracted from the get-go. Now she knew there was so much more about him that interested her.

But only until tomorrow.

Unless…

Only until tomorrow!

"Please," she whispered. "We only have until morning and I really don't want to waste it sitting here waiting for the pizza to cool off."

Apparently hearing her sincerity, he no longer hesitated. He waved to their waitress, then murmured, "But I do reserve the right to ask you if you've read any good books lately on the ride back to the hotel."

"Books. Okay, I can do that."

And she could. Books were fine. So were movies and politics and sports and anything else that didn't really require intimate conversation.

He just couldn't ask her about her past relationships, her family background or her footloose lifestyle. She wouldn't share details of her aversion to small towns, home, hearth, wholesome values or anything else resembling the world in which she'd grown up.

And she definitely didn't want to talk about her slightly hardened heart. Or the fact that some people didn't even seem to think she had one.

5

Thanksgiving

"SO, I'VE BEEN MEANING to ask you, how'd your folks take you not coming home for the holiday weekend?"

Sprawled back in a comfortable, cushy chair in the rec room of her friend Jazz's parents' house, Amanda resisted the urge to unsnap her khakis. After the two full plates of Thanksgiving dinner, plus the pumpkin pie and the teensy sliver of pecan that she'd simply had to taste, she should be glad the snap hadn't just popped on its own.

"Manda? Were they upset?"

Tryptophan kicking in, she yawned and shook her head. "Actually, I think they were relieved."

Jazz, who supervised the mechanics who kept Clear-Blue Air flying, curled up in her own chair, her head barely reaching the top of it. She was petite, five-foot-four, but you'd never know that by the way she ran her mechanics' shop or the magic way she coaxed the best performance out of an airplane.

The two of them were hiding down in the converted basement. They'd finished dinner a few hours ago and

Jazz's big family had just begun saying their goodbyes. Neither of them being the air-kisses type, Amanda and Jazz were waiting out the big huggy scene downstairs. Once the coast was clear, they would go back up and let Jazz's mother make a big fuss out of loading up plates of leftovers for the "single girls" to take home.

It was becoming a tradition. Somehow, hanging out with Jazz's big, loud, crazy family on holidays was easier than going home and sticking out like a sore thumb in her own small, quiet, proper one.

"Relieved why?"

"You know Abby got engaged?"

Jazz nodded with a big roll of her dark eyes. She'd met Amanda's younger sister last year when Abby had come to the city for a spring shopping trip.

Abby was okay, at least when their parents weren't around and she didn't have to play Miss Perfect. But the stick up her ass only ever came out so far, and Jazz was not the type around whom Abigail Bauer would ever let down her guard.

Jazz was an exotically beautiful, loud-mouthed, crass, wild-child. Abby was a demure, classically beautiful, prodigal one. Oil and water.

Which made Amanda, what…the vinegar to their Good Seasons salad dressing?

Yeah, tart and sour.

She thrust that thought away, preferring to think of herself as flavorful and zesty.

"How do you like her fiancé?"

"He's a douche."

Back to tart and sour.

Jazz snorted, sipping from the glass of wine she'd smuggled down from the kitchen. "Figures."

"He's as cold as my father and as reserved as my mother. And he comes from a family of people just like him. His parents invited my folks over for a prewedding holiday meal today."

"Gotcha. No bad girls allowed, huh?"

Amanda lifted a brow, feigning offense. "Look who's talking."

Jazz bent her head and smiled into her glass. "I'm not the one flying off tomorrow to have a weekend of illicit sex with a guy I barely know."

Sucking her bottom lip between her teeth, Amanda reached for her glass of water. Because damn it, yes, she was doing exactly that.

She'd left Cleveland absolutely certain she'd never see Reese Campbell again. She'd felt sure she'd gotten him out of her system. They'd had a great time, built some incredible memories. Plus they'd done just about everything two people could do together sexually.

Okay, that was a lie. She could think of about another four or five things she'd like to do with the man. Or five dozen.

The point was, they'd had amazing sexual encounters twice now, and twice was once more than the one-night stand she'd intended. So how crazy was she to go for number three?

Third time's the charm.

She'd been unable to resist. Hearing his voice on her voice mail the other day, she'd gotten shaky and weak all over again. When he'd asked her if she wanted to meet him in Florida to see if they could get kicked out of a theme park for having hot sex in public, she'd been unable to say anything but yes. She hadn't even insisted that he promise to put on any mouse ears.

She had something else in mind for the fantasy part of their sensual weekend. Something a little more risqué than a theme park.

"Where are you meeting him?"

"Daytona."

"Warm. Sounds good. So, uh, when are you going to let me meet this guy?"

"Never."

Her friend pulled a hurt look. "Come on, I introduce you to all my boy toys."

"He's not my boy toy. He's…"

"He's what?" Jazz asked, leaning forward and dropping her elbows onto her knees.

Good question. She couldn't really call Reese a stranger anymore. They not only knew and had explored every inch of each other's bodies, they'd also spent time together doing nonsexual things. Damn it, she'd gotten roped into pillow talk that last time.

Even worse, they'd actually chatted about his family the morning after. Mainly because his teenage sister had called him at the butt-crack of dawn to ask him to intervene with their mother for permission to go to some party.

Even adorably tousled and sleepy, Reese had been kind and patient with the girl, whose loud voice Amanda could hear from the other side of the bed. She'd watched him during the conversation, seeing the great guy, the caring brother.

He'd told her a little about his family after the call. That his father had died, that he'd taken over as head of the family business. He hadn't had to tell her he'd taken on his father's role in his younger siblings' lives, too. She'd heard it in the tender—and a little over-whelmed—tone when he talked about them.

Those were about a half-dozen more details than she had ever intended to learn about him. Especially be-cause every one of them just made him that much more appealing.

She absolutely should have steered well clear after that. So how dumb was she to have said yes to this weekend's get-together? Extremely. And yet, she was already almost breathless with excitement when she thought about the fact that she'd be with him again in under twenty-four hours.

"I guess he's just a pretty big distraction right at the moment," she finally admitted.

"I'm glad," Jazz declared. "It's about damn time."

"I know. Now I don't have to give up my membership card to the sexually alive club."

"I don't mean that." Jazz finished off her wine, then got up and crossed to a well-stocked bar, digging around in a fridge for another bottle. She held it up question-ingly, but Amanda shook her head. She'd had one glass with dinner. That was her max, considering she was flying the next day.

"So what did you mean?" Amanda asked, once her friend returned to her seat.

"I mean, it's about time you stop thinking about what that creepazoid Dale said to you when you dumped his sorry ass. You're not cold, you're not ruthless and you're no heartbreaker."

Amanda couldn't help humming a few bars of the Pat Benatar song under her breath.

Jazz ignored her. "He was a tool."

True.

"And that fake-overdose shit also proved he was one taco short of a combination plate."

Also true. But he wasn't the only man she'd ever let down. Something her loyal friend was apparently trying to ignore.

"Face it," Amanda said, "moss doesn't grow under my feet. In thirty years, I'm going to be like Uncle Frank. I'll be the one flying off to the Bahamas to hook up with some hot divorcée for the Thanksgiving holiday."

Hell, she was already like Uncle Frank. Suddenly, she wished she could have that second glass of wine.

"If you're swinging that way in thirty years, I might just have to be the hot divorcée."

Amanda snorted with laughter, as Jazz had obviously intended her to. Because the girl was about as flaming a heterosexual as she'd ever known. Jazz often said her favorite color was purple-veined penis.

"Give yourself a chance," Jazz murmured, her smile fading and her tone turning earnest. "Don't decide what this is before you have the opportunity to really find out."

Amanda opened her mouth to respond, but didn't quite know what to say. So she said nothing and simply nodded.

They fell silent for a minute or two. Then, from upstairs, they heard the tromping of feet and the slam of the back door, which meant that Jazz's mother was ushering out the rest of her guests. They'd managed to successfully avoid the big so-great-to-see-you-let's-do-this-more-often goodbye. The two of them lifted their glasses in a silent toast.

To hiding out when the going gets tough, and avoiding emotional entanglements.

She just had to keep reminding herself of that thought for the next couple of days. And not think about the silent promise she'd just made to her best friend.

As he drove his rental car closer to the beachfront hotel where Amanda awaited him, Reese had sex on his mind. Wild sex. Steamy sex. Crazy, never-thought-it-could-be-this-good sex.

That had been on his mind for days. Ever since he'd driven away from that Cleveland hotel room, unsure of whether he would ever again see the beautiful woman who'd slept in his arms the night before.

This time, he'd played it a little smarter. He hadn't called or e-mailed her right away. Despite how much it killed him, he'd let a full of week go by before he'd tried to contact her.

And it had paid off. Amanda had let her guard down enough to admit she missed him and wanted to see him again. She'd agreed that Thanksgiving weekend in Florida sounded like a perfect holiday.

He should have known it wouldn't stay entirely perfect. Nothing ever did, right?

"Damn it," he muttered, seeing a blue light come on behind him, and hearing the brief trill of a siren.

He was a good driver. But when it came to these getaways with the most exciting woman he'd ever known, even his foot got excited and pressed down a bit too hard on the gas pedal.

He could see their hotel, an older place with a sign showing a blue dolphin leaping through the waves. The thought that Amanda was waiting behind the door of one of the rooms, while he was going to have to spend the next fifteen or twenty minutes just a few yards away dealing with a ticket was frustrating in the extreme.

He put the car's emergency flashers on and pulled into the hotel parking lot, praying the cop was in a good holiday mood. Considering it was Black Friday, however, and he'd probably been chasing credit-card-crazy shoppers clamoring to make it from door-buster to door-buster, Reese somehow doubted he'd be that lucky.

The cop who'd pulled him over spoke from a few feet away as Reese lowered the window. "License and registration?"

Reese started at the female voice, glancing over and seeing the shapely woman standing beside the car door. She was dressed in a formfitting uniform, and wore dark sunglasses even though it was just after sunset. She stared down at him, not taking them off.

"Good evening, Officer," he said slowly. "Is there some kind of problem?"

"You were doing forty in a twenty-five."

"Really? Are you sure about that?"

She bent down into the open window. "You saying I'm wrong?"

"Not wrong. Just maybe…mistaken?"

"You have a smart mouth. Maybe I should haul you in."

He offered her his most charming smile. "I'd really appreciate it if you didn't. I've got a busy night planned."

She fisted her hands and put them on her shapely hips. "You think your night's more important than the safety of everyone else on the road?"

He hesitated, giving it some thought.

"Step out of the car," she snapped.

Reese didn't argue but did as she ordered. Removing

the keys from the ignition, he opened the door and stepped out into the thick Florida night. Despite the fact that it was November, heat assaulted him. Though it was already evening, the air was still heavy and hot, with that not unpleasant smell found only in the south. A mixture of citrus, flowers, paper mills and suntan oil.

And spicy, sultry female cop.

"Don't you think we could come to some kind of arrangement, Officer? Can't you get me off…excuse me, I mean, let me off, with a warning or something?"

Her lips tightened. "I don't think a warning will do."

He lifted both his hands, palms up. "There must be some kind of arrangement we could reach. Something I could do for you so you'd feel comfortable forgetting about my speeding?"

She rubbed her hand on her slim jaw, her lips pursed. Then, as if she'd come to some decision, she slowly nodded.

"Okay, then. Maybe you can sweet-talk me into not writing you a ticket."

"Talk?" he asked, moving closer, until the tips of his shoes touched hers and the fabric of their pants brushed. "You sure that's all you want from me? Conversation?"

She swallowed visibly, her throat moving with the effort. Reese lifted his hand, tracing the tip of his index finger from her full bottom lip, down her chin, then her throat, her neck. All the way to the top button of her blouse.

This time, her hard swallow was preceded by a shaky sigh.

"Which room?" he asked, urgency making his voice weak.

She lifted a shaky hand and pointed to the nearest one, on the end.

"Key?"

Tugging it out of her pocket, she handed the key card to him, then put her hand in his and let him lead her across the parking lot. Just before he opened the door, he glanced back at the car, and the motor scooter—obviously a beachside rental—sitting directly behind it.

Smirking, he said, "Not even a real motorcycle? It's not terribly intimidating."

"Maybe not," she said with a wicked smile. Then she reached into her pocket and pulled out something... something metal. Something that jangled. "But these are definitely real."

Handcuffs. Oh, yeah. They were real. And they were most definitely intimidating.

He just wondered what his sexy-lover-playing-cop was going to say when he got the upper hand and used them on *her*. She might think she was in charge this time, but she'd played that role in Cleveland. It was his turn.

"Okay, Officer Bauer. I guess I'm your prisoner."

At least for a few minutes. As soon as he could gain the upper hand, he'd be the one calling the shots, leaving her vulnerable and helpless against every bit of pleasure he could possibly give her.

AMANDA DIDN'T KNOW WHAT happened. One second, Reese was lying on the bed, his shirt off, pants unfastened, arms upstretched toward the headboard. The next, *she* was flat on her back and wearing one of the sets of handcuffs.

She sputtered. "What are you doing?"

He didn't answer at first, too busy double-checking the cuffs that attached her left hand to the headboard. The other set was lying on the bed, but instead of reaching for it, he hesitated. "We don't have to use both...if you're not comfortable."

She had fully intended to use both sets on him, wanting him totally at her mercy. How wonderful Reese was to take it just far enough, but then pause to make sure she was okay with what he was doing.

Not a lot of men would do that. Of course, not a lot of women would say 'to hell with it' and offer up her other wrist for restraint, either.

But they weren't exactly your average couple.

"Go for it," she said with a sultry smile as she twisted on the sheets, suddenly so aroused she could barely stand it.

He reached across the bed, fastening her other hand, then came back to center, brushing his mouth against hers.

"I've wanted you since the last time I saw you," she told him.

"I know."

He wasn't being arrogant, she realized. He knew because he felt the same way.

"Okay, you've got me, big guy. Now what are you going to do?"

Reese had been almost undressed when she tried to take over, but Amanda hadn't removed so much as her shoes. Which would probably present a bit of a problem when it came to her top. But she trusted him—he was a very resourceful kind of guy.

And it buttoned up the front. Thankfully.

"I'll think of something." He frowned down at her. "So, madam police officer, are you used to trading sexual favors for legal ones?"

"Only in very special circumstances."

He rose to his knees, reaching for her waistband, and unfastened her pants. Amanda lifted up a little so he could slide them down over her hips and bottom, feeling the slow glide of his fingertips down to her very bones.

"What circumstances would those be?"

"Well, when I haven't had a man in a very long time." She licked her lips. "And I stumble across one who looks like he could satisfy me."

He tsked. "Didn't we have this conversation in a beer closet once? Is there any doubt that I can satisfy you?"

Giving him an innocent look, she asked, "A beer closet? Why, I don't know what you mean."

He reached for her tiny panties, catching the elastic and pulling them off the way he had her pants. This time, she didn't help. She let him work them down, liking the way he couldn't take his eyes off her body as he revealed it.

Those blue eyes darkened as he stared at her hips, her pelvis, the curls at the top of her sex. But he didn't touch, seeming content to drive her mad with just a stare.

He could set out to be as slow and deliberate as he wanted. Amanda knew, however, that his strength would only last so long.

She'd been there, done that, and brought home the orgasms to prove it.

Bare from the waist down, she casually lifted one leg, letting her thighs fall apart so he could see the glistening effect he'd already had on her.

He hesitated for a second, then, as if unable to resist, he reached for her. Tracing her pelvic bone with his fingertips, he finally slid them down to swirl over her clit.

Amanda jerked, her hips lifting off the bed. He didn't go any faster, or further, he just continued to toy with her, to pluck her like a fine instrument, until she was gasping. Then he moved his hand away and reached for the bottom button of her blouse. He unfastened it, pressing his mouth to the bare skin of her belly. The next button—and that wicked, wonderful mouth moved higher.

By the time he reached her midriff, his tongue was involved and he was taking tiny tastes of her, as if he was nibbling delicately on some luscious dessert. She twisted beneath him, arching toward that questing mouth and those careful fingers.

For the first time, she got a sense of just how difficult this being restrained was going to be. Because she desperately wanted to twine her hands in his hair, to caress his handsome face, cup his strong jaw.

She also wanted to pull him up a teensy bit faster. Her breasts were throbbing with need, her nipples scraping almost painfully against the rough, starched blouse— part of her phony uniform. And having his mouth on her skin, his breaths blowing hotly against her, all she could think about was how incredible his tongue felt on other parts of her anatomy.

But she could do nothing: couldn't hurry him, couldn't

touch herself to provide some relief. She could only lie there, silently begging with every quiver of her body.

"What's wrong?" he asked, and there was laughter in his voice.

She faked it. "Not a thing."

"Uh-huh. Sure."

He moved up again. One inch closer to where she needed him to be. Or one inch farther from where she needed him to be. She honestly couldn't decide.

Well, of course she could. She wanted both. Wanted him sucking her nipples and also giving her the kind of mind-blowing oral sex that she'd had erotic dreams about for weeks.

"Please..."

He moved again, this time his slightly roughened cheek scraping the bottom curve of her breast. His lips followed, kissing away the irritation, and she flinched with the close contact to her sensitized nipples.

Finally the right button. He looked down on her and shook his head. "No bra? Is that standard uniform attire, Officer?"

She twisted, trying to push her nipple toward his mouth, needing him to suck and squeeze and twist.

"Your breasts are a work of art," he mumbled, dropping his aloof act.

She didn't totally agree, always feeling at least a cup size less adequate than most women. But they were pretty, nicely shaped and high. Plus her nipples had so many nerve endings it was a wonder she didn't come when she wore a silk blouse.

"Suck me, Reese," she begged.

"That an order?" He pulled farther away, deliberately tormenting her.

"Let's call it a polite request."

"Well, since you're being polite."

He said nothing else, gave her no warning, merely bent to capture the taut tip between his lips. He sucked her once, then deeper, reaching up to catch the other mound in his hand.

She cried out, her hips instinctively jerking toward his jean-covered legs. Twisting her thigh over his, she tugged him closer, gaining satisfaction from the brush of his jeans against her sex.

She was all nerve endings, all sensation, and between the deep, strong pulls of his mouth on her nipple and the rub of his strong, masculine thigh between her legs, she felt herself begin to climax. The wave began, and she let out a hitchy little cry.

Reese moved suddenly, removing all that physical connection. He covered her mouth with his, swallowing down the sound with a kiss. And the orgasm dissipated like morning fog baked away by the rising sun.

"Not yet," he whispered. "Not just yet."

Oh, God. She was going to kill him. "Paybacks are hell," she snapped.

"Yeah, I know." He moved his mouth to her neck, sucking her skin into his mouth and biting her lightly. "Consider this a payback for November 11th."

Oh. Yeah. The day she'd kept him on the brink of climax but hadn't let him go over the edge until she was good and ready.

"Can I just cry uncle, say you win and take my orgasm now, please?"

"Nope."

Damn. She'd been afraid of that.

Reese was as good as his word. For the next hour,

he tormented her, delighted her, toyed with her, thrilled her. There was magic in the man's hands and heaven in his mouth. And he used those hands and that mouth on every last inch of her.

Her shoulders became sore from twisting around on the bed while her arms were restrained above her head. But, to be honest, Amanda didn't mind. There was something incredibly freeing about being at the sexual mercy of someone she trusted completely. There was no quid pro quo, no reciprocity. She just had to lie there and let him give her pleasure, just take, take, take and not feel one bit of guilt about it.

It wasn't until she was sobbing with the need to come that Reese finally decided to grant her an orgasm. He'd been moving his mouth and tongue across her groin, her upper thighs and the outer lips of her sex, but not lingering long enough. Finally, though, perhaps hearing the sobs of pleasure mingled with frustration, he did linger.

Oh, did he linger.

Swirling his tongue over her clit, he flicked and sucked, then upped the intensity by moving a hand to her swollen lips. He wet his finger in her body's moisture, then slid it into her. Then another, moving slowly, deeply.

"Oh, yes," she said. "More, please."

He gave her more. More pressure, more suction, more delicate stabs of his tongue. And he began to withdraw his fingers, then plunge them in again, filling her as best he could until he could use the part of his anatomy she really wanted.

"Oh, God, finally!" she cried as the waves of pleasure erupted. Nothing could have held them back this time.

Her body had reached its very peak of sexual arousal and the explosion that rocked her seemed to last for a solid minute. She almost had an out-of-body experience, she was so in its grip.

By the time it finally released her, she realized Reese had moved away long enough to strip out of his clothes. His erection was enormous, looking bigger somehow, as if seeing her so entirely lost had aroused him more than he'd ever been before.

He paused only long enough to pull on a condom, then moved between her splayed thighs. Amanda immediately tilted up to greet him, wrapping her legs around his hips, wanting him as deep as he could possibly get.

They knew each other now. Knew what they wanted, what they liked, what they could take. So there was nothing tentative, no gentle easing like there'd been the first time, when he'd almost seemed worried he might hurt her.

This time, Reese drove into her in one thrust. Though she was dripping wet and took him easily, Amanda let out a little scream of pleasure. He filled her thoroughly, stretching out a place for himself, making her wonder how she withstood the emptiness when he wasn't inside her.

She wanted her hands free, wanted to wrap them around his neck and hold on tight. But he was too hungry for her to consider asking him to pause to find the keys.

Oh, what the hell.

Amanda didn't even think about it. She easily slid her hand out of the left cuff, twisted the right and tugged that one free, too. Reese had been so tender and sweet about it, not wanting to hurt her, that he hadn't fastened the damn things tightly enough.

His eyes flared in surprise when she lifted her hands to his thick, broad shoulders. "Sneaky woman."

"You don't have to be gentle," she told him, not just referring to the cuffs.

"I know." His eyes glittered as he withdrew, then slammed back into her, hard, deep, almost violent.

Nothing had ever felt so good. Nothing. Not ever.

Amanda raked her nails across his back. Wanting even more, she tilted farther until her legs were so high, he took them and looped them over his shoulders.

"Yes, yes…."

Smiling down at her, Reese bent to catch her mouth in another hungry kiss. His warm tongue thrust deeply against hers, catching the rhythm of his thick member moving in and out of her body. She matched both movements, taking everything, giving it back again. Until finally, in a lot shorter time than he'd allowed for hers, he came close to reaching his own ultimate level of fulfillment. She knew, by his hoarse groans and the strain on his face, that he was almost there.

Not willing to be left behind, yet not wanting to give up one centimeter of that deep possession, she reached down between their bodies, rubbing at her most sensitive spot with her fingertips. Reese looked down, and she followed his stare. It was incredibly erotic, seeing her fingers tangled in her curls, and below, his big, thick cock disappearing into her.

The sights, the sounds, the weight of him, the smell of him, and, oh, the feel of his body joined with hers… all combined to drive her up to that ledge again. And once he saw she was right there with him, Reese brought them both as high as they could possibly go…and then just a little bit further.

THOUGH THEIR PREVIOUS encounters had, literally, been one-nighters, this trip to Daytona was actually going to last two. Amanda had booked the hotel room through Sunday, and Reese wasn't about to ask her why. She again wanted to change the terms of their…whatever it was. Well, that was just fine with him. Double the pleasure, double the fun.

Problem was, by Saturday afternoon, he could see she was beginning to regret it. Her smiles were forced. She kept averting her gaze during their brief talks. And whenever he began any kind of real conversation, she tried to seduce him.

Not that he minded being seduced. Seriously. But he was only human and while the mind was willing, his dick was just about worn-out after six or seven rounds of cops and robbers.

Amanda had even resisted going out to eat, having filled the small fridge with food before his arrival. He knew without asking that she was remembering their dinner at the Italian place in Cleveland. Her aversion to anything that looked, smelled or sounded anything like a date had come through loud and clear. He didn't know why she felt that way—how could he?—but the message had definitely been received.

Still, he'd had enough of grapes and cheese. Not to mention enough of her skittishness about doing anything that didn't involve some part of his anatomy connecting with some part of hers. And that was why, at three o'clock Saturday, he put his foot down, insisting they get out of the hotel room and actually see the ocean they could hear pounding right outside their window.

"I didn't bring a bathing suit," she muttered as he nudged her toward the door.

"I didn't, either. The water's not exactly swimming temperature, is it?" Though, judging by the clear blue sky and blazing yellow sun he could sort-of see through the tired, smudged windows, he figured it had to be as hot as a typical summer day in Pittsburgh. "A walk on the beach doesn't require special clothing. And I might be lucky enough to find a hot dog vendor or something. Because if I have to eat nothing but cheddar cheese for the rest of the day, I'm going to fly to Vermont and shoot someone."

Though a grin pulled at her mouth, she visibly subdued it. With her brow tugged down, she looked like someone trying to get out of some difficult chore. "Fine. We'll walk."

"You know, if I hadn't already seen just how daring you can be, I'd have to conclude you were a total chickenshit."

Her eyes flared wide in surprise. "What did you call me?"

"You heard me," he said with a shrug.

"I'm not afraid of the beach," she insisted.

He'd lay money she intentionally misunderstood. "I didn't say you were."

"Then what are you saying?"

Putting a hand on her elbow, he led her out the door while she was distracted being all pissed off. "I'm just wondering something. Are you scared that if you take your hands out of my pants for too long, you might actually start to like me?"

Her face flushed, but, as he'd figured, she kept on walking, now challenged more than anything else.

It took a full minute for her to respond. As they crossed the wooden planking over the dunes and stepped down onto the sandy beach, she finally muttered, "I don't dislike you."

"Progress."

She fell silent again while they stopped to kick off their shoes. As he'd suspected, it was blazingly hot out, at least fifty degrees warmer than it had been yesterday in Pittsburgh. While he definitely could appreciate the warmth, he honestly didn't think he'd ever actually enjoy living someplace like this. Wearing shorts while watching football on Thanksgiving day just sounded wrong on all kinds of levels.

Carrying their shoes, they made their way down toward the water. They skirted the pasty-skinned sunbathers, on vacation from cold northern cities, who were sprawled on colorful towels and slathered with lotion. Only when the warm ocean surf lapped at their feet did they turn and proceed north.

Heading away from the hotels, the beach grew less and less crowded. Soon the voices of shouting kids, radios and gabby teenagers had disappeared. There was nothing but the churning of the waves, the hiss of the breeze and the squawk of overhead seagulls. And the very loud silence of his companion.

It was probably a good ten minutes before Amanda said a thing. When she did, it was in a whisper he could barely hear above the strong lapping of the surf against his ankles.

"I actually like you a lot, Reese."

He said nothing, just reached for her hand and laced

his fingers through hers. He'd touched her in so many ways, but this was, as far as he could recall, the first time he'd simply held her hand.

Amanda had such a strong, confident personality, he sometimes forgot how feminine she was. Her slender hand, delicate fingers and soft palm reminded him that, despite the swagger and the attitude, she was still vulnerable. More than she'd ever want anyone to realize.

"I probably like you too much already." She sounded as though she'd just admitted to liking tuna-and-peanut-butter sandwiches.

"I wish I could say I understand why that's such a bad thing."

"I told you I didn't want anything serious."

"Who said liking each other meant we were about to exchange rings?"

She stopped, but didn't pull her hand away. Tilting her head back to look up at him, she pushed her sunglasses up onto the top of her thick hair, as if wanting to ensure he understood what she was about to say. He did the same, seeing confusion in her green eyes.

"Here's the thing. I am poison when it comes to men and relationships. My name might as well be Ivy."

He didn't laugh, knowing she was dead serious. She really believed what she said. "Why do you think that?"

"Because I've been *told* that. I break hearts and hurt people, Reese."

"Intentionally?"

Her brow furrowing in confusion, she shook her head slowly. "No, I suppose not. But what difference does that make?"

Leaning down, he pressed his lips onto her forehead,

kissing her tenderly. There was nothing sexual in it, just warmth and a bit of consolation for this beautiful woman who seemed to see herself so differently than the way he saw her.

"It makes all the difference in the world," he murmured.

She remained stiff, unyielding. "Not to the guys whose hearts I've broken."

"Armies of them, I suppose?"

She wasn't teased out of her dark mood.

"Platoons?" Reese put his arms around her shoulders, tugging her against him, making her take the support and connection she tried so hard to resist. "Squads?"

"I don't know how big those things are," she mumbled into his shirt, her voice sounding a little watery.

He didn't tease her, didn't pull back to see if those really were tears dampening the front of his shirt or just the misty spray off the ocean.

"I don't, either. And I honestly don't care."

He meant it. He was a grown man, and she'd warned him from the get-go. He could take care of himself.

He only wondered if she was really as tough as she tried to make herself out to be, or if all these protestations and fears were more about protecting her own heart than anyone else's. Not that he was about to say that out loud. Not when she had, at last, seemed to let down her guard, at least a little bit.

"Let's just go with this—no more rules, no more walls. And see where it takes us. Okay?"

No answer. Instead, quietly, slowly, she relaxed against him. After a few moments, she even slid her arms around his waist, holding him, if not tightly, at least comfortably.

They stood that way for a long while, on the edge of the water, with the waves splashing against their legs. And in the quiet stillness of the moment, he felt the tension leave her, felt her give up some of the control she'd been trying so very hard to maintain.

And finally she murmured, "Okay."

He didn't respond or react in any way, knowing the decision had been a difficult one for her to make. He also knew they'd just agreed to something that could end up not working at all.

Because what was happening between them was unpredictable, as uncontrollable as the currents sending the salty ocean water splashing over their feet. He didn't know where they were going or how long it would take to get there. Or how long they'd stay.

He was just glad Amanda had finally appeared to decide to continue the journey with him.

6

December 7

SEEING THE NUMBER ON HER caller ID as it rang very late one weeknight, Amanda almost didn't answer the phone. Not because she didn't want to talk to Reese, but because she *did* want to...a little too much.

They hadn't spoken since they'd parted at the airport the Sunday after Thanksgiving. Yes, they'd exchanged a few e-mails, but neither of them had pushed it, both realizing things had changed during their walk on the beach.

Amanda hadn't yet decided how she felt about that change. Going from a holiday fling to a long-distance relationship was such a big step. An enormous one, at least for her. So the cooling-off period had seemed like a very good idea. Mentally, she'd been hoping her common sense would slowly edge out her libido and she'd somehow find the strength to tell him she had changed her mind and it was over.

Not seeing him again was the best course of action. They hadn't gone too far yet. At this point, he couldn't decide to hate her and blame her for leading him on.

Couldn't accuse her of taking his heart and crushing it beneath the heel of her boots when she left.

Logically, she knew all that. But as the days had dragged on, she'd begun to realize how much she missed him. She missed *everything* about him. She wanted to hear the laughter in his voice, and the sexy way he said her name. She missed the whispers about how much he wanted her when they made love. She even found herself missing the way he kept trying to get her to talk about her past, her family and her lousy romantic track record.

She missed his touch.

Third ring. Fourth. She swallowed hard, twisting in her bed, the covers tangling around her legs. Her muscles flexed, the blood rushing a just bit harder through her veins. Her senses perked up, the scratch of the sheets on her bare skin, the image of his face, the thought of his hands and his mouth.

She hadn't reached for her little sex toy in a few weeks, and if she answered the phone, she had the feeling she would need it. Hearing his voice, wanting him but not having him, would take the low, edgy need throbbing deep inside her and push it up like lava rising in a volcano.

Of course, not answering would still leave her needing it. So she might as well enjoy it. "Hello?"

"Do you realize that today is National Cotton Candy Day?"

She chuckled, wondering how the man could amuse her when she was suddenly so damned horny. "Funny, I had figured you were calling because it's Pearl Harbor Day." She had half thought about it herself, sticking to their holiday theme.

"That's too somber," he said. "Cotton candy's a lot more cheerful. It's very pink."

"I'm not a pink kinda girl."

He didn't even pause. "It can also be blue."

"An expert at cotton candy, are you?"

"Let's just say I'd like to become better acquainted with it. Especially with what I'm picturing right now."

She settled deeper into the pillow, the phone nestled in the crook of her neck. "What are you picturing?"

"You. Wearing nothing but a lot of fluffy cotton candy."

Laughing softly, she said, "Sounds sticky."

"Sounds delicious."

"You really think you could eat that much?"

"I could dine on you for days, Amanda Bauer."

Okay, definitely gonna need the vibrator tonight. Sighing in utter pleasure at the sound of his need for her, she kicked the covers totally off. She bent one knee, letting her legs fall apart, barely noticing the cold night air. The heat of his whispers warmed her enough.

"Where are you?" he asked, his voice thick, as if he'd suddenly realized she was no longer thinking light and flirty thoughts, but deep and sultry ones.

"I'm in my great big bed, all by my lonesome."

"Mmm. And what are you wearing."

"Not a blessed thing."

"Hold it…ahh, now you are. I see you. All wrapped in blue fluff just waiting for me to eat it off you."

Amanda licked her lips, then slid her hand across her stomach, tracing her fingertips along the bottom curves of her breasts. "Where are you?" she asked.

"In bed. Of course, I don't have as much privacy. I'm not alone like you are."

She stiffened, though realistically she knew he wouldn't be calling if he had a woman with him. Especially because he knew if he did, she'd fly to Pittsburgh and punch him.

"Get down, Ralph."

Hearing a low woof in the background, she realized who he was talking about. "Ahh. Your dog."

"Out you go, buddy," he said. She heard the click of a door as the dog apparently got sent out of the bedroom for the night. Then Reese admitted, "He's not as cuddly as you are."

Cuddly? Her? Ha. "I'm as cuddly as a porcupine."

His soft laugh told her he didn't believe her instinctive protestation. "You're very nice to hold, Manda. I can't decide which I like better—holding you in my arms while you sleep, or just watching you."

"You watch me sleep? Why?"

"You're soft when you're asleep," he explained simply.

Soft. He didn't mean her skin, or her hair. She knew what he meant, that he had seen her with her guard down, emotionally vulnerable, no barriers. And he sounded happy about it.

Her heart twisted a little. Then she kicked her legs restlessly. "Get back to the cotton candy," she ordered, preferring sexy talk to the gentle, tender stuff. It was safer. Less risky.

"God, you're so predictable."

Gasping, she snapped, "I am not!"

"Yeah, babe, you are. You wanted to reach for your sex toy and let me whisper you through an orgasm and I went and got sappy on you."

Okay. So she was predictable. She didn't reply at first,

nibbling her lip, finally asking, "Does that mean no phone sex?"

"Are you kidding? Hell yeah to the phone sex." His voice lowered, all amusement fading from it as he admitted, "I'm lying here with my rock-hard cock in my hand, just thinking about all the places in your body I want to fill with it."

"Oh, my," she whispered, a few of those places reacting instinctively. Her mouth went dry, her sex very wet. She moved her hand in a long, slow slide down her bare stomach until she reached her hip. "Tell me more."

He did, speaking in a hoarse whisper. "I want to take you in every way a man can take a woman."

She closed her eyes, the very word *take* making her quiver. Amanda was not one to give up control. But oh, how she had enjoyed it that Friday night in Daytona. Giving herself over to him, knowing he wouldn't hurt her and only wanted to give her pleasure had been one of the most exciting sexual experiences of her life.

"But first we'd have to get rid of all that cotton candy."

"You want to take a shower together?" she teased.

"Not right away. No, first I want to lie on my back and pull you up on top of me."

Her pulse pounded, her breath became shallow.

"I want you sitting on my chest, your legs open for me so I can lick all that sugar off the insides of your creamy thighs."

Amanda's legs clenched reflexively. She moved her hands to the curls between them, sliding her fingertip over her clit, hissing at how hard and sensitive it was. Every word he uttered was an invisible caress, the mental picture he created almost drugging in its sensual intensity.

"It'll be soft and fluffy at first. So sweet. But the closer I get to you, the more pure sugar I'll find. Because you'll be so hot and wet it will already have melted."

"Oh, Reese." She arched on the bed, stroking her clit harder, then sliding her finger between the lips of her sex. *Hot and wet* most definitely described what she felt.

"Do you know how much I love having my tongue on you…in you?" he asked. "How good you taste to me?"

She reached for the sex toy in the drawer beside the bed. Now, more than ever, she wished she had a big, thick rubber one rather than just the thin plastic vibrator. She wanted to be filled. *Taken.*

"Manda?"

"I'm here," she whispered as she flipped the switch and moved the device right where she most needed it. Then she clarified, "Actually, I'm not here…I'm almost *there.*" Hearing his deep breaths, she knew she wasn't alone. "Tell me what happens next. After you've licked away every bit of sweetness."

"You tell me," he countered.

"Easy. I'll slide down your body. Slowly. Tormenting you."

"No fair. I didn't torment you."

He was tormenting her now. Giving her fantasy when she wanted reality. But fantasy would have to do, at least for now.

"But I wouldn't be able to hold out," she conceded. "I'd be so desperate to have you inside me, the second I felt the tip of your cock against me, I'd slide down onto it, welcoming you in one deep thrust."

He groaned. Hearing that deep, primal sound of pleasure, recognizing it from all the times Reese had come inside her, Amanda pressed the vibrator a little harder. The waves of her climax rolled up. Higher. Faster. She couldn't speak anymore, couldn't listen, couldn't even think. She could only feel as the pleasure exploded in a hot rush, filling her body.

But it was short-lived. Very short. Not nearly the kind of satisfaction she got in Reese Campbell's arms.

Silent and spent, gasping on the bed with the phone still beside her ear, she had to admit it, if only to herself. She'd become addicted to him.

And she knew, without a doubt, she'd do just about anything to be with him again. For as long as she could have him.

Christmas

SOME YEARS, THE CELEBRATION of Hanukkah coincided with Christmas. Fortunately, however, this year was not one of them.

Which meant two real holiday getaways in December.

They'd spent the first one in a room in a New York City hotel. Reese had met Amanda there, not sure what she had up her sleeve for them. The venue had been far different from the place in Florida where they'd spent Thanksgiving weekend.

Not that he'd complained. Just wanting to be with her again, he really hadn't cared where they went. That desire had grown exponentially after their Cotton Candy

Day phone sex, and he probably would have agreed to meet her in the middle of a war zone if that was the only way he could get her.

So, yeah, anyplace would do, as long as it had a bed and was far away from the real world where nobody knew them. A place where Amanda could relax and forget she wasn't the settling-down type, that she didn't want a relationship, was just fine with him.

Especially since, whether she liked it or not—whether she would admit it or not—they *had* a relationship.

Far from a beachfront dive, the Manhattan high-rise had been all about luxury and indulgence. He'd understood her reason for choosing it when she'd finally revealed herself…and the game. Reese had nearly had a heart attack when she'd snuck out of the closet in their room, dressed all in black from head to toe. She was playing the part of a cat burglar who'd just been caught in the act.

He'd really liked the way she'd taken possession of his most valuable jewels.

He'd liked it just as much that she hadn't resisted when he'd whisked her out of the hotel for dinner at an upscale restaurant. And that she'd given him a loud, smacking kiss when he'd presented her not with tickets to a Broadway show but with ones to a hard-rock concert at the Garden.

During the trip, she'd been relaxed—sexy as always, but not so guarded. She'd laughed easily, talked more. It was as if she'd done some thinking after their walk on the beach, and had decided to just go with this for as long as it lasted.

His Easter eggs were looking brighter already.

The thought of it made him smile. Especially since he was going to be seeing her again so soon.

"I still can't believe you're taking off for Las Vegas on Christmas. That's so mean!"

Ignoring the disgruntled tone of his teenage sister, Molly, he forced his thoughts off tomorrow's trip—technically, the day *after* Christmas—and turned them back to the matter at hand: the board game which was set up on the kitchen table. Playing games after Christmas dinner had been a Campbell family tradition since he was a kid.

That his father had been the game fanatic made the ritual one everyone seemed to want to keep alive. Including Reese, even though, on any other day of the year, he'd rather eat moldy fruitcake than play Risk.

Then again, it could be worse. There had been those Pretty, Pretty Princess marathons all those years ago when his sisters were young and got their way most of the time.

Hmm. Not that much had changed. Even though he wasn't the pushover his dad had been when it came to the Campbell girls, they still managed to get what they wanted for the most part.

Like now.

"Wahoo! I just took over Australia! You keep thinking about the chick you're hooking up with in Vegas, big brother, and I'll keep taking your countries."

Reese frowned at his sister Debra, nine years his junior and halfway through her second year of college. She smirked, lifting a challenging brow, daring him to deny what she'd said.

"What?" Molly asked, her eyes widening. "You're meeting someone? Who?" The sixteen-year-old, who hadn't yet figured out that the world didn't revolve entirely around her, pouted as she added, "Is that why you won't take us, even though you *know* how much I'm dying to go to Vegas? Because you want to hook up with some girl? Talk about shitty."

"Watch your mouth," he said, the reply automatic. Funny, considering when he was sixteen, his bad language had prompted their mother to squirt a bottle of dish detergent all over his dinner one night. But he figured it's what Dad would have said.

"Why would *you* want to go, anyway? All you'd do is shop for clothes and text with your friends, just like you do here."

That was the longest sentence Reese had heard out of his kid brother Jack's mouth all day. The fourteen-year-old had eased up on his I-hate-everyone-because-I'm-a-teenager schtick a little bit today, and for him, the remark was downright chatty. He even went on to add, "Who's the girl, Reese?"

As pleased as he was that his sullen brother, who'd been only twelve when their father had died, was actually interested in having a conversation, that was one talk he didn't want to have. "Ignore her. She's trying to distract you so she can take over Southeast Asia."

"Is she hot?"

Incendiary. "Are we playing or are we talking?" He glanced at his watch. "Because it's almost eight and I'm outta here at nine whether I control the entire world or not."

Jack wasn't put off. Neither were his sisters. Like three dogs sniffing after a bone, they stayed on the subject. He was just lucky his other two sisters—Tess, a hard-assed, divorced man-hater right now, and Bonnie, the bleeding heart who wanted to save the world—were in the other room watching Tess's kids play with their new toys.

"Is your new girlfriend the reason you went away for Thanksgiving weekend?" asked Molly, that whine in her voice making his eye twitch.

"Friend," he clarified.

Molly rolled her eyes. "Does she live far away?"

"Chicago," Debra said.

Reese gaped. "How the hell do you know that?"

"Aunt Jean told me," she said with a broad, self-satisfied grin. Debra had outgrown any teenage whininess and now just loved playing her role of family shit-stirrer.

Reese didn't ask how Aunt Jean knew. The old woman had spies watching her spies. Besides, if he wanted to know, he could ask her himself. She should be here soon; they would be the last stop on her around-Pennsylvania visits to all her nieces, nephews and distant family members.

But he didn't want to know. In fact, he didn't want to see her at all, knowing she'd take one look at him and crow with triumph. Obviously, if she was telling his kid sister about his trips to meet Amanda, she knew damn well he'd taken her advice—well, her order—to go out and live a little.

Nobody said "I told you so" like an old woman who really *had* told you so. With any luck, he'd be gone before she got here to say it.

"Why hasn't this 'friend' come to meet us?" asked Molly.

"Maybe because you'd scare her into the next state."

"Oh, a real Miss Priss, huh?" the sixteen-year-old said with a tsk. "No balls?"

Jack grunted. "I sure hope not. If Reese switches sides and starts tea-bagging, I'm giving up on this family for good."

His jaw hanging open, he stared at his kid brother. "If I start *what?*"

"You know, it's when you…"

Reese threw a hand up, palm out. "Enough. I know what it is." Glancing at his sisters, who made faces ranging from ewwwy to grossed-out, he saw they knew what it was, too.

Jesus, how had his father ever stood it? Teenagers were a damned nightmare.

"What's her name?" Molly asked.

"None of your business."

"None of Your Business Campbell. Has a nice ring to it," said Debra, her pretty eyes dancing with laughter. She was the mischief-maker of the bunch, playing that middle-child role like she'd invented it. "You can name your kids Go Away and Bite Me."

"Go away," he mumbled, closing his eyes and rubbing at them with his fingers.

"Bite me," she said sweetly.

"That's not very polite, young lady."

His eyes flying open, he looked up to see his great-aunt Jean standing in the doorway. Surveying the scene, she looked matriarchal, though her lips twitched with amusement. He suspected she'd been there for a while.

His sisters both rose from the table to greet their aunt who, though an eccentric one, was also everybody's favorite. He suspected that was partly due to the fact that she always came loaded for bear with presents.

"Help me unload my car, will you? I brought a few goodies."

The girls raced toward the door so fast the Risk board almost went flying. Which would have been fine with him.

"Gonna help them, bro?" Reese asked Jack, who had slouched down in his seat, not wanting to appear eager or excited about anything. Around the immediate family, he'd lowered his defenses for a little while today. Aunt Jean's arrival had put that guarded look back in his eyes.

Reese's heart twisted. The kid had once been a happy-go-lucky, smiling Little Leaguer. But not anymore. Four-teen was bad enough. With the weight Jack had been carrying around for two years, it was a lot worse.

The boy shrugged. "Whatever."

As his brother got up and walked by, Reese couldn't help offering a small, encouraging nod, and a slight squeeze of his bony shoulder. *Be a kid. Just for tonight, even. Tomorrow's soon enough to go back to being mad at the world.*

Jack didn't smile in return. But his spine might have straightened a little and his trudging footsteps picked up. It was something, anyway.

"He'll be all right," Aunt Jean murmured, her eyes softer than usual as they watched Jack walk out the back door.

Reese sincerely hoped so.

"Now, let's talk about *you*."

He had known that was coming. "I hear you already have been. Thanks a lot. I really love getting the third degree from my sisters."

"And a merry Christmas to you, too."

Curiosity won out over embarrassment. "So how'd you know?"

She merely shrugged, guarding that mysterious, all-knowing, all-seeing reputation. Then, glancing at her diamond watch, she shook her head. "Hadn't you better be heading home for the night? It's a long trip to Las Vegas." She shrugged. "I'm afraid I don't have very much for you in the car, because I think I've already given you a big enough gift this year."

Well, he supposed her urging him to go out and have an adventure for himself did count as a gift. Because, whether he wanted to admit it or not, the past few months had been the best he'd had in a long, *long* time.

Reese's mouth widened in a smile and he crossed the room to kiss her powdery, paper-thin cheek. "Thank you, Aunt Jean."

"You're welcome. Now, go. Have fun. Be wild." She waved a hand, gesturing around the kitchen. "This domestic bliss will all be here waiting for you when you get back."

Whether that was a promise, or a threat, he didn't know. Nor did he really want to think about it. Because he already had other things on his mind.

He had the rest of a holiday to celebrate. And a woman he was crazy about to share it with.

AMANDA WASN'T MUCH of a Christmas person. Her parents had not believed in spoiling her or her sister, so the season had never really entailed presents or parties. The holidays comprised a lot of volunteer work, the requisite Bing Crosby songs, quiet dinners and church. Some years, they hadn't even gotten a tree, her frugal father finding the expense excessive.

The Christmases she'd spent with Uncle Frank had been completely different. Big parties, lots of drinking, dancing, jetting off to some hot spot for New Year's. There had definitely been no popcorn stringing or chestnuts roasting.

The closest she ever came to a normal American family holiday were the years she'd stayed in Chicago and had gone to Jazz's parents' house. But she'd always felt a bit like an outsider. She didn't quite get the lingo, had never felt completely comfortable receiving socks and bras from Jazz's mom, who treated her just like one of her own.

Christmas, she had long ago decided, just wasn't her thing.

So when Reese Campbell walked into their hotel room with a suitcase full of presents for her, she didn't know what to think. "Oh, God, are you kidding? I only got you one small gift!"

A small, sexy gift. A small, sexy, *funny* gift.

But she didn't think the men's velvet boxers with the Rudolph head—complete with blinking red nose—was quite equal to the ten or so packages he pulled out and tossed onto the big bed.

"I'm so bad at this," she groaned, not elaborating. He knew what she meant: this whole *girlfriend* thing. No, they weren't using the word, but it was about the only one she could come up with. And as girlfriends went, she totally sucked the big one.

Metaphorically speaking. Well, literally speaking, too, but thinking about that wasn't going to help right at this particular moment.

"I don't care. Christmas isn't about getting, it's about giving."

"You're giving me a guilty conscience," she wailed, staring at the brightly wrapped boxes.

Funny, a few months ago, her first instinct would probably have been to give in to the tightness squeezing her chest, turn and walk out the door. She'd always wanted to visit London during the winter. Prague sounded good. Amsterdam.

No. You're not doing that. Not this time. Not to him.

She'd come here this weekend knowing full well what it meant. After their conversation in Florida, she knew the terms had changed yet again. Their New York trip had been fun, but Christmas and a whole week in Vegas together added up to something more. And while she'd managed to convince herself nothing would be really different, that this was just another sexy holiday getaway, deep down she'd known Reese might treat it as a genuine one between two people who were involved.

And she'd shown up with damned fuzzy Rudolph boxer shorts.

Tart, sour and heartless. That was her.

"Don't even think about it," he warned, obviously seeing something in her eye.

She didn't need his warning. Because even without it, she'd already kept her feet planted on the floor.

The pressure in her chest gradually eased until she could breathe normally again. Then, instead of frowning and accusing him of taking things too seriously, getting her gifts like they were some kind of real couple, she couldn't help but smile.

"You're serious? All these are for me?"

"Well," he admitted as he threw himself down on the bed, "some of them are for me, too." He wagged his brows suggestively as he rolled onto his side, resting on his bent elbow. "I think a fashion show is in order."

She bit the inside of her cheek to keep from laughing. "Okay, but only if you promise to do one, too, with what I got you."

"You're on."

Oh, boy, was he going to regret that one. But Amanda could hardly wait.

Well, giving it some thought, she realized she could wait. There was a way to salvage this situation. "Listen, let's hold off on the presents until tomorrow, okay? Give me a little time to at least come up with an ugly tie, a bowling ball or a bottle of Hai Karate for you to open."

He snorted a laugh. "You just described every one of my father's Christmas mornings. But, bad news. I don't bowl."

"Okay. Maybe I can come up with something else."

He sat up, reaching for her hand and tugging her forward until she stood between his legs. "You really don't have to."

"I know." She wanted to. Suddenly, the idea of giving her lover a real Christmas gift sounded like exactly the right thing to do.

There was something else she wanted to do, as well. Something that had been on her mind for days, ever since she'd realized they were going to sin city. She had a fantasy in mind, one she suspected he was going to enjoy sharing.

"You do realize today is a holiday, too. It's Boxing Day."

"I'm not into boxing, either," he said, his eyes twinkling.

"It's a big deal in some countries." She shimmied out from between his strong legs. "What I'm trying to say is, I would very much like to *play* with you on this holiday."

He nodded slowly, the twinkle turning into a gleam of interest. Hunger.

"So here's what I want you to do." She dug a piece of paper out of her pants pocket and shoved it toward him. "Go to this address and wait for me. I'll be there in an hour."

He glanced at it. "Is it a restaurant or something?"

She shook her head. "No. Just wait outside."

Still appearing puzzled, he rose to his feet. But he didn't leave immediately, pausing to cup her chin and tug her toward him for a soft, slow kiss goodbye.

She almost relented, giving up on the fantasy for some good, old-fashioned, lovely sex. But she'd been thinking about this for a long time. After showing up without any presents for him, the least she could do was try to give him the kind of fantasy he would never forget.

And just about every man in the world had one fantasy when it came to Vegas. Reese's was going to come true.

Pushing him toward the door, she said, "Go. One hour."

He lifted his hand in mock salute. "I can hardly wait."

The minute he was gone, Amanda raced to her suitcase and began yanking clothes from it. She'd done a little more eBay shopping, looking for another costume. Not a stewardess this time, she was going for someone quite different.

She intended to transform herself completely. And

fifteen minutes later, when she looked at her reflection in the mirror, she knew she had succeeded.

"Hot damn," she whispered, smiling as she checked herself out from bottom to top.

The boots were even more kick-ass than her Halloween ones. Black leather, spiked, coming all the way up over her knee. They were wicked and screamed sex.

Above them was a large expanse of fishnet-covered thighs. And finally a few inches of hot pink miniskirt that barely covered her ass. It was made out of something that felt like cellophane and crinkled when she walked.

The teensy, tie-front white top covered her shoulders and her breasts and not much else. And the short, platinum-blond wig completed her transformation from Amanda Bauer, professional pilot, to Mandy the hooker.

After all, what guy hadn't fantasized about being picked up by a sexy call girl in Vegas?

"Whatever the customer wants, that's what he's going to get," she whispered, smiling as she headed for the door to the room. She paused only to grab her long coat off the back of a chair. Not only because it was chilly out, but also because there was no way she wanted any hotel employees to see her entire costume. The place was five star all the way, and the *Pretty Woman* look probably wouldn't be welcome in the lobby.

"Okay, sweet man, get ready, because here I come," she said under her breath as she descended in the elevator. Every minute ensured her certainty of one thing.

Reese Campbell had no idea what kind of night he was in for.

$$7$$

Boxing Day

SHOWGIRL OR STRIPPER? Paid escort? Call girl?

Reese wasn't sure which Amanda was going to show up tonight. He only knew that whichever woman met him here on this slightly seedy corner, one block off the northernmost end of the Strip, she was going to blow his mind. Just like she always did.

"Come on, it's been over an hour," he muttered, glancing at his watch as he leaned against a light post. She'd better show up soon, or one of the real working girls might decide he was looking for some company.

She'd been adorable when pushing him out of the room back at the hotel. Had she really thought he didn't know, that he couldn't figure out what kinds of games she'd want to play in Las Vegas? Seriously, what could be more obvious?

Still, maybe it wasn't as clear to her as it was to him that he knew her so well. Better than he'd ever imagined when they first met. Better than she'd ever wanted him to, that was for sure.

He was even beginning to understand why. Despite

those careful walls she'd kept around herself in the beginning, during their last couple of get-togethers, she had started to reveal bits and pieces of herself.

She'd talked a little about her family back home, hinting at a lack of connection that saddened him on her behalf. His own family might drive him crazy, but he'd been raised in a house filled to the brim with love.

He suspected Amanda had never been assured of that emotion from her parents.

She'd also asked about his upbringing, and in her slightly wistful tone, he'd heard much more than she was willing to say out loud. He'd known, somehow, that despite how much she claimed not to need anyone, a part of her might actually wonder what such connections might be like.

One thing she hadn't talked any more about was her past love life. But, hell, she didn't need to. He knew she'd had a few rocky relationships. He also knew they'd ended badly, and that she still kicked herself about it.

She was human, wasn't she? Human and only in her late twenties. Who the hell didn't do dumb things in their twenties, things they regretted for a long time after? Amanda simply hadn't realized yet that she wasn't much different from anybody else. Including him.

"Hey stranger, you lookin' for some company?"

Call girl.

Excitement washed over him as he turned to stare at the woman who'd spoken from a few feet away. She stood just outside a puddle of illumination cast by the streetlight, and he couldn't see her well. But he'd know her anywhere. That voice, that scent. The very air seemed filled with static electricity, snapping with the excitement that always surrounded her. He reacted to it on a visceral level, as he had since the moment they'd met.

"Maybe," he admitted. "Are you offering to keep me company?"

"I might be willing to do that. If you offer me enough…incentive."

She sauntered closer, into the light, and Reese had to suck in a surprised breath. Good thing he'd had that moment of instant recognition, all his other senses confirming her identity. Because for a brief second, when he saw her, he feared he'd been mistaken. At first glance, she looked like a completely different woman. An incredibly sexy woman. A woman he wanted with every cell in his body.

"Wow," he muttered.

Her wig was short, blond, curling just past her chin. The style emphasized the heavy makeup she wore. Amanda's face was already lovely, but with the added coloring—the thick mascara, the ruby-red lips—she looked exotic and oozed sex appeal.

The clothes, however, took the sex appeal from oozing to gushing.

Her long, black overcoat clung to the very edges of her shoulders. Completely unbuttoned, it gaped open to reveal the skimpy outfit beneath. What little of it there was.

Her white top was not only incredibly tiny, plunging low to tie beneath her breasts, it was also thin, nearly sheer. Even in the low light, he could make out the dark, puckered nipples and hunger flooded his mouth. It had been too long since he'd tasted her, touched her. He should have insisted on at least a few minutes back at the hotel to satisfy the raging need he'd been feeling ever since they'd parted ways in New York.

Her midriff was entirely bare, down all the way past her stomach. The skirt, which didn't even reach her belly button, merely pretended to clothe her hips, and was so tight he could see the line where her thighs came together underneath. And oh, those fishnet-clad thighs beckoned him, tempting him to taste the tiny squares of supple skin revealed between the black, stretchy bits of fabric.

The boots were, without a doubt, his favorite part of the whole thing. And he already knew he was going to rip those hose off her body so she could leave the boots on to wrap around him as he pounded into her.

"So, whaddya say, mister?"

"To what?"

"To a date?"

"A...date? With you?" he asked, pretending reticence he in no way felt.

"No," she said with a definite eye roll. "With that light post holding you up."

He still didn't move.

"Come on, admit it. Haven't you fantasized about spending a night with a girl like me?"

He couldn't answer that. Not truthfully. Because if he answered in the game, as if she were really a call girl, he'd have to say no. He'd never even thought about being with a prostitute.

If he answered as himself, the real Reese Campbell talking to the real Amanda Bauer, then the response was unequivocally yes. He wanted to go out with *her,* be a half of a couple with her—Amanda—almost as much as he wanted to take her back to the hotel and do her until she screamed with pleasure.

"I promise you, I'll let you do things to me that your nice little wife or girlfriend back home has never even heard of."

Interesting. The corner of his mouth lifted in a half smile. "I think I might need to hear more about these things before I make a decision."

She moved closer, her gait slinky, the sway of her hips exaggerated. When she reached his side, she lifted her hand to his chest. "Let's just say you can do anything you want to me. Absolutely *anything*. And I'd let you."

He shook his head, feigning confusion. "I'm still not sure I know what you mean."

She lifted her chin and her eyes narrowed as she heard the challenge in his voice. Then, with a smile of pure wickedness, she leaned up on her toes, coming close enough for her beautiful lips to graze his cheek. With a nip on his earlobe, she told him one *very* naughty thing she wanted him to do to her.

Damn. Heat and excitement flared and he slid his hands into her coat, cupping her waist. Without a word, he turned her around, so her back was to the light pole, then bent down and kissed her. Licking his way into her mouth, he met her tongue with his and thrust lazily. Their bodies melded and he heard her tiny groan when she felt how hard he already was for her. She pressed against him, grinding her groin against his erection, wrapping one long leg around his to cup him more intimately between her thighs.

They were on a public street and it was only ten o'clock at night. Fortunately, though, the cool weather had people staying inside the closest casino gambling, not outside cruising the block. So as far as he could tell, they didn't have an audience.

That was good. Because he couldn't stop. No *way* would he stop. Not when her lips were so sweet and her body so willing. Not when she'd whispered such wanton, erotic desires in his ear, promising their fulfillment with her dreamy-eyed stare.

When he finally ended the kiss, lifted his head and looked down at her, he saw the dazed look of pure want on her face. Her lids half covered her green eyes and most of her lipstick had been kissed off. She looked sensual and awakened, ready for sin and sex and more of everything they'd ever done together. And some things they hadn't.

He had to have her. *Had* to.

"Let's get out of here," he muttered, already stepping toward the curb to flag down a taxi.

"Absolutely," she whispered, her voice shaking.

Traffic wasn't heavy, and not a cab was in sight. Figured. When he saw one crossing the next block, Reese stepped off the curb onto the street, whistling loudly. But before he could see whether the cabbie had heard him and made a last-minute turn, he was startled by a shout that split the night air.

"Stop, thief!"

Reese froze, jerking his head to stare in the direction of the voice. The cry had sounded like it was coming from the closest building, which had a sign identifying it as a pawn shop.

He was a split second slow in reacting. If he'd been thinking more clearly, he would have immediately jumped back up onto the sidewalk, grabbed Amanda and shoved her safely behind him. In his surprise, though, he hadn't done it.

So she was right in the path of the black-cloaked figure that came hurtling out from behind the building.

"Manda!" he cried, seeing the shape emerge from the darkness.

Before she had time to react, the running man barreled into her. They stumbled around together for a second, their legs and coats tangling.

"You son of a bitch." Reese dove toward them, knocking the man off her, but falling, himself, in the process. "You're dead," he snarled.

The thief, obviously realizing there was only one thing that would stop Reese from chasing him down and beating him to a pulp, whirled around toward Amanda and shoved. Hard.

The blow sent her careening toward the street. Those high-heeled boots wobbled, making it impossible for her to catch her balance. Right before she fell off the curb into the path of the cab, which had indeed turned and was rapidly cruising up the block, Reese lunged to his feet and grabbed her around the waist, hauling her back to safety.

"My God, are you okay?"

She nodded, though her whole body was shaking, especially as a taxi screeched to a stop right where she would have landed in the street.

"That rotten bastard," Reese snapped, his feet nearly in motion to go after the man in black. The thief had just darted down the next alleyway, heading across a debris-laden, abandoned construction site that separated this road from the north strip.

"No, Reese," she insisted, holding on to his arm. "I'm

fine, really. And you are *not* going to go chasing after some robber. You could get hurt."

"He was a scrawny runt."

"Who might be armed. You're staying right here."

Before he could reply, a heavyset, balding man with flaming red cheeks jogged up to them. "Did you see him? Did you get a good look? Rotten thief robbed my shop!"

"I saw him," Amanda replied, sounding weary.

The shop owner peered at her, narrowed his eyes and sighed heavily. "Oh, that's just *great*."

The man's sneer toward Amanda, whom he obviously took for a real lady of the evening, tempted Reese to let the guy deal with his own problems. But his rage toward the thug who'd so callously tossed her into the street was greater. So he admitted, "I saw him, too. Now why don't you go call the police so we can give them a description." He tightened his arm around Amanda's shoulders. "And hurry. We've got things to do tonight."

OF ALL THE WAYS she'd envisioned spending their first night in Vegas, standing in a dingy pawn shop, talking to two officers from the LVPD, hadn't been in the top thousand. Especially because said cops had spent the first ten minutes of their interview trying to figure out whether they needed to arrest her for prostitution and Reese for solicitation.

Talk about a convincing costume. She and Reese had finally had to come clean about what they were up to, showing their credentials, including Amanda's pilot's license. Ever since, the younger police officer had been trying to hide a smile and was casting quick, sneaky glances at Amanda whenever he thought he could get away with it. The older one hadn't even tried to hide his amusement. She'd swear she heard him mumbling something about how much he wished his wife would wear thigh-high boots.

That so didn't help.

"Okay then, miss, sir, I think I've got everything I need," said the older officer, who'd introduced himself as Parker. Standing in the well-lit entranceway of the shop, they'd just finished answering all his questions. "You did a good job remembering details about this guy."

Amanda didn't think she would soon forget the pale, pockmarked face of the man who'd so readily shoved her toward what could have been her death. His glazed brown eyes and long, greasy blond hair weren't going to leave her mind anytime soon, either.

"The owner of the shop says the thief got away with some valuable diamond jewelry," Parker added. He snapped his notebook closed and tucked it into his uniform pocket.

Reese glanced around the small, nondescript shop, which was a little dusty and unimpressive. "Really?" he asked, sounding doubtful. "It doesn't look exactly top shelf."

"You'd be surprised," offered the younger officer, whom the older one kept calling Rookie. His voice low, he looked around for the owner, who'd disappeared into the back to do yet another check on his inventory. "A lotta these places are mob-owned, legit businesses where money goes to get nice and clean."

"Would you shut yer yap?" said Parker. With a glare, he explained, "We're really not in the habit of making unfounded comments about members of our local business community."

The younger guy snapped his mouth shut and didn't say another word.

"If we're finished, are we free to go?" Reese asked.

"Sure thing." Smiling, Parker tipped his hat at Amanda. "Hope you two enjoy the rest of your visit to our fair city. And might I suggest that next time you, uh, confine your field trips to the lobby of your own hotel?"

Though she'd been embarrassed at first, now all Amanda could do was chuckle. Parker seemed like a nice guy, and, really, it was either laugh or cry. Laughing seemed the much better option.

"You bet," she said. Winking, she added, "And if you get your wife a pair of these boots, be sure to get one size larger than she usually wears. They're pretty painful."

He threw his head back and guffawed. "If I came home with a pair of those things for her, she'd use them to kick my ass."

With a polite nod, Reese led Amanda out of the shop by the arm. She was still chuckling as they emerged outside, knowing she was going to have to share this whole story with Jazz. Her friend would love it.

So would Uncle Frank, if she was ever able to get over the whole embarrassment factor and tell him, too. But it was the kind of situation that would horrify her parents, and reinforce their firm belief that she was a reckless wanton who cared nothing for her own reputation. Or theirs.

Caught up in thought, she didn't notice that a small crowd had gathered outside the pawn shop. About a dozen people milled around on the sidewalk, likely drawn by the flash of the police lights and the whispers of a robbery in the neighborhood.

"Hey, what happened?" somebody asked.

"You'll have to let the police fill you in," Reese said, sliding a hand around her waist as he tried to lead her through the crowd.

It was only when she felt the warmth of his fingers against her very bare skin that she realized she hadn't re-buttoned her coat, which she'd unfastened in the heat of the store. Gaping open, it revealed her costume in all its glory to the wide-eyed strangers. She reached for the edges of it, intending to yank it closed. But before she could, a male voice called, "Hey, sweet thing, how late you working tonight?"

Another one added, "Got a business card?"

Though she knew she should be absolutely mortified, and maybe even a little nervous, more laughter bubbled up inside her. The size of the crowd, the presence of a few normally dressed women and tourists, and the two police officers right inside the closest building eased her hint of fear.

And the embarrassment? Hell, she was so far past that, she couldn't even remember what it felt like.

Beside her, Reese made a small sound. Worried, she glanced over and saw his lips twitch. Relief flowed through her. His anger and concern had finally eased up and he was beginning to see the humor in the situation, too.

"Sorry, guys, she's retired," he said, tugging her closer to his side.

"Since when?"

Following his lead, she sidled closer to Reese. Glued to his side from ankle to hip, she slipped her arm around his waist, too. Dropping her head onto his shoulder and simpering a little, she pointed toward a small white building across the street. "Since I roped myself a man tonight at that wedding chapel over there. Jeez, what's a girl gotta do to enjoy her wedding night?"

The two potential clients groaned, but the others surrounding them started to laugh and call out congratulations. They were probably going to go back home and tell their friends and family they'd stumbled into a real-life version of *Pretty Woman*.

Reese, wicked amusement dancing in his eyes, took full advantage, playing to the crowd. Without warning, he tugged her closer, turning her so their faces were inches apart, then he caught her mouth in a deep, intimate kiss.

She forgot about everything for a full minute. The robbery, the thug, the cops, the onlookers. When Reese kissed her like this, all hot and wet, with delicious strokes of his tongue, everything else just ceased to exist.

When they finally ended the kiss, it was to the sound of applause. "Way to go, girlfriend!" someone yelled.

She didn't have to force the note of breathless excitement as she asked, "Can we please get outta here, hubby-cakes?"

"You got it, sugar-britches," Reese replied, compressing his lips, trying so hard not to laugh.

He amazed her. From sexy playmate, to hero who'd literally saved her butt, to serious witness, to passionate lover, and back to the most playful, good-humored, self-confident man she'd ever known, all in the span of an hour.

She'd known before tonight that Reese Campbell was a great guy. But as she let him lead her away, holding her protectively, lovingly, like a new husband with his bride, she had to acknowledge that he was even more than that.

He was special. Very special. The kind of man women read about in romance novels and dreamed about actually meeting.

He was, to use his favorite word, just about perfect.

Perfect for her? Well, that she wasn't ready to concede, at least not in the long term. But for right now, there was simply no place else she'd rather be…and no one else on earth she'd rather be with.

New Year's Eve

THEY SPENT THE ENTIRE holiday week in Las Vegas. And this time, after that first night when their game playing had nearly gotten them into legal trouble, they'd let all the other identities fade away. It was just Reese and Amanda, spending every minute of the day together.

They gambled, they saw a few shows, they walked the strip and shopped. They laughed over pizza dinners and shared a bucket of popcorn as they went to see a movie, which neither of them had done for so long.

And finally, eventually, they even talked.

"You're sure you don't mind leaving before midnight?" Amanda asked as they reentered their room at around eleven-thirty on New Year's Eve.

"My ears have been ringing all week from the sound of the slot machines. Add a few thousand voices screaming 'Happy New Year' and I might go deaf." Before he'd even reached back to lock the door, he drew her into his arms and kissed her cheek. "In other words, no, I most definitely do not mind sharing a quiet celebration with you."

Though he had never seen her drink much, Amanda had enjoyed a couple of glasses of champagne at the hotel's holiday party downstairs. Though not drunk, he'd have to describe her as slightly tipsy. Her eyes sparkled and her always beautiful smile flashed a little wider. Though nobody would ever call her giddy, when she kicked off her shoes and spun around the room with her arms extended straight out, she looked pretty darn close.

She also looked damn near adorable—young and carefree. Her black cocktail dress was tight to the waist, but flared on the bottom and it swirled prettily around her bare legs.

"I love New Year's," she admitted once she stopped twirling.

He never had understood the appeal of the holiday himself, having grown up hearing his father calling it amateur night: the night normally smart, rational people drank too much then drove drunk. In their line of work, they knew way too much about it. The Campbells had always stayed home on New Year's Eve.

"It doesn't sound like the kind of holiday your family would be into," he said, his tone careful, as always, when the subject of her family life came up.

Amanda laughed out loud. "Are you kidding? Hell no, they weren't into it." Her voice lowered and her brow pulled down in a deep frown. "'This holiday is just an excuse for people to use poor judgment and do things they know are immoral and indecent. No daughter of mine is going to participate in public drunkenness or lewdity.'"

The imitation had to be of her father, though, honestly, he couldn't imagine this woman having grown up with someone like that. "Not exactly Mr. Tender Loving Care?"

She snorted. "I don't think he knows the meaning of any of those words." She thought about it, then clarified. "Well, *mister* he gets very well. He has kept my mother in her place since the minute he proposed to her. But *tender, loving* and *care* just aren't part of his vocabulary. Not toward her, not toward *anyone*." She yawned widely, as if she were discussing something mundane rather than utterly heartbreaking. "And I guess living with him all these years has rubbed off. Because my mother is about as warm as a guppy, too."

He glanced away so she wouldn't see the sudden flash of sympathy—and even anger—in his face. There was no malice in her. This wasn't an adult kid blaming her poor, unknowing parents for some imaginary slights. She didn't even sound resentful. She'd simply accepted their frigidity as a fact and moved on.

How much of their coldness had she unintentionally absorbed? How deeply had it affected her own life, her choices, the face she showed to the world? Seeing her like this, hearing the truths she'd been trying to hide from him since the very beginning, he understood so much more…and he liked her all the more for it. Even though he knew she would probably resent any sympathy he tried to offer.

He forced the thoughts away, as well as the unpleasant subject of what her parents had or hadn't given her in her childhood. Not wanting her to even think about it anymore, he changed the subject. "So when did you become a New Year's convert?"

She plopped down onto the edge of the bed. "In college. My freshman boyfriend took me to my very first

New Year's Eve party and I got completely caught up in everyone else's excitement and good mood."

He hid his interest in the "boyfriend" part.

"I loved all the resolutions, the anticipation of a clean slate, a fresh start. And I suddenly saw it as a chance to reevaluate, figure out what went wrong in the past year and plan on how to make it right in the coming one."

Interesting. He had to wonder what she had evaluated and planned on this particular holiday. But he knew better than to ask. He shrugged out of his suit jacket and tossed it aside, then sat in a chair opposite the bed, eyeing her. "What did you decide that first year?"

"To dump my boyfriend."

Caught off guard, he had to chuckle. While that subject had been taboo up until now, Amanda laughed, as well. "He was a creeper," she admitted.

"A…creeper?"

"He had moist hands and he was sneaky, always touching me. That was when I was only nineteen, and still a virgin."

She'd held on to her virginity longer than most girls he knew. Considering her family background, he wasn't entirely surprised. He doubted there had been much dating or teenage partying in her household.

"So we have the creeper," he murmured, lifting his index finger to count off. "Who was next?"

Probably because she'd had a couple of drinks, Amanda didn't immediately freeze him out and change the subject. Instead, she threw herself back on the bed, her brow scrunched as she thought about it.

"I dated around when I was a sophomore. Kind of a lot." The way she nibbled her lip told him what that meant. She'd lost that pesky virginity and had gone for a walk on the wild side.

"Then I hooked up with a guy named Scott for several months. I broke up with him when I caught him copying the answers from my take-home exam for a class we had together. After that came Tommy…he drove a Porsche and I think I liked the car more than I liked him, which he eventually figured out."

"Completely understandable," he pointed out.

She ignored him. "Rick was nice, but the first time we slept together and I realized he was lousy in the sack, I stopped taking his calls."

Again, completely understandable, at least for a college-aged kid. Not that he intended to interrupt her again, not now, when she seemed to really be getting to the nitty-gritty.

She was now the one with her fingers up. Mumbling under her breath, she lifted another, then another, and then moved on to her next hand. Up came the index finger. The middle one, then a third…which she quickly put back down. "Wait, Josh doesn't really count."

"Why not?" he asked, amused by this frank, open Amanda talking about her past. Even if she was only being that way because she'd had one too many sips of champagne.

"Because I was just a beard. I found out he was in the closet on our second date, but kept going out with him just 'cause he was a nice guy. Plus he had a crush on my roommate's boyfriend, who I hated, and it made me laugh to keep him around." Sitting up quickly, she gave him a stricken look. "Oh, that was bitchy, wasn't it? I *told* you."

"Yeah, yeah, you're cast-iron, babe."

So far, from what he could tell, she'd had about the same number of boyfriends as his twenty-something-year-old sisters. The difference being, from what he had pieced together in the past, that she had always been the one to walk away.

That refrain repeated in his mind. *She always walked away.*

He should have taken that as a warning sign, proceeded with caution. But he hadn't...mostly because he wasn't at all convinced Amanda was as anti-love-and-commitment as she claimed. She'd just never been involved with the right man. Whether that was pure happenstance, or by design—since her upbringing had to have soured her on the whole idea of personal relationships—he didn't know.

"Come to think of it, I don't feel so bad," she suddenly said with a firm nod. "I didn't break his heart or anything, so he had no business joining that Facebook group." Her voice lowered. "No business at all."

"What group?"

She hesitated, the finally admitted, "The 'Dumped by Amanda Bauer' group."

He threw back his head and laughed...until he saw that she wasn't smiling. Instead, her eyes held a hint of moisture and her bottom lip quivered. The tough girl actually looked vulnerable. Hurt.

Mentally kicking himself, he got up and joined her on the bed, pulling her into his arms. She burrowed into his chest, sniffing a tiny bit, and he suddenly had the urge to hunt down the pricks who'd formed the mean little club and made her cry.

Talk about ridiculous—holding on to some bullshit college gripes and sharing them with the world years later, no matter who you wounded. It was one way in which the Internet age definitely had not improved life.

Amanda let herself relax against him for a minute or two, then she began to tense, shifting uncomfortably. He recognized the signs and knew what she was thinking: too much emotion, too much talking, too personal, too dangerous.

He released her, forcing a smile. "It's almost midnight."

She didn't smile back, her beautiful face still wearing that same sad, stricken expression. Amanda stared at him for a long moment, her green eyes revealing her every thought as her gaze traveled over his face, as if to memorize him for the not-too-distant future when she wouldn't see him anymore.

"He wasn't the last one," she admitted.

"You don't have to do this...."

She ignored him. "The last guy I dated decided if I wouldn't just *give* him my undivided attention and devotion, he'd take it from me."

He didn't like the sound of this, not one bit.

"We had a fight, I broke it off, then he called in the middle of one night saying he'd just swallowed a bottle of pills."

Oh, God. Whether she wanted it or not, he had to hold her, tightly, giving her the support and tenderness she never asked for. He kissed her hair, whispering, "It wasn't your fault...."

She immediately shook her head. "No, he didn't die or anything."

Thank God.

"Because he was lying. The whole thing had been a setup, just to play on my emotions."

"What's his name?" he snarled, ready to kill a guy he'd just been thankful hadn't died.

"It doesn't matter. It's all over, all in the past. The point is…" She hesitated, then, with a voice as shaky as her slowly indrawn breath, whispered, "Don't love me, Reese."

His heart broke a little. For the pain of her past affairs, for the heartbreaks, and for the cold family life she'd endured. They'd combined to create a beautiful, extremely lovable woman who didn't think she was capable of returning the emotion.

She was wrong. She wouldn't admit it, not now, maybe not for a long time. But he knew Amanda Bauer had feelings for him, deep ones. Just as he did for her.

Reese was no fool, however. So he said nothing, merely nodded slowly, as if agreeing to her command.

The bedside clock glowed red, catching his eye as the numbers shifted from 11:59 to 12:00. And suddenly it was a whole new year. A new future had opened up and the mistakes of the past seemed destined to be washed away, with only good things coming toward them.

"Happy New Year, Manda," he whispered, leaning close to brush his lips against hers. "I hope this upcoming year is one neither of us will ever forget."

Her soft lips parted and she kissed him back, sweetly, tenderly. In that kiss she said all the things she would not say out loud—that she wanted more, but was afraid to let herself ask for it.

She'd changed a lot in the two months he'd known her. The hard shell had started to crack, whether she liked it or not. One day, sooner or later, Amanda was going to realize she was capable of a lot more than she gave herself credit for. She was capable of loving, and of being loved.

He only hoped she let him stick around until that day came.

8

Groundhog Day

"HONEY, WHY DON'T YOU just fly to Pittsburgh and see him?"

Amanda averted her eyes, not wanting to hear another lecture from Ginny, their administrative assistant, who stared at her from across her paper-laden desk. The older woman had figured out months ago that Amanda was involved with someone. She had finally gotten her to talk about Reese after the holidays. Probably because Amanda had walked around with a constant frown on her face since she'd arrived home.

As she'd flown back to Chicago on January 2, she'd wondered if it was time to end the affair. The intimate conversation she'd shared with Reese, and the way he'd made such sweet, tender love to her afterward, had convinced her she had to at least call a time-out, if not quit the game altogether.

Damn the man for slipping past her defenses, breaching her outer walls. Somehow, he'd worked his way into her previously brittle heart. That could be the only explanation for why she'd opened up to him the way she never had to anyone else before.

She'd told him such dark, ugly things about herself, it was a wonder he hadn't run screaming into the night.

It wasn't that she minded so much that she cared for him. The problem was, caring for him meant she wanted to be with him, to keep going with this thing that had sprung up between them. And that, she greatly feared, would not be good in the long run…for Reese. Having feelings for the man meant she didn't want to see him hurt. And she especially didn't want to be the one doing the hurting.

But it was inevitable, wasn't it? Just a foregone conclusion? When the going got tough, Amanda hit the skies.

"Would you talk some sense into her?" another voice said.

Jazz had come into the office, wearing a pair of her mechanic's overalls. A smear of grease on her cheek and the sweat on her brow made her hard labor obvious, but didn't diminish her earthy beauty one bit. "I swear to God, Manda, if you don't call the dude, I'm gonna leave a wrench in your aft engine and just let you fall out of the sky and put us all out of your misery."

Amanda rolled her eyes, feeling very much ganged-up on. "I saw him on Martin Luther King day, and I talk to him every few days."

The government holiday had been a busy one, and a weekday. She hadn't been able to take time off for any out-of-town tryst. But she had arranged for a three-hour layover at the Philadelphia airport. Reese had driven all the way there…and spent those three hours doing incredible things to her in the cockpit of her plane.

She thrust away the warm, gooey feeling those memories inspired. "It's not like I've ended it."

"Uh-huh. But you're planning to," Jazz said knowingly. Ginny nodded in agreement. "Definitely."

She glared at both of them. "It was never meant to be serious. My God, we live in two different states."

"And you fly a plane for a living," Jazz retorted. "An air trip from Pittsburgh to Chicago would probably take less time than commuting in from the suburbs on the El every day."

That was crazy talk. Jazz almost made it sound like she thought Amanda could actually *move* to Pittsburgh and live with Reese. Make something permanent out of what was just a holiday fling.

Wouldn't that be nice? Her, Amanda Bauer, the heartbreak queen of Chicago living a couple of blocks away from Reese's perfect, all-American family with a house full of siblings who adored him and would absolutely hate her guts.

I don't think so.

She stood abruptly, silently telling them the conversation was over. Jazz and Ginny exchanged a frustrated look, but they didn't say anything else, knowing her well enough to know she was already mentally halfway out the door.

Glancing at the clock, she said, "It's late. Time for all of us to call it a day, right?" Forcing a laugh, she added, "Wish that stupid groundhog hadn't seen his shadow this morning. I don't know if I can stand another six weeks of winter."

Jazz muttered something under her breath. Something that sounded like ice-queen, but Amanda ignored her.

Ginny, a little less blunt, walked over and put her hand

on Amanda's shoulder, squeezing lightly. "We love you, honey. We just want you to be happy."

Love. Happy. Two words that hadn't even been in her vocabulary for the first eighteen years of her life. One of them still wasn't.

Not true. Not entirely, anyway. She did love. She loved Jazz and Ginny and her uncle Frank. She loved her sister, if in a somewhat pitying way. She supposed she even loved her parents, because for all their inattention and coldness, they were still her mother and father, after all.

How crazy was it to imagine she might widen that circle and actually let herself love a man? One man?

Maybe it bore consideration.

"I know," she finally replied, giving Ginny a brief hug. Normally not demonstrative, she knew the impulsive act had probably taken the older woman by surprise. Jazz's wide eyes said she felt the same.

"I'll see you guys tomorrow."

Grabbing her keys and her bag, she left them and walked through the quiet office wing of the airport where Clear-Blue Air was housed. As always, it took a while to make her way to the car, and even longer to drive to the city and park in the garage by her building. The entire time, she tried to pull her thoughts into order, to focus and make sense of everything that was going on and how she felt about it.

Feelings and all that stuff so weren't her thing. She just didn't know what to *do* with them.

"Hell," she muttered as she got out of her car, stepping into the frigid Chicago night. It was very dark out, and even inside the parking garage, the wind whipped wildly off the nearby lake. Its gusts made eerie whistles through the openings of the structure, making her freeze for a second before locking up and heading toward the elevator.

As she punched the button and waited for it, an unnerving sensation began on the back of her neck. She glanced side to side, then turned to look behind her. Nobody was around, not a single car moving. She'd gotten home after most commuters but before the club crowd started hitting downtown.

"Okay, cool it," she told herself, knowing she was imagining things. Still, she didn't drop her key chain into her bag, keeping it in her hand with long, sharp keys protruding between her fingers. Just in case.

The elevator arrived and she quickly scanned it to make sure it was empty before stepping inside. She remained close to the control panel, ready to jab the "open" button if somebody she didn't like the look of suddenly came out of nowhere and joined her. But nothing happened, not a sound, not a soul.

She breathed a sigh of relief, laughing at her own foolishness as the doors began to slide closed.

That's when she saw him. A man stood a few yards away, not far from her own car. Fully visible beneath an overhead light, he must have intentionally moved toward it because he had not been there a few seconds ago.

She caught a good look at his face right before her door shut, blocking the view. That glimpse was enough to capture a few quick impressions. Short, compact body clothed in black. Longish, stringy blond hair. Dark-eyed glare.

And suddenly, she remembered him.

"No way," she muttered, her hand tightening on the keys.

But she knew it was true. She'd just seen the thief, the guy who'd mown her down back in Las Vegas.

"You rotten bastard," she added, wishing the door hadn't closed before she'd identified him. Because her first impulse was to go after him and punch his lights out for shoving her into the street.

Then, of course, the wiser head that had kept Reese from doing that very same thing back in Vegas whispered wisdom in her brain. He could be armed, and he'd already proven himself dangerous.

Within seconds, the door reopened on the ground level of the garage. There was no way he could have beaten her here, not unless he'd sprouted wings and flown. He'd been far away from the stairs and the other elevator was clear on the opposite side of the deck. So she wasn't nervous as she stepped outside. Merely very curious. And worried.

"What are you doing here?" she whispered.

It couldn't possibly be a coincidence. The guy had tracked her down, come all the way to Chicago for some reason. But instead of confronting her, he'd played a sneaky game of hide-and-seek, trying to scare her.

But why?

Right outside the garage, people passed by, a nearby bar already swelling with regulars. She put her keys away, though she kept very focused, constantly looking around as she walked the few yards to her building. The doorman offered her a pleasant nod, and once she was inside, she breathed a small sigh of relief.

Not that she was truly frightened. Creeped out, that was a much better way to put it.

"Thanks, Bud," she said to the doorman as she headed toward the elevator. Before she'd reached it, however, she heard a distinct ring. Her cell phone. Grabbing it, she answered with a distracted, "Hello?"

"Is this Amanda Bauer?"

The voice was unfamiliar and throaty, as if the person were trying to disguise it. "Yes, who is this?"

"Long time, no see. You look a little different without the wig."

It was him. The guy from Vegas...the one from the garage. Tense, she stepped into a corner, not wanting to be distracted by the voices of people coming in behind her. "What do you want?"

"I want what's mine. That night when I bumped into you, I dropped a bag of my stuff. The police report says they didn't recover it, which means only one thing. *You* kept it."

"Bullshit," she said with a snort.

He hesitated, as if surprised she wasn't quivering with fright. Which only made her more convinced he was nothing to be afraid of. If he'd had any kind of a weapon, and had the guts to use it, he would have grabbed her in the parking deck and forced her to take him to his so-called loot.

"I'm calling the cops."

She could almost hear his sneer. "What are you going to tell them? That the guy you stole the jewelry from is after you?"

"Oh, I stole your merchandise, huh?"

"Yeah, you did. And I want it. More important, the people I work for want it."

People he worked for? What was there some ring of thieves in Vegas led by a modern-day Fagin and the Artful Dodger? Ludicrous.

"Look, you're crazy. I don't have any jewelry and

you've just wasted a trip to Chicago," she said, feeling more annoyed than fearful. "Maybe you should go back and check all the storm drains or something. It probably fell down one when you tried to kill me."

"Drama queen."

"Psycho asshole."

He hesitated, as if at last realizing he wasn't scaring her one little bit. "Then your boyfriend has it."

She stiffened, suddenly wary. If he'd tracked her down, he might have done the same thing with Reese. "No, he doesn't."

Her tone must have betrayed her tension, because Mr. Robber's voice got a tad more confident. "Oh, he has it, all right. I think I'll have to make a trip to Pittsburgh now."

Damn it. "How did find out who we are?"

"You're famous, lady, don't you know that?"

She had no idea what he was talking about.

"Plus, the people I work for have a few friends in the LVPD. Your names and contact information were right on the police report."

That didn't exactly inspire confidence in the Las Vegas Police Department. She suddenly had the urge to call Parker and tell him to stop worrying about his wife's footwear and start looking for dirty cops.

"I guess I'll be seeing ya," he muttered with a laugh.

"Wait, he doesn't have them, I swear to…"

But she was talking to dead air. The creep had hung up on her.

She quickly flipped back to her caller ID, not surprised that the last incoming call had been from an unavailable number.

Nine-one-one? Officer Parker? Who to call first?

Of course, the answer was neither of those. Without hesitation, she thumbed to her address book, highlighting Reese's contact information on the tiny screen.

She started with his cell number. "Come on," she said when it rang and rang. When his voice mail came on, she didn't bother leaving a message, just moved on to the next one on the list, his house. Again, she got the same result.

"Damn it, where are you?"

The elevator had come and gone a couple of times, and it returned again with a loud ding, letting off a couple who lived on her floor. She smiled impersonally, bringing the phone up to her face to avoid any conversation.

The elevator door remained open and she stared at it. She was in the lobby of her own building, a few floors down from her apartment. But she suddenly found herself unable to walk through the open door and take the short ride upstairs.

An entire evening of trying to track Reese down, to warn him about the crazy thug from Vegas, sounded unbearable. And Jazz's claim about how quick the commute was between Chicago and Pittsburgh kept repeating itself in her head.

She gave it about ten seconds' thought. Then she turned and strode toward the exit. "Bud, would you flag me a cab?" she asked, knowing she couldn't go back for her own car. El Creepo could still be lurking around, and she didn't want him knowing she was heading to the airport, going to warn Reese.

"Sure, Ms. Bauer," the doorman said.

A few minutes later, as she got into the taxi, Amanda

had to smile. Because, as usual, when in crisis mode, she was taking off, hitting the skies. This time, though, instead of running away, she intended to fly *toward* the very person who'd been filling her head with confusion and her heart with turmoil.

Trouble could be heading Reese's way. But she fully intended to get to him first.

WHEN SOMEONE knocked on his front door at ten o'clock that night, Reese immediately tensed. The reaction was instinctive. Even now, two years later, the ring of a phone awakening him out of a sound sleep, or an unexpected knock on the door this late brought him back to the moment when his whole world had changed.

He'd been the one who'd answered the door when the uniformed police officer had come to inform his mother of his dad's accident.

He thrust the dark thoughts away. His family was just fine. He'd left them a half hour ago, happily eating birthday cake at Aunt Jean's mansion, where they'd been celebrating her seventy-whatever'th birthday. Nobody was entirely sure how old she was since she'd lied about the number for so many years.

The only other person he truly cared about was Amanda, and nobody even knew they had any connection. So it wasn't like anybody would be coming to him if something had happened to her.

Besides, he had no doubt she was just fine. Right about now, she was probably in her bedroom, wearing something plain but incredibly sexy, staring at the phone. She would likely be having a mental debate about whether to call and entice him into some serious phone sex, or to continue to try to be strong and resist him, showing them both she didn't *really* need him...at least until she just couldn't help herself.

God, the woman drove him crazy. In a good way, as well as a bad one. And oh, how he adored her for it.

The doorbell rang, then rang again, as if his visitor had become impatient. He forced himself to relax and headed over to answer it, reminding himself not to worry. Still, he couldn't deny his pulse sped up when he turned the knob and pulled the door open.

Seeing who stood there, he jerked in surprise. "What are *you* doing here?"

His four sisters, his brother, his mother, his young niece and nephew and his great-aunt all pushed their way into his house, babbling a mile a minute, all talking over one another.

Reese froze, trying to make his brain process what was happening.

A gaggle of insane people had just turned his quiet respite into a loony bin. Ralph, smart dog that he was, got the hell out, dashing toward the laundry room, probably to snuggle between the dryer and the wall, his favorite hiding spot when he'd done something bad.

"My God, Reese, how could you be so damned irresponsible? How am I supposed to raise my kids to make good choices when their uncle does something so incredibly *brainless?*"

"Reese, are you okay? I'm so sorry if you felt you couldn't share this with us."

"Oh, I've failed you. What would your father say? How could you do such a thing? Where did I go wrong?"

"Were you ever going to tell us, you sneak? I can't wait to meet her."

"Man, wait'll I tell the guys. They're gonna shit bricks."

"How could you! I'll never be able to show my face at school again!"

"When I said to have an adventure, dear boy, I didn't know you'd take it quite *that* far."

All the voices swelled, a chorus of them, but one comment, his sister Debra's, pierced through the cloud of confusion.

"Wait. *Her* who?" he asked, staring at his second-to-youngest sister.

"Reese, are you listening to me?" his mother asked, waving a hand in front of herself, as if to fan away a hot flash. She was red-cheeked, and appeared a bit woozy, although that could have been from the brandy Aunt Jean had been shoving down her throat before Reese's departure.

"Do go sit down before you faint," said Aunt Jean, pushing his mother toward Reese's leather couch. "Molly, take the little ones into the kitchen and get them a snack. They weren't happy that they didn't get to finish their cake."

The sixteen-year-old cast a furious glare at everyone, then grabbed Reese's young niece and nephew and marched them toward the kitchen.

"Jack, why don't you go find Ralph. I'm sure he's scared to death at all of us barging in like this," Aunt Jean said.

Jack frowned darkly. "I'm not a kid."

"No, you're not, which is why you are mature enough to recognize that a poor animal is hiding and frightened in the other room and you should go help him," Aunt Jean said.

Jack had always been a sucker for animals, and he really loved Ralph. Sometimes he came by just to play with the dog, throwing a stick for him, bringing a toy. So the quiet request worked like nothing else would have.

Finally, when it was just the older females of his family, and him, the lone man—Lord, talk about painful torture: estrogen poisoning—Reese repeated his question. "Which *her* are you talking about? What the hell is going on here?"

"Don't act all innocent. The truth is out. Oh-ho, is it out, in a major way," said Tess, the oldest of his siblings. She was the mother of the two kids who were probably right now whining that they had to make do with dry crackers because Uncle Reese didn't have any cookies or good snacks in his pantry.

Seeing Reese's open laptop on the coffee table, since he'd been checking his e-mails before bed, hoping for one from Amanda, Tess grabbed it and began punching letters on the keyboard. "Talk about irresponsible. And stupid!" she snapped, as always, voicing her opinion and not caring how anyone else felt about it.

"Will someone *please* talk to me?"

His mother sniffed, then waved a hand toward the computer screen. Reese turned his attention toward it, wondering why in the name of God everyone was so worked up about a YouTube video.

Then the video started.

"Hey, sweet thing, how late you working tonight?" a male voice said from off camera.

The voice was unfamiliar, but the words rang a bell, though he couldn't place them right away. Nor could he make much out in the dark, grainy image.

Then the focus kicked in, the picture brightened

and cleared. And another voice said, "Got a business card?"

"Sorry, guys, she's retired."

That voice he recognized. "Oh, hell," he muttered, unable to believe it, but knowing what he was looking at. Especially now, as the image got nice and sharp and the screen filled with an easily identifiable couple.

Him. And "Mandy" the hooker. In all her wicked glory.

He glanced away, scrambling to remember everything they'd said and done, wondering if the sly videographer had caught the sexy kiss. Or, worse, the line about…

"…I roped myself a man tonight at that wedding chapel over there. Jeez, what's a girl gotta do to enjoy her wedding night?"

He leaned back in his seat, dropping his head onto the back of the couch and staring up at the ceiling.

This couldn't be happening. It just couldn't.

"You're married?" his mother cried. "How could you get married and not tell us?"

"Worse, how could you marry a poor, down-on-her-luck prostitute? Do you know anything about her? Where is she? Did you abandon her?" asked Bonnie, his twenty-four-year old sister, who shared the middle-child title with Debra but was extremely empathetic and had never seen a tree she didn't want to hug.

"Look," he said, not even sure what he was going to say. "It's not what you think."

"Then what is it?" Tess asked. "Did you or did you not either go temporarily insane or get roofied, and marry some trashy Vegas whore?"

That made him sit straight up and snap, "Watch your mouth." He cast his sister a stare so heated she actually drew back a little. Her mouth remained shut, her lips compressing tightly.

Beside her, watching like the proverbial cat that swallowed the canary, was his aunt Jean. Her mouth was tightly shut, too, only it wasn't because she was trying to control her anger. The wicked old woman was instead trying desperately not to laugh. It was a wonder she didn't hyperventilate from lack of oxygen as she held her breath, trying to contain her merriment.

She was loving every minute of this. Probably taking full credit for pushing Reese completely over the edge.

"I'm just *thrilled* that you're so happy," he said, his voice dripping sarcasm.

She sucked her bottom lip in her mouth, then finally let out a whoosh of air. Rushing toward the kitchen, she said, "I think I'll go check on Molly and the children."

Well, that was one for the record books, a red-letter moment. The ballsiest woman he knew had cut and run. Add that to the rest of this funfest and this might just go down as the strangest night of his decade.

"So tell us, brother dear, what's the story?" asked Debra as she leaned back in a chair and lifted her feet onto the coffee table. She looked to be enjoying this almost as much as Aunt Jean had, but she didn't race for the kitchen in an effort to hide it. "When do we get to meet our new sister-in-law?"

He didn't reply. Instead he stared again toward the computer screen. The video had ended, but he wasn't focused on that, anyway. No, what had drawn his eye was the small counter that indicated how many people had viewed it.

Thousands. Many of whom had left five-star reviews and salacious comments.

He could only shake his head in disbelief.

"Well?" prompted his mother. "Don't you have anything to say for yourself? Not a single explanation?"

Hmm. Which would be worse? Letting his family believe he'd married a hooker during a wild night of partying in Vegas? Or admitting that, for months, he'd been traveling all over the country to play naughty, sexy role-playing games with a woman he was falling head over heels for?

He wasn't sure what he was going to say. Truth or consequences? Either way, he came out looking like a total jackass.

Before he could figure it out, he was, quite literally, saved by the bell. The *ding-dong* was the perfect sound effect for the insane situation in which he'd found himself.

"Good heavens, who can that be?" asked his mother.

"Not a clue," he replied, hearing an almost cheerful note in his own voice.

"Who on earth would simply show up here unannounced at this time of night?" she added.

"Can't imagine. Rude, isn't it?" he muttered, certain the sarcasm would go over her head.

Reese didn't know who had landed on his doorstep this time. He only knew he was grateful to the bastard for giving him an excuse to get up and walk away from the inquisition.

Maybe he'd get lucky and it would be a fireman saying the whole neighborhood had to be evacuated due to a gas leak. Maybe he'd get even luckier and just blow up with it. Anything to escape having to share embarrassing fiction or even *more* embarrassing truth with his nosy, incredibly obnoxious family was a-okay with him.

Whatever he'd been imagining, though, it didn't even come close to reality. He thought he'd been surprised to find his family barging in twenty minutes ago? Hell, that was nothing compared to the shock he got when he opened the door.

Of all the times he'd imagined Amanda Bauer coming to his home, being part of his real world, it sure hadn't been under circumstances like these. Yet there she was, staring at him with uncertainty in her eyes and apologies on her beautiful lips.

"Reese, I'm sorry to just show up like this, but I need to see you and it's not just to jump your bones, even though that's exactly what I'd like to…" Her words trailed off as she looked past him into the house, obviously seeing a bunch of wide-eyed, openmouthed females who'd heard her every word. Her babbling nervousness segued into a momentary horrified silence.

Gee. The night just got better and better.

"Oh, man, *please* tell me you're having a late-night Pampered Chef party, and that's *not* your entire family sitting over there," she said in a shaky whisper.

"'Fraid I can't do that." He forced a humorless smile, stepped back and extended an arm to beckon her in. "Welcome to the asylum."

To give her credit, she didn't run. A few months ago she probably would have. But tonight, she took one tentative step inside, and then another, her curious stare traveling back and forth between him and the women watching wide-eyed from a few feet away.

The silence lengthened, grew almost deafening,

and finally, the sheer ludicrousness of the whole situation washed over him. This was like something out of a movie—a romantic comedy where the hapless hero went from one humiliating situation to a worse one, constantly looking like an idiot in front of the smart, witty heroine.

Fortunately, this smart, witty heroine had a couple of skills that could come in really handy right now. First, she wasn't the type to pass judgment. Second, she was really good at adapting to new situations, as evidenced by her aptitude at role-playing. And finally, she had one hell of a sense of humor. So, with laughter building in the back of his throat, he squeezed Amanda's hand and drew her toward the others.

He opened his mouth to make a simple introduction, trusting that she looked different enough from the woman in the video to be unrecognizable.

He should have known better. Eagle-eyed Tess leaped out of her seat, hissing, "She's the one—it's her!"

Amanda flinched, obviously having no clue what the other woman was talking about. Reese kept a strong, comforting arm on her shoulder. And then, though he didn't really plan to say the words until they left his mouth, he introduced her to the judgmental women watching them with expressions ranging from pure curiosity to horror.

"Amanda, this is my family." He draped an arm across her shoulder and tugged her against him. "Campbell family, meet the little woman."

9

TEN HOURS LATER, the shock of the previous night still hadn't sunk in. Amanda felt dazed whenever she thought about it.

"I just can't believe you did that. Your family must hate me," she said as she walked into Reese's bathroom the next morning. She'd spent the night, of course, having nowhere else to go and not a single piece of luggage.

She now wore one of his T-shirts, which barely skimmed her thighs. Not that she'd needed anything to wear last night. Oh, no, he'd kept her quite warm while making love to her until just a few hours ago, when they'd finally fallen into an exhausted sleep.

She liked the feel of the shirt, liked that his smell clung to it, and she felt perfectly comfortable intruding on him in the bathroom, hopping up to sit on the counter,

Strange that they were already so comfortable with each other, like longtime lovers. Strange, but nice.

"Don't worry about it," Reese said, glancing at her in the mirror. He stood over the sink, shaving, amusement warring with lazy sexual satisfaction in his eyes. "I'll tell them the truth and they'll fall all over themselves apologizing."

The truth? That she was his holiday mistress who'd had him play-acting all across America since Halloween? Oh, lovely.

"But you told them I was your wife."

"No, they told *me* you were my wife and waved their 'evidence' in front of my face to prove it."

The damned video. She still couldn't believe it. Someone had been videotaping them that night, possibly with a cell phone, and they'd never even realized it. Heaven help her if any of their corporate clients stumbled over the clip.

At least she hadn't been *too* easily recognizable. Unlike Reese, who'd been completely uncostumed.

"But you confirmed it. My God, Reese, what were you thinking?"

"Well, I was thinking that my family is composed of a bunch of nosy busybodies and they deserved a little payback." Grinning, he swiped his razor along one more strip of lean jaw. "If my aunt Jean hadn't ducked out the back door before you arrived, I would have seriously considered dropping a pregnancy bombshell, too."

"Whoa, big boy," she said, knowing she sounded horrified. She leaped off the counter and backed out of the bathroom, both hands up in a visible "stop" sign. "That's not even funny."

He didn't look over, that half smile still playing on his mouth as he shaved around it. Ignoring her dismay, he said, "You didn't meet my aunt Jean."

No, she hadn't. Nor did she think she wanted to. She'd met quite enough of the clan last night and didn't care to expand on, or to repeat, the experience.

She slowly shook her head. "I should have denied it."

"I'm glad you didn't."

He could laugh. He wasn't the one being mentally murdered by a group of women who thought she'd either trapped or drugged their brother and son.

Yeah. Denial would have been the way to go. But she'd been so surprised by Reese's claim, she could only watch in silence as his shocked family quietly rose and headed for the door. She'd said nothing when they'd murmured their apologies to Reese for the intrusion and left the house, giving her looks that ranged from disgust to pity. They'd been gone within five minutes of her arrival.

Something else she could have done—followed them out. It would have been even better to have just stayed home in Chicago and kept trying to call Reese all night long rather than flying off to play superhero and protect him from the bad guy.

Superhero my ass. She'd come in person because she'd wanted to see him. That was all there was to it. Excuses about Vegas thugs be damned.

She'd stayed for the same reason. Stayed despite the crazy lie, despite the sheer misery it had been to come face-to-face with the women in his family, playing the girlfriend—no, *wife*—role as if she had some actual right to it. Stayed after facing down the women who all thought she had sex for money.

She felt like throwing up.

Backing up, she stopped only when her legs hit the edge of his enormous bed, then slowly sat down on it. What the hell had she gotten herself into? And she wasn't even referring to the fact that an angry robber had followed her halfway across the country and could be parked outside Reese's door right now, just waiting to break in.

Not that Reese seemed to care. In fact, when she'd told him what had driven her here last night, he'd spent about five minutes being utterly enraged and the next thirty muttering all the ways he intended to punish the guy if he actually had the nerve to show up.

She'd just wanted to call the police. Which was exactly what they were going to do in a couple of hours, once they'd made up the time difference in Vegas and had a good chance of catching Officer Parker on the job.

In the meantime, she didn't quite know what to do with herself. She'd already called Ginny and had her rearrange her schedule. Fortunately, the week looked pretty light and Uncle Frank was able to pick up today's trip. A part-time pilot they contracted with when they were extra busy was on for tomorrow.

Not that she intended to spend another night here. Uh-uh. She had no clothes, and she was already itching to get back to her real life, away from Reese's admittedly beautiful house and ultranormal one.

She wasn't ready to play the role of domestic goddess, or even live-in girlfriend. No matter how nice it had been to wake up in his bed this morning and watch *him* sleep for a change.

Time to run, girlfriend.

But she couldn't leave just yet. Not until they'd reached Officer Parker and found out what he wanted them to do about their unwelcome stalker. They might need to get in touch with the local police. Or she might have to go right back and report to the Chicago ones. She just didn't know.

"Forget it," Reese said, watching her from the doorway of the bathroom. He wore a white towel slung around his lean hips and looked so utterly delicious she wished she'd said yes when he'd offered to share his shower.

"Forget what?"

"You're not going home, not until we've dealt with this guy."

"So, what, I'm supposed to just move in here?"

He shrugged, a non-answer, but the quirk of his lips said he didn't mind the idea.

She forced away the flash of pleasure that gave her, knowing she couldn't let herself be distracted by the realization that Reese really wanted her to stay. "I don't have any clothes."

"It's not the Magnificent Mile, but we do have stores here in Pennsylvania."

She ran a hand through her hair, which she hadn't even brushed yet this morning. "I have a job."

"Your plane's sitting at the airport, isn't it? Who's to say you can't fly from here to go pick up your passengers?"

That was a good point, and was, in fact, exactly what she would have done if she hadn't been able to get coverage for today and tomorrow. But she wasn't ready to give up. "I really shouldn't."

"Yeah. You really should."

The sexy, cajoling smile widened and he walked toward her. She swallowed as that hard, muscular form stopped in front of her, and she couldn't resist reaching out to rub her fingertip along the rippling muscles of his stomach.

"What's more, you really want to," he whispered, stroking her hair and then her cheek.

Amanda leaned closer, wanting to taste that hot skin. She pressed her mouth to the hollow right below his hip, which was uncovered by the low-slung towel. "How will I spend my time?" she asked, brushing her lips across him, toward the long, thin trail of dark hair that led from his flat stomach down into the white terry cloth.

The fabric began to bulge toward her as he hardened right before her eyes.

"Mmm."

He lifted his other hand and twined those fingers in her hair as well, but he didn't guide her closer, didn't force her anywhere she didn't want to go.

She was capable of deciding that all on her own.

A quick flick of her fingers and the towel fell to the floor. His rock-hard erection jutted toward her, and she blew on it lightly, hearing him hiss in response.

She knew what he liked, knew how to please him. But she also knew how to draw out the pleasure. So instead of opening her mouth and sucking him in, she continued to press those featherlight kisses on his groin, letting her cheek brush against his shaft, knowing every soft caress sent his tension—his want—skyrocketing.

"Manda…" he muttered, already sounding near the edge of control.

She moved her hand, sliding it across his strong thigh, one goal in sight. When she cupped the delicate sacs in her palm, handling them carefully, Reese jerked toward her. Only then did she open her mouth and lick at the broad tip of his cock.

"More?" she asked.

His hands tangled a little more in her hair, but he still didn't take what he wanted, merely accepting what she chose to give him.

And what she chose to give him was the pleasure of sinking that throbbing maleness into her mouth. She took as much of him as she could, then tilted her head to take a little more. Using her tongue and soft, gentle suction, plus the careful strokes of her hand between his legs, she soon had him groaning in pure sexual pleasure.

She was ready to go all the way, loving the taste of him and the power of knowing how much he loved what she was doing. But he suddenly pulled back, gently pushing her off him. Then he lifted her under the arms and tossed her back onto the bed, following her down.

He didn't say a single word, didn't kiss her, or stroke her, seeming beyond all capacity to do anything except have her.

It didn't matter. Because when he plunged into her, she was creamy-wet, completely ready for him.

She arched up, taking everything, meeting him thrust for thrust, not even minding that he began to reach his climax long before she was ready for him to. Especially not when he muttered, "I'm sorry. I swear, I'm going to make you come so many times tonight that you won't remember what it feels like not to be having an orgasm."

That sounded like a pretty okay deal to her.

Then he couldn't say anything else, he could only groan as he exploded in a hot rush inside her. Having long since gone on the pill so they wouldn't have to use condoms, she savored every sensation, loving that there was nothing separating skin from skin. Having this man empty himself into her body made her feel connected to him in a way she'd never been with anybody before.

Or maybe it was more than that. Perhaps it was the knowledge that, for the first time in her life, she hadn't just opened her legs to a man.

She had begun to suspect she'd opened her dusty heart to him, as well.

HIS FAMILY KEPT their distance for the next few days. Reese didn't get a single phone call, not one e-mail, and didn't have to endure any fact-finding trips disguised as casual dropping-by-the-brewery-to-say-hello visits.

That was fine. Just fine. No, he wasn't still furious at them for barging in on him the other night, whether they thought they had the right or not. But he just didn't want to deal with that part of his life right now.

Not when the rest of it was going so very well.

Amanda might not be his wife, she might not even be ready to admit she loved him, but she was sleeping in his bed at night. She was sitting across his table for breakfast each morning, and curling up on the couch to watch a movie with him during the evening. She used his toothpaste and she slept in his undershirts, her shopping trip that first day not including a stop for a nightie.

She'd even done as he'd first suggested and gone back to work from here, flying in and out of Pittsburgh. Her origination point didn't really matter, considering she picked up people all over the country and shuttled them where they wanted to go. So it wasn't a difficult adjustment—he took her to the airport in the morning and picked her up at night.

They were playing a whole new game: normal couple. And he'd never enjoyed anything more.

The only imperfection in the whole thing was that they were playing this game because some sleazy criminal from Vegas might be after her. There hadn't been much progress in the case, though they kept in touch with Officer Parker, a detective from Chicago and a local cop, all of whom were monitoring the situation.

Parker had been furious to learn the thief had been able to access police records to track down the witnesses against him. And their first conversation with him had been quickly followed up by one with someone from the Internal Affairs office.

There was one bit of good news: they'd at least identified the guy. Parker had had a few leads on suspects, and when he found out about the thug's visit to Chicago, he'd narrowed them down even further, focusing on any who had left Vegas. A faxed mug shot later and they'd both identified their man as one Teddy Lebowski, age thirty-six, occupation petty thief and all-around scumbag.

Hearing the criminal was loosely connected with one of the Vegas crime families hadn't made their day. But the fact that he had never been charged with a violent crime, and that Parker considered him little more than a blowhard who didn't have the balls to actually try to hurt anyone, brought a hint of relief.

Sooner or later, the bastard would be caught. Reese half hoped he was stupid enough to show up in Pittsburgh. He'd sincerely like the chance to beat the guy to a pulp for what he'd done to Amanda, both in Vegas and when he'd stalked her in Chicago.

"Hey, you," she said, interrupting his thoughts as he finished locking up his desk for the night. She hadn't had to fly today, and had agreed to come to the brewery for a few hours this afternoon, to see where he worked.

The afternoon had stretched into evening, as a crisis had arisen with one of their distributors. But Amanda hadn't appeared bored, insisting she'd enjoyed touring the place, inspecting the enormous vats and watching the plant workers running the equipment and observing the bottling line.

She'd done a tasting, declaring their amber lager the best, then had sat quietly in a corner while Reese dealt with putting out the fires. Now that the last phone call was done, he stood and wearily rubbed at his temples.

"You look like you could use a massage," she said, rising from the couch that stood against one wall of his office.

"Mmm. You want to play massage therapist now?"

"I think that could be worked into my repertoire," she said flirtatiously.

Arm in arm, they walked outside. A few night workers remained within, but Reese paused to lock up. Then, taking her arm again, they headed for his car.

They hadn't even made it down the outside steps when he saw a familiar vehicle pull into the parking lot.

"Oh, hell."

Beside him, Amanda tensed, going on alert. "What is it?"

"More like *who* is it." The Caddy came to a halt directly in front of them. "You're about to meet my great-aunt Jean."

"Oh, terrific. I can hardly wait for this one," she said, her tone saying exactly the opposite.

He had a lot to say to his great-aunt, both for her leading the charge over to his house the other night—which he had no doubt she did—and for the way she'd slunk out the back door after getting everyone completely stirred up.

The door opened and the elderly woman stepped out of the driver's seat, into the shadows of the parking lot. Then she walked around the luxury auto, approaching them without a hint of wariness, her obnoxious red-leather cowboy boots clicking merrily on the blacktop.

He was about to open his mouth to warn her against saying anything out of line to the woman at his side when Amanda made a small, confused sound. "Mrs. Rush?"

"Hello, Amanda my dear," the old woman said as she reached the steps and walked up them. She leaned over to press a kiss on Amanda's cheek. "I can't tell you how happy I am to see you here." She wagged her drawn-on brows at Reese. "And under such delicious circumstances."

Reese couldn't move, couldn't speak, couldn't put a thought together. He could only stare, wondering how in the name of God his great-aunt knew his lover.

"I don't understand," said Amanda, sounding a little dazed.

But Reese did. Or he was beginning to. "Damn it. You manipulative old…"

His aunt waved aside his anger, as if it were a pesky odor, then lifted her cheek for his kiss.

He didn't give it to her. "You set this up. This whole thing."

"Oh, no, of course I didn't."

"Wait," Amanda said, finally catching on. "*You're* really Reese's great-aunt Jean?"

"Guilty as charged," said the woman.

"Son of a bitch," Amanda muttered, taking the words right out of his mouth.

"Oh, you two, please stop acting as though I had anything at all to do with this fine mess you've gotten yourselves into." She tsked and shook her head, though her lips twitched with merriment. "I merely pushed you in each other's direction. Arranged for your first meeting after I'd planted a few suggestions in Reese's mind—" she turned toward Amanda "—and made sure you were suitably dressed and loosened up for the occasion, thinking you were going to be part of my in-flight costume party."

Her Halloween costume. His last-minute flight. All a setup.

The light dawned. "You called old Mr. Braddock and had him call me to get me to come to Chicago that day."

Her bracelets tinkled as she clapped her hands, as if pleased he'd put it together so quickly. "Yes!" Then she made a cross-my-heart motion and said, "But that was all. Everything else is all on your heads." She almost beamed at them, so wrapped in approval and self-satisfaction she could barely contain herself. "Oh, my, playing such wicked games in Las Vegas." She tapped her fingertip against Reese's chest. "You're a naughty one, Reese Campbell."

He crossed his arms, almost forgiving her, considering she had, in fact, done him one of the biggest favors of his life. But he wasn't quite there yet. "Did you have anything to do with that video clip showing up on YouTube?"

She shook her head hard. "Absolutely not." Then, averting her gaze, she admitted, "Though, I must admit, it was one of my friends whose daughter spotted you in it and sent me a link. I fear that video has gone, what do they call it, viral? You're right smack-dab in the middle of your own fifteen minutes of fame."

Lucky him. And he'd had absolutely no clue. One more reason he wasn't so crazy about the Internet age.

"Let me guess. You just had to show it to the rest of the family after I left the other night."

"Yes. I would say I'm sorry, but you know I'm not."

Of course she wasn't. The woman had never been truly sorry for anything she'd done. Damn, she must have led his great-uncle on a merry chase.

"So, all's well that ends well!"

"No, it's not," he protested. "In case you've forgotten, my family is convinced I'm married to a hooker."

She waved an unconcerned hand. "No, they're not. I straightened that all out."

Almost not sure he wanted to know, he asked, "How?"

"I told them you were flamingly angry and embarrassed that you and Amanda had been caught on camera at a New Year's Eve costume party in Las Vegas. That it was all a joke and you were punishing them for assuming the worst of you."

It wasn't a bad story, come to think of it.

His aunt reached over and pinched Amanda's cheek, apparently not noticing that she'd been almost completely silent. "I knew you'd be perfect for him...and that *he'd* be perfect for *you*. Do forgive an old woman's meddling. It's just that when I see two wounded people who so obviously belong together, I can't stand not doing something about it."

Without waiting for a reply, she turned around and

skipped down the steps like a woman one-third her age. She gave them a cheery wave before getting back into her car and driving away, leaving them staring after her in silence.

He didn't move for a long moment, just stood there absorbing the fact that he'd been completely manipulated by a family member. How much worse must it be for Amanda? God, she barely knew his great-aunt, who, apparently, from what they'd said, was one of her regular customers.

He should have known, should have suspected when his aunt simply insisted he take her place on the private flight to Chicago on Halloween.

"Amanda?" he finally murmured. "Are you all right?"

She hesitated for a moment, then, tilting her head sideways, with her brow furrowed, she replied, "Your family is freaking nuts, you know that, right?"

Startled, relieved, he could only nod and grin. "Yeah."

"I mean, certifiable."

"I repeat…yeah."

She paused again, shaking her head, still staring off down the road where his elderly relative's car had disappeared. When she spoke again, her confusion was gone. So was any hint of anger. "You know, I like that crazy old woman."

"I do, too, when I don't want to strangle her."

"We really have to plan our revenge."

His heart getting lighter by the minute, he nodded in agreement. Plotting together made it sound like she planned to stick around for a while.

Which sounded just about perfect to him.

10

AFTER THEY'D LEFT HIS OFFICE, Reese insisted on taking Amanda out for a late dinner. It was after eight, they were both wiped and a steak was the least he could offer her considering she'd just come face-to-face with the person who'd been pulling her strings for months, even though she hadn't known it.

They went to one of his favorite places, not too far from home. It was low-key with good food and great service. There was no play-acting, not even a whisper of suggestion to be anything other than who they were. He didn't mention it, not wanting Amanda to think for a minute that disappointed him.

On the contrary, he couldn't be more pleased that she continued to drop those walls, let down her guard and just be herself…the woman he had fallen in love with.

He knew she didn't want to hear it, and that she'd warned him against it, but there was no hiding the truth, especially not from himself. He'd fallen hard for the woman. Fallen head over heels into the kind of love he had seen in others—like his parents—but hadn't had time to consider he might find for himself.

By the end of the meal, they were laughing as they

tried to outdo each other with extreme revenge plots against Aunt Jean. He had also promised her a dozen times that if and when she met his family again, they were going to be falling over themselves to make up for their assumptions and their coldness toward her.

That would happen even if he had to order, blackmail and browbeat everyone in his family to make absolutely sure of it.

Once they were finished eating, they walked to the car. Night had grown deeper, and she shivered in the frigid air.

"You okay?" he asked, dropping an arm over her shoulder and tugging her closer.

She nodded, clutching her coat tighter around her body. "How can it be colder here than in Chicago?"

"It isn't."

"It sure feels like it."

"I'll warm you up," he offered.

She glanced at him from the corner of her eye. "I'm counting on it."

Once inside the car, Reese watched as Amanda fastened her seat belt, then he put the key in the ignition. But he didn't turn it right away. Instead, he glanced over at his companion, wondering what she was really thinking, wondering if her good mood was covering up any last, lingering resentment over his aunt's confession.

Finally, he just asked. "Are you *sure* you're okay?"

"Uh-huh. I'm about as fine as somebody being chased by a crazy Vegas mobster and mistaken for a prostitute can be." Shaking her head woefully, she added, "It's really not fair that I can be accused of being a hooker and not have the sordid experience to show for it. And called a thief and not have any jewels."

Any final threads of tension evaporated, and Reese had to admire the way she'd taken everything that had come her way in the past several days in stride. Just like she did everything else.

Some women would have left that first night, after she'd been treated so harshly by his pushy family members. Others might have resented being moved around like a pawn on a chess board by a rich old busybody who liked getting her own way.

But Amanda just went with it, laughed and never complained about what she couldn't change. He found that incredibly attractive.

He also really liked the way she teased him about it as they drove back to his place, asking what his sweet old aunt would think if she knew the wild things he'd done to her the night before. As if wanting to remind him, she put her hand on his thigh. Then she began sliding it up, inch by inch.

Suddenly, though, when she went too high, whispering something about making the ride home more enjoyable, he dropped his hand on hers and squeezed, shaking his head in silence.

He didn't have to say anything. She immediately understood. Sucking in an embarrassed breath, she pulled away. "Oh, Reese, I'm sorry."

"It's okay," he murmured, knowing she understood why he was such a careful driver.

There were some games he'd never play, some risks he would never take. No matter what. He'd learned that lesson all too well.

"I'm an idiot." She sighed heavily. "An insensitive twit." She curled up one leg, wrapping her arms around it and resting her chin on her upraised knee, staring pensively out the windshield at the oncoming traffic. With a hint of wistfulness in her tone, she added, "He must have been a wonderful man for you to have turned out to be such a great guy yourself."

"Yes, he was."

He fell silent, not elaborating at first. Talking about his father was probably as difficult for him as talking about hers was for Amanda. Not for the same reasons, of course. Her wounds were old and scarred, and she no longer felt the ache. His were fresh and raw, and he just didn't feel like poking at them and starting the bleeding all over again.

But he could tell by the continued silence that she felt like crap for even suggesting they fool around while he was behind the wheel. The last thing he wanted to do was make her feel worse. So he began to speak.

"His name was Patrick, and he died way too young."

She turned her head to look at him, wide-eyed and tentative. "You don't have to…"

"It's okay. Actually, it's kind of nice to be able to say his name without someone bursting into tears."

She wasn't crying, but he could tell, even in the low lighting of the car, that her eyes were moist.

"He'd worked late, as usual. And he was driving too fast, trying hard to make it to one of Jake's basketball games. He'd missed the last few because of work, and they'd had a big fight about it the day before. He'd promised he'd make the next one. Only…he didn't."

"Oh, God, poor Jake," she whispered, immediately grasping the situation. "That's a lot of weight for a kid to bear."

"Tell me about it. He's been the one I've been most

worried about. He's angry at the world, sometimes mean and rebellious, sometimes still just a lost kid wondering what happened."

Amanda reached across for his hand, this time lacing her fingers through his in a touch that was all about sweetness and consolation. And because she didn't ask any questions, didn't pry at all, just letting him say whatever he wanted, he felt okay about saying it.

He told her about that night. About the nights that followed. About how fucking hard it had been to pick out a casket and decide on a headstone and keep his mother upright and his sisters from sobbing and the business functioning and his brother from blowing his whole life out of guilt, and still maintaining his own sanity amid his own deep, wrenching grief.

It was like someone had pulled a plug on all the words that had gone unsaid for two years. And it wasn't until he'd let them out that he realized just how much he'd needed to say them. Being the strong one, the stoic one, the steady one had also left him the one who'd never been able to release the anger and the heartbreak that had been locked inside him.

By the time he finished, they were sitting in his driveway, and had been for several minutes. They were silent, neither of them even looking at each other, or moving to get out of the car. But finally, once he'd taken a deep breath and realized the world hadn't ended just because he'd admitted to someone else that he sometimes resented his life and his family and even his father, he looked over at her and saw the kind of warmth and kindness Amanda Bauer probably didn't even know she possessed.

"It's all right," she whispered. "Everything you're

feeling is completely understandable." She lifted his hand to her mouth, pressing a soft, gentle kiss on the backs of his fingers. "I'm sorry you and your family had to go through that, Reese. So damn sorry."

"Thank you," he said, rubbing his knuckles against her soft cheek. He opened his mouth to continue, to both thank her and to tell her she needn't feel sorry for him. He also felt an apology rise to his lips, feeling bad for dumping everything on her like that. But before he could say a thing, something caught his eye.

A shadow was moving around the corner of his house.

He stiffened, leaning over to stare past her, out the window, but saw nothing. Thinking about what he'd seen, he knew it hadn't been Ralph. He never left the dog out if he wasn't home. Nor had the shape looked like any other kind of animal.

It had been man-size.

"Stay in the car and lock the doors," he ordered, reaching for the door handle.

"Huh?" She swung her head around to see what he'd been looking at. She figured it out almost immediately. "Is it him? Wait! Don't you dare…"

But he had already stepped out into the cold night, quietly pushing the door closed behind him. Maybe that bastard Lebowski didn't know he'd been spotted.

Reese paused for one second to glance back at Amanda, who watched wide-eyed from inside the car. Making a dialing motion with his hand, he mouthed, "Call 911," then crept across his own front lawn.

Though Parker had said the thief wasn't considered dangerous, Reese wasn't taking any chances. As he passed by the front flower bed, he bent over and grabbed the ugly ceramic gnome one of his sisters had given him as a gag housewarming gift. The thing had weight, it was solid in his palm. And if knocked against somebody's skull, he suspected it would hurt like crazy.

It'd do.

The night was moonless and cold, wind whipping up the few remaining dead leaves still lying in the yard. Reese moved in silence, approaching the corner of the house, carefully peering around it before proceeding.

He spotted Lebowski immediately. The robber was trying to use a credit card to jimmy the lock on the side door leading into the utility room. Muttering curses under his breath, the robber appeared clumsy and not terribly quiet, as if he'd gotten spooked when he'd heard them pull up in the driveway and was now on the verge of panic.

Reese suspected the man had been at it for a while. The fact that the guy hadn't been scared off when he and Amanda had returned said a lot about how desperate Lebowski was to get whatever he thought Reese and Amanda had.

The guy might be sly, but he wasn't much of a criminal. He didn't even notice Reese moving up behind him, jerking in shock when Reese pressed the pointed tip of the gnome's hat against the small of his back. "Make one move and you're dead."

"Aww, shit, man," the guy whined. "No, don't shoot, please don't. I wasn't gonna hurt anybody. I just wanted to get what's owed me and get outta here before you got back!"

"Yeah, so why'd you feel the need to threaten my girlfriend?" he asked, digging the point a little harder into the bastard's back.

"Are you kidding me? I didn't threaten her. The crazy bitch is hard-core, she ain't afraid of nothin'. *She* scares *me!*" The other man risked a quick peek over his shoulder, paling a little more when he saw the obvious rage in Reese's face. "Sorry."

"I most certainly am not hard-core," a voice said, cracking through the cold night as sharp and forceful as a whip.

He was going to kill her. "I asked you to stay in the car." He had to push the words through tightly clenched teeth.

"I did. I called the police, they'll be here any minute. When I saw you had things under control, I thought I'd come back and see if you could use this." She held out her hand, extending the long waist-tie to her overcoat.

Smart thinking. He'd gotten Lebowski to remain still, but hadn't thought ahead to how to keep him that way until the cops came. If the little toad figured out he was being held in place by a ceramic gnome's head, he might not be in the mood to stick around and wait to be arrested.

"Fine. Tie him up."

She moved closer, carefully. "Put your hands behind your back."

"I swear, I just wanted my jewelry. I owe some money to some of my colleagues and if I don't come up with it, they're gonna kill me."

"Well, hopefully they won't be able to get to you in a jail cell," Amanda said, sounding distinctly sour and a little bit pleased at the thought. Not that the guy didn't deserve it.

As she tied Teddy Lebowski's hands behind his back,

yanking the fabric so tight the other man winced, she also said one more thing.

"And you can call me the biggest bitch in the known universe. But I am *not* crazy."

REESE HAD NEVER TOUCHED her more tenderly, more lovingly than he did that night after they'd watched Teddy Lebowski being taken away by the local police. They'd walked upstairs with their arms around each other's waists, her head dropping onto his shoulder in utter weariness.

But once they'd slipped out of their clothes and met in the middle of his bed, sleep had been far from Amanda's mind. And from Reese's.

He'd spent hours stroking her, tasting every inch of her skin, teasing her with soft kisses and slow, deliberate caresses. Every brush of their lips had included a sweet whisper, each embrace a sigh of delight.

Even as he aroused all her senses, bringing her every nerve ending to its highest peak, he'd made her feel... cherished.

Adored.

There had been absolutely no frenzy. They exchanged long, slow kisses that didn't prompt any urgency, didn't make them want to go faster or hurry on to whatever came next. They were delightful just for how good they felt, how intimate and personal and right.

Kissing *was* an incredibly intimate act, she saw that now. She'd always considered it more a prelude to other things, but in Reese's arms, under his rapt attention where every touch brought waves of sensation, she gained a whole new appreciation for a simple kiss.

She'd never experienced anything like it. Never

dreamed that emotional tears would fill her eyes as a man slowly slid into her body. She hadn't ever pictured every slide becoming a declaration and each gentle thrust a promise.

Nor had she ever imagined that when it was nearly over, when she'd lost herself to climax after climax, and had known he was reaching his, too, she'd actually feel her heart split in half at the sound of the words he'd softly whispered in her ear.

I love you.

He'd done it—the unthinkable. The thing she'd warned him not to do. He'd fallen in love with her. And he'd told her so.

Part of her wondered why she hadn't already left, slipping out the minute he'd fallen asleep. The old Amanda would have headed for the hills or the plains or another continent where she didn't have to deal with someone else's feelings that she simply didn't return.

She didn't have to wonder for long. The answer was simple, really. She *did* return them.

And that broke her heart even more.

Lying in Reese's arms after he'd fallen asleep, Amanda couldn't stop thinking about that moment she'd been sitting in the car, when she'd watched him disappear around the corner of the house. She'd heard the expression about your heart going into your throat when terror had you in its grip. But she'd never experienced it…until then.

It didn't matter what Parker had said, or that he'd been right in pegging Lebowski as a cowardly punk who didn't have the nerve to commit real violence. There'd been no way to be sure of that. As the seconds had passed, when her ears had still rung with his sad, grief-stricken whispers about his father, whom he had so loved and lost, she could only imagine the worst.

Losing him, something happening to him…she wouldn't be able to stand it. And though she had no real liking for his family yet, given their behavior the other night and the fact that his mother had looked at her like she was something that had crawled up from out of a toilet, she suddenly felt boatloads of sympathy for them.

The pain of losing someone you deeply loved had to be unimaginable. Which was, perhaps, one reason she'd never wanted to experience the emotion.

Too late. She, the stone-cold, heartbreaking bitch had fallen in love. Completely, totally, irrevocably in love. The ice had melted, her heart had begun beating with renewed energy and purpose. And the man she'd fallen in love with incredibly sexy, smart, funny, loyal… and great.

Yet, instead of that realization filling her with joy, she could only lie here in the dark and wonder just how long it would be before she screwed it up.

What would be the first callous thing she'd say to start piercing at his feelings for her? What trip would she take, what birthday would she forget, what need would she ignore, what promise would she not keep? How soon before she felt constricted, restrained, and just needed to *go?*

Because those things were inevitable. That was her M.O. No, she'd never gone as far as falling in love before, but it didn't matter, did it? She always let men down, always hurt them, always bailed.

She was just like Uncle Frank. Feckless, reckless, lovable but unreliable Uncle Frank. Everybody said so.

She suddenly wanted to cry. Because how badly did it suck to finally fall in love, *really* in love, and realize you liked the person too much to inflict yourself on him?

Reese was too good, way too good for her. She didn't want him hurt.

Not only that, he had a million and one things on his plate, was obviously at the end of his rope in terms of all the demands placed on him by everyone around him. So how could she add to that, become one more thing for him to worry about, one more weight on his shoulders?

Funny, when he realized she was gone, he would probably think it had something to do with his family, his responsibilities, his ties that bound him so tightly to this place and these people. All the things he'd told her about on the ride home tonight.

In fact, none of that really mattered. She'd told herself she never wanted to be stuck in place, living the same kind of life her parents had lived. But it didn't take a genius to see she didn't have to. She'd been in Reese's house for almost a week, and the world hadn't come to an end. She'd kept going to sleep each night and getting up each day. Kept breathing in, then out. Kept working, kept flying, kept living.

They *could* make this work.

If only she weren't so damned sure it wouldn't last.

It was that certainty that drove her out of bed just after dawn. For a moment, the thought of just leaving, heading for the airport, occurred to her. It had been her standard operating procedure in the past.

But Reese didn't deserve that kind of treatment. Besides, she wasn't that person anymore. Cowardice and immaturity had led her to make those decisions in the past. Now, she wasn't afraid, and she was looking at this through calm, adult eyes.

They couldn't work. Not in the long term. So *he'd* be better off getting out in the short one.

Sitting at his kitchen table, with Ralph—sweet dog, she was going to miss him, too—at her feet, she sipped a cup of coffee and waited for the chill of morning to leave her bones.

It didn't. Not one bit. She just sat there cold and sad, waiting for him to come down.

Finally, he did. When he walked into the kitchen, she could only stare at him. He wore low-riding sweatpants, no shirt, and she gazed at the strong arms that had held her during the night, the rough hands that had brought her so much pleasure. The broad chest against which she'd slept.

God this was hard. Love was hard.

He knew before she said a word that she was leaving.

"Do you need a ride to the airport?" he asked, not meeting her stare.

"Reese…"

He waved off her explanation. "I know. Game's over. Bad guy's caught. It's not even a holiday, so there's no reason for you to stay."

There were a million reasons for her to stay, but one really good one for her to go. All the men in the Dumped by Amanda Bauer group could attest to that. She just wasn't cut out for a serious, loving relationship.

"I did the unthinkable," he added, sounding so tired, and looking so resigned, her heart twisted in her chest. "I fell in love with you when I told you I wouldn't."

He finally met her stare, watching her closely. He

seemed to be looking for something—a sign, a hesitation, a hint that she was happy he loved her.

It took every bit of her strength not to give it to him.

Finally, with a short nod that said he'd gotten the message, he broke the stare. "So, do you need a ride?"

"I can get a cab," she murmured.

"Fine. Goodbye, Amanda."

He didn't say anything else, merely turned and walked back out of the kitchen. His footsteps were hard as he walked up the stairs, and from above, she hard the slamming of the door as he went into the bathroom.

The shower came on. It would undoubtedly be a long one. He didn't have to tell her he hoped she'd be gone when he got out. That was a given.

She followed him up, quickly threw her new clothes in the shopping bags they'd come in. Not really thinking about it, she crossed the room, walking toward the bathroom door. She lifted her fist, half tempted to knock. But her hand unclenched and flattened. She pressed it against the wood, fingers spread, almost able to feel the steam-filled air on the other side of it. Closing her eyes, she leaned her forehead against the door, picturing him in the shower, already hurt by her when it was the very last thing she'd wanted to do.

Better now than later.

Her eyes opened. Her hand dropped. She picked up her bag. Then Amanda Bauer walked out of Reese Campbell's bedroom and out of his life for the last time.

11

Valentine's Day

REESE WISHED THE ONE DAY of the year set aside for lovers took place in March. It would help him out a lot if he could talk Saint Valentine into switching places on the calendar with Saint Patrick, just this once. Maybe Hallmark wouldn't appreciate it, or the flower or chocolate industries, but he could really use an extra month before the big day meant for romance and love—all the stuff he'd had a couple of days ago, before Amanda had walked out of his house.

All the stuff he intended to have again. With her.

It had been hell watching her go. But the minute he'd walked into the kitchen and seen the sad, resigned expression on her face, he'd known she was leaving. He could do nothing but let her, not because of that "If you love something set it free" bullshit, but because he knew her well enough to know there was no point trying to talk her out of it.

As he'd gone upstairs, he'd briefly hoped that seeing how calmly he'd taken it—even though inside he'd been a churning mass of anger, frustration and want—she would realize she was making a mistake and change her mind. Hearing her come up to gather her things, he'd waited in the bathroom, not in the running shower, but standing right on the other side of the closed door. Half wondering if she'd knock. Pretty sure she wouldn't.

She hadn't.

As strong as she was, Amanda wasn't the type to make important decisions on the spur of the moment. She was the retreat-consider-evaluate-then-cautiously-edge-forward type.

He only wished he was able to give her more time to sit in Chicago considering, evaluating, before edging back in his direction. That's why it would have been better if Valentine's Day were a month away. With one month to think about it, he knew—without a doubt—that she'd be calling, e-mailing or showing up on his doorstep.

Maybe not for emotional reasons. Not for commitment and marriage and a lifetime together. It could be just because she *wanted* him, and would send him an invitation to come to D.C. to play a game of senator and naughty aide. Sex. Not love. She was as sexually addicted to him as he was to her, and within thirty days, she'd be jonesing for the kind of hot, wild intimacy the two of them had shared from day one.

So, yeah. She'd call, or write or text.

And he'd go.

It was okay. She could use him to satisfy her deepest needs, because he knew he'd be filled with the same hunger for her. And their game would begin again.

Mainly, however, he'd go because deep down, he knew that one of these days, she was going to finally figure out she loved him, too.

She did love him, of that he had no doubt. Amanda just hadn't acknowledged it yet. Or else she had come up with a million reasons why it couldn't work and had decided not to *let* herself love him.

That was okay, too. He didn't need her to say the words. Sex was enough to intertwine their lives until she was ready, and in a month, she'd be dying for it.

"Curse you for being born in February, St. Valentine," he muttered.

Because while thirty days would have done the trick, five might not be enough. In the short time since she'd left, she might have gotten just a little edgy, but she was stubborn. She could probably hold out longer than that, no matter how incredible the sex between them had been during those nights when she'd slept in his bed.

He had no choice, though. It was February 14, and the romantic in him just couldn't let the day pass without at least giving his best shot at seduction. For the first time in his life, he was in love with the right woman on Valentine's Day. He had to do something about it.

And that was why he was sitting on a plane that was right now landing at O'Hare Airport. He'd booked the best room he could get on such short notice at an exclusive Chicago hotel. Tonight, he would either be there with her, reminding her she'd made the right choice in showing up.

Or he would be sitting in it alone, tossing a box of chocolates into the trash, watching the rose petals strewn all over the bed wilt, and wishing he hadn't wasted a case of champagne by pouring it into the bathtub. Not to mention regretting the oysters he'd already ordered from room service.

He was definitely hoping for option A.

Fortunately, he had an accomplice in his plan to whisk Amanda away for a night of sexy romance. As much as he'd hated to do it, he'd gotten in touch with Aunt Jean and asked her who at Clear-Blue Air would be the best person to ask for inside info on Amanda's schedule. This Ginny woman she'd recommended had been extremely helpful, either because she liked his great-aunt, or she loved her employer. Maybe a combination of both.

From what the woman had said, he had a few hours before Amanda returned to Chicago from her day trip to Cincinnati. A few hours to check into the room, set the scene, then call her and ask her if she had the nerve to see him again this soon.

Asking her probably wouldn't do it. Daring her just might.

All those things churned through his mind as he followed the long stream of passengers off the plane and into the terminal. One more thought occurred to him, too: if this didn't work, he might just have to come back next month and check out the green river and a few Chicago pubs. Amanda would look cute as hell in a leprechaun hat. Or sexy as hell if it was all she was wearing.

Smiling at that thought, he headed not for the taxi stand, but rather toward the offices of Clear-Blue Air. He'd told Ginny he would come by when he arrived, just to touch base and make sure Amanda's schedule hadn't changed. He probably could have called for the information, but he suspected the woman wanted to check him out.

Speaking of calling...*phone*. As he walked, he tugged his cell phone out of his pocket and turned it on. A quick glance at the bars confirmed he had no reception. So maybe Ginny wasn't sneaky and a hopeless romantic, just used to spotty service inside the airport. Though, it could be both.

Making his way through Security, who had his name on the list of authorized visitors to the office wing, he followed the directions Ginny had given him. The airport was huge, he'd always known that. But he'd never imagined the amount of space the public never saw. The hallway seemed to go on for blocks.

Of course the Clear-Blue office was at the end of that hallway. His steps quickened as he realized what time it was. He'd figured this errand would take a few minutes.... It had been thirty since he'd stepped off the plane.

When he was finally within a few feet of the door, he saw it open from the inside. He stepped out of the way to let the person out, not really paying attention. At least, not until a woman emerged. The very woman he did not want to see, at least not until tonight.

"Oh, hell," he muttered as all his plans went up in smoke.

Amanda stared at him, wide-eyed, wide-mouthed, not saying a word. She probably feared he'd turned into some psycho stalker.

"Hey," he said softly, wondering if she'd duck back into the office and avoid him altogether.

Instead, she did something far more shocking. Something that rocked him where he stood.

Without a single word, Amanda dropped the small overnight case she'd been carrying, stepped toward him, threw her arms around his neck and kissed him like she hadn't seen him in at least…a month.

HE WAS HERE. She couldn't believe he was really here, that he'd come to Chicago for her for Valentine's Day.

Kissing Reese, feeling the warmth of his body, inhaling his scent and reliving all the pleasures of his mouth, she found tears rising to her eyes. She loved him, she'd missed him. And she had finally found the man who might give her the freedom to fly when she needed to, but would always be waiting for her when she got back. Or else he'd simply come after her.

Finally, their kiss ended and she smiled up at him. "You came."

"Of course I came." Shaking his head and narrowing his eyes in confusion, he said, "You're supposed to be in Cincinnati."

A quick stab of worry made her ask, "Oh, God. You didn't expect me to be here? You didn't come here to see me?"

He threw back his head and laughed, tightening his arms around her waist. "Crazy woman, of course I came here to see you. But I had this big seduction plan all worked out and you didn't give me as much as an hour to get over to the hotel and set it all up."

"There's a couch in my office," she said, her tone dry. "For you and me, that's about all it would take."

"True." He leaned down and kissed her forehead, murmuring, "But I want to give you more than that."

She sighed, turning her face up so her soft cheek brushed his rough one. "I guess that's okay, then. Ginny's desk *is* right outside my door."

"Hotel it is."

Sounded just fine to her. Anxious to go, to be alone

with him somewhere so she could tell him about all the wild thoughts that had gone on in her head, and the wilder feelings that had her ready to burst emotionally, she slipped out of his arms and bent down to grab her overnight bag. He took it from her, slinging it over his shoulder with his own.

She didn't argue—it wasn't much of a burden, because there wasn't much in it. A silky red teddy, a pair of thigh-high stockings. Just the necessities. Not what she typically packed for working trips, because she most definitely had not been on her way to Cincinnati when she'd run into him. Ha! No wonder Ginny had kept looking at the clock and stalling her with inane questions. She'd been worried Amanda would fly to Pittsburgh while Reese was flying here.

"So why aren't you somewhere in or over Ohio?" he asked as they began walking toward the terminal, his arm around her waist, their hips and thighs brushing with every step.

"I had someone else take my flight," she told him. "Too flipping cold in Ohio."

Even as he laughed at that, given the fact that it had to be ten-below-cold-as-shit here in Chicago, he jiggled the overnight bag. "So where *were* you headed?"

There was a hint of amusement in his voice, as if he knew the answer. Well, of *course* did. He knew she'd been coming to see him. He hadn't realized it before he'd arrived here, obviously, but once he'd seen her, once she'd thrown her arms around him and kissed him with all the love she felt for the man, how could he not know she'd want to be with him on *this* of all holidays?

"Where do you think, hotshot?"

"Daytona? It's certainly warmer."

"Not as hot as Pittsburgh."

He stopped when she confirmed it, turning her in his arms so he could kiss her again. This time it wasn't sweet and soft, but deep and hungry, as if he'd been thinking about her since the minute she'd left his house, wanting her all that time.

Or maybe she was projecting how she'd been thinking and feeling. Whatever. All she knew was the man's sweet mouth was covering every millimeter of hers and she never wanted it to end.

Finally, though, because a nearby office door opened and voices intruded, it did.

"Let's get out of here," she whispered, looping her arm through his and leading him back toward the terminal. "I think we have some talking to do."

But not yet. She didn't want to have any deep, important conversation as they walked through the public area of the airport. It was filled with travelers frantic to make their destinations and groaning their way through the long lines at Security.

Since "I'm sorry, I was stupid and I love you" was out, she used the time to fill him in on something a little less personal.

"You're not going to believe the phone call I got this morning." She had intended to tell him about it when she saw him at his place tonight. At least, as long as he let her in the front door.

Not that it would have stopped her if he hadn't. She already knew one of his windows didn't lock right—thank goodness their visitor from Las Vegas hadn't realized it.

"From who?"

"Officer Parker. I guess he was really curious why a sleazy thug would follow us all the way to Chicago, and then Pennsylvania, if he hadn't *really* dropped the jewelry he'd stolen."

Reese eyed her in interest. "Did he have any theories about what happened to it?"

"Yep. Turns out the store owner was apparently just as sleazy. Our friend Teddy *had* dropped his bag of goodies that night—right outside the door of the shop. The owner found it, hid it, then filed a false insurance claim. Parker got him to confess the whole thing."

Reese nodded, appearing as relieved as she had been at the news. "So no more worrying about Mr. Lebowski."

"Correct." Smiling, she added, "Which means you don't have to update your garden gnome for a .357 Magnum."

He chuckled, and a companionable silence again fell between them. It continued as they reached her car and got in it, neither saying much of anything once he'd given her the name of the hotel where they were staying. It was as if he already knew she had a lot to tell him, and didn't want that conversation to start until they were completely alone. She wanted no distractions caused by nosy onlookers, or the need to keep her hands on the wheel.

Besides, a little silence was good. She needed the drive time to put everything into words.

She'd figured she'd have a few hours before arriving on his doorstep in Pittsburgh, armed with a coffee can in one hand, and a teabag in the other. "Coffee, tea or me?" had seemed like a good opening line. Getting him to smile might ensure he didn't slam the door in her face for being such a cowardly bitch and running out on him the other morning without giving him the courtesy of an explanation.

Finally, they arrived at the hotel. She whistled as they walked into the lobby, duly impressed. The man was going all out for this little holiday getaway.

"Don't get too excited," he murmured as they approached the front desk. "I just made the reservation yesterday. They're probably desperate to take advantage of every holiday sucker they can get, so we might end up sleeping in a tiny bed stuck inside a janitor's closet."

She laughed, but honestly didn't care. As long as they could be alone, and a bed was in the vicinity, that was just fine with her.

A few minutes later, when they arrived at their room, she realized Reese needn't have worried. Neither of them were laughing as they walked inside and looked around. Despite the last-minute reservation, the room was beautiful, with a huge, plush bed, elegant furnishings and enormous windows that looked down on bustling Michigan Avenue. She didn't doubt he'd paid several times the rate it would have been on any other night of the year.

"Not bad," he conceded.

"It's amazing," she whispered, not really talking about the room, but about one spot in it.

He had obviously been specific with his requests,

because spread all over that plush, turned-down bed were what looked like hundreds of red rose petals.

"What game are we playing here?" she asked, suddenly a tiny bit cautious and wary.

This looked like wedding-night stuff. And while she'd mentally acknowledged she could not let Reese go without giving the feelings they had for one another a chance, she was in no way ready for rings and white veils.

Liar.

Okay, maybe the thought *had* crossed her mind. But only in a "someday, possibly" kind of way. Definitely not soon.

He accurately read her expression. "Don't worry, if I wanted to play honeymoon, I would have whisked you off to one of those places in the Poconos with the heart-shaped beds and the raised, champagne-glass bathtubs."

She punched him lightly in the arm, instinctively replying, "We are not spending our honeymoon in Pennsylvania!"

Only after the words had left her mouth did she realize what she'd said. And acknowledged the implications.

Seeing the warmth in his eyes, she put a hand up. "Wait. That's not what I meant. I'm not saying…"

"Would you shut up?" he asked, sweetly, tenderly. He lifted a hand to her face, brushing his thumb across her cheek. "Just stop thinking about it, stop talking about it and love me."

It was as simple as that.

She nodded, rising on tiptoe to press her lips against

his. Just as sweetly, just as tenderly. When the kiss ended, she kept her arms around his neck and stared into his handsome face. "I do love you."

"I know."

She kissed him again. "I shouldn't have run out the other day without admitting it."

"I understand why you did."

Her brow furrowing, she lowered her arms and slowly sat down on the edge of the bed, careful not to disturb the flower petals. "You do?"

He pulled a chair closer and sat opposite her, bending over with his elbows on his knees, hands dangling between his parted legs. His expression was serious as he said, "All the difficulties you're sure we have can be dealt with. My family, your family, our jobs, our homes. That whole geography thing they no longer teach in schools."

He didn't have to go on. She had already realized none of those problems really mattered. They could be worked out. In fact, she'd already talked to her uncle about modifying her work schedule so she could, as Jazz had suggested, commute out of Pittsburgh.

Uncle Frank had been incredibly supportive once he'd found out why. Urging her not to let his own bad example lead her to a life as lonely as his, he'd offered to do whatever it took to accommodate her.

"Reese, I…"

"Let me finish, please." The corner of his mouth lifted in a half smile as he completely bared his heart to her.

"I love you. And after we talked the other night in

the car, I realized life is just too damned precarious not to be with the person you love."

She understood. Those very same thoughts had crossed her mind the other morning…only she'd taken the cowardly way out of having to deal with any future pain, loss and heartache. She'd cut and run. Reese was far more daring, willing to risk whatever happened tomorrow for the good things they could have today.

That kind of emotional bravery at least entitled him to the whole truth. "I didn't leave because I was scared for myself, but because I was afraid for you."

"What?"

"I don't want to hurt you, Reese. I love you too much. I've just grown used to the idea that I'm destined to hurt men because I'm not cut out for relationships."

He shook his head. "That's crazy, you wouldn't…"

"I know that now. Sitting at home for the past few nights, going over it in my mind, I realized all those failed relationships I *wasn't* cut out for had one thing in common."

"What's that?"

"They weren't with you."

He pulled her off the bed into his arms, settling her into his lap. Amanda cuddled against him, sucking up his heat and his essence, then said, "How can any loving relationship work if only one person is actually in love?"

"It can't."

"Exactly. And once I realized that, once I acknowledged that I have never been in love with *anyone* until now, I was finally able to let it go. The guilt, the regret, the shame."

He squeezed her. "You have nothing to be ashamed of."

"Tell that to Facebook," she mumbled. But she quickly thrust the thought aside. No room for darkness now, there was only light and happiness, passion and possibility. Love.

"There's nothing wrong with me," she admitted, to both of them. "I just don't fall in love easily."

"Neither do I."

"Which means neither one of us is going to fall out of it easily, right?"

He kissed the top of her head, vowing, "Neither one of us is going to fall out of it at all."

He couldn't know that. No one could know such a thing. But she believed him. With all her heart, with every instinct she owned, she believed him.

"I can't promise not to be insensitive and self-absorbed sometimes," she warned. "Can't say I'll never do something selfish and hurt you."

"Well," he replied after giving it some thought, "I can't say I'll always remember to put the toilet seat down or not squeeze from the middle of the toothpaste tube."

She laughed softly.

He thought about it some more. "I can't promise to let you handcuff me the next time we play cops and robbers…but I might agree to a few silk scarves."

Her laughter deepened, as she knew he'd meant it to. Then Reese got more serious.

"I can't say I'm never going to work late. Or that I won't sometimes just need to be alone with my thoughts. Some days of the year my mood will be dark and I won't want to talk about it."

Hearing that hint of sadness she'd heard in his voice the other night, she understood that. Completely.

"Okay. But I can't promise I'm not going to try to kidnap you away from work once in a while so I can fly us to Aspen to do a little skiing."

He grinned. "That sounds great. Especially because *I* can't promise we won't have one or another of my PMS-ing sisters calling in the middle of the night because she had a fight with her boyfriend and needs a ride."

His family was part of his life. She knew that. The way he cared for them was one thing she loved best about him. Still, the memory of their first meeting intruded. Nibbling her lip, she asked, "Do they all hate me?"

"No! Not one little bit. In fact, two of my sisters showed up at my place last night asking me why I hadn't left yet to come here and win you back."

She breathed a sigh of relief. Though she hadn't wanted to admit it, the idea of a wedding had, indeed, flitted around in her mind once or twice. She'd immediately done her Amanda-thing and started worrying about how she could handle having bridesmaids who hated her guts in her wedding party.

Plus Jazz. Plus her sister, Abby. Oh, Lord.

Not thinking about that now.

"You should also know, my mother called to apologize and asked me to tell you that despite her behavior that first night, she would not be a Monster-In-Law. Which is true—she's sad lately, but she's never been pushy or tried to interfere in my life before. I've been the one hovering."

"That's because you're a good man," she whispered.

A really good, funny, *sexy* man.

A man she deserved.

For the first time, she allowed herself to believe it was possible. She *could* make the right man happy. She *did* deserve him.

Reese was that right man.

Though the rose petals beckoned, and she truly wanted to slip out of her clothes, and get him out of his, so they could express their love in the most elemental, sensual way possible, she had to add one more thing. One more promise, that she intended to keep.

"I won't ever run from you, Reese."

"Sure you will." He smiled tenderly. "But I'll always follow."

* * * * *

THE DRIFTER &
TAKE ME IF YOU DARE
(2-IN-1 ANTHOLOGY)

BY KATE HOFFMANN & CANDACE HAVENS

The Drifter

Charlie Templeton is a wanderer, an adventurer. But one thing scares him: the chance that he's permanently lost the woman he loved, the woman he left. He's going back to Eve...

Take Me If You Dare

Mariska Stonegate's new man is secretly a CIA agent on the run. And he'll do just about anything to stay alive, including seducing Mariska one hot, steamy night at a time!

AMBUSHED!
BY VICKI LEWIS THOMPSON

Gabe Chance is blown away by the feisty redhead who unexpectedly lands right in his bed and, soon enough, his heart! He realises that Morgan's everything he wants, but she may be attracted by his ranch...

SURPRISE ME...
BY ISABEL SHARPE

Seduced by his fantasy woman. She's overlooked his intellect and dodgy haircut. He's totally in love; until he realises *she thought she'd climbed into bed with his bad-boy brother*!

On sale from 18th February 201
Don't miss ou

Available at WHSmith, Tesco, ASDA, Eas
and all good booksho
www.millsandboon.co.

0211

A STORMY SPANISH SUMMER
by Penny Jordan

Duque Vidal y Salvadores hated Fliss Clairemont—but now he must help her claim her inheritance! As their attraction takes hold, can Vidal admit how wrong he's been about her...?

NOT A MARRYING MAN
by Miranda Lee

Billionaire Warwick Kincaid asked Amber Roberts to move in, but then became distant. Is her time up? The chemistry between them remains *white-hot* and Amber finds it hard to believe that her time with Warwick is *really* over...

SECRETS OF THE OASIS
by Abby Green

After giving herself to Sheikh Salman years ago, Jamilah Moreau's wedding fantasies were crushed. Then Salman spirits her off to a desert oasis and Jamilah discovers he still wants her!

THE HEIR FROM NOWHERE
by Trish Morey

Dominic Pirelli's world falls apart with the news that an IVF mix-up means a stranger is carrying his baby! Dominic is determined to keep waif-like Angelina Cameron close, but who will have custody of the Pirelli heir?

On sale from 18th February 2011
Don't miss out!

*Available at WHSmith, Tesco, ASDA, Eason
and all good bookshops*
www.millsandboon.co.uk

TAMING THE LAST ST CLAIRE
by Carole Mortimer

Gideon St Claire's life revolves around work, so fun-loving Joey McKinley is the sort of woman he normally avoids! Then an old enemy starts looking for revenge and Gideon's forced to protect Joey—day *and* night...

THE FAR SIDE OF PARADISE
by Robyn Donald

A disastrous engagement left Taryn wary of men, but Cade Peredur stirs feelings she's never known before. However, when Cade's true identity is revealed, will Taryn's paradise fantasy dissolve?

THE PROUD WIFE
by Kate Walker

Marina D'Inzeo is finally ready to divorce her estranged husband Pietro—even a summons to join him in Sicily won't deter her! However, with his wife standing before him, Pietro wonders why he ever let her go!

ONE DESERT NIGHT
by Maggie Cox

Returning to the desert plains of Kabuyadir to sell its famous *Heart of Courage* jewel, Gina Collins is horrified the new sheikh is the man who gave her one earth-shattering night years ago.

On sale from 4th March 2011
Don't miss out!

Her Not-So-Secret Diary

by Anne Oliver

Sophie's fantasies stayed secret—until her saucy dream was accidentally e-mailed to her sexy boss! But as their steamy nights reach boiling point, Sophie knows she's in a whole heap of trouble…

The Wedding Date

by Ally Blake

Under no circumstances should Hannah's gorgeous boss, Bradley, be considered her wedding date! Now, if only her disobedient legs would do the *sensible* thing and walk away…

Molly Cooper's Dream Date

by Barbara Hannay

House-swapping with London-based Patrick has given Molly the chance to find a perfect English gentleman! Yet she's increasingly curious about Patrick himself—is the Englishman she wants on the other side of the world?

If the Red Slipper Fits…

by Shirley Jump

It's not *unknown* for Caleb Lewis to find a sexy stiletto in his convertible, but Caleb usually has some recollection of how it got there! He's intrigued to meet the woman it belongs to..

On sale from 4th March 2011
Don't miss out!

Available at WHSmith, Tesco, ASDA, Eason and all good bookshops

www.millsandboon.co.uk

THE *Royal*
HOUSE OF NIROLI

The richest royal family in the world—united by blood and passion, torn apart by deceit and desire

The Royal House of Niroli: Scandalous Seductions
Penny Jordan & Melanie Milburne
Available 17th December 2010

The Royal House of Niroli: Billion Dollar Bargains
Carol Marinelli & Natasha Oakley
Available 21st January 2011

The Royal House of Niroli: Innocent Mistresses
Susan Stephens & Robyn Donald
Available 18th February 2011

The Royal House of Niroli: Secret Heirs
Raye Morgan & Penny Jordan
Available 18th March 2011

Collect all four!

INTRIGUE...

INTRIGUE...

2-IN-1 ANTHOLOGY

THE LIBRARIAN'S SECRET SCANDAL
by Jennifer Morey

No one believes Lily has changed, except sheriff Wes. And, though she's determined to keep her secret, she and the sheriff certainly give people something to talk about.

DR COLTON'S HIGH-STAKES FIANCÉE
by Cindy Dees

In the dark, forced in the same place, Finn and Rachel confide in each other about their high-school days; yet can they rekindle an old flame?

•••

SINGLE TITLE

ONE HOT FORTY-FIVE
by BJ Daniels

A woman in trouble was like the call of a siren for Lantry Corbett. And while Dede was in over her head, she was off limits...until a lethal threat bound them together.

On sale from 18th February 2011
Don't miss out!

0211/46b

2 FREE BOOKS
AND A SURPRISE GIFT

We would like to take this opportunity to thank you for reading this Mills & Boon® book by offering you the chance to take TWO more specially selected titles from the Blaze® series absolutely FREE! We're also making this offer to introduce you to the benefits of the Mills & Boon® Book Club™—

- **FREE home delivery**
- **FREE gifts and competitions**
- **FREE monthly Newsletter**
- **Exclusive Mills & Boon Book Club offers**
- **Books available before they're in the shops**

Accepting these FREE books and gift places you under no obligation to buy, you may cancel at any time, even after receiving your free books. Simply complete your details below and return the entire page to the address below. You don't even need a stamp!

YES Please send me 2 free Blaze books and a surprise gift. I understand that unless you hear from me, I will receive 3 superb new books every month, including a 2-in-1 book priced at £5.30 and two single books priced at £3.30 each, postage and packing free. I am under no obligation to purchase any books and may cancel my subscription at any time. The free books and gift will be mine to keep in any case.

Ms/Mrs/Miss/Mr_____ Initials _____

Surname _____

Address _____

_____ Postcode _____

E-mail _____

Send this whole page to: Mills & Boon Book Club, Free Book Offer, FREEPOST NAT 10298, Richmond, TW9 1BR